The Cowboy and the Angel

Also by T. J. Kline

Rodeo Queen

The Cowboy
and the Angel

T. J. KLINE

AVONIMPULSE
An Imprint of HarperCollinsPublishers

Excerpt from *Rodeo Queen* copyright © 2013 by Tina Klinesmith.

Excerpt from *Full Exposure* copyright © 2014 by Sara Jane Stone.

Excerpt from *Personal Target* copyright © 2014 by Kay Thomas.

Excerpt from *Sinful Rewards 1* copyright © 2014 by Cynthia Sax.

EPub Edition AUGUST 2014 ISBN: 9780062370075

Print Edition ISBN: 9780062370099

JV 10 9 8 7 6 5 4 3 2 1

For my Mama and Daddy:
the two people who bought me my first horse
and always pushed me to reach for more, never settling.
You taught me how to fly.
I can never thank you both enough.

Chapter One

"ANGELA, CALL ON line three."

"Can't you just handle it, Joe? I don't have time for this BS." It was probably just another stupid mom calling, hoping Angela would feature her daughter's viral video in some feel-good news story. When was she ever going to get her break and get some hard-hitting news?

"They asked for you."

She sighed. Maybe if she left them listening to that horrible elevator music long enough, they'd hang up. Joe edged closer to her desk.

"Just pick up the damn phone and see what they want."

"Fine." She glared at him as she punched the button. The look she gave him belied the sweet tone of her voice. "Angela McCallister. How can I help you?"

Joe leaned against her cubicle wall, listening to her part of the conversation. She waved at him irritably.

It wasn't always easy when your boss was your oldest friend—and ex-boyfriend. He quirked a brow at her.

Go away, she mouthed.

"Are you really looking for new stories?"

She assumed the male voice on the line was talking about the calls the station ran at the end of several news programs asking for stories of interest. Most of them ended up in her mental "ignore" file, but once in a while she found one worth pursuing.

"We're always looking for events and stories of interest to our local viewers." She rolled her eyes, reciting the words Joe had taught her early on in her career as a reporter. She was tired of pretending any of this sucking up was getting her anywhere. Viewers only saw her as a pretty face.

"I have a lead that might interest you." She didn't answer, waiting for the caller to elaborate. "There's a rodeo coming to town, and rodeos are full of animal cruelty and abuse."

This didn't sound like a feel-good piece. The caller had her attention now. "Do you have proof?"

The voice gave a bitter laugh, sounding vaguely familiar. "Have you ever seen a rodeo? Electric prods, cinches wrapped around genitals, sharp objects placed under saddles to get horses to buck . . . it's all there."

She listened as the caller detailed several incidents at nearby rodeos where animals had to be euthanized due to injuries. Angela arched a brow, taking notes as the caller continued, giving her several websites she might research that backed the accusations.

"Can I contact you for more information?" She heard him hemming. "You don't have to give me your name. Maybe just a phone number or an email address where I can reach you?" The caller gave her both. "Do you mind if I ask one more question—why me?"

"Because you seem like you care about animal rights. That story you did about the stray kittens, and the way you found them a home, really showed who you are inside."

Angela barely remembered the story. Joe had forced it on her when she'd asked for one about a local politician sleeping with his secretary, reminding her that viewers saw her as their local sweetheart. She found herself reporting about a litter of stray kittens at the local shelter, smiling as families adopted their favorites, while Jennifer Michaels broke the infidelity story and was now anchoring at a station in Los Angeles. She was tired of this innocent, girl-next-door act.

"I'll see what I can do," she promised, deciding how to best pitch this story to Joe and whether it would be worth it at all.

"What was that all about?" Joe waved at one of the news crew as they passed. She recognized the man as one of the nameless camera crewmen she routinely worked with, but she didn't even remember his name.

"Hey, Greg." Joe called.

Greg, that's right. She knew she'd forget again in minutes. The only thing she could afford to think about right now was how this story might advance her career. She needed to get her father out of their neighborhood and

4 T. J. KLINE

quickly. He hadn't come home again last night, and she prayed he was sleeping off his hangover somewhere safe. She opened her laptop and ran an Internet search for rodeo animal cruelty.

"Well?"

"Give me a few minutes to see if it's even worthwhile." She clicked on the first result, bookmarking several videos to watch.

"You know you make me nervous when you get secretive." She turned toward him, smiling broadly, her eyes flashing with excitement and a curl of tension winding in her stomach the way it always did when she was on the right track for a good story. "Man, I know that look."

Joe shook his head and jammed his hands into his pockets. "Let me know before today is up or it's a no-go. No wasting time chasing dead ends."

"Mike," Derek called, shifting his straw hat farther back on his forehead. "You need to come do another interview."

Tossing the last of the alfalfa over the fence to the cattle, he narrowed his eyes as the news van stopped at the back gate of the rodeo arena. He didn't want to be seen on camera with sweat trickling down his back and staining his t-shirt nor did he have the time. They had only a few hours left before the last rodeo performance of the weekend, and every minute was essential.

"I don't have time for this today, Derek." Mike's voice was muffled as he unloaded the saddles from the tack compartment of the stock trailer. "I don't really run the show anymore. You kids do. You can tell them the same thing I would: No comment." He poked his gray head out from the side of the horse trailer and glanced toward the back gate. "It's probably just another local story anyway. Besides, they'll want a good-looking guy like you on camera before they want my grizzly face on there."

"Fine," Derek sighed, dusting alfalfa leaves from his pants as he headed toward the van.

So far, Derek was pretty sure he didn't like his new position as arena director. his brother, Scott, had stepped down recently, taking a behind-the-scenes role at the ranch after his marriage and the birth of his daughter, so Derek recognized it was time he "cowboy up" and help out more in the family business even though he'd never been *that* guy. Derek was the fun-loving, irresponsible one, and he liked it that way. As the youngest in the family, he'd been mothered by his older sister after their parents died and she'd spoiled him rotten. They all knew it and accepted it, but as Mike pointed out when Derek became an uncle, it was high time he "suck it up," accept the responsibility, and become the man they all believed he was.

As Derek walked by the trailer his sister Jennifer shared with her husband, Clay, one of their rodeo pick-up men, she poked her head out and looked toward the back gate. "Another one?"

Derek tickled the foot of the newborn boy she held in her arms. It still surprised him that she attended the rodeo with his nephew, but knowing her devotion to Mike and their company, it probably shouldn't have.

"Yes. I get so tired of this," Derek complained.

He paused mid-step as the side door of the white news van slid open and revealed a firm female behind encased in tight black jeans. The owner bent over and searched for something inside as he arched a brow and a slight smile crept to his lips. *This interview just started getting interesting.*

He stood at the locked gate, crossing his arms over the top rail and leaning against the warm metal while waiting for her to notice him.

"Skip, hurry up!" the woman called impatiently. Derek heard equipment shifting and looked back at Mike over his shoulder, starting to grow impatient himself. As much as he might enjoy flirting with this reporter, he still had animals to get ready before the rodeo started, and she was wasting what little time he had. He jabbed the toe of his boot in the dusty driveway, kicking up puffs of dirt and willing her to hurry up.

He leaned his body to the side, hoping for a glimpse of the woman. Derek couldn't help but chuckle at the way she'd tucked her pants inside the city-girl, high-heeled dress boots. He could see the back of a plaid Western shirt and some sort of rhinestone belt. As she stood she plopped a cheap, black cowboy hat on the back of her head. He grinned and wondered when a television station would send out a news crew who knew how to get dirty. His laughter died when she turned around to face him.

This woman was gorgeous.

Not in a fake, medically enhanced, airbrushed way either. Her auburn hair caught the sunlight and shone like fire under the black hat, and her large emerald eyes pierced him as they met his. She had flawless porcelain skin, too light to have spent much time outside, and her body banished any coherent thought left in his brain. She was the kind of woman fantasies were made of, with curves that no real woman should have. Her long legs flared into rounded hips before tapering to a miniscule waist and rounding again at her . . .

"I'm up here, cowboy," she warned, pointing a freshly manicured finger at her face. The man he assumed was Skip snorted and she cut those green eyes at him, glaring. He immediately headed back to the side of the van.

Derek swallowed and, regaining his composure, gave her a cocky grin and stood to his full six-foot-four stature. He adjusted his hat on his head before hanging his hands over the rail of the gate. "How might I help you, ma'am?" he drawled.

"I'm Angela McCallister with Channel 12 News. I was hoping to talk with the stock contractor for a few minutes."

Her lips were moving, but he was having difficulty concentrating on the words coming out of them. He was too busy imagining himself kissing them—long, sweet kisses that made you savor the moment, forgetting the past or the future. Hell, her lips might make him forget his own name. He dragged his thoughts back to the present, where he stood in a sweaty t-shirt, his face smudged with dirt and grime.

"Sorry, as much as I'd like to chat with you, we don't have time for interviews this morning. Maybe later." Derek winked at her, turning on the heel of his dusty boot.

She stopped him with her hand on his bicep. "Wait, couldn't I just ask you a couple of questions?" Her voice was sultry, almost seductively sweet, and she batted her long dark lashes at him.

He paused as warning bells sounded in his brain. This woman was trouble, and as much as he might want to spend a few minutes causing "trouble" with her, he couldn't let Mike or the rest of his family down. He'd already been conned by Mike's daughter, Liz, and that stupid move had nearly ruined his family. He wasn't about to fall prey to another conniving woman. He was determined to prove to them he could work just as hard as Scott and take care of the family business just as well as he had. That didn't include wasting time flirting with reporters.

"You'd look good on camera, you know." She circled her finger over the back of his hand and wrist. "What's your name?"

Derek wondered how Scott would've handled this situation. He frowned, torn between following his natural instinct to have fun with this incredibly attractive woman and becoming the dependable rock for his family the way his brother had always been. Responsibility won out. "No interviews," he repeated. His voice was gruffer than he'd intended and he cleared his throat, feeling like a jerk.

"Okay," she agreed, holding up her hands, acknowledging her defeat, "I just thought that maybe I could get a behind-the-scenes look at the rodeo. It might be good publicity for you," she suggested, glancing at him coyly and batting her lashes dramatically.

Derek had a hard time keeping his laughter at bay as he forced himself to be stern. She was a terrible flirt. She couldn't possibly think this act was working. "Our publicity is just fine. If you want to see the rodeo, you'll have to buy a ticket like everyone else." He glanced back to the stock trailer and saw Mike watching him. He couldn't waste any more time when the early events were due to begin soon.

"There's no need to get fired up, cowboy. I just wanted to talk to you."

She leaned toward the fence, giving him a bird's-eye view of her ample cleavage since she was at least eight inches shorter than he was, and pouted. A sizzle of heat shot through him and centered in his groin. Derek arched a single brow and gave her a lopsided grin. He knew Mike needed him, but he couldn't help but enjoy the redheaded vixen's awkward attempt at seduction.

"About what?" Derek said.

"If you open this gate, I have some coffee in the van. We could chat over a cup." She ran her fingers over his forearm before playing with the frayed edge of his t-shirt where it stretched over his bicep.

Derek couldn't hold back his laughter any longer. "That's the best you've got? I'd have thought that someone who looks ..." He eyed her well-endowed frame.

"Well, like you, would at least know how to flirt better. You're gonna have to work harder than that to get me to do an interview."

She narrowed her eyes as they flashed with emerald fire, her full lips pinched together with fury at being thwarted. All pretense of seduction disappeared. "Look, I have a press pass your boss issued our station last week." She jabbed her finger against the hard wall of his chest. "Are you going to honor it or not?"

"That press pass entitles you to attend the rodeo, not to distract me from my job. Feel free to come back when the gates open and watch the show. Interview the cowboys then. Hell, I'll even give you a *private* interview if you want," he said, wiggling his brows and laughing at her.

She wrinkled her pert little nose at him and rolled her eyes. "No thanks. Dust-covered manure jockeys aren't my thing."

Normally, he'd have been offended by her insult, but right now he couldn't help wanting to kiss that smart mouth of hers. He glanced at Skip, who awaited her orders at the van. This uptight city girl was probably used to men lining up to do her bidding, but out here she was on his turf and, desirable or not, he wasn't letting her have the upper hand.

Derek chuckled, jerking his chin at her clothing. "By the way, your urban cowboy look is going to make you stick out like a sore thumb. You might want to do some research on what to wear to a rodeo before you come out later." He walked away, glancing back at her over his shoulder. "Although, I must admit, those pants do make your butt look great."

"YOU MIGHT WANT to pucker up, cowboy, because the next time you see me, you can kiss it," she yelled after him.

Angela eyed his retreating back. No man outsmarted her, and she wasn't about to let a smelly cowboy have the last word. She wasn't normally a violent person, but if she'd seen a rock nearby, she'd have thrown it at the cocky redneck. She wasn't buying his "good ole boy" act any more than he'd believed her coy ruse to get through the gate. She certainly wasn't going to acknowledge the electric jolt of pleasure she felt when her hand touched his or again when his bicep had flexed beneath her fingers.

She needed this story and she was going to get it, no matter what. She wasn't about to let some Podunk, backwoods hick stop her from scooping this story for her reel and getting the hell out of this town, no matter how drop-dead gorgeous he was. This exposé about the abusive treatment of rodeo stock was her ticket out of this small time, local gig. Petty events and feel-good pieces were getting her nowhere, and she couldn't stand reporting another grocery store opening or ribbon-cutting ceremony.

She couldn't even think about what would happen to her and her father if she wasn't able to get him away soon. If he stayed much longer, his guilt was going to eat him alive, leaving her alone. She had to protect him, even from himself. He was all she had left. She needed this story to change their circumstances, and no redneck cowboy was going to get in her way.

She spun on her heel, nearly tripping over the clunky cowboy boots, and yanked open the passenger door. A blush heated her skin, rising from her chest to her cheeks, and she prayed he'd missed her less-than-graceful exit. She tossed the microphone to the floor and slammed the door as the sound of his laughter carried to her ears. *So much for prayers.*

She wasn't even sure why she was letting this guy get her so worked up. She'd never been one to lose her cool—not with businessmen, politicians, or actors—so, why in the world would a *cowboy*, no matter how sexy he was, get her flustered? And why was a phony dalliance causing her mind to conjure up images of their bodies pressed together, sending heat coursing through her veins? It's not like she was really flirting with him. She shook her head, trying to clear the image from her mind.

"What was that all about?" Skip asked, turning the key in the ignition.

"Just shut up and drive," she muttered. "Go to the diner on the corner so I can figure out our next move." She pulled a laptop out of her bag and powered it up. "First, I need to find out more about this particular stock contractor and the idiots he has working for him." She pulled her hat off and tossed it behind her, recalling his parting words. "On second thought, let's go find something else for me to wear."

"Didn't research that?"

"Who researches rodeo clothes?" She shot him a sideways glance in time to see him trying to hide a grin and glared at him. She knew the names others at the station called her behind her back: Ice Princess, Snob, and Queen Bitch. She deliberately kept herself closed off from most of her coworkers. It was easier to undercut them, stab them in the back, or bail on them completely if she didn't feel a connection. It was a cutthroat industry and she might hate herself later, but right now, being a cold-hearted witch was the only way to survive. If that meant being the Channel 12 Ice Princess, then so be it. But most of them would love to see her fall on her face like this. She probably should have put more thought into what to wear, but she'd been in such a hurry to get her animal rights information in order that she hadn't studied trends in rodeo wear.

"If you mention this again, I'll make sure the only videos you take will be home movies, got it?" she threatened. She felt guilty as she glanced at the wedding ring on his hand, but she wasn't going to let him spread word that some cowboy had beaten her at her own game.

"Done already? Why don't the reporters that interview me look like that?" Mike winked at him and pulled the cinch on the saddle tight.

"I didn't do an interview." Derek frowned, deciding in an instant he didn't like being the guy in charge. It made him feel like an egotistical ass.

"Something wrong?"

Derek wasn't sure how to explain his frustration to Mike. The man raised him after his parents died and could read his every emotion like Derek was his blood. He shook his head, hoping to clear the vision of the redheaded spitfire from his mind. "Just getting my head in the game for today."

Derek didn't want to admit that a woman he'd met only minutes ago had him second-guessing his ability to do this job. He could barely focus on the rodeo that was about to start because he was doubting his decision to not kiss her sassy mouth. *Great, now I'm as bad as one of those randy bulls.*

"So, what'd she want?" Mike bent over to clean a horse's hoof. "Did you even find out?"

"Not really. She was a snob."

Derek regretted it as soon as the words left his mouth. It was a fair assumption given her insult, but he'd been a jerk, taunting her. It wasn't fair to be so judgmental of her because he was thrust into a role he didn't feel prepared for. He should've ignored the van from the start, or asked Jen talk to them. Instead he'd flirted with her and tormented himself with glimpses of creamy skin where the buttons of her shirt pulled. He wrenched his thoughts from the tantalizing path they were taking.

"She had a press pass, so she may be back later. You can talk to her next time."

There was no way he was getting caught within ten feet of that succubus again. She was too much of a distraction, and he needed to prove to his family he was capable of handling this responsibility. Unlike the last time they'd trusted him.

Chapter Two

THAT VIXEN MIGHT have changed her clothes, but Derek wouldn't mistake those curves for anyone else. He wasn't sure who'd dressed her this time around but, had she been astride a horse, she could've passed for any of the barrel racers circling the warm-up arena. She no longer looked like she'd just stepped out of a bad 70s Western. His eyes drifted to the press badge hanging on a lanyard between her breasts.

Down boy, you don't need this kind of distraction.

His feet ignored the warnings his brain offered. He stepped up behind her while she watched the chute crew slipping horn wraps over the steers for the team roping event. Derek placed a hand on either side of her shoulders, along the top of the metal panel railing.

"Still looking for that interview?"

"Not from you, cowboy." She didn't even bother to turn and face him.

"Ugh! You wound me." He clapped a hand to his chest, just above his heart.

Derek wasn't sure if she'd known it was him or didn't care who it was. He caught a whiff of vanilla and peaches and inhaled deeply, feeling a jolt of desire strike him in the gut. Her deep-red hair shone like fire from under the new black Stetson, and his fingers itched to see if those tresses were as soft as they appeared. She glanced over her shoulder, pinning him with an irritated glance as he grinned down at her.

"I highly doubt that. I'm sure there are plenty of other women around here for you to harass." She turned back to the animals milling in the large pen behind the chutes.

"Look, maybe we got off on the wrong foot." He looked down at the back of her head and wondered again if flirting with her wasn't a huge mistake. "I get the feeling you think I'm a jerk."

"Oh, I don't think you're a jerk," she interrupted, glancing back at him. He arched his brows in surprise. "I *know* you're a jerk." He laughed as she shoved his arm from the fence so she could pass, causing him to stumble forward.

"Now if you don't mind, I have a job to do and an interview with Mike Findley." She shot him a coy smile. "I guess your boss sees an interview with me as good publicity after all. Maybe that's why he's the owner and you're, well, you."

With a twirl she headed back toward her news van. The waves of her red hair swayed at her waist, making her back seem ablaze and he felt his stomach tighten, wondering how it was possible that he still smelled vanilla and peaches over the pungent scent of cattle and dust.

Yep, she's trouble with a capital T.

"MR. FINDLEY, HOW long have you been a stock contractor?"

Angela flipped her hair back over her shoulder and smiled at the older gentleman. He had kind eyes that crinkled with laughter as they joked before turning on the cameras. He seemed like a genuinely nice man. A twinge of guilt stabbed at her conscience, but only for a moment, as she recalled the atrocities she'd found in her research of the cruelties stock contractors had been accused of.

"I started this company with my partner about twenty-five years ago. I can't imagine doing anything else."

She smiled brightly at him, attempting to lure him into a false sense of security. "Did you always love rodeo?" She glanced at her cameraman, Skip, and gave him a signal to zoom in on the old man. His reaction when she swooped in for the kill would be ratings gold.

"Rodeo's in my blood. My father was a bronc rider, his father, too. I learned to rope a steer right after I learned to walk." He chuckled and shifted his hat, readjusting it on his head nervously. "I guess you could say I was practically born in a saddle."

"So, it would be accurate to say you've been abusing these poor animals for most of your life?"

The man frowned as if he hadn't understood the question. "What? I . . . no," he stammered.

"Mr. Findley," she began, deliberately tilting her head toward him in a way that would appear hard-hitting but feminine on camera, her tone as condescending as if she were scolding a wayward child. "Do you expect us to believe that these animals aren't abused?"

Mike Findley straightened, still looking confused. Remorse gnawed at the edges of her conscience. Just because he was a nice man, or the fact that his family had never been forced to take responsibility for their actions, didn't mean he shouldn't be made to answer for the wrongdoing, she reasoned. And if exposing the mistreatment of his livestock earned her a ticket to a bigger television station and a better life for her and her father, then she'd ignore her conscience and do what was best for her family.

"We have never allowed, nor would we ever allow, any abuse of our animals," said another voice from behind her. She recognized *that* voice immediately. "These animals are treated with the utmost care and dignity. Without them, we couldn't make a living."

"Not according to my research. I could show you hundreds of sites online that show examples of the abuse I'm talking about. Eyewitness accounts, news stories, court documents, police reports." Angela spun to face Derek's massive, broad shoulders.

"Is this the same research that had you dressing like some 70s spaghetti Western?" Derek mocked.

"I'm sorry, but you already refused my interview. Now

I'm conducting one with Mr. Findley." She flipped her hair from her shoulder and tried to ignore him.

She didn't want Derek to be a part of this interview, and damn him for looking incredibly sexy in his long-sleeved Western shirt, tight Wranglers, and rodeo chaps. Women would eat him up if he appeared on camera, which wasn't her intention for this story. It was bad enough to have a sympathetic old man, but there was no way she would be able to turn this stud into a villain. He was going to ruin her interview.

"I'm not sure we were ever properly introduced. I'm Derek Chandler, one-third owner of Findley Brothers." Derek held out his hand to shake hers. She glanced down at it and he smiled, leaning closer. "Don't worry, I think I got all of the manure off."

She signaled to Skip with a slash of her fingers at her chin. "Cut." Angela dropped the microphone to her thigh as Derek Chandler moved to stand beside Mike Findley, looking like a bodyguard. "Is this some sort of game?"

Derek laughed sardonically. "You think *we're* playing games? What about you, pretending you to want an interview when you're just another protestor?"

Mike placed a hand on Derek's shoulder, and she realized that these two would stand together against her. Her chance at an interview was becoming less likely with every second. "We don't need to defend rodeo. This country was founded on the backs of ranchers."

"Not to mention animal cruelty," she added quickly. "Or do you just assume that because something has been

done a certain way for generations that makes it right?"
She pointed a finger at the men standing across from her.
"Do you even realize that what you're doing is barbaric?
There are far more humane methods for raising cattle,
even for consumption, and this *sport* doesn't bear any re-
semblance to cattle ranching."

Derek snorted. "When have you ever been on a working cattle ranch?"

Angela glared at him, irritated that she'd underesti-
mated a bunch of cowboys. She'd thought a little cleavage and a toss of her hair would convince these guys
she was harmless, but they hadn't fallen for it and her
mistake annoyed her. He'd already called her out on her
ridiculous clothing when she showed up looking like a
dime-store cowboy, but she wouldn't tolerate him in-
sulting her as a journalist. She might not have been as
thorough researching clothing, but it didn't take a visit
to a cattle ranch to read the research and watch footage
of animals being injured, maimed, and, in many cases,
killed.

"I find it hard to believe that cowboys jump on the
backs of bulls on the range." She arched a brow, daring
him to take up her argument.

"Whoa, whoa ... both of you need to calm down."
Mike Findley glanced from her face to the cowboy
beside him.

While she was certain anyone could see the fury in
her eyes, Derek remained as maddeningly unperturbed
as ever, with his thumbs hooked in the front of his chaps
and giving her that cocky, playboy grin of his. He was

so confident he could win this argument. It took every ounce of self-control to keep herself from smacking him. She decided she'd better try a different tactic before Findley escorted her out once and for all. She wasn't about to be outsmarted by this arrogant, pig-headed cowboy.

"Mr. Findley," she began, facing the older man and ignoring the infuriating mass of muscle beside him, "while I understand rodeo is how you make your living, you must understand it isn't exactly a civilized method. It's perpetuating the mistreatment of animals. You have them doing things they would never do in nature. In the past, horses were obviously tamed for riding but not by scaring them to the point that they would hurl themselves into fences. Can you deny the many injuries rodeo stock receive each year?"

Mike held up a hand, halting her in the middle of her diatribe, and laughed. "Young lady, have you ever actually been to a rodeo before? Or seen a horse being broken to ride?"

Angela cocked her head to the side. "Not in person, but in my background research—"

"I'm not sure what sort of research you've done, but I'd be happy to show you around so that you can actually see the animals, see the measures we take to protect them, and talk to our judges and vets."

Angela took a step back, surprised by his offer, and glanced toward Derek. "You'd do that? I was led to believe that you would try to avoid the press and any sort of videotaping of your animals."

Derek shook his head and pursed his lips. "What kind

of propaganda have you been reading?" He rolled his eyes. "If you'll excuse me, I have a rodeo to get started. And animals to take care of," he added for her benefit.

She narrowed her eyes at him as he left, wishing she could burn a hole in his back with her thoughts. *Arrogant jerk.* He probably thought she was a pushy, obnoxious shrew who should learn her place, but she wasn't going to pretend to be a simpering, barefoot-and-pregnant country girl who would fall for his drawling, hillbilly charm. Her mother had fallen for a cocky, swaggering man and paid dearly for it. She would never be a submissive, weak female and no man would dominate her. If that made her a bitch, then she was happy to let narrow-minded brutes think so.

Mike caught her staring after Derek and smiled, his head cocked to the side. "Young lady, I'd be happy to show you around the rodeo and explain what we do." He tapped his index finger against his lower lip. "But if you really want a story, and I think you do, I have a better idea." His eyes glimmered mischievously and she wondered what this man had up his sleeve.

DEREK TRIED TO ignore the gorgeous redhead all day, but she seemed to be everywhere he looked. He couldn't help but notice the sway of her hips as she climbed the steps to the chutes when Mike showed her the saddle bronc equipment. Later, as she watched the calf roping with intensity, he noticed the way she pursed her lips in concentration. While she was deep in thought, he couldn't help but be mesmerized by her eyes, a deep shade of emerald green he'd never seen before.

This was exactly the kind of distraction he hadn't wanted to deal with. By the middle of the barrel racing event, he found himself concerned about the pink tinge her skin had begun to take, her hat doing little to protect her pale skin from burning. While part of him warned him not to feel any concern for this woman bent on ruining their reputation, he refused to even consider letting her suffer. It just wasn't in him to ignore someone in need.

He pulled his horse to a halt behind her as she focused on the pen of bulls. "You might want to find some sunscreen." He couldn't help being a bit amused when she jumped and moved away from his gelding as he dismounted. "Don't like horses, huh?"

"You just surprised me." She flipped her hair back from her shoulder, and he could read the lie in her eyes.

Tiny beads of sweat clung to her upper lip. Working in a newsroom obviously hadn't prepared her for withstanding this kind of heat in long sleeves, and he bit back his condescending smile. She pressed her fingers against her cheeks, testing the burn.

"Ow!" She pulled her hands away from the tender skin. "I didn't realize I was so bad."

"Let me guess, you don't have sunscreen?" He arched a brow.

"Well, I didn't exactly plan on staying out here all day."

"Just a quick morning attack?" he filled in.

"Interview," she corrected, giving him a dirty look.

"If that's what you want to call it." He motioned for her to follow him as he led the horse toward one of the trailers. "Here." He reached inside and handed her a bottle of lotion. "Your cheeks and nose are getting the worst of it, but be sure to do the back of your hands, too."

She sniffed at the sunscreen and squeezed some onto her fingertips, rubbing it on her cheekbones and nose. She hissed as the cold lotion hit her cheeks. "I guess it's worse than I realized." She eyed him warily. "Why are you being so nice all of a sudden?"

Derek shrugged and leaned against the trailer. "Maybe I just don't want you to accuse me of mistreatment." He fought the grin tugging at the corners of his mouth.

Angela glared at him. "Thank you." She tossed the bottle back at him. He quickly moved in front of the horse and caught the bottle in midair.

"This ole boy doesn't mind, but most horses will spook if you throw things around them," he warned. He looped a halter around the horse's neck and buckled it.

He moved closer to her and was immediately assaulted by her peach-vanilla scent. How in the world could she still smell so enticing after being in this heat all day? "You really don't know much about rodeo, do you?"

"Do I look like I know anything about rodeo?"

"More so than you did this morning. I do miss your other pants, though." Derek winked and laughed when she glared at him, tucking his thumbs in the front of his chaps. "So, why take this assignment?" He wasn't even sure why he asked. Something about her drew him in. In spite of her obvious dislike of him and his chosen career, he wanted to get to know her better, to find out what would make a woman like her brave the unknown for a news story.

"I'm not sure." She dipped her head, looking toward her boots before meeting his gaze. "I knew it would be a controversial topic."

"And you like that?" He could hear the logical voice in his head insisting he walk away from this conversation now, turn his back and get as far from her as he could. He ignored it. "Controversy?"

"I guess. It gets ratings, and I like those." She shrugged slightly but a hint of a smile curved the corners of her lips.

She looked innocent, young, and fresh with the sunburn coloring her cheeks and her eyes lit up with excitement as she talked about her job. He could just make out a faint smattering of adorable freckles on the bridge of her nose. His fingers suddenly itched to bury themselves in the fiery length of her hair. He gripped the belt of his chaps, refusing to give in to the need to touch her, and took a step away from her. He'd never wanted to kiss anyone so badly.

What was he thinking? This woman wanted to destroy Mike's business—their *family* business—for ratings. She was a selfish, conniving witch, no matter how attractive. He hated himself for the desire still churning through his veins. *Typical Derek, thinking with the wrong brain*. He had to get a grip on himself before he betrayed his family again.

"I guess it doesn't matter how you get them, right? Who you might ruin along the way?"

He saw her eyes cloud over, becoming as hard as the gems they resembled. "I'm a journalist, Mr. Chandler. I simply report the truth, even if you don't like it."

"At least your skewed version of it," he corrected. He turned back to his mount and unbuckled the halter. "I have to get back to work."

"I guess we'll see soon enough how skewed my version is," she answered with a haughty note.

Derek mounted the gelding and curled his lip in derision. "I'm sure Findley Brothers will manage to come out unscathed, if your earlier outfit was any indication of the depth of your research skills."

"Well, since Mr. Findley has invited me to stay on the ranch and join him as his guest for the next few rodeos, I should be able to do plenty of in-depth research on every aspect of your job, don't you think?"

"He what?"

She tilted her head, looking confused, and he wasn't sure if she was legitimately surprised that he didn't know about Mike's invitation or just a great actress. "Mr. Findley suggested I follow you guys with a small crew and see how the animals are"—she searched for a suitable term—"handled." She shrugged. She knew there was a good chance they would try to keep the less savory parts of the operation under wraps and hidden from her view. But they had a rodeo to run, which meant she'd have plenty of time to snoop around on her own without them watching over her shoulder. So far, it didn't seem like they saw anything wrong with the way they operated though. In which case, she wouldn't need to sneak around at all.

"Wonderful," he muttered. He forced himself to swallow the lump lodged in his throat as he clenched his jaw. "Then I guess this is your official welcome to the crew, Ms. McCallister."

He needed to find Mike *now*.

Chapter Three

"Mike, you've been the only father I've ever known, and I mean this with all due respect . . ." Derek ran his fingers through his hair before slamming his hat back on his head. "What in the hell were you thinking? You cannot let her do a story on us."

"Derek, it's not a big deal. We've got nothing to hide, and this will prove it. It should get animal rights activists off our backs." He shook his head. "Trust me, your sister and Sydney will set her straight pretty quickly if she gets out of line. I almost feel sorry for her. Besides, she's harmless." He chuckled at the thought.

Derek glared at Mike. "Just because that woman looks like an angel doesn't make her one."

Mike's brows shot to his hairline and he chuckled. "An angel?"

"Damn it, Mike, this isn't funny." Derek sighed, irritated that he'd let the comment slip, and threw his gloves on the side of the trailer. His gelding twitched at the sound as a cloud of dust rose from under them.

"What's not funny?" His sister walked up to them with the baby in one arm and patted Derek's horse on the neck.

"Mike just invited that reporter to stay at the ranch in order to prove we don't mistreat our animals."

"We don't. So, what's the big deal?" Jen agreed, shrugging. "She'll follow us around for a few days, get some video, realize she was wrong, and go home. No story and no harm done."

"I don't think this one will give up that easily," Derek argued.

"Oh, are we talking about that redhead you've been watching all day?" Jen didn't wait for an answer. "Is my baby brother afraid of a little girl?" she teased. It irritated him that she didn't bother to hide her patronizing smile. "Is that pretty girl being mean to you?"

"Shut up, Jennifer," he muttered. "Is either of you even considering that she could spin anything we do to make it look really bad for us? She could cause a lot of trouble." He glanced toward the arena, where the announcer was cracking jokes with one of the rodeo clowns, indicating the end of the break from events. The bull riding was next, and he needed to be in the arena with Clay. "You know Scott will agree with me. But you're not calling him to ask his opinion, are you?"

"Who still runs this company?" Mike asked, tapping his chin, pretending to contemplate the answer. "Oh, right! It's me. Now, get your butt back into the arena.

We have one event left and we're heading out in the morning—*with* that reporter," he added.

Derek knew any discussion regarding a certain pain-in-the-ass reporter was finished. Mike was calling the shots and, as usual, Derek's opinion was overruled. It frustrated him that even when he tried to step up, his family treated him like an irresponsible child. He clenched his jaw so tightly he felt his pulse throbbing in his temple. He jumped into the stirrup and swung his leg over the saddle.

"This is a mistake, Mike."

"YOU REALIZE THIS is a crazy idea, right?" Joe, Angela's station manager and ex-boyfriend, shook his head as she paced. "Why in the world do you feel the need to go traipsing to a cattle ranch to get a story? I think it's a bad idea."

"Viewers love stories like this, you know that."

"We'll find you something else. I promise I'll put you on a bigger story. Maybe something with that realtor that was embezzling from clients."

"That's local, Joe. A big exposé is going to get the attention of bigger stations. And a story that encompasses a national pastime . . . The only thing better would be if it were about football or baseball. People see cowboys as larger than life. If they aren't the heroes, well, *that* is a story that gets attention."

"So this is about leaving the station again?"

"Joe, you know I need this. I have to get Dad out of

this place." She waved her hand around the sparsely furnished, two-bedroom apartment she shared with her father.

He frowned at her. "There is nothing wrong with this place. This is home. You've grown up here."

"As long as he's here, guilt will keep eating at him. He drinks to forget. I have to get him away from everyone who's enabling him. Do you realize the bartender at O'Reilly's has a cot for him in the back room?"

He pulled her arm and urged her to sit beside him on the worn-out couch. "Your mama is buried here. This is where we should be, together." He curled his fingers around her hand.

Angela bit her lower lip. She cared about Joe; she had since they were children. He was one of the only men she'd considered trusting even a little. Joe was the only person who knew the truth about her father and his drinking problem, but she couldn't see him as anything other than a friend and her boss. She'd tried to force herself to feel more for him, and at his pleading she'd agreed to date him. But she broke it off after only a few months. It had felt too much like dating her brother.

She knew he thought he was in love with her, but she just couldn't return the emotion. There was no spark there no matter how much she wished she could pretend there was. She couldn't lie to him, and she cared about him far too much to ask him to settle for a loveless relationship. Maybe her parents' dysfunctional relationship had jaded her on love. Maybe the death of her mother at such a young age had hardened her heart and she would never find love. Whatever the reason, it was just another to add to the long list convincing her to move on from this place.

Angela slipped her hand from his grasp. "I have to get him away from here. You know that. As long as we're here, he's going to continue drinking."

"You don't know that leaving will help him. What if it doesn't or if it makes things worse?" He sighed and clenched his jaw, his pulse ticking in his temple. She could see the war in his heart between wanting to see her happy and wanting her for himself. "How will I manage if you leave?"

She smiled sadly, cupping her hand against his smooth cheek. "We can only be friends, Joe. We tried to be more, remember?" She could only hope that Joe would find someone who would appreciate the love he had to offer. It simply wasn't her.

He nodded, his dark hair falling into his defeated blue eyes as he hung his head. She wanted to brush the lock of hair back but knew he'd misconstrue the gesture. "I'll try to get you a small crew, but I can't send more than one or two guys. You'll have to do all your own research. But bring back a good story." He stood up, looking down at her still on the couch. "You know I love you."

His voice was so forlorn, it squeezed at her heart. It killed her to hear the ache in his voice. She wished she could love him in return. "I love you, too, but it's not like that. I think we both need this to work out so that Dad and I can move out, and you can move on."

"I'll never move on," he whispered as he looked back at her from the front door. Joe shook his head and closed the door.

IT WAS WELL past midnight when her cell phone chimed from the battered nightstand. Angela reached for it, knocking over a bottle of perfume and a picture of her mother in the process. Her finger closed on the pebbled case but she couldn't find the button to connect the call before it stopped ringing.

"Damn," she muttered as she scooted into a seated position against the pillows. She glanced down at the screen, extra bright in the darkened room. "Damn," she repeated, recognizing the number on the screen. No law-abiding citizen should have the police department on speed dial.

Angela pushed her mussed hair back over her shoulder and listened to the message. She rubbed her eyes, trying to wake herself before she called back. She waited as it rang several times before an officer picked up the phone.

"Fort Mills Police Department, is this an emergency?" Angela repeated the extension left in the message.

She instantly recognized the deep, masculine voice of the officer who had called her numerous times over the past ten years. "Officer Miller," he answered.

"This is Angela McCallister. You called me a few moments ago?"

"Yes, Angela. We have your father in custody again."

Angela bit down on her bottom lip, trying to calm the anger bubbling in her chest, and took a deep breath, exhaling slowly. "What did he do this time?"

"Same as always, drunk and disorderly." The officer sighed into the receiver. "Angela, you have to get him some help."

Get him *some help? What about me?*

"I'll be there in a few minutes, Officer Miller."

"We'll have him in holding, like usual."

Angela arrived at the police station in time to hear her father's voice singing at the top of his lungs from one of the holding cells. She couldn't make out his words but she'd recognize his Irish baritone voice anywhere.

"I'm here to pay the fine for my father, Robert McCallister."

"Sign right here." The officer on duty pointed at a line on the form in front of her. "And here." He tapped a finger on the next page. "Last time."

"How much?" She cringed as her father's voice echoed past the closed door again. She slipped her checkbook onto the counter and prayed her dwindling savings would magically have enough to cover the fine for the second time this month.

"One thousand dollars, ma'am."

Her breath hitched in her throat and the officer looked up from the paperwork. "Are you all right?"

"Fine," she answered quickly. "Just a little hiccup." Angela flashed the officer a dazzling smile, praying she could convince Joe to give her yet another advance. She wrote out the check, hoping Joe would come through again, her fingers gripping the pen hard enough that she worried it might break.

As much as she loved her father, there were times she wished she could run away, abandon him to his drinking, and find a life without the responsibility of looking after him hanging over her head. She wanted to turn her back on him and the choices he made, but she knew it just as often was an illness he couldn't control. She couldn't explain it.

He was her father, the only family she had left since her mother died when she was eight, but he was a drunk and had been as long as she could remember. He was the reason her mother had left that night, the reason her mother ran out of the apartment into the rain, the reason she didn't see the car speeding down the wet street. He was also the reason that Angela hadn't been allowed to go to the hospital and say goodbye to her mother before she slipped away. All because he couldn't loosen his grip on a bottle.

Angela shook her head, clearing the bitter memories. Nothing would bring her mother back, but she refused to end up like her. She was going to find a way to give them both a second chance for a better life. She'd spent her entire youth dragging her father home from local bars because he passed out. Too many bartenders knew her by name and kept her phone number by their registers. Tonight would be the last time she bailed him out. She couldn't waste any more time letting her father's addiction drag them both down. They had to get away from this place, its memories and pain, and this rodeo story was the first glimmer of hope for escape. She had to grasp it with both hands and make it work.

"Oh look! That's my Angie-girl." She heard him slur the words as Officer Miller escorted him through the doors.

"Yes, Bobby, I know."

He gave Angela a sad smile as her father fell forward, hugging her. He might be a poor excuse for a father, but he loved her as much as he was able to in his agonized heart. "You look just like your mother," her father whispered loudly.

She could see the sadness in her father's eyes at the mention of her mother, but she was finding it difficult to dredge up sympathy for him when she thought about how she'd just spent their rent. The embers of anger flamed to life.

"Let's go, Dad." She just wanted to get him home and into bed so she could pack and leave first thing in the morning before she had to nurse his hangover.

DEREK AND MIKE had just finished loading the last two horses into the stock trailer when the blue sedan stopped at the back gate of the arena. Jen shot her brother a playful grin as the redhead emerged from the driver's seat to open the gate for herself.

"Your girlfriend's finally here."

"Shut up, Jen," Derek muttered, glaring at his sister as he slammed the back of the trailer shut and latched it.

Jen arched a brow and caught Mike's eye before making her way back to the truck she was riding in with her husband.

"You might as well go let her know we're about ready to leave." Mike tossed the lead ropes into the tack compartment. "We'll be pulling out in about thirty minutes."

"Are you kidding me, Mike?" Derek sighed and shook his head, jamming his hands into his pockets. "This stupid idea was yours, so I don't see why I'm the one dealing with her."

The old man slapped his shoulder. "Think of it as a good chance to set things on the right foot again. Go apologize for yesterday." He chuckled. "Use some of that Chandler charm you boys are famous for."

Derek rolled his eyes. He was beginning to wish he'd never set eyes on this sexy, smart-mouthed, city girl. "You owe me, Mike."

"Don't worry, Derek," Mike called after him. "You can thank me later."

Derek made his way toward her, dragging his feet with every step. Mike's entire plan was ridiculous and doomed to backfire. Derek was sure of it. He glanced at her through hooded eyes, a baseball cap shading his face from her view.

At least she was nice to look at. She looked different with her hair pulled loosely back at the base of her neck. She'd dressed casually today in blue jeans and a plain green t-shirt that matched the deep emerald color of her eyes. She appeared relaxed and comfortable. He wondered if it was because she didn't feel the need to play the part of the hard-hitting journalist. As he got closer he could see she'd worn only minimal eye makeup and marveled how it actually made her look prettier. She looked innocent and young with her cheeks pink from the sun yesterday, the sunburn fading to a slight tan, her green eyes glinting brightly with excitement. Without the pretentious glare she sported yesterday, she seemed almost approachable. Desire circled and settled deep in his belly. The simple fact that he wanted to approach her irritated him.

"Morning," he muttered as he walked up to her.

"I'm so sorry I'm running late." She was flustered and brushed a loose tendril of hair behind her ear. "I had a bit of a hang-up at home and got out later than I'd planned."

He unlatched the chain that locked the gate with a loud clang on the metal and held it open for her. "Go ahead and park by my truck over there." He pointed at the black pickup in front of the stock trailer. "We'll be leaving soon."

"Is there anything I can help with?" she asked, climbing back into her car.

His brow arched in surprise. "We can check with Jen and see if she might have something for you to do."

She drove the sedan slowly to his truck. Was this the same pretentious woman he'd met yesterday? He was curious about the overnight change in her. The woman who'd tried to interview Mike yesterday wanted to shut them down, but this morning she seemed considerate, jovial even. It would be easy to fall for her performance, especially when she looked as sweet and innocent as she was acting, but he knew better than to trust her. Trust was a luxury he didn't have to offer anymore. He wasn't going to fail his family again.

ANGELA FELT ELATED. She was trying to hide her excitement, mainly because no one would understand the huge weight that seemed to drop from her shoulders with every mile she drove away from her apartment. She'd packed up her meager belongings and left her father with a glass of water, some aspirin, and a note promising to collect him after her assignment finished; her father was still sleeping off his hangover. The refrigerator and cupboards were full, but every trace of alcohol was cleaned out of the house. Joe had promised to check on him twice a week for the next few weeks. There was nothing left for her to do but get in her car and drive toward their future, their freedom. She knew that eventually she would need to call and check on her father, but she was never returning to that apartment. It was now a part of her past, and she was heading to their future. This was the first step on her way to a better life for them both. This breath of freedom would become the first of many.

She parked the car and jumped from behind the wheel. "Who is Jen?" she asked Derek as he walked toward her. "I don't think I met her yesterday."

A scowl marred his handsome features. He looked

like he wanted to throw her off of the property again, and she wondered if she hadn't been too aggressive yesterday. Angela chewed at her lower lip nervously. It looked like she was going to have to do some damage control with this cowboy.

"Look, I want to apologize for yesterday. I might have been a bit overeager for my story. Can we start over?" The words rushed out in a tumble as she thrust out her hand, praying that he would accept her peace offering at face value. She knew she had an ulterior motive, but he didn't realize how badly she needed this story to move ahead with her plan for her future.

He simply stared at her hand as if it were a snake about to strike, his dark eyes narrowing with distrust. "Overeager," he repeated, sarcasm tingeing his voice. "Yeah, I guess that's one way to describe it."

He crossed his arms over his broad chest, and she tried to ignore the way his biceps bulged, stretching the arms of his t-shirt. *How in the world did a cowboy get this muscular?* He looked as if he spent hours in the gym. The t-shirt stretched across his chest and her mouth went dry. Her pulse skipped a beat before racing ahead, and she felt a blush creeping up the back of her neck. Knowing it would show on her face immediately and not wanting him to see how he was affecting her, she turned back toward the car, pretending to busy herself with the boxes in the backseat.

"Mr. Chandler, I hope we'll be able to work together without any problems. I'm coming into this with an open mind. I was hoping you might do the same." She glanced at him over her shoulder as he continued to glare at her.

"What's all that?" He jerked his chin toward the pile of luggage and boxes crammed into her backseat. "Planning on moving in permanently?"

"No, but a girl never knows what she might need," she joked. She tried to cover her nervousness with a laugh, but what slipped past her lips came off sounding near-hysterical. She had to get control over herself. She wasn't about to confess that she'd packed everything she owned into her small car.

Angela turned and leaned back against the car door before shrugging. "I like to be prepared for every circumstance. There's a lot of equipment we'll need," she lied, hoping he wouldn't realize her deception once she unpacked her car.

He sighed, not bothering to hide his irritation with her presence. "Jen's in that trailer." He pointed toward a fifth-wheel trailer already hitched to a truck. A huge cowboy was loading plastic totes into the compartment on the side. Derek turned to walk away.

"But . . ."

"What?" he asked, turning back, exasperated. "I'm sure you can introduce yourself. You didn't have any problem with it yesterday."

His eyes darkened from coffee to cocoa and she wondered if he wasn't testing her, being deliberately challenging in hopes she would give up and go home. She lifted her chin slightly, determined to prove to him that she could match his defiance.

"Fine." She clicked the button on her car alarm, signaling to him that it was locked and she was finished with their conversation. Shoving the keys into her pocket, she walked away from him, leaving him standing alone at her car.

That's what you call damage control, Angela?

Chapter Four

ANGELA SIGHED AS she glanced at her vibrating cell phone. This was the sixth call she'd received during the three-hour drive to the ranch she would soon be calling her home, at least temporarily. She recognized Joe's number again on the caller ID. She knew she couldn't avoid him forever, so she pushed the button on her earpiece.

"Hey, Joe. What's up?" She prayed her father wasn't already causing trouble.

"Almost there?"

"I think so. The crew will be there in the morning, right?"

"About that." He hesitated. "The station isn't too happy sinking money into this. They want you to come back."

Panic flooded her chest, drying her mouth and closing her throat. She'd barely made it out of town. She couldn't let them kill this story before it happened. It was going to be the one opportunity that would change her life; she could *feel* it. Every journalist knew to trust their gut instinct above logic, and hers was screaming at her to keep moving forward.

"Joe, you have to convince them. You know what this means to me," she pleaded. She hated begging, but she couldn't admit defeat this easily.

"I've tried, Gigi." She cringed, wondering how many times she had to tell him she hated that nickname.

"I won't give up on this. You know as well as I do that there's a story here."

"No," he argued. "I don't. I know that you want to run away and you're grasping at this as a way to do it."

Angela's eyes darted to the rearview mirror and the cowboy driving the black truck. She could come up with far more friendly places to run away to than one run by a stock contractor who already hated her. Nothing would make Derek Chandler happier than for her to turn around and head back without any story, her tail tucked between her legs in defeat. He'd made it perfectly clear that he wasn't welcoming her on the ranch and wouldn't be any help getting her story. Without the backing of the station or even a cameraman, she wasn't sure she could do this. How could she conduct an interview and videotape it at the same time?

"Don't I have vacation time coming?" *Please be my friend instead of my boss now.*

"It's not like you've ever used any of it, so I'm sure you do. Why?" She could hear the irritation in his voice, just like when she'd outsmarted him as kids.

"Give me the next few weeks off. If I can prove there's a story, will you send the crew?"

He sighed into the mouthpiece of the phone, and she knew she was testing his patience. She seemed to be doing that a lot with the men around her lately. "I don't like this idea one bit, Gigi. You don't know these people."

"Please, Joe? I'll be fine, and if I don't have anything in two weeks I'll come back, no complaints. I promise."

"Two weeks?" His voice cracked and he cleared his throat. "Angela, I don't think they'll let you take two weeks off together."

Angela? Either he's furious or someone just walked into the room. Since he didn't lower his voice, she assumed he was angry at her. She might as well push the envelope now.

"Two weeks," she repeated, praying that she could dig up something promising before then.

Ideas and theories weren't going to be enough. She needed concrete evidence and a killer story.

Desperation gripped her chest and squeezed as she realized that in less than two weeks, she might have to destroy the livelihood of the very people welcoming her into their home.

DEREK WATCHED THE woman in the car in front of him as they pulled through the gates, declaring their arrival on the ranch. Not long ago she'd been pretty animated in the car, and he assumed she'd been talking to someone on her cell phone. She slowed as her tires left the paved road and met with the crunch of gravel. Her small car kicked up dust and pebbles, so he slowed the truck, letting it fall farther behind so that the tiny rocks wouldn't damage his windshield. Each one was fairly harmless, but given the right velocity they could become dangerous ammunition. Like the redhead in front of him. He was afraid she would take any little detail she found and twist it into a destructive news story. One sick animal or accident and she could cause the downfall of everything his family had built together.

He watched the stock trailer with the cattle peel off and head to the north pasture while the trailers with the bulls split and went toward his sister's house. He wasn't surprised to see Sydney exit the barn and wave, carrying his niece on one hip as they pulled up the drive. The blue sedan made its way toward the front of the house as he parked his truck near the barn. Several more rigs followed them down the drive as the crew hurried to unload the animals and get them settled. It was always hectic unloading after a rodeo, but with an extra set of judgmental eyes, Derek worried over every detail.

"Hey, take it slow with those bulls," he yelled as one of the boys passed. The driver waved a hand, letting Derek know he'd been heard. "Let's get these horses out," he ordered, reaching for another, newer crew member.

He glanced toward Angela in time to see her slip out of her seat and stare at the activity, her eyes wide with awe. He was reassured to see her overwhelmed by the busyness around her. Maybe realizing just how hard they worked, how important their livelihood was to their family, would send her home empty-handed and apologetic.

"Sydney," he called, hurrying over to his sister-in-law. "Where's Scott?" He looked back over his shoulder as Silvie, their housekeeper, came out and enveloped a hesitant Angela in a warm embrace. He frowned as he turned back to her. "We have trouble."

"Scott's in the barn. Who's she?"

"A reporter." He couldn't help the distaste coloring his voice. "She's doing a story on the abuse of rodeo stock."

"Then why is she here?" she asked, adjusting her daughter, Kassie, on her hip while she played with her necklace.

"Mike invited her to travel with us for a while. Won't that be fun?" He shook his head, his voice dripping with sarcasm.

She sighed, looking skeptical. "Scott's not going to like this."

Derek held his hands up in defense. "I had nothing to do with it. I tried to stop Mike." Kassie saw that he had his hands up and leaned toward him. He scooped her out of her mother's arms and kissed the curls on top of her head.

Sydney looked from Derek to the woman Silvie led toward the house. "This was Mike's idea?" A slow, confident smile spread over her face, her eyes lighting up. "Looks like he's at it again."

Derek glanced up as his brother came out of the barn and draped his arm around his wife, leaning down to kiss her cheek. "At what again?"

He and Scott hadn't always gotten along well. It had been worse when Sydney arrived at the ranch as Mike's new horse trainer. But over the past year they'd been able to put the past behind them and begin mending their strained relationship. Scott set a high standard. Derek had big shoes to fill in the company business, and at times Derek felt like it was nearly impossible. No matter how hard he tried, he struggled to be the man his brother was. Derek felt the need to continually prove himself.

"Mike's matchmaking again." She directed Scott's attention toward Angela. "He invited a reporter to stay." Sydney untangled Kassie's fist from Derek's t-shirt just before the little girl leaned forward, reaching for her father's hat.

Scott's eyes narrowed suspiciously. "Why would a reporter come here?" Derek explained the situation to them. "Why didn't anyone call us? I know you were busy, but Jen could've called."

"Jen went right along with Mike."

Derek was glad his brother shared his resentment at Angela's presence. Technically, Scott had the final say on all business matters with the company, being the majority shareholder after buying out Mike's shares and distributing them equally between the three of them, but they had all unanimously agreed to allow Mike to continue running it as he saw fit. They loved him too much to ever ask him to step down. None of them could forget that Mike had taken them in and raised them after their parents were killed. None of them would turn their back on that kind of loyalty.

"Scott, you know Mike." Derek handed Kassie off to her father as she leaned toward him. "He does what he wants. I guess he's decided that, right now, he wants a reporter snooping around during our busiest time of the year. I don't understand it, I don't like it, but there's not a damn thing I can do about it." Derek threw a look over his shoulder where the woman had disappeared into the main house. "Doesn't look like you can either."

"Wanna bet?" Scott started toward the house, determination etched on his brow.

Sydney put a hand on Scott's shoulder, stopping his tirade. "Just wait." Her voice was soft but stern. "I'm sure Mike has his reasons for having her here. You didn't want me here either, remember?" She arched her brow at him, and Scott twisted his mouth into a grin.

"Fine, for now," he agreed grudgingly. "Come on, little lady," he cooed to his daughter in his arms as she stared up at him, a smile of delight spreading over her face. "Daddy's gonna show you the big horsies."

As Scott walked back into the barn, Derek turned to Sydney. "How did you manage to turn my macho brother into the world's biggest softie?"

Sydney glanced back at her husband and daughter as the two entered the barn and laughed. "It wasn't me. That was all Kassie's doing."

Derek eyed his brother, trying to ignore the stab of jealousy piercing his heart. He wanted what Scott and Sydney shared, what his sister and Clay had together. He wanted his own family someday, complete with someone who would light up whenever he walked into the room.

He wanted to find someone he could be vulnerable with without worrying that he was going to disappoint them. For a while, he hoped he'd found it with Sydney. It had been difficult when she chose his brother over him even if he knew it was the right decision, so he went on the road with Mike for the start of the rodeo season. Time had given him the perspective he needed, and he realized they'd never shared what she had with Scott. Those two were meant to be together, but seeing them made him wonder whether there was actually someone who could fill the emptiness he felt inside.

ANGELA WASN'T SURE how to respond as the housekeeper wrapped her in a warm hug only moments after meeting her. She'd never been overly affectionate and was uncomfortable with touchy-feely people who didn't seem to understand the concept of personal space. However, she also didn't think it would be in her best interest to alienate the very people welcoming her into their home, so she tolerated the hug and pretended to return the sentiment.

She didn't have to try hard; it was difficult not to like Silvie immediately. She looked exactly the way Angela imagined her grandmother would have if she'd ever known her, complete with gray hair, apron around her rounded hips, and ample stomach. Wrinkles of laughter and joy crinkled around her eyes and the curve of her mouth.

"Come inside, dear. You must be hungry after that drive." She shuffled Angela up the porch stairs and toward the house. "Those men never stop and eat," she fussed. "And just look how thin you are! You look like you need a few good meals."

Angela glanced back toward the barn in time to see Derek frowning in her direction before turning back to his conversation with the woman holding an infant. He looked angry again and she had the unreasonable urge to apologize. She wasn't sure why she should feel remorseful or why she cared if he hated her presence, but the feeling remained just the same.

She saw him tip the front of his hat toward her slightly, acknowledging her. She narrowed her eyes, assuming he was somehow mocking her, and on a whim blew him a kiss as she turned on her heel and followed Silvie into the house. She immediately regretted her childish impulse and scolded herself for her lack of self-control.

"Silvie, I'm fine. Really," she insisted, hurrying to catch up to the woman who was surprisingly nimble for her age. "I'm not that hungry. If you show me where I'll be staying, I'll just start unpacking my car." *And hide in my room doing research.*

"Oh, pshh." Silvie waved her off. "Don't you worry your pretty head about that. I'll get the boys to bring your things into the house and we'll get you settled in a bit. Right now, sit, and I'll get you something to tide you over until dinner."

Left with little choice in the matter, Angela slid into one of the chairs surrounding a large kitchen table. She slid her hand over the well-worn surface, feeling the nicks and scratches. No doubt they had shared several family dinners around this table, filled with deep conversation and raucous laughter. She'd seen enough at the rodeo to know that Derek was fiercely protective of his family and their business. She thought of the meals she and her father had shared throughout the years, most consisting of deafening silence while he drank his entree from a bottle and she warmed some sort of frozen dinners from boxes. There'd been no laughter in her childhood, no father-daughter conversations or tenderness. Even when her mother was alive, mealtime had been an experiment in sensory deprivation, where she and her mother remained as quiet as possible to allow her father to sleep off his latest hangover. Most nights, even the silence didn't help, and the war between them would rage while Angela hid in her room.

"So, Angela," Silvie's voice interrupted her depressing thoughts of the past. "What will your story be about? We really don't see many reporters around here."

Silvie bustled around the kitchen, filling the coffee pot with water before opening the oven to check on the food cooking inside. As soon as the oven door opened, the delicious scent of sage and garlic filled the kitchen. Angela inhaled the heavenly scent of yeasty homemade bread, and her stomach growled loudly. She covered it with her hand quickly, but Silvie had already heard it and laughed sweetly.

"You see? You are hungry." She reached for a plate of cookies on the counter and slid it on the table. "Try these for right now."

Angela stared at the plate. Homemade chocolate chip cookies. She tried to blink back the tears that sprung up from deep within her heart. She hadn't eaten a homemade cookie since before her mother died. She'd been too busy taking care of her father, putting herself through school, and, later, working to spend time on anything as frivolous as making cookies. Just the sight of those baked treats conjured up the memory of a too-short period of her life when someone had taken care of her, when she remembered at least a modicum of happiness. The memories of her lost childhood burned in the back of her throat, and she tried to swallow her unbidden tears.

"Angela?" She looked up to see Silvie's brow furrow in concern as she pulled out the chair at the end of the table. "Aw, honey, are you okay?"

"I'm fine," she managed to whisper as she blinked back the threatening tears. "It's just been a long day. I'm a little tired."

"I'm so sorry. I should have taken you right up to your room." She rose and took Angela's hand in hers. "Come on. Let's get you settled upstairs."

Silvie led her up the stairs to a small room on the right of the hall. Angela crossed the threshold and couldn't help but smile in spite of the emotional exhaustion quickly overtaking her. The room reminded her of the room she and her mother had always dreamed about when she was a child—bright and sunny with double windows on one wall covered by lace curtains billowing in the late afternoon breeze. A queen-size bed against the back wall was draped with a snow-white bedspread dotted with cheery yellow flowers. Everything about the room made her feel happy and safe, something she'd rarely felt before.

"This will be your room for your stay. Please, make yourself at home," Silvie instructed. "When your crew arrives, we've already made arrangements for them to stay in the bunkhouse with some of the boys."

Angela's stomach did a flip at the mention of the crew. If she didn't get evidence of a story quickly there wasn't going to be a crew coming, but she wasn't about to admit that to anyone. She would make sure she found an angle for this story; she *couldn't* fail, for her father's sake. She just hoped it wouldn't mean twisting the facts to make a story. She knew reporters did it all the time, but so far she'd avoided that trap. But she'd do it if she had to. She steeled herself against getting emotionally attached. Her future had to come first.

"Thanks, Silvie. This is perfect." She made her way into the room. "Is there a bathroom where I can freshen up?"

"You'll share the bathroom at the end of the hall with Derek. His room is across the hall, and Mike's is at the other end. Mine is downstairs, so if you need anything, just come and let me know."

Angela's heart skipped a beat at the mention of Derek. She'd hoped she could avoid him for the most part, but it didn't look likely with his room mere steps away. His dark, brooding eyes filled her mind. She bit her lower lip and wondered how difficult he was going to make it for her to get the information she needed.

"Dinner will be ready in an hour, if you want to get cleaned up or lay down for a few minutes. I'll send Sydney up to get you when it's ready."

"Sydney?" Angela glanced back at Silvie in the doorway before turning her attention toward someone yelling outside the window, moving the curtain aside to look out.

The view from her room was incredible. She could see the entire front pasture, where several cowboys unloaded horses. She smiled as they removed the halters and the horses ran away, twisting and bucking, tossing their heads. They looked carefree, and for a moment she felt a camaraderie with the animals, sharing their pleasure at being released from captivity. A broad-shouldered cowboy caught her attention, and she knew, even without seeing his face, it was Derek. He had several inches on most of the cowboys she'd seen at the rodeo over the weekend and he was definitely more muscular. Most of the cowboys she'd seen were on the lean side, but he seemed to have muscles upon muscles. She couldn't deny he was gorgeous with his dark brown hair and caramel-colored eyes. When he decided to turn on the charm, she bet every female heart within a twenty mile radius melted.

She chewed at her lower lip. Handsome as he was, it wasn't his looks that continued to pull her eyes to his frame standing in the pasture. She couldn't explain it, but when they'd flirted over the gate at the rodeo arena, she'd seen something familiar in his eyes. She'd recognized the same haunted look she knew was in hers. They shared a sad desperation most people didn't show. In those few moments of conversation, she knew they had both unwillingly shared an unspoken secret neither meant to reveal. Even during their faux seduction, they'd been unable to hide their desire for something more.

Angela suddenly realized Silvie was still talking to her, but she'd missed the conversation. "I'm sorry, what were you saying?" She moved away from the window, letting the curtain fall.

Silvie walked to the window and glanced outside, a knowing smile gracing her lips. "I said, Sydney is Scott's wife. She's our horse trainer. Scott is Derek's older brother," she clarified. "You've already met Jen, his sister, and her husband, Clay, right?"

"This morning at the arena." Angela nodded.

Silvie walked back to the door and glanced at Angela over her shoulder, bracing her hand on the doorframe. "You'll find we're a close family. We take care of each other."

Angela wasn't sure if Silvie was issuing a warning or a promise.

Chapter Five

ANGELA PACED THE room, feeling like a caged animal. She'd tried to relax but her mind wouldn't settle. Even doing research online, which usually helped calm her nerves, wasn't doing anything to still the panicky uneasiness. She couldn't help but worry about the story or, more precisely, her lack of a story. This would be the most important story of her career, either raising her to new levels or ruining her reputation at the station completely. Maybe some fresh air would help her get some ideas for her story and settle her nerves. If nothing else, a walk around the property would give her a chance to do a little snooping and give her a better sense of what direction her story might take.

Angela tiptoed down the stairs without alerting Silvie and snuck out the front door. None of the cowboys gave her more than a quick glance as she meandered toward the barn, as if strange women walking around the ranch were a common occurrence. She recognized a few faces from the rodeo the previous weekend, but none that she'd interviewed. As a third cowboy shunned her gaze, she began to wonder if they weren't under specific orders to avoid her. Were they told *not* to give interviews, and if so, what were they hiding for their boss? She tried to ignore the small spark of hope that burned in the pit of her stomach as she poked her head inside the barn and thought of running into a certain hulking cowboy.

"Hello?" The only sound that greeted her was a soft rustle from the stall and what sounded like a stomping hoof. She heard a snort from deep in the barn, but there were no voices. She walked inside, grateful for a few moments of solitude to organize her thoughts into a viable plan of action.

In order to get her father the kind of help he would need, she needed to get him away from their neighborhood, away from the haunts that had become more familiar to him than their apartment. To do that, she needed to take a huge leap up the corporate ladder by getting picked up by a large station as an anchor and garnering a paycheck fitting the position. None of that was possible until she had a story—an exclusive—worthy of the large stations looking for her. It had to be controversial but, as controversial stories did, it was bound to cast a negative light on one of the parties involved. It was the nature of the news. There was no gray area; someone would take on the role of the bad guy and, in this case, it would likely be the stock contractor. Unfortunately, she really liked Mike Findley. Trying to resolve the guilt squeezing the air from her lungs, she moved toward the nearest stall and watched the horse eating grain from a flat, black bucket.

The animal was obviously well cared for, its shiny coat gleaming like copper satin where the sunlight streamed in through the open back door, and she wondered how she was going to prove these animals were abused. So far she'd only seen them given the utmost care.

If she was successful, if she found the proof she was looking for, what would the story do to Mike and his family? They relied on this business for their livelihood. She knew there was far more at stake here than just a story or her future.

What if the story broke and no one cared or she didn't get a better station to take notice or hire her? She didn't want to destroy this family's business needlessly. She felt her mind at odds with her heart. She knew better than to allow herself to become emotionally invested with the subject of a story, but none of her subjects had ever welcomed her into their home to share meal or been so hospitable. So far, Mike and Silvie had offered her a taste of family she'd hadn't felt since her mother had died. She'd never known what it was like to come home with someone to greet you at the door with a hug. She'd known only whispers and apprehension.

Would she have been this pessimistic if her mother had lived? Would they have ever escaped her father's addiction, or would they have continued to live under the shadow of his drinking? It was hard to remember a time when her father's alcoholism didn't color her memories. The ones she did have were so distant she couldn't be sure she didn't make them up. She knew her mother had done her best to protect her from her father's disgrace, but it hadn't always been possible.

She crossed her arms over the stall door and laid her chin on her wrists, watching the animal as it ignored her and continued eating, still wondering which decision was the right one. Angela smiled in awed delight as the horse lifted its head and sniffed at her arms, revealing a colt hidden behind it.

"I wasn't sure you knew how to smile."

The horse jerked its head up as Angela jumped back, moving away from the stall, yelping in surprise. "You scared me," she accused as Derek leaned on his shoulder against the wall of the stall with his fingers tucked into the pockets of his jeans.

She'd been so lost in her thoughts that she hadn't heard him come into the barn. His stance appeared casual but his eyes spoke of tension within, and she could feel distrust emanating from him.

"Silvie sent me out to find you and let you know dinner will be ready in about fifteen minutes."

"How did she know I was out here?"

A wry smile slipped to his lips. "She's raised me and Scott. If we couldn't sneak past her, there's no way you'll be able to." He shrugged. "There isn't much that goes on in this house she doesn't know about."

He was teasing, but his words hit too close to the truth. "I wasn't sneaking anywhere. I was simply going for a walk." She turned back to the animals in the stall, dismissing him.

"I see."

Instead of leaving, he bumped her hip with his and mimicked her stance at the stall door, looking inside as well. She was puzzled by his playfulness but wondered if Mike hadn't had a hand in his change of heart regarding her presence.

"See that little colt?" He jerked his chin at the baby trying to eat its mother's grain from the bucket. "He's our last foal out of Sydney's stud horse."

She wasn't sure what he expected in response so she remained silent. He cocked his head sideways and looked at her, his chin still on his forearms. His baseball cap on backward made his jaw look even more chiseled, and she felt her heart trip in her chest as his eyes locked with hers. "He's going to be part of the foundation of our breeding program."

"Sydney, your sister-in-law?" She edged away from him, giving herself a few more inches of space between them, trying to catch her breath and calm the nervous skipping of her heart.

He turned and faced her, standing upright, so she did the same. He took a step toward her, closing what little distance she'd created between them, and she felt his breath fan against her cheeks. She looked up at him. He was close enough that, had he wanted to, he could kiss her. Her heart lodged in her throat and her breath came in shallow gasps. She felt surrounded by him as he blocked her view of anything else. The scent of him, like leather and horses with a touch of cinnamon, heated her senses. She forced herself to stand her ground when everything in her warned her to back up and move away. She'd never allowed a man to have the upper hand before, and she didn't want to start now with this cowboy.

Several moments passed and he hadn't moved or touched her. He stood inches from her with his hands loose at his sides, staring down at her, waiting. She met his gaze and held her breath as his eyes darkened, becoming almost black, and she wondered if he might kiss her. She found herself wavering between wanting to press herself against him, feeling his fingers buried in her hair with his lips against hers, and running back to her car, returning to her apartment, and forgetting she'd ever met him.

"Why are you really here?" His voice was husky but gentle, coaxing the truth from her.

"I don't know what you mean." She resisted, barely able to put words together, let alone think of a logical explanation. Her heart pounded heavily against her ribs.

"I can't let you ruin our business. I won't let you destroy what Mike and my parents built." His words should have sounded like a threat, but his voice was seductive, belying the warning. "You have to know that."

"I don't want to destroy anything," she whispered, unable to tear her eyes from his mouth. She dug her nails into her palms, trying to refocus her attention on the pain instead of the desire swirling within, igniting dormant emotions.

"Why can't I seem to stay away from you?" he growled quietly. Derek took a step toward her, pressing her back against the wall of the barn, his hand slipped up to cup her jaw.

She barely heard his question as blood rushed through her veins, shooting flames of desire through her limbs, burning through her clothing. She curled her fingers against his chest, feeling the muscles tense under her fingers, and wondered why she didn't push him away. She could feel every inch of his hard frame pressed against her, holding her upright against the wall. His thumb brushed over her cheekbone, lighting a fire that spread over her skin. She could see the day-old beard growth dusting his jaw and imagined how that rasp would feel against her skin. A shiver of anticipation coursed through her as she met his hooded gaze. He leaned down toward her and she closed her eyes, expecting the touch of his lips on hers.

"Damn it," he cursed and she opened her eyes. Derek pushed himself away from her, and cold air filled the space between them. "I can't do this."

Disappointment flooded her, permeating the lonely places she tried to hide behind her work and caring for her father's needs. She'd never wanted a relationship with anyone before, never needed a man for anything, so why this one? She obviously wasn't his type any more than he was hers. They had nothing in common, especially considering she was likely to destroy everything he held dear. She covered up the dull ache of dejection with sarcasm, refusing to let him see how his rejection hurt.

"Just like a cowboy," she scoffed, "eight seconds and you're done." She shot him a disdainful glance as she pushed herself from the wall. "I'll remember to keep my interview with you short and sweet."

Angela brushed past him and flipped her hair from her shoulder, refusing to acknowledge how her skin still tingled from his touch or how her heart continued to race the entire way back into the house.

ANGELA'S PARTING COMMENT echoed through his mind, her eyes taunting him as she reminded him how, once again, he'd almost betrayed his family. Derek fisted his hands at his sides, his jaw clenched so tightly he thought it might break. He slammed his fist into the wall. Pain exploded in his hand before radiating up his arm and into his shoulder, but it did nothing to temper the ache in his chest. No wonder his family didn't trust him. Hadn't he learned his lesson when Liz used him to try and con them out of the ranch? He was still the same irresponsible Derek he'd always been, more interested in ladies and fun than in his obligations.

"What is wrong with you?" he muttered to himself, shaking his hand. "Idiot."

He made his way back to the house slowly, cursing himself with every step as he heard the family gathering in the kitchen. She would already be sitting down with them at the table. He considered staying outside but rejected the idea quickly. There'd be far too much explanation needed, and he didn't really want to examine what had just happened too closely.

He opened the back door in time to see Angela slipping into the chair between Sydney and Jen. Little Kassie was in her high chair at the corner of the table between her mother and father. Clay took the seat across from Jen with Silvie beside him. The only spot left was directly across from Angela.

Wonderful, now that contempt can stare me in the face all through dinner. Bitterness was already ruining his appetite as he slid into the chair.

"Now that you've met everyone, we can eat," Silvie said. "Derek, there you are." She reached out for his hand and squeezed. He cringed as pain radiated up his arm but hid it behind a soft smile.

Derek couldn't help but feel tenderness toward the only mother he could remember. He'd been young when their parents died and Silvie had stepped in; she'd cared for all three of them as best she could. He leaned over and pressed a kiss to her plump cheek.

"Just making sure everyone in the barn got the TLC they needed," Derek said. He glanced across the table at Angela and winked. Her eyes widened as she caught his meaning.

"Casanova's okay?" Sydney asked.

Derek's eyes never left Angela. "Content with his mom, isn't that right?"

"Um, he seemed to be," Angela stammered uncomfortably, glaring at him.

"What was it about rodeos that interested you, Angela? It's not something reporters are usually drawn to," Sydney asked.

Derek arched a brow and gave her a smug grin. Sydney

might sound like she was making conversation, but he knew her well enough to know she was fishing for information, trying to draw out their guest's motives.

"Actually, I don't know much about them other than what I've learned in my research. Last week I had an anonymous caller warn me that there would be animal cruelty at the rodeo. I wanted to investigate the claims further." She smiled. "That led me here."

Derek spooned some of Silvie's famous chicken pot pie onto his plate and shoved a heaping forkful into his mouth, forcing himself to keep his mouth shut. There was no sense in attacking her again, at least not until she did something that would warrant it.

"So, you're still doing research?" Mike asked. "Or have you already chosen your side of the argument?"

He dished up his own plate and indicated that Angela should hand him hers. He spooned a large helping onto it before passing it back to her.

"Well . . ." She paused, looking conflicted. "I don't know. What I've found in my research doesn't look promising for the sport in general." Derek watched her play with her food, poking at it with the fork nervously. "But, I don't really choose sides. The news is impartial. I report the facts and let viewers make their own decisions."

"Bullshit." Derek's outburst caused every adult at the table to turn and stare at him. "You know damn well people believe whatever the media says, right or wrong. You're making the decision for them when you go on the air and your mind was made up when you showed up at that gate yesterday." He pointed his fork in her direction.

Her eyes blazed with emerald fire, reminding him of a cat stalking prey, but her voice remained calm—too calm. "I am reviewing both sides of the evidence, Mr. Chandler. That is my job. As I was saying"—she looked at Derek pointedly—"so far, it doesn't look favorable for the sport of rodeo. There are multiple incidents of injury, abuse, and mistreatment of animals but I'm here so you can show me another side of rodeo, and to experience it firsthand. Unless, of course, you plan on showing me only the favorable side of rodeo."

"And if we prove to you that we don't mistreat our animals? That's the story you'll report?" Derek scoffed. "Isn't that a bit *boring*?" He arched a brow in disbelief. "It won't get those ratings you said you're looking for."

Angela opened her mouth to argue, but Scott spoke before she could answer. "Then I assume you'll be heading out with us on Thursday to our next rodeo?" Scott's voice was tight, and Derek could tell he was barely holding his temper.

"I believe that's what we had planned." She glanced at Mike for confirmation.

Mike nodded. "Yep, although we'll need to figure out some sort of sleeping arrangements before we leave. Maybe you can stay with Sydney. Scott and Derek can bunk together."

Derek shot a look at Mike. "And in the meantime? Is she just going to wander around the ranch? Who knows what kind of trouble she'll get into or where she might sneak a camera?"

"I'm still sitting right here," Angela pointed out. "And

I have plenty of online research to do before we leave on Thursday."

"Actually," Mike interrupted, "the best way for you to see what we do is from the back of a horse. Have you ever ridden?" Derek saw her eyes widen and the color drain from her face at the suggestion.

"I . . . um, I've never been around animals," she admitted. "Except a few stray cats I fed in our neighborhood."

"Then you're in for a treat. While you're here we'll teach you how to ride and how to take care of cattle." Mike winked at her, beaming as if someone had just told him tomorrow was Christmas morning and he was playing Santa Claus. "Maybe we can even teach you to throw a rope. You'll learn all the ins and outs of a ranch."

Derek shook his head and took a long swallow of his tea, wondering what Mike was thinking.

Scott was the only voice of reason. "Are you going to teach her all of that, Mike? I will be in the north pasture fixing the fences this week. Sydney's taking care of the foals, and Jen and Clay will be at the auction tomorrow."

Everyone at the table turned to look at Derek expectantly. He saw the blush staining Angela's cheeks. He leaned back in his chair and crossed his arms over his chest, feeling his pulse throbbing against his temple. He was unsure if it was anger or frustration, but he couldn't deny the burst of desire that settled below his belt buckle. He made no attempt to hide his displeasure.

"So I get to babysit?"

"I really do have plenty of research to keep me busy until we leave," she insisted.

"Derek," Silvie scolded, frowning at him as she slapped his shoulder. "Don't be rude. You can at least show her how to ride tomorrow and take her around the ranch."

He clenched his jaw and glared at his plate. Of course he *could*, but it irritated him that they'd all assumed he had nothing better to do than to show this city girl how useless he was in the business. He didn't want to have her here at all, let alone be stuck playing tour guide for her. When he looked up Angela met his gaze, and he could see the audacious glint in her eyes.

Her eyes flashed and a slow smile spread across her face. "We could get your interview out of the way. I'm sure it won't take long."

To anyone else it might appear she was flirting, but he knew better. He wasn't about to let her attempt to mock him slide without a retort.

"I guess that all depends on how long you think you can stay in the saddle." He winked at her, giving her a confident grin, and slid his chair back from the table. "Thanks for dinner, Silvie. I've got a few things to get done."

Chapter Six

THE REST OF dinner passed with a blur of conversation. Angela couldn't keep up with the discussions about which cattle were sick, where they wanted to move them, and which horses needed extra work. Most of the terminology they used went over her head, and she made mental notes to go online and look several of them up. If she was staying here, she'd need to keep from making a complete fool of herself. Apparently that also meant figuring out how to ride before tomorrow morning.

The prospect of spending the day with Derek Chandler could prove to be a double-edged sword. The man was a tempting enigma. He was definitely antagonizing and didn't fail to make it clear at every opportunity that he didn't want her anywhere near the ranch, but at the same time there was something about him that consumed her thoughts. She longed to discover the burden that hovered in the depth of his eyes. He had secrets he wasn't revealing, and she wondered if she recognized the fact because she carried a few of her own well-hidden secrets.

Who are you kidding? It wasn't his secrets that made her want to rip his shirt from his body and let her fingers trace every creviced muscle she'd seen though the thin material of his t-shirts. Then there was the mischievous, playful side she'd caught a glimpse of in the barn. Secrets or not, Derek Chandler was sexy as hell. She glanced toward the door he'd exited and wondered where he might be now.

After dinner Jen and Clay excused themselves, saying that their baby had been coughing. Mike headed to his office with Scott to finish some paperwork, leaving Angela, Silvie, and Sydney in the kitchen. Sydney grabbed a washcloth and wiped off the baby's face, scooping her out of the high chair and holding her out to Angela.

"Would you mind holding Kassie for a second?"

"I guess." Angela stared at the baby for a moment, unsure of what to do. She'd never been near a baby before but held her hands out as Sydney placed Kassie in her care. She tucked her hands under the baby's armpits as Kassie cooed with a wide smile and shoved a fist into her mouth, kicking her little feet like she was riding a bicycle.

Silvie laughed and moved to adjust her hands. "Here, like this." She settled the baby on Angela's hip and wrapped her arm around the little girl's waist and back before returning to the sink and stacking the dishes. "Angela, I'm sorry about Derek. He's not usually like that."

Angela stared down at the Kewpie-doll face and felt something deep within her soften as the child stared back with innocent, chocolate-colored eyes. "It's fine. I know he's not happy I'm here or that I'm doing this story. I don't know that I'd want me here either."

"I'm curious, Angela. What do you actually hope to accomplish with this story?" Sydney sounded interested, but Angela could sense Sydney didn't trust her completely and was worried about her motives.

It felt like an offensive move, and Angela stood, wondering if she needed to prepare for an oncoming attack. She answered with every ounce of professionalism she'd learned as a journalist in the past two years.

"Like I explained to Derek and Mike last weekend, viewers are attracted to controversy. Even the rumor of animal abuse creates controversy and ratings. I know what I've found in my research. When I interviewed Mike last weekend, he suggested that I come see the evidence for myself and spend some time watching more than one rodeo to see how a ranch is operated. He wants me to see how your animals are treated on a daily basis and use that as evidence for my story as well."

"He's hoping you'll realize there's no abuse," Sydney clarified.

Angela found herself rocking slightly from side to side with the child. "I think so, too," she agreed. She glanced down at the baby's wide eyes staring up at her so innocently, and she wondered if she could actually report something that might cause this child to lose her home. "I'm keeping an open mind, but I'll report what I see even if that means exposing the fact that animals are abused or mistreated."

"And if it's your misunderstanding?" Sydney pressed. She didn't seem concerned that Angela might find anything detrimental.

"Well, I suppose that's part of why I'm here. For your family to make sure that nothing I report is a 'misunderstanding.'"

Sydney nodded and put her hands to her hips, leaning back against the counter. Her gaze bored into Angela, making her shift in the chair. "I still think there's a lot more that you're not telling us. You just seem like you're hiding something." She bent over and loaded the last few dishes into the dishwasher. Sydney turned and faced Angela, wringing the kitchen towel with her fingers. "But I don't think you want to hurt us, so I'm willing to give you a shot."

Angela cleared her throat, unsure of how to respond. Silvie laughed, breaking the tension, and swatted at Sydney with a kitchen towel. "Listen to you. Go on, take Kassie and head home. I'll finish this mess."

Angela let Sydney scoop her daughter up, feeling slightly bereft. Something about the little girl had tugged at her heart and she blinked slowly, trying to clear the quiet ache of jealousy forming in her chest. She'd never even thought about having children. Who was she kidding? She'd never thought past getting her father sober, let alone wasting time hoping for a marriage or family of her own.

Angela hurried to the sink to help as Sydney kissed

Silvie's cheek. She could see the affection between the women and felt like she was intruding. "I'll help you, Silvie. I can at least earn my keep." She smiled at the older woman.

Silvie passed her a towel and shooed Sydney out the door. "I'd be happy to have you help. And you," she said, swatting Sydney on the rear end, "go home to your husband. I'll see you tomorrow." She turned back to Angela, who waited for instructions. "That girl fusses too much. She's going to wear herself out one of these days."

Even in her criticism, Angela heard tenderness in Silvie's tone. It was obvious she adored Sydney. In fact, it was quite clear from her doting attention to her family that she loved them all. What would it have been like to have someone like Silvie in her life, helping her grow up, watching out for her as she navigated the troublesome teen years?

Don't do this. Don't become attached. This story isn't likely to end well for them.

"She's right to worry though." Silvie interrupted Angela's train of thought. "About you."

"Me?" Her voice came out with a squeak, and she cleared her throat.

Usually Angela didn't care what people thought of her. She wasn't one of those women who felt the need to be liked. She was more likely to allow people to underestimate her, content to disappear into the background until she decided to surprise them. She certainly never cared about upsetting people when she was trying to scoop a fellow reporter for a story. It was the nature of this business. So far, it hadn't bothered her when she heard others describe her as a "bitch." But, for some reason, the thought of this family thinking of her that way disturbed her. Maybe it was because they seemed unassuming or because they'd been kind to her. Either way, she wanted to change their opinion of her and quickly. She bit her bottom lip.

"I agree with Sydney that you're not being completely honest." Silvie narrowed her eyes, curving her finger around her pursed lips, but smiled. "But, I'll listen if you want to open up. I get the feeling you're carrying a pretty heavy load on those tiny shoulders."

Angela reached for a dish, unsure how to respond, wondering how this woman was able to read her so easily. She didn't like being the subject of her accurate scrutiny and wanted to change the subject. "How are Mike and Derek related?"

Silvie shot her a sideways glance, concern written on her brow, but she must have decided it was safe to share. "Jennifer is the oldest and Derek is the youngest. Their parents were partners with Mike when they were killed in a car accident on the way home from a rodeo." She sighed. "The kids were all young when they died, but Derek was only about five or six. So, other than his brother and sister, Mike and I are the closest thing to family he's ever known."

"That's terrible," Angela muttered. She hadn't expected that she and Derek would have a childhood tragedy in common. Perhaps she understood the burden he carried better than she'd imagined.

"Yes," she agreed. "But that boy has been nothing short of a delight. He's such a sweetheart." She glanced at Angela before putting the dried glasses into the cupboard. "He's going to make some lady very happy someday."

Angela arched a brow. "Are you sure we're talking about the same guy?"

"Please." She flipped the dish towel at Angela. "Don't tell me that you're buying his macho cowboy act. That boy is just trying to prove he can protect his family." She pursed her lips, looking disapproving. "I think he's still trying to measure up to his brother. He doesn't realize that the man he's become is just as honorable as Scott."

Ah, so there were brother issues. Angela had learned that if you let people talk long enough, eventually they would tell far more than if you questioned them. She looked through the kitchen window as she dried the last plate and caught a glimpse of a cowboy in the barn. It looked like Derek's broad frame, and she felt a twinge of sympathy for him. Her life had been difficult without her mother, but losing both your parents and trying to live up to a standard someone else had set would have made it near impossible.

"Go on," Silvie said, noting the direction of Angela's gaze. "Maybe if you open up a bit, he'll act more like the Derek I've helped raise."

Angela bit her lower lip nervously and wiped her hands on her thighs, glancing back at Silvie as she waved her toward the door. If she was going to spend all of her time with this family for the next two weeks, she should make sure it was on good terms. She had a feeling that by the time her story aired, none of them would ever want to see her again.

"HEY, COWBOY."

She strode into the barn like she owned the place and it infuriated him even as desire swirled in his gut. He'd come out here hoping the physical labor and a quiet place to think would help him figure out how best to protect them from the disaster he was sure this nosey redhead was going to rain down on them. Part of him wondered if he wasn't just being melodramatic, but he could feel it in his gut: This woman was dangerous.

Instead of putting her out of his mind, he hadn't been able to stop thinking about her or the way she'd felt in his arms or how soft her skin felt under his fingertips. As if his thoughts had conjured her she appeared in the barn. Derek frowned as he lifted the heavy bale of straw from the stack and tossed it into the wheelbarrow.

"What do you want?" He wheeled the straw into the empty stall and broke it open, spreading it around with a pitchfork. Sweat trickled down his bare back, but he was grateful for the physical labor. Normally, he would have cleaned stalls in the morning when it was cooler, but he'd needed to get some perspective, and the mindless task had done that. At least, it had until she'd come in.

She leaned against the open doorway of the stall, watching him work. "I thought we might talk," she suggested.

"So, talk," he said, barely glancing at her before focusing on the straw at his feet again.

"I know you don't want me here."

He laughed out loud. "And here I thought I was hiding it so well."

"But Mike invited me and this is my job." She folded her arms over her chest. "We can either get along or . . . Well, it'll be a miserable couple of weeks for us both if we can't manage to at least tolerate one another."

He stood up, leaning on the handle of the pitchfork and trying not to notice the way her folded arms made her breasts fill out her shirt. He forced himself to focus on her eyes but even that was dangerous territory. "Just how do you propose we do that? Should I just ignore the fact that you're hell-bent on proving something about us that's simply not true?"

She stared silently at him for a moment, biting her lower lip, before her gaze slipped from his face and down to his bare chest, slick with sweat, dotted with straw chaff. Her eyes darkened with desire, and the corner of his mouth curved upward in a cocky grin as he waited for her reply.

"Earth to Angela?" he teased.

Her eyes jerked upward and she blushed furiously, her fingers fidgeting with a ring hanging from a gold chain at her throat. "I . . . I should go back." She glanced toward the house. "Maybe this was a bad idea."

"Chicken," he taunted.

He wasn't sure why he wanted to goad her, but the desire he could see in her eyes sent a white-hot jolt of need through him, shocking him. He was convinced he must be completely irrational to continue to entertain the visions of her hands on him. The heat of his body suddenly had less to do with physical exertion and more to do with the intensity of her gaze.

She lifted her chin in defiance, as if daring him to challenge her. "Is it really that hard for you to believe that I just want to do my job?"

"When you look at me that way, it is." Derek laughed quietly at the blush that crept over her cheeks.

"Don't flatter yourself." He arched a brow in disbelief as she played with her necklace a moment longer before tucking her fingers into her pockets. "What are you so worried about anyway? You keep saying that you take good care of your animals. If that's true, then that's what I'll report."

There it was, the ice-cold reporter he'd seen when he'd turned her away at the rodeo. He wondered which woman was the real Angela: the emotionless ice queen he saw now or the blushing temptress he'd pinned against the wall earlier. Derek tossed the pitchfork into the wheelbarrow and moved it toward her, forcing her to exit the doorway and stand in the aisle of the barn.

"I seriously doubt you're concerned at all with the truth." He shut the door to the stall and stood in front of her with his arms crossed. "You're looking for something, but it's not the truth. And I'm not going to let you use my family for ratings."

She cocked a hip to the side and looked thoughtful. "You know, you protest an awful lot for someone with nothing to hide."

"Who me? I'm an open book." He shrugged. "Ask me anything you want." He pushed the wheelbarrow to the back of the barn and reached for his t-shirt, which lay across a nearby bale of straw. He slapped it against his thigh to knock off the bits of straw, slid his arms through the holes, and slipped the material over his head. "You wanted an interview? Now's your chance."

"Open book, huh? Okay, I'll call your bluff." A flash of curiosity lit her green eyes and she gave him a slight smile.

His mouth felt like he'd swallowed cotton balls, and he clenched his fists to keep from burying his fingers into her hair and taking her mouth hostage. Derek shrugged, pretending that her nearness wasn't tying his stomach in knots, and sat on a bale of alfalfa stacked in the aisle of the barn. "Give it your best shot."

She arched a brow and stepped in front of him, immediately falling into her reporter persona. "Tell me about yourself."

"That's not a question," he pointed out with a lopsided grin. "What do you want to know? I'm the youngest of three. You met Jen and her husband, Clay. She's the oldest, then Scott."

"He and Sydney are newlyweds, right?"

Derek nodded. "They were married about seven months ago." He wasn't sure where her questions were leading, but so far they seemed harmless.

"What about Mike's wife?" She tipped her head to the side and crossed her arms in front of her.

Derek narrowed his eyes and wondered at her defensive gesture. He was the one under the barrage of questions, yet she felt the need to put up barriers? "She died when I was just a baby. I never knew her. Silvie has never married, but she's worked for Mike as long as I've been here. Anyone we've forgotten?"

She reached for the necklace again; her other arm stayed wound around her waist and twirled the ring between her fingers. "What about you?"

"What about me?" He shrugged again but leaned back against the wall and crossed his ankles in front of him. "You applying for the open position?"

He was teasing, but she glared at him. "Again, you flatter yourself. I mean, what about your parents? Mike mentioned that he started the company about twenty-five years ago with a partner. I'm assuming he meant your parents?"

Derek nodded. "My dad. He and Mike were traveling partners and rodeoed together. They passed this property several times before they earned enough prize money to pool it together to get this place and go into business. They went from being rough stock riders to stock contractors."

"Silvie said they were killed in a car crash when you were very young?" Her voice was soft, almost sympathetic, and she gripped the ring on the chain.

He noticed her hand trembling and cocked his head to the side. He uncrossed his ankles and reached for the hand at her throat, pulling her between his thighs. "Hey, are you okay?"

Derek wasn't sure what was going on in that pretty head of hers, but something about their discussion had upset her. When she didn't answer him, he pried her fingers from the necklace gently and picked up the ring on the chain, examining it. She gasped as their gazes met. He felt like she'd reached into his chest and squeezed his heart. The raw pain he saw in her eyes made his chest ache. For a moment, he could only think of replacing the hurt in her eyes with something far less agonizing.

His fingers found her chin and he slid his thumb over her jaw, watching as her anguish was replaced by the hunger he was certain was reflected in his eyes. "You're going to be my downfall, aren't you?"

He didn't give her a chance to respond as his lips met hers in a feather-light caress. His fingers curled at the back of her head, twining in her hair. Her fingers grasped his t-shirt and he deepened the kiss, his free arm circling around her back and pulling her close. He felt lighting shoot through him, centering in his loins, igniting a fire that would consume them both if he didn't stop this now. His brain insisted he break the contact, but he'd fantasized about doing this for days. His lips refused to release her, and he licked her lower lip. Her mouth opened with a slight gasp and he slipped his tongue inside, meeting her own and tormenting him with the taste of her. He smiled against her lips, momentarily content in the knowledge that she tasted like the peaches and vanilla that made up her unique scent. Their tongues dueled even as alarms sounded in his brain.

Ignoring the warning, his hand slid along her spine before his thumb trailed over her ribcage, his other hand settling at her waist. She leaned into him, arching against

THE COWBOY AND THE ANGEL 83

him, and made a soft whimpering sound, pressing her breasts against his chest. He couldn't break away from her without one final taste of her honeyed sweetness, and he sucked at her lower lip as he broke the kiss. Derek pressed his forehead against hers and took a deep breath, inhaling the intoxicating scent that had haunted him since their first meeting. Her eyes met his, glimmering with desire that matched his own.

"It's a good thing you're not applying for the position," he said, grinning down at her.

He saw the irritation ignite in her eyes, shining from within, and she shoved him away. "Jerk," she muttered, turning to storm from the barn.

Derek's hand snaked out and grabbed her by the wrist, tugging her back toward him. "Wait a second," he chuckled. "Don't get all bent out of shape. You were kind of freaking out and I wanted to distract you."

"By molesting me?" She jerked her hand away from him.

"Well, by definition, molestation would be undesired and you didn't seem to mind at all."

He grinned at her and reached for her hand. He wasn't sure why he had this overwhelming need to touch her again. He'd never felt it with any other woman, but he was quickly realizing Angela wasn't like any woman he'd ever known. This time she didn't fight him and his hands settled on her hips. It was a gesture meant to keep her close without seeming too intimate. He didn't want to risk her running away from him.

"Will you answer a question for me?" He pulled her with him as he sat back down on the alfalfa, and she stood between his thighs. He hoped that by appearing relaxed, it would make the question seem less threatening.

"I suppose." She followed him, her movements jerky and stiff, as if she distrusted his motives.

We have that in common at least. Neither of us trusts the other.

"What's with the necklace?"

"My necklace?" She reached up and touched the ring hanging at the base of her throat. He traced the line of the chain with his fingertip and watched her pulse jump, her chest heaving in an effort to breathe naturally. His finger traced her collarbone and she dropped the ring as if it were on fire. "It's nothing."

She was lying. He had no doubt that the necklace had a tremendous amount of meaning for her and wondered why she wouldn't share it, especially considering she had just been grilling him about his family. What was she hiding?

"So you're *not* an open book."

She backed away from him, just out of reach, retreating behind nonchalant coolness. "Trust me, cowboy, this isn't a book you'd want to read."

He watched as she turned on her heel and walked out of the barn, back toward the house. Derek wondered if kissing her had been one of the biggest mistakes of his life, but if that were the case, why was he imagining what would happen if he followed her into the house and lost himself in those emerald eyes again?

Chapter Seven

ANGELA HEARD THE early morning commotion downstairs and rolled over to see the sun glaring through the open window. Dishes clattered, a baby cried, and laughter floated up the stairs to her bedroom as she pulled the sheet over her head. Sounds of early morning breakfast with siblings—a close-knit family—all sounds she'd longed to hear for the past fifteen years, so unlike the silent mornings from her childhood with no one to help her get ready for school and no one to greet her when she arrived home. She pulled the sheet from her head and wondered if the family downstairs realized how lucky they were to have one another and how many people would give everything to have what they had.

She swung her legs over the side of the bed just as a knock sounded at the door. "Angie, are you up?" Silvie's voice was sweet but insistent. Angela caught her breath—no one but her father called her Angie. She felt a rush of emotion crash over her, realizing she needed to call him and see how he was doing.

She reached for a sweatshirt at the foot of her bed and pulled it over her head. Burying the tears that threatened to spill over, she hurried to open the door a crack. "I'm up. I'll be down in just a couple of minutes."

"Derek is already waiting for you at the barn when you're finished eating."

"Already?"

Silvie smiled at her sympathetically. "Our day starts early around here. We're usually up and out the door before seven."

Seven? She was used to doing the evening report with a follow-up late at night. Most of the time she didn't even get to bed until two or three in the morning. She was never up early. In the interest of getting her story, it appeared she was going to need to adjust to the early morning hours they kept here at the ranch.

"I'll be right down," she assured the older woman.

She closed the door and heard Silvie's footsteps making their way back downstairs. She hurried to the dresser, deciding to forgo the shower until after her time with the horses, and pulled out old jeans and a t-shirt she'd unpacked. She could feel the morning sun already heating up the air, and she shoved the t-shirt back into the drawer in favor of a tank top. She glanced at her image in the mirror and wrinkled her lip before rubbing her eyes.

"You look like you haven't slept in a week," she said to her reflection.

In truth, she had tossed and turned most of the night, sleep eluding her. As much as she wanted to blame her sleeplessness on the conversation with Derek stirring up memories of her mother, she knew it was because of his kiss. She couldn't put it out of her mind, nor could she forget the way her body had responded to him.

She'd kissed plenty of boys in high school and men in college, even afterward, but none of them had left her shaking with need, hungry for more. The simple touch of Derek's hand on hers had sent icy shivers of longing down her spine. Her entire body had melted in liquid heat when his lips had touched hers, leaving her body quivering with unsatisfied desire. She pressed her fingers to her lips, remembering the way his mouth had moved over hers, coaxing her to respond, and how his hands warmed her skin, teasing the yearning in her belly to an inferno that couldn't be extinguished by sleep.

She forced her focus back to the present and pulled her hair into a ponytail, the red tresses hanging to the middle of her back in loose waves, before hurrying to the bathroom to wash her face and brush her teeth.

Angela made her way down the stairs, taking them two at a time, fully prepared to skip breakfast and head out to the barn. She didn't want to keep Derek waiting. After last night, she didn't want him to have any ammunition to use against her. After the promiscuous way she'd responded to his kisses, he had enough ammunition already.

As much as she wanted to feel his hands on her again, she couldn't get involved with him. Falling for the subject of one of her stories, especially one she was certain wouldn't end well, was a recipe for a broken heart, namely hers. And if anyone ever found out about her father, that would sound the death knell on her career. Newscasters, like politicians and beauty queens, were supposed to be above reproach. That meant they weren't allowed to have alcoholic parents or fathers in rehab.

Silvie was waiting for her in the kitchen, loading the last of the breakfast dishes into the dishwasher. Without turning, she reached into the cupboard and took down a coffee cup. Angela laughed and took the cup from the older woman.

"Derek's right. You really do know everything that goes on in this house, don't you?"

Silvie joined her laughter. "After all of these years and raising those two boys, I don't think anything would surprise me anymore." She turned back to the dishes. "How'd you sleep?"

"Rough night," Angela admitted.

"Well, I guess that's to be expected in a new place." Silvie eyed her suspiciously as she turned on the dishwasher. "Or maybe you have something on your mind you need to get settled." Her expression shifted as she moved toward the refrigerator. "Did you want me to fix you some breakfast? I can make you some eggs if you want."

"Oh, no, don't even worry about me, Silvie. I'll just get a cup of coffee and grab an apple." She reached for the fruit in the bowl on the kitchen table.

"Coffee is fresh and there's cream in the fridge. I keep

a pot going all the time since the boys are in and out all day." She wiped her hands on the towel. "I'm going to be here in the house with the little ones if you need anything today."

Angela could hear the excitement tingeing the woman's words, making her sound years younger. She couldn't help but smile at Silvie's sense of adventure when the thought of spending the day with babies would send Angela into a frenzied panic. "Sounds like you'll have your hands full today. Don't worry about me."

"You take care of Derek today," she ordered. "I already packed a lunch for the two of you. Derek'll have it in the office. Remember to have some fun today and don't let him work you too hard. I think a little fun is exactly what you need."

Silvie exited into the living room and Angela poked her head out the back door, looking toward the corral where she saw two horses tied and waiting patiently for riders. A ripple of anxiety centered in the pit of her stomach at the sight of the animals. She poured a cup of coffee, topping it off with cream. Rubbing the apple on her pant leg, she pushed the door open and prepared to meet her fear head-on.

Several cowboys passed her on the way to the corral. A few made their appreciation known, but she pretended not to see their sidelong glances. She saw Derek coming out of the barn wearing his usual t-shirt and jeans combination, his baseball cap on backward, carrying a saddle over one shoulder. She couldn't help but appreciate the breadth of his chest and the way his muscles rippled with each movement. As he reached one of the horses, he tossed a Navajo blanket over its back. She was surprised to see that the animal's back was almost as tall as his chin, which was impressive considering how tall he was. She sipped her coffee as she watched him in the corral.

"You should come learn to do this," he suggested, barely glancing her way. "First rule of rodeo, know how to saddle and unsaddle your own mount."

"Tomorrow, I promise." She hoped he believed her, but she wanted to look up how to do it on the Internet before she tried her hand at it. Later today she planned on spending a lot of time online researching several things, including how to groom and saddle a horse.

He bent over and reached for the leather belt under the saddle, pulling it tight and latching the buckle. "Doesn't that hurt him?"

Derek unhooked the stirrup from the top of the saddle and snapped it to the side. The horse didn't even flinch or move from its bored position, its head hanging as if it were asleep. He leaned his elbow against the saddle and looked at her. "Does it hurt when you put a belt on?"

She sipped the cooling coffee. "No."

"Exactly." He reached back and buckled another belt on the back of the saddle, this one much looser before clipping a strap under the horse. "This is a flank cinch. It's not going to serve much of a purpose for you today, but if we were roping, it would keep the saddle in the right position on the horse."

"Is that the same kind of flank strap you use on the

bucking stock?" she asked, curious about the gear he was putting on the horse. The last thing she wanted was to be on her butt in the middle of the corral as she learned to ride. She wouldn't put it past him to sabotage her attempt to get her to leave.

"Similar, but different purpose. This one holds the saddle in place when you're roping and something is tugging on it." He glanced at her before waving her over to him. "She won't buck. Come here."

"Are you sure? He doesn't look happy." She eyed the enormous animal warily.

Derek laughed. "That might be because you keep calling her a *him*. She's the gentlest horse we have on the ranch. She's big but she won't hurt you."

Angela paused at the fence, eyeing the man and beast cautiously before slipping a leg through the wooden slats and bending to slide through. She yelped and jumped backward, feeling horse lips on her arm. "I thought you said she was nice!"

Derek laughed out loud. "I probably should've warned you about that apple. She thought you were giving it to her." He pushed the horse's head away from the woman caught against the fence and tried to stop laughing. "I'm sorry." He twisted his mouth, unable to hide his smile.

Angela stood with her hands on her hips and glared at him. "Why do I get the feeling you did that on purpose?" She glanced at her breakfast on the ground where she'd dropped it and picked it up, attempting to dust it off on her pants. It was a lost cause. "I guess she might as well have it now."

Derek moved behind her, slipping his large palm under the back of her hand, and her heart stopped beating. "Like this," he instructed. His voice was low and husky as he flattened her palm in his and placed the apple on it. He leaned close to her ear. "Keep your palm flat so she doesn't mistake your fingers for carrots."

"What?" She twisted her head to look at him over her shoulder, but the movement brought their lips within inches of one another. She gasped at his nearness, inhaling the heady scent of him as heat sizzled down her back where his chest was pressed against her.

His other hand rested on her shoulder as her body molded against his, sending waves of desire rippling down her limbs and making her wonder how she was able to continue standing upright, let alone take a breath. His fingers slipped down the side of her arm, and she fought to keep from dropping her head back against his shoulder.

"She won't hurt you. I'll make sure of it," he promised.

The horse flipped her upper lip at the apple before grabbing it from Angela's hand with her teeth. Her lips were like velvet on her palm, tickling it. She tried to pull away, but Derek held her hand in place. Trying to step away from the animal only pressed her more fully against the wall of his chest, burning her skin with the heat from his body.

"See?" he asked releasing her hand, letting his rest on her hip. He glanced down at her feet. "I had a feeling that's what you'd wear." She looked down at the sneakers on her feet. "Those are too dangerous for riding, but I'm sure Jen or Sydney has extra boots in the barn. What size are you?"

"Eight." She was surprised by how breathless she sounded.

"I'll go check. Wait right here," he ordered.

He left her alone with the horse in the corral, and she stared at the animal in front of her. "You better be as nice as he says you are. I've never done this before, and I don't want to end up on the ground." The horse gave her a dispassionate glance before looking away and blowing air through her lips. "If I do, you'll be glue, I swear."

"And you call us abusive?" Derek shot her a lopsided grin, sending her heart racing double time, and hung a pair of boots over the fence. "Try these."

She took the boots, eyeing the horse as she changed her footwear. The boots were like those she'd seen people wearing at the rodeo and around the ranch, rounded at the toes with a low heel, lacing up past her ankle. She was surprised at how comfortable they were and pulled her jeans over the top of them, hoping it didn't look ridiculous.

"Much better," Derek said with a wink. "This is Honey's bridle. I'll show you how to put it on and then you can try." She watched as he cupped the metal bar at the bottom in his palm before slipping it into the horse's mouth, lifting the leather straps over her head. "See?" She frowned at how easy he made it look. Derek slipped the straps off the horse's head. "Now, you try."

Angela took a deep breath and reached for what looked like a torture device. She cupped her palm around the metal piece the way he did and put it against the horse's lips. The stubborn animal stood there, unmoving, ignoring her attempt entirely.

"Come on," she muttered, pushing the metal bar against the animal's mouth just a bit harder. Still nothing.

She glanced over her shoulder at him and saw he was trying to hide a smile. "Try putting your thumb in the corner of her mouth, right here." He slipped his thumb into the corner of the horse's mouth and she immediately opened her mouth. "See?"

"Ew." Angela wrinkled her nose. "You said not to get my fingers in her mouth, that she'd think they were a carrot," she pointed out, grimacing as she pushed her thumb into the wet corner of the horse's mouth.

The animal immediately started chewing on the metal bar. "Pull it up over her ears now." Under his watchful eyes, she lifted the bridle over the horse's ears carefully. "They don't have teeth right there, so you're safe. You did it."

Angela stepped back and admired her accomplishment. "I did, didn't I?" She patted the animal's neck. "We might become friends after all."

The horse tucked her head against Angela's stomach. She was almost touched by the sweet, trusting gesture and reached to pet the horse's neck. The animal flipped her head, knocking Angela backward off her feet. Strong arms circled her, caught her, and lifted her back onto her feet even as Derek's chest vibrated against her back with his deep laughter. Embarrassment flooded her face, coloring her cheeks as she realized his arms were pressing against her breasts. So far, the only good coming from this lesson was how often his hands were ending up on her.

"ARE YOU ALL right?" Derek felt her tremble and the laughter died in his throat. This wasn't the way he'd hoped this would go. This lesson was quickly turning into a disaster. "Angela?" He turned her to face him, his hands on her hips.

"I'm fine," she said as she looked up at him. Laughter bubbled from her throat and he decided in an instant that he loved her laugh. She tossed back her head and let the humor of the moment overtake her. "Either you're a horrible teacher or I'm the world's worst stu—oh!" She squealed as Honey flipped her nose into Angela's lower back, throwing her into his arms again.

He caught her against him, his arms encircling her, but this time the mirth died in his throat as their bodies pressed together. He felt his desire ignite like a wildfire, his jeans suddenly becoming incredibly uncomfortable. With her breasts pressed against his chest, her soft curves molding against him, and the silken skin of her shoulders under his fingers, he inhaled deeply, enjoying the sweet scent of her. None of the women he'd held had ever tormented his senses and scattered his logic like this one.

"Maybe that's enough ground work for one day." His fingers slid over the satin skin of her upper arm.

Derek forced himself to step away from her, hating that the movement was almost as painful as if he was tearing a limb from his body.

This is bad.

Derek knew better than to allow himself to fall for any woman as dangerous to his family as this one. He needed to keep his mind focused on the task at hand, which meant showing her that her theory about animal abuse was unfounded and escorting her from the ranch as quickly as possible. He took a deep breath. The churning desire made it difficult to keep his hands off of her. He shoved them into his pockets, shifting awkwardly.

"Let's get you into the saddle and we'll work on the basics in the corral before I take you out." He stood at the mare's head, holding the reins. "Just put the ball of your left foot in that stirrup and pull yourself up. Then swing your right leg over the saddle, but be careful not to kick Honey in the rump."

She did as he instructed, looking uncertain, but he could see a glimmer of excitement in her eyes as she sat down in the saddle. He moved to the other side of the horse and slid the stirrup over her foot, letting his hand linger on her shapely calf a moment longer than was necessary; he was unable to fight the need to touch her.

He returned to her left side. "Take the reins in the fingers of your left hand loosely. Keep it in front of the horn."

"This thing?" she asked, pointing at the saddle horn.

"Yep. Now Honey neck reins, which means if you want her to go right, lay the reins on the left side of her neck." He moved her hand and showed her. The horse immediately responded by taking a step to the right. "Why don't you try walking her around the corral? But make her turn where you want her to go."

Derek moved to the center of the corral, leaving his gelding tied on the fence while he watched her. She sat tall but stiff in the saddle, causing the mare to pull at the reins.

"Relax; I'm not going to ask you to do anything you're not comfortable with." She glanced his way before quickly looking back at the animal, clearly not trusting him. "Whoa," he called out. The mare stopped and stood still.

Angela looked at him as he approached her. "She stopped."

"I told you, she's well trained." He laid his hand on her knee, trying to ignore the electricity shooting up his arm and centering in his chest. The mare fidgeted, pawing at the ground. "See that? Horses can read the emotions of the people around them. They mimic what they feel coming from you. If you're angry, she'll act up. If you're nervous, she'll be antsy." He put his hand on her ankle. "Drop your heels, sit deeper into your butt. Let your hips rock with her movement. Put your hand on top of her neck. It's like sitting in a moving chair."

"Like this?"

He watched as she continued circling the corral, doing better, but he knew it would be easier just to show her what he meant. He hurried back to his gelding as she continued to circle the corral. Settling himself in the saddle, he rode beside her.

"See how my hips stay relaxed?" She frowned and bit her lower lip, her attention focused on his lower body and matching his movements. Derek fought back a groan as her eyes caressed him and he watched her hips rock in time with the movement of the animal between her thighs. His thoughts began to stray, thinking of those hips under his hands only moments before. He knew he was only tormenting himself.

"I think you'll do fine as long as we stay at a walk," he growled as he led her to the corral gate. He needed to put some space between them and gain control of his carnal fantasies.

Chapter Eight

EVERYTHING WAS STARTING to hurt, from the balls of her feet all the way to the spot between her shoulder blades that she desperately needed to stretch. They had ridden in silence for the last thirty minutes with him leading the way. Normally, she would've enjoyed the quiet, but every muscle in her legs and lower back was screaming at her, aching with a need to be massaged. Derek promised that they would stop as soon as they reached the lake, but that was when they'd first left the corral and she didn't know how much more agony her muscles could stand. What she really wanted was a few minutes to soak in a hot bath.

She glared at his muscular back as she'd been doing for what felt like miles of open pasture. He should have felt her eyes burning holes in his shirt by now. She twisted in the saddle, looking to see how far they'd come from the main house, and saw nothing but grassy hills and pastures dotted with Corriente cattle they used for roping.

"Um, are we getting close to that lake?" She flexed the muscles of her thighs and grimaced in discomfort. He ignored her, not even turning around to look her way. She stuck her tongue out at his back. She knew it was a child-ish gesture, but she couldn't figure him out. One minute he was kissing her, his hands creating a yearning in her she'd never known, and the next he snubbed her, content to forget her very existence. "Hello?" she called.

"It's just up ahead."

"Up ahead where?" she muttered, patting the side of Honey's neck. "At least you've been nicer to me than he has."

Derek was right about the horse: Riding her was like sitting in a slow-moving rocking chair. But that didn't make the ride any easier on her sore backside. As they crested the hill, the horse picked up speed and began trotting down the hill as Angela bounced uncontrollably in the saddle, grasping the saddle horn with both hands.

"No, wait, stop!" Her horse passed Derek in her hurry toward the water now coming into view at the bottom of the hill. "Ow, you damn horse, stop!"

"Pull back on her reins," he ordered, not even both-ering to hide his irritation. Before she could follow his instructions, he was by her side, reaching for the reins. "Whoa, girl," he murmured to the animal.

Her traitorous horse immediately betrayed her and halted. Derek glanced at her, his face screwed up with disgust. "This isn't nearly as hard as you're making it."

He cued his horse to walk toward the lake, leaving her staring at him, openmouthed, while her disloyal mount pawed at the ground, wanting to follow.

Deal with it, you stupid horse.

She swung her leg over the saddle and dismounted. She'd walk the rest of the way to the lake—and back to the ranch, if necessary—but she'd wasn't about to give him the satisfaction of knowing how sore she was. She clenched her jaw, stuffing her irritation within when she really wanted to throw something. She hadn't wanted to come for this ride in the first place. She'd have been just as happy touring the ranch with anyone else or, better yet, doing research online in her room. She took a deep breath to control her temper.

She could see him ahead, tying his horse to a branch under one of the trees before loosening the saddle. His horse immediately dropped his head and began grazing on the grass nearby. Derek moved to sit on a rock near the water, not even looking to see if she was riding down or not. It annoyed her that he was certain she would follow him but the thought of riding, or walking, back to the ranch was too much to contemplate. He picked a glorious spot, shaded by several trees. The breeze barely blowing across the water caused small ripples while sparrows played at the edge. She made her way slowly, trying to loosen the tight muscles of her thighs, hating him a little more with every step.

He glanced up as she neared. "It's about time." He rose and took the reins from her hand, careful not to touch her, and tied the horse to a branch near his own, slipping a small pack from where it hung over the back of her saddle.

"What's that?"

"This?" He held up the pack. "This is lunch."

She frowned at him. "If I'd known I had it, I would have headed back to the ranch."

He handed her a bottle of water, tipping his toward her before twisting the cap and taking a long drink. "You're welcome."

"For what, being a jerk?"

He held a sandwich out to her. "What did I do?"

She arched a brow and snatched the sandwich from his hand. "Oh, absolutely nothing at all," she answered dryly. She was certain he knew exactly what he'd done.

He sat on the ground in front of her and took a bite from his own food. "Fine, why don't you tell me how you want me to act. Should I follow your every move like a puppy on a leash? Or maybe I should act more like a tour guide?" He waved his hand elaborately to the side. "Everything you see around you is our north pasture. This is where we keep most of the cattle that are used in the calf and team roping. We have about three hundred head of cattle we choose from so that we don't overwork any of the animals." He took another swig from the water bottle. "Is that what you want?"

She shook her head at him. "It helps, smart aleck." She sipped the water. "You know, you could have warned me that the horse might take off running toward the water—or at least reminded me how to stop her when she did."

"I showed you in the corral." His eyes softened as he glanced her way. "But, you're right," he conceded, "I probably should have reminded you how to stop her. This *is* your first ride. I'm sorry."

She wasn't sure what she'd expected from him, but it wasn't an apology. It immediately diffused her irritation.

"Thank you." She looked back toward the water and the birds still twittering at the edge. It was a perfect location for a relaxing picnic, if she could calm the nervous flutter of her stomach.

He bumped her foot with the toe of his boot. "How are your legs doing?" His voice held a note of concern it hadn't a few moments ago, and she wondered at the change in him.

"How'd you know?" She smiled in spite of herself.

Derek shrugged. "You're not the first person I've taught to ride."

A stab of jealousy caught her by surprise as she envisioned him teaching women far prettier and less troublesome. She wondered if the entire routine in the corral, feeding her horse and being pushed into his arms, hadn't happened hundreds of times before. Did he always finish his riding lessons here with a picnic? She frowned, eyeing him warily.

"I'm sure I'm not. I'll bet you're in high demand as an *instructor*."

She caught the glimmer of humor in his eye as he didn't even bother to conceal his cocky grin. "Everyone goes through it. We'll walk part of the way back. That should help alleviate some of the soreness."

She noticed he didn't deny her accusation. She refused to let him think that she'd be envious of any bimbo he might have hooked up with. Why should she care who he took riding? Her gaze slid over his broad shoulders to his narrow hips, changing the direction her thoughts had taken. She instantly regretted the new course they'd taken.

"Like you've ever been sore," she muttered.

Derek laughed. "You'd be surprised. Up until about six months ago, I was pretty scrawny." She tilted her head and gave him a disbelieving look. "I swear," he said, holding up one hand.

"How is that even possible?" She didn't intend to stroke his ego, but she couldn't believe his admission. The man was a mass of bulging muscle, a magnificent specimen of manhood with broad shoulders tapering to a six-pack most men would kill for. His thighs stretched his jeans as much as his t-shirts strained to fit around his biceps. Even his hands were manly, calloused and work-roughened. There was nothing about this man that didn't speak of masculinity. He was a woman's dream of sculpted perfection with only one flaw she could see: a tiny scar over his right eye. "You're so . . ."

She blushed, unsure of how to finish without sounding like a lovesick teenager. He leaned back on his elbow, basking in her praise, and arched an eyebrow, waiting to see what she might say next. He certainly didn't need her to feed his ego.

"Well, look at you."

He laughed again. "It's funny what a few months of hard work out here will do for you. Taking care of cattle, tossing hay bales—all of it makes weightlifting look like child's play. Although Clay and I do have a makeshift gym at his place."

"I knew it. You're a gym-junkie," she teased. "All brawn and no brains." She was finding it difficult to stay angry at him when he stopped giving her his death-glare and began to relax around her. She could glimpse the mischievous boy Silvie talked about.

"Hardly." He frowned and she detected a note of bitterness in his voice. "Now that Scott stays here at the ranch and I'm arena director, I'm on the road far more than I'm ever here."

"You don't like it?" He shrugged but she could see it was meant to redirect their conversation and didn't take his bait. "Are you and your brother close?"

"We're closer now than we have been in the past." She could see him shutting off as he rose and made his way to the horses. "You finished?"

She arched a brow, not distracted so easily. "Changing the subject? What happened to that 'open book'?" He looked back at her, and she could see he was trying to decide whether or not to answer her questions. "Why weren't you close before?"

Derek sighed and turned back toward the horses. "When our parents died, Scott decided he had to be the one in charge. He wasn't very old but he's always been the serious one and he tried to act like my father. I didn't like it. It caused friction."

She rose and made her way toward him, wincing with every step but intent on seeing his expression. She knew what he left unsaid was just as important as anything he admitted. "Friction?" She edged closer.

He kept his attention focused on his horse. "Up until

this past year, I haven't exactly stepped up to help with the family business the way I should have."

She moved to stand in front of him, placing her hand on the rump of the horse beside her. "Why not?"

He shrugged again, but she wasn't about to be deterred and remained in his way. He crossed his arms over his chest. "I guess because I didn't have to. Scott was always right there to take the lead or pick up whatever I let slide."

She could see the shadow of disappointment flicker in his eyes and the tension bunching his shoulders even as he was trying to maintain his usual blasé attitude. The reporter in her wanted to press him with more questions, to delve further into the family dynamic and see what secrets might be hidden, but she could see him closing himself off to further discussion. She needed to earn his trust before he'd reveal much more, which just didn't seem possible with their current circumstances.

She glanced at the water over her shoulder and Angela saw him stiffen slightly in preparation for her next question. "So, how many other girls have you brought here?"

She saw his relief at the change of subject. "One or two." He winked at her as she twisted her mouth in disbelief.

"Right. I'd bet that between you and your brother, there isn't a girl on this side of the state who hasn't been to this lake."

He laughed out loud. "Maybe it was a few more than that. You know, Scott used to call it 'Make-Out Creek.'" He arched a brow and a playful grin spread slowly over his lips, making her nervous. "Come on."

He reached for her hand and pulled her toward the water. She tried to ignore the electric jolt of pleasure that shot up her arm, sending needles of desire into her chest. "Where are we going? Slow down," she groaned, running behind him stiffly.

Derek stopped at the edge of the water and pulled his boots off, dropping his socks inside, and reached for the hem of his t-shirt.

"What in the world are you doing?" She felt her cheeks burn, but she couldn't tear her eyes from the bronze expanse of skin he revealed.

"Going for a swim. Coming?"

She spread her hands in front of her indicating her clothing. "In jeans?"

"Or not," he suggested, his eyes gleaming mischievously as he unlatched his belt, sliding it through the loops and dropping it on his boots. He popped the button on his jeans and her eyes widened.

"Are you serious?"

His eyes darkened as her gaze slid over his chest and back to his face. She forced herself to keep her eyes above his neck when he slid his pants down his thighs. Even as she tried to catch her breath, her imagination ran wild with images of what he would look like without his pants.

Derek shrugged, unabashed, and tossed his baseball cap on top of the pile of clothing. "Suit yourself, Angel." He turned and headed for the inviting water.

She couldn't help but break her vow, allowing her gaze to wander down his chiseled back to take in the dark boxer briefs that cradled his firm round butt as strong thighs flexed with his every step. He walked until the water hit his knees before diving in, surfacing and swiping water away from his face and through his dark hair.

"You're really not coming in?" He was teasing her but he almost sounded disappointed.

She forced herself to walk away from the edge of the water. She spotted a large rock along the shore and sat down. "No, I'm really not."

Removing her boots and socks, she rolled up her pants to her knees and dipped her toe into the water. It wasn't as cold as she'd expected, so she slid both feet in, letting the weeds underwater tickle the bottom of her feet. Derek swam toward her slowly and she narrowed her eyes at him, pointing a finger his direction.

"Don't," she warned.

"You should probably take off anything you want to stay dry." His eyes gleamed, and he shot her an impish grin. "Riding in wet clothes sucks," he pointed out.

She tried to remember what sort of underwear she'd put on in her rush to get dressed this morning, praying that she'd opted for something at least somewhat substantial. She jumped up from the rock as he reached for her ankle.

"Fine, but you go over there, cowboy." She pointed toward the middle of the lake and glared at him, trying to stay angry at him and finding it increasingly difficult when he turned on the charm. "Why do I get the feeling it wasn't your brother who named this place?"

Derek laughed as she unbuttoned her pants and slipped them to her hip, relieved when she saw her striped bikini underwear.

They cover as much as bathing suit bottoms.

She stalled for time, sliding her jeans over her thighs and folding her pants, laying them on her borrowed boots. She refused to look at him as she edged closer to the water and walked into it up to her waist, the hem of her tank top getting wet.

"Leaving your shirt on?" She glanced his way in time to see him standing in waist deep water, his eyes glittering with desire and something she hadn't seen yet. He was completely relaxed. She'd seen him playful and teasing, but this was the first time she'd seen him without the shadow of worry and doubt that seemed to dog every conversation.

"Yes, I am."

"Party pooper," he whispered, moving closer and reaching for her wrist.

"I prefer 'cautious.'" His fingers closed over her hand while his other arm found her waist, pulling her against his chest, stealing the breath from her lungs as he moved farther into the center of the lake.

"Chicken?"

"Guarded," she admitted.

"I promised you earlier, I won't ask you to do anything you're not comfortable with."

Derek wound his other arm around her waist and let his hands knead the tense muscles of her lower back, sending spirals of longing along the length of her spine. Water swirled around their shoulders, her toes no longer touching the bottom of the lake as he held her to him. She could feel his arousal pressing against her through the thin barrier of their undergarments and she trembled, wishing for the first time that she could follow her desires instead of common sense. Letting him touch her, gripping the slick muscles of his forearms, feeling her nipples tighten in her bra, she would give anything to give in to her hunger for this man. But she knew giving in would be a mistake. Maybe not tomorrow but next week, or the week after, when the story aired, when his family was forced to suffer the repercussions from protestors and possible investigations, he would hate her.

"I won't hurt you," he promised, lifting one of her arms to his shoulder. "Relax. Trust me."

"That's a lot more dangerous than it sounds."

"Angel, I think I have more to lose here than you do." Derek gave her a lopsided grin and brushed a lock of hair from her face.

"You might be surprised," she whispered at his chest, unable to meet his eyes.

He tipped her chin up, forcing her to look at him. "Open book?"

She couldn't admit to him why this story was so important. He couldn't possibly understand the need to escape with her father, especially when it would jeopardize his future. Everything in her wanted to open up, to allow his broad shoulders to bear some of the weight she carried each day. She'd been caring for her father and hiding his problems since she was a child. She would have given anything for someone to tell her it was no longer necessary. And if Derek wanted her to trust him . . . What was she thinking? She barely knew him. With his arms around her, sapping at her will to remain distant, she almost gave in to this fantasy he created. She pushed away from his shoulders and swam away, trying to get some distance from him to help her think clearly.

She turned to face him from the bank, wishing she didn't feel the dull hopelessness creeping over her. "I never claimed to be an open book." Angela sat on the rock and drew her knees to her chest, ignoring the water coursing down her legs and back and puddling on the ground.

"Fair enough," he agreed, still watching her intently. "Then where does that leave us? What can we talk about?"

She rested her chin on her knees and wrapped her arms around her legs, creating a barrier between them. "Rodeo, I guess. It's why I'm here." She shrugged, wishing that they could have met under different circumstances. "According to you, I have a lot to learn in a very short time. So teach me."

"Rodeo," he repeated as he walked to the edge of the water and made his way to his clothing. He watched her, narrowing his eyes intently as if trying to read her thoughts. Derek's gaze was warm but piercing, reaching into her soul, imploring her to confide in him.

She tried desperately to avoid his penetrating eyes, which caused an entirely different problem. Her gaze shifted to the droplets of water as they fell from his chest, down the planes of his stomach and lower. Her breath caught, his wet clothing leaving little to her imagination.

She deliberately turned so she faced the horses until she heard the clink of his belt. Angela turned back in time to see him tighten the belt before running a hand through his wet hair, causing it to stand up at odd angles. He slapped his hat onto his head and frowned at her.

"Angel, I can think of a hundred things that would be more fun to do with you instead of talking about rodeo." His voice was husky with desire as he reached for his shirt, but he broke the tension with a quick kiss on her cheek. "I guess you're all work and no play, huh?"

She laid her cheek on her knee and looked up at him, wishing that for a moment she could follow her heart instead of her head, regardless of the consequences. But her heart wasn't going to pay for rehab for her father; her heart wasn't going to find a way out of the guilt her father's drinking had doomed her to live in.

Derek reached for her and gently caressed her cheek with his thumb. He acted as if he wanted to say something but restrained himself. It wasn't what she expected and made her feel like a tease, drawing him close then pushing him away. Derek didn't react the way most men would. He intrigued her as much as he confused her.

"Rodeo it is, then," he agreed, sitting on the ground beside her. "Let's start with the first event."

Chapter Nine

DEREK HADN'T MEANT to ignore her on the way to
the lake, but he needed to get a grip on the desire rushing through his veins, threatening to consume him.
Space had been the only way to accomplish it, and even
that hadn't been enough to cool the longing pulsing in
time with his heartbeat. He'd never wanted a woman
the way he did Angela. Maybe it was because she was
dangerous, off limits, but when she was in his arms, she
sure didn't feel forbidden. She felt willing and sweet and
tempting. He hadn't meant to reveal anything about his
family to her, but when she turned those emerald eyes
on him, she had a way of getting him to let his guard
down.

He watched as she finished grooming the mare, wanting to sneak behind her and press his mouth over the
bared curve of her neck, to kiss her shoulder and feel her
tremble the way she had in the lake. He wanted to cause

the goose bumps to rise on her flesh again and felt his body answer with his own unfulfilled need.

She dusted her hands off on her jeans and turned toward him, catching him mid-fantasy. "Take her back to the stall?"

She was learning quickly, and by Thursday's rodeo, she would probably be able to saddle her own horse. He leaned against the corral fence. "You remember how I showed you to lead her?"

Angela nodded, her ponytail flipping over her shoulder, making her look innocent and ... well, adorable. What he wouldn't give to press a kiss to her pretty pink lips.

Down, boy. This filly is pretty skittish.

But, damn, if she didn't make him want to gentle her, even when she was being obstinate. He wanted to find out what it was that drove her, what was going on behind those green eyes that made her so sad at times. He wanted to know what caused the near impenetrable wall that protected her heart. Something had her scared, and he was determined to find out what it was.

"You coming?" She stopped and looked back at him nervously.

"I think you have this." Derek didn't want to push her too hard and hoped she'd make the next move. He winked at her. "Unless you want me to come?"

She rolled her eyes. "Whatever you want to do, cowboy. First stall, right?"

Derek nodded. He was disappointed but he wasn't going to let it deter him. He had a few more days of her undivided attention to get her to warm up to him. He hung back at the corral, his hands unsaddling his gelding while he watched her from the corner of his eye.

"How'd it go today?" Mike asked as he leaned against the corral fence, watching Angela in the barn. "She's putting Honey away by herself?"

"She did well. We checked out most of the north pasture, to the lake at least, and she asked a lot of questions about rodeo."

"Enough to know what she's looking at this weekend? I'm so tired of hearing that using a flank strap is abuse."

Derek shrugged and nodded. "She will by Thursday." He pulled the saddle from his gelding's back and set it on the fence, turning the animal loose in the corral. "You realize she's hiding something." Mike cocked his head to the side in question. "I don't know what it is, but . . ." Derek let his words falter, unsure what else to say.

"Silvie and Sydney said the same thing. Something's haunting that girl. I saw it in her eyes that first day." Mike shrugged his shoulders and waved a hand. "Who knows, maybe that's why I invited her."

He clapped the older man on his shoulder. "Your soft heart is going to get us into trouble one of these days. You can't keep taking in every stray and trying to fix every broken heart."

Derek knew he was wasting his breath. It was just one of the things that made Mike who he was. After all, he'd taken in three homeless kids and raised them as his own. Derek couldn't help but wonder if Mike hadn't bitten off more than he could chew this time. Angela was tenacious. She wanted a story, for whatever reason, and she didn't seem inclined to give up until she had one.

ANGELA PUSHED HER computer away from her on the bedspread. She couldn't watch another gruesome video. She'd seen enough animals with broken limbs being tormented or shocked with electric prods to make her sick to her stomach. How could Derek or anyone else defend these actions? The image of frightened baby cattle trying to run from the arena with legs obviously broken burned behind her eyes. Rubbing her forehead with her fingers, she sighed, wondering if these videos were indicative of what she was going to have to watch on a daily basis for the next few weekends.

Her fingers found the ring on her necklace and began rolling it between her fingers, wishing, as she often did, that her mother would give her a sign, some sort of advice, on which direction to take. She was met with only the silence of her room and the steady thud of her heartbeat.

After unsaddling the horse she'd begged off eating with the family, claiming she wanted to do some research. In reality she'd needed to put some space between Derek and her raging hormones. That man was enough to make a nun forget her vow of chastity. It barely took a look from those dark chocolate eyes of his and she melted into a puddle of quivering desire. It had taken every bit of self-control at the lake for her to keep from wrapping her legs around his waist and letting him satisfy the need she felt burning inside her. She'd never ached for a man before or craved the feeling of his hands on her skin and fantasized about what it would feel like to finally give in to him. Every feeling was completely foreign and frightening. It was the fear that made her feel the need to hide.

After disappearing into her room, she'd decided to distract herself from thoughts of him by researching the rodeo events online. It hadn't been hard to learn the basics of the events, so she started looking for sites discussing the management of the animals and was shocked by what she'd found. A few sites touted the humane treatment of the animals, but they were outnumbered by pages of anti-rodeo articles, pictures, and videos. Animal cruelty abounded throughout the sport and most of the time was dismissed as just part of the performance. She didn't think she could stomach being surrounded by it day in and out for the next few weeks.

Angela rose and walked to the window, staring out at the corral below where Sydney rode a gray horse in circles. It was going to be difficult to separate fiction from reality with this story. She couldn't talk with anyone directly connected with the sport because they'd be biased. She needed to find a large-animal veterinarian to interview about the animal care, something she had no experience with, in order to clear up arguments between the two sides. She bit her bottom lip before grabbing her cell phone and dialing Joe.

"Hey, Gigi!" She cringed at his nickname for her. She hated it with a passion. At least he seemed to be in a good mood.

"Joe, I need a big favor." She heard his dramatic sigh. "Oh, come on, it's not *that* big of a favor."

"Gigi, I have the station breathing down my neck to get you back from your 'vacation' early as it is."

She pressed on as if he hadn't spoken. "I'm heading to the first rodeo on Thursday. I don't suppose we could get someone out there?"

"Doubt it. First, I don't have the manpower for it. Second, I told you, you're on your own until you bring me something substantial." She heard someone in the background talking to him and he covered the mouthpiece of his phone to answer. "I have to run. An issue with one of the teleprompters," he explained.

"Can you set up an interview for me with a local large-animal vet? Someone not involved with this stock contractor or rodeo. I want a completely unbiased opinion."

"That I can do for you, but I can't promise it will be in the same town. Small towns may not have too many vets, and since you want to be particular, we might have to go to the next town."

A smile of relief appeared. She could always count on Joe. "That shouldn't be a problem. I'd like to interview them before I head out on Thursday."

"I'll text you all the details. Keep me posted."

"Thanks, Joe."

"By the way, your dad is doing okay. I had to take him home last night, but he wasn't too far gone. I think he misses you. You might want to give him a call." She could hear the note of disappointment in his voice.

"I'll call him as soon as I get a chance." The guilt pricked her conscience. She'd been gone only a day, but it had felt good to be free from the constant worry.

"Just make sure you do." Joe sighed again. "You know, I would take care of both of you if you'd just let me."

She didn't get a chance to answer before he disconnected the call.

SYDNEY LOOKED UP and waved as Angela made her way to the corral, her legs and rear aching with every stiff step she took. She hoped she didn't look as awkward as she felt, but the more she concentrated on the pain in her lower half, the more uncoordinated she felt. Sydney laughed and brought the horse to the fence.

"That bad?" She dropped her hand with the reins to the horse's neck. *Gelding*, Angela corrected herself.

Angela laughed in spite of the pain. "Yes, isn't there something I can do?"

Sydney shrugged. "I went through it after having Kassie when I hadn't ridden for a few weeks. My best advice is to do a lot of walking."

"But that's what hurts." She exaggerated a pained expression. "Who's this?" She reached through the fence and petted the gelding on the forehead.

"This is Bully. He'll eventually be one of the horses used by the pickup men."

"Bully?"

Sydney laughed. "Yeah, he tends to pick fights with the other horses in the pasture and likes to challenge the pecking order. He's a bit of a bully to the younger horses, so the name stuck."

Angela looked up at the woman on the horse. She looked like she was about the same age as Angela, but she also seemed to have a sense of composure and serenity that Angela didn't possess. "How long have you been riding and working with horses?"

"As long as I can remember." Sydney dismounted and led the gelding to the gate. "Come with me to do the barn. We can talk while I unsaddle him." Angela tried keep up with Sydney, grimacing as she moved her limbs. "My parents have a cattle ranch near West Hills so I've been riding horses and working cattle forever."

The gelding nudged Sydney on the shoulder, demanding attention as she clipped his halter and began to unsaddle him. "He likes you," Angela pointed out. "They all seem to."

Sydney put his halter on and opened her hands, using her fingertips to rub just below his eyes. The gelding stuck his nose near hers, and she watched Sydney kiss him. "You're a good boy, aren't you?" She patted his forehead before reaching for the saddle and disappeared into the tack room.

The gelding turned his attention to Angela, nosing her arm. She reached out a hand, tentatively petting his cheeks, staring into his soft brown eyes. He was a smoky-gray color, with lighter spots covering his coat and white down the middle of his face and his front two legs. Sydney came out of the tack room and led the gelding into one of the empty stalls, patting him roughly on the shoulder as she removed the halter.

"Doesn't that hurt him?" Angela asked.

"What?" Sydney looked at her, confused.

"When you hit him on the shoulder that way?" Sydney hung the halter on the outside of his stall and she followed Sydney to the tack room where she hung up the bridle.

Sydney glanced at her. "No, horse hide is much thicker than ours. Come into the office," she said, leading Angela into what she had assumed was another tack room.

She looked around her, surprised by her mistake. Windows graced the sides of the room, one looking into the barn and the other looking out toward the corral. The back wall was lined with bookshelves and file cabinets. Sydney moved to the first cabinet and withdrew a folder, tossing it onto the desk. Angela moved to a studded leather couch against the wall.

"Thirsty?" Sydney opened a small refrigerator in the corner. "I have sodas or water."

"Water is fine." Angela took the bottle from Sydney, noticing several boxes with medication on the shelf of the refrigerator. She made a mental note of the labels: boxes of Phenylbutazone paste and sealed packages of vials and syringes with "Fluvac" written on the outside. She recited the names in her head, determined to look them up online when she went inside. She'd read about rodeo stock being drugged to perform and wanted to see if there might be truth to the rumor.

"Other than being sore, how was your first day?" Sydney asked, taking a seat behind the desk and opening the file.

"It was . . . fine." She didn't want to relive the moments with Derek today. She wasn't even sure why she was letting him affect her the way he had. She'd been pretty effective at pushing men away in the past, but Derek didn't seem inclined to take the hints she was dropping.

Sydney smiled. "That doesn't sound good." She twisted her lips, trying to hide a smile. "Derek can be difficult at times, but his heart is in the right place."

Angela smiled at her, thinking about how patient Derek had been while teaching her to ride. "It wasn't Derek," she lied. "I just need to be careful to keep my point of view impartial, and I get the feeling he's trying to keep me from doing that."

"Probably," she admitted, jotting down a note in the file before looking up at Angela. "Derek won't let anything threaten this family, especially now."

Angela leaned forward. "What do you mean, now?"

"He didn't tell you?" Sydney leaned back in the chair, giving Angela her full attention. "Up until this past year, Derek and Scott have been at odds about his place in the family business. Derek stepped up when Kassie was born, so Scott could spend more time at home with us."

"He mentioned some friction between them."

Sydney nodded, her lips twisting to the side. "That's a nice way of putting it." She put the file back into the cabinet and took a soda out for herself, popping the top with a soft *whish*. "Derek hasn't always made the best decisions. But he's been a great friend to me since I came here. Scott and I wouldn't be together if it weren't for him. He made us face our fears in order to find a future." She smiled and tipped the can toward Angela. "I think, maybe, he's trying to do the same for you."

Angela stood quickly, not wanting Sydney to analyze the situation between her and Derek for fear she might dig into Angela's past. "I should probably let you get back to work."

Angela didn't even realize she was twirling the ring on her necklace until Sydney rose from behind the desk and reached out to take it between her fingers. "It's pretty. An heirloom?"

She glanced up at Sydney, surprised to see friendly interest instead of judgment. "It was my mother's wedding ring," she answered, her voice strained.

Sydney met her gaze and must have seen the pain she felt at the mention of her mother in past tense. "I'm sorry," she said, dropping her hand.

Angela shrugged, erecting the walls surrounding her emotions again, refusing to let anyone see the emptiness that had left a gaping hole in her heart for the last fifteen years. "It's been a long time. I don't remember a lot," she lied.

Sydney smiled sadly. "You and Derek have more in common than I realized. He lost his parents young, too. Sometimes it's nice to have someone who understands to talk to." She tipped her head and looked at Angela oddly before drinking the last of the soda and tossing the can into the garbage. "Mike wanted me to iron out the sleeping arrangements before Thursday. We'll be going this weekend instead of Jen and Clay. Their baby has been coughing, so Jen wants to keep him home."

Angela frowned at the quick change of subject, wondering if she'd be staying with Sydney in the trailer now. *Please, let that still be the plan.*

"Kassie will come with us, but she'll stay in the trailer with you and me. She's a good baby and sleeps a lot." She smiled tenderly at the mention of her daughter. "It makes my job a lot easier."

"Hey, Syd!" The women both turned as Derek entered the barn. Angela saw his eyes grow hot as they caressed her. "Sorry, I didn't know you were busy." His voice was husky and he stared at her lips.

Sydney glanced between them before giving Angela a knowing smile. She prayed that Sydney wasn't able to read her thoughts. She certainly didn't want anyone to realize the way her heart raced when he walked into the room or the way her limbs felt like they'd turned liquid. Or how heat spread down her spine, warming her every nerve ending and making her feel like she was slowly being consumed by fire.

"I should get back to my research," Angela muttered. "Thanks for the heads up, Sydney." She brushed by Derek, unable to avoid touching him, and fought to hold back a groan of pleasure as her breast brushed against his arm as she snuck past him in the doorway before limping back to the house. She closed the front door and leaned her back against it, reaching for the ring. "Oh, Mama, what have I gotten myself into?" she whispered.

Chapter Ten

ANGELA WOKE STILL fully clothed, lying on top of the covers of her bed. She glanced at the blank computer screen in front of her. She must have fallen asleep while she was doing research, and it had gone to standby. Rubbing her eyes, she pushed herself up and shoved her thick hair back from her face, pulling a hair tie from her wrist to draw it back. Her fingers deftly plaited it and banded the bottom as she wandered toward the window. Night had fallen, covering the sky like an inky blanket, but lights glowed in the barn. She reached for her cell phone to check the time, realizing she must have slept right through dinner. Ten thirty?

Her stomach protested, growling loudly, and Angela wondered if it would seem rude if she raided the refrigerator. She tiptoed downstairs, pausing with every creak, trying not to wake anyone as she made her way into the kitchen to open the pantry door. Her brows shot upward as she took in the massive quantity of food before her: everything from canned goods, fruit, jams, and sauces to staples like beans, pastas, and baking goods. She wished she were a better cook because Silvie's kitchen was a chef's paradise. She couldn't even guess where to start and gave up, reaching for bread and peanut butter from the shelf. She started to close the pantry door when a shadow in the corner of her vision caught her attention.

A gasp of fear escaped, and she dropped both items as she spun to face the intruder.

"Hey, it's okay," Derek whispered quickly. "It's just me."

"Crap!" She felt her heart leap into her throat. "What the hell, Derek?" She lowered her voice. "You scared me half to death." She bent and scooped up the bread and the container of peanut butter. "Why are you sneaking around this time of the night?" she asked through clenched teeth, trying to control her racing heart.

He shot her a lopsided grin, took the items from her shaking hands, and put them back into the pantry. "I could ask you the same thing. Here." He opened the refrigerator and handed her a plate covered with aluminum foil. "Silvie figured you'd wake up hungry, so she made a plate for you. Just heat it up."

Angela stared at him, unsure what to say. Gratitude flooded her chest, filling her eyes with tears. The last time anyone had given even a second thought to her needs was when she was eight, before losing her mother. She'd been the caregiver for her father as long as she could remember, the one who kept his dinner warm, not the other way around. She wanted to hold the tears back, but the harder she tried the more they threatened to spill. Finally, she gave in.

"Hey ... Aww, man," Derek muttered, taking the plate from her hands and helping her into one of the kitchen chairs. "It's nothing to cry about. It's just dinner." He slid the plate into the microwave and hit the buttons.

Angela buried her face in her hands and continued to cry, hating that this man, out of everyone at the ranch, was the person to see her break down. "It's not about dinner. It's ..." Angela threw her hands in the air as Derek slid the warm plate in front of her. "I don't know."

He sat next to her, and she felt his hand squeeze her knee gently. "Angel, if you want to cry, I've got two free shoulders. But, if you'd rather, we can just talk."

Angela cupped her hands around her eyes and sniffed. The thoughtfulness of this family was something she'd never experienced from anyone before. Throughout most of her life, she'd been surrounded by people clawing to get ahead, no matter what damage might be caused in the process. She'd spent every waking moment living just like them, scraping and struggling to get by and dragging herself into the circle of success, ignoring the wake of bruised and battered people left behind. In her business, it was the only way to get ahead. In a few short days, this family was forcing her to rethink every belief she held.

Her stomach growled loudly in spite of the turmoil going on in her heart, and Derek laughed out loud. "That lasagna isn't going to stay hot much longer." He shook her leg gently. "Eat. We'll talk after." He stood and walked to the refrigerator, giving her some much needed space to compose herself.

Angela wiped her eyes, her fingers coming away with smeared mascara. *Great, I probably look like a raccoon.*

She dug into the cheesy pasta with a fork, grateful that Derek hadn't made fun of her tears. For someone who'd managed to hide her emotions for the last fifteen years, she hadn't been doing a very good job over the past few days.

"Thirsty?" Derek stood in the doorway of the refrigerator, glancing back at her, his forearm resting against the top. "There's water, tea, soda, beer ... What's your pleasure?"

She nearly choked on her food and wondered if he realized the double meaning of his words. She covered her mouth with her hand and turned toward him, sizzling heat slithering to her stomach and warming her limbs. His lopsided grin told her she'd given him the reaction he'd been looking for, and she tried to frown at him even while she couldn't help the smile pulling at the corners of her mouth.

"Come on, that was funny. You know it was," he insisted as he slid a cold beer in front of her. "I'm guessing you're more of a wine girl, but you seem like you could use something to take the edge off." He slid into the chair. She glanced at the beer in front of her, instantly wondering which bar her father was likely frequenting at this moment.

"No thanks, I'll just have water." She returned the beer to the refrigerator and took out a bottle of water.

"You ate that already?"

Angela smiled unapologetically. "I was hungry."

"I guess," he agreed, widening his eyes. "For someone so tiny, you've got a healthy appetite." Derek shook his head and took the plate to the dishwasher.

"You know, I could do that," she said.

Derek shrugged. "I suppose, but I'm already finished. Want to go out to the porch?"

Angela rose and followed him out to the front porch where he reclined on the wicker loveseat, crossing his ankles on the tabletop and patting the spot next to him. She shook her head at him disapprovingly. "What would Miss Silvie say?"

"She'd say, 'Derek, relax, you work too hard.'" He winked at her and patted the cushion again.

Angela eyed him warily. "You promise to behave this time?" She wasn't sure what had possessed her to ask him. *Nothing like letting him know you've been thinking about his kiss all day.*

"Cross my heart," he said, demonstrating.

She sat beside him, careful to keep several inches between them, and took a long sip of the cool liquid, dropping her head onto the backrest and staring out toward the corral. "What are you still doing up this time of night? Don't you have to get up with the chickens?"

"I guess. I'm sort of a night owl," he answered after taking a swig from his bottle. "Tomorrow should be interesting for you. You'll get to see some of the bucking stock up close."

She lifted her head and eyed him with distrust, hoping he didn't hear the tremor of apprehension in her voice. "How close?"

Derek chuckled quietly. "Still don't trust me?" He looked down at her.

Angela looked up and their eyes met. She could see laughter in the depths of his but there was more—a yearning that made her want to meet him halfway. The raw need for understanding ate at her resolve to remain detached. "I don't *distrust* you."

He laughed quietly. "I guess that's a place to start."

She looked out over the front yard and corral, her eyes lifting to the indigo sky filled with sparkling stars, which were brighter than she'd ever seen and faded into a distant abyss. She could see the dark shape of a horse in the corral and trees behind, but they were all small shadows in the distance, creating an eerie feeling of insignificance under the huge expanse above her. They sat in silence for several minutes, and she wondered how she could be so comfortable with a near-stranger beside her, late at night, in the middle of nowhere.

"It must have been pretty amazing growing up out here," she murmured, deliberately breaking the silence that was lulling her into a false security. She wanted to steel herself against his charm, but right now, under the stars with him, she was finding it more impossible than ever.

Derek put his empty bottle on the porch near the corner of the loveseat. "I always had an escape plan. I

THE COWBOY AND THE ANGEL   131

thought I wanted to live in the city until I went there," he said, slipping his arm around her shoulders.

It was an unspoken request for her to move closer, to eliminate the physical and emotional distance between them. By moving toward him willingly, she would become vulnerable, allowing him access to the hidden corners in her heart where she remained safe from further loss. If she allowed him in, she risked losing everything she'd worked for, including the freedom she was fighting to obtain.

Angela remained rooted to her cushion, stubbornly refusing to look at him. She wanted to move toward him, wanted to open up to him, but her fear was greater than her desire.

Derek wasn't about to be deterred so easily, and he scooted closer to her on the couch. She pressed her lips together and looked at her lap. If he didn't send her heart racing out of control with a mere glance, she would have dismissed him long ago for being such a pushy, alpha male. Usually she couldn't stand guys who demanded her attention, not that she'd had time for more than a few men, but something about Derek made her crave his presence even as she dreaded what it might cost her.

"How could anyone want the city over this?" She dropped her head back against his shoulder and soon found herself moving her head to rest against the wall of his chest. "I've never seen stars so bright."

Derek laughed quietly, the sound rumbling under her ear. "Same stars, Angel, but with no street lights you can actually see them all."

His arm hung loosely around her shoulder and she felt the warmth from his body radiating through his shirt, relaxing her tense muscles and making her wonder if this wasn't her opportunity to become the woman she'd always wanted to be. She glanced up at him. His jaw was mere inches from her lips and she watched him try to hide a smile. There was just a shadow of a beard darkening his skin, giving him a roguish appearance. She desperately wanted to press a kiss to his jaw, to feel the day's growth of stubble against her lips, but she settled for inhaling his personal scent—horses and grass with a hint of cinnamon—and tore her gaze from him, sighing against his chest.

"Why do you keep calling me that?"

"Calling you what? Angel?"

His voice was thick and she was afraid to speculate on the cause. She didn't want to hope for more than these brief stolen minutes in his arms. Thinking about the future would only bring disappointment. She wanted to savor this moment, where they had no past, no future, only *now*.

She nodded against his chest and felt his hand slip the hair tie from the bottom of her thick braid. He ran his fingers through the tresses, separating the strands, causing them to fall around her shoulder, and she bit back a moan of pleasure.

"Why would you ever pull this back?" he whispered. His hand rested at the base of her neck, his fingers absently moving along the flesh, sending silvery flames of desire over her shoulders and down her spine.

She dropped her head backward into his hand. "What are you doing?" Her voice was husky with desire. Her body was on fire and she was dizzy from trying to deny herself.

"I'm seducing you. Is it working?" His eyes were shadowed in the darkness. She couldn't tell if he was teasing her or not, so she remained silent. His fingers grazed the clasp of her necklace, and Derek cleared his throat. "Are you ever going to tell me about your ring?"

"My ring?" His question jolted her from the spell he'd woven on her senses. She felt goose bumps break out over her arms as she looked up at him, her cheek still pressed against his chest. She'd already told Sydney about her mother, so it shouldn't be so difficult to tell him. But the tenderness she could see in his eyes unraveled her. "It belonged to my mother. It was her wedding ring."

"Why do you have it?" He brushed her hair back from her forehead, heat trailing wherever his fingers touched.

"I ..." She couldn't think clearly. "She died." The words tumbled from her lips, and she wished she could take them back as she saw him frown. She should have at least tempered the words with some dignity instead of sounding crass. What was wrong with her?

He brushed his fingers over her cheek and took her chin between his thumb and finger. "I'm sorry, Angel. I didn't know. Something else we have in common."

Something else? She wrinkled her brow in confusion. "What's the other thing?" She was finding it difficult to catch her breath, and her chest was heavy; every inhalation intoxicated her with his scent.

A boyish grin spread over his lips. "We both want me to do this."

He lowered his head, gently brushing her lower lip between his lips before allowing his tongue to explore her mouth. He tasted and teased, his fingers winding into her hair. She curled her hands against his chest, bunching his t-shirt in her fists as he groaned and pulled her closer. He turned toward her on the couch as he pressed her backward. Angela slid her hands up to his shoulders, grasping the solid wall of muscle beneath her fingers, twining them behind his neck, and pulling him more fully against her.

She lost herself in the ecstasy of his kiss, her desire exploding in her stomach and her heart bursting with pleasure at being wanted instead of needed. Derek's fingers found the edge of her shirt, slipping just below the hem and grasping her waist as her back arched, pressing her against him, seeking a deeper connection. His hand trailed over her ribcage. His palm covered her breast, burning her skin through the thin lace covering her aching flesh. Derek's lips found the tender skin of her neck as his fingers slipped past the material, and her head tipped back, her fingers burying into his hair. A whimper of delight escaped her lips unbidden as his other hand slid up her thigh.

Derek pulled away. "Angel, you make me forget that I'm supposed to stay away from you." His breath was ragged as he whispered against her lips. "If we don't stop now, I'm going to take you upstairs." His promise hung in the air.

Shame flooded her. A few moments more and she would have willingly disregarded everything she was working to achieve for her father. His ability to chip away at the flimsy barriers she'd erected was going to be her downfall. She needed to avoid him whenever possible without making it look like it was intentional, or she might as well give up ever seeing her father sober.

As if sensing her retreat, Derek pressed a quick kiss to her swollen lips. "Don't do that, Angel."

"What?" She scooted into a sitting position, moving away from him.

"You're putting that wall back up. I can see it in your gorgeous green eyes." He reached for her hand and twined his fingers with hers, facing the corral, turning his attention back to the stars. "Tell me about your mother."

"My mother?" The fire he ignited in her made her brain fuzzy and her body prone to act without any thought to consequences.

He chuckled as if he understood her confusion. "Tell me about her. What was she like?"

"She was pretty." She glanced at their hands, which were clasped on his knee.

"I could have guessed that." He gave her a heated gaze that made her toes want to curl with longing. "What was her favorite thing to do?"

Angela had avoided thinking about her mother for more years than she could remember. Memories did nothing but expose pain. But when Derek asked, she found herself thinking back with fondness, remembering some of the fun she'd had with her mother. "She sang, a lot. She used to sing while she unloaded the dishwasher, and we would use wooden spoons as microphones."

"You sing?" His thumb was lazily tracing circles on the back of her hand, making it difficult to concentrate and remain emotionally distant.

"Not well," she pursed her lips. "What about your mother?"

"I was too young to remember much. I remember her telling us bedtime stories. Scott and I shared a room, and she would pretend the bed was a rocket or pirate ship or race car."

The sweet memory made her heart ache for the little boy he'd been. She could feel her heart waging a war with her mind, and logic was bound to lose if she didn't distance herself. "I should go inside."

Derek shook his head and slumped his shoulders. "And, there it is."

She pulled her hand away from his and frowned at him. "What?"

"That wall. It's about ten feet tall, made of bricks, and covered with electrified razor wire. You know, Angel, it's not going to kill you to let someone get close."

Angela stood up and glared at him. "I'm no angel. Anyone who thinks I am is going to be disappointed." She spun on her heel, leaving him on the porch.

She hurried up the stairs and closed her door, trying to ignore the wrenching ache in her chest. Would a time ever come when she could be vulnerable or allow someone to see the authentic woman she hid behind this bitchy façade? But doing that meant sacrifice, and she couldn't make that sacrifice yet. Someday, but not yet. Her father still needed her to remain focused. Maybe when he was well. Until that day, it didn't matter how much she liked this family or how much Derek made her heart race and her mind spin; she had a job to do. This was the first time Joe had let her take the lead on a serious news story. There wasn't room for failure. This story was the only way she would ever find freedom to live her own life.

DEREK SAT ON the porch as Angela bolted up the stairs, listening to her footsteps. The fact that she ran let him know he'd hit the mark. She was afraid to allow anyone close, and she shut down anytime he asked personal questions. This wasn't about her job.

Derek waited until he heard the door upstairs close. He needed a cold shower, and he doubted even that would cool him off. He'd always been a flirt, but when he was near Angela, he couldn't stop the slow burn that encompassed him. She had a way of turning him into a fumbling teenage boy again. He groaned, his pants becoming too tight, as he thought about their kiss and how, right now, she was preparing to climb into a bed only feet from his. His fingers still tingled from the contact with her silken skin; his clothing still carried her unique scent, teasing him. She was a vixen, tormenting him. But his need for her wasn't confined to the way she set his body into a spiral of desire. There was pain in her eyes he longed to see disappear. He couldn't put his finger on why it mattered to him, especially since he barely knew her.

But he could sympathize with the torment he recognized and wanted to be the one who made the shadow of fear in her eyes vanish. Tonight she'd shown him glimpses of the woman behind the icy veneer, and he was determined to draw her out. He just had to make sure it wasn't at the expense of his family.

Chapter Eleven

"MORNING, ANGEL. SLEEP well?" Derek smiled at her as she came into the kitchen before handing her a cup of coffee, complete with cream.

She took the cup and sipped the strong brew, grimacing. "No, and stop calling me that."

As a matter of fact, she had spent the entire night tossing and turning before giving up at four in the morning, but she wasn't about to tell him that. She was frustrated—with him, with herself, with her situation—and saw no solution in sight.

He grinned as he reached for his own cup, plopping a straw cowboy hat onto her head. "You're gonna need this today."

It was at least two sizes too big. She could only imagine that she must look twelve with it on. "Why?"

"Because today we're going to be out riding a bit longer and I don't want you to burn that pretty ivory skin of yours."

She groaned at the thought of another day in the saddle and glared at him. "I have sunscreen."

"Trust me, you'll want the hat once the sun comes up." He finished his coffee and tossed her a banana. "Unless you'd rather have another apple," he said, deliberately reminding her of their lesson yesterday when she ended up in his arms. Derek laughed. "No? Then let's get moving. There are stalls to clean." He led the way out the front door with her stumbling behind him.

"I'm cleaning what?" Why did she feel like she was constantly asking him questions without ever getting a straight answer? She followed a few feet behind him.

"Grab Honey and clip her on the lead, here," he pointed at the rope hanging from the outside of Honey's stall. "Then grab the wheelbarrow and pitchfork and clean her stall. When you finish, the brushes are in the tack room. I'll bring the saddle and blankets out so you can saddle her." He turned away and disappeared into the office, closing the door behind him.

Angela raised her brows in disbelief. Just because she watched him do it yesterday didn't mean that she was ready to try it on her own. She threw the hat at the ground and reached for the halter, muttering curses under her breath. She wondered briefly if feigning helplessness might convince him to do it for her again. She played with the nylon lead rope for a moment, unsure what caused his dismissive attitude. Was he mad she rejected him last night?

"I'll show him," she muttered. She slid the stall door open and Honey glanced away from the last of her breakfast as she slipped the halter over her nose. Angela smiled at the mare's cooperation as she dropped her head, allowing Angela to buckle it easier. "At least you'll help me out, won't you?" She patted the animal's neck as she led her from the stall and into the aisle of the barn.

After clipping her outside the stall, Angela twisted her lips and lifted the end of the wheelbarrow to guide it to the stall. It teetered tentatively, almost toppling. She would never admit it to Derek, but she'd never used a wheelbarrow and it was harder than it first appeared. She reached for the pitchfork inside, dragging it into the stall behind her. She slipped it under the manure, wrinkling her nose in disgust, and lifted it toward the wheelbarrow in time for the manure to slip through, leaving only straw stuck to the tines. Sighing, she tried again. This time it fell on the side of the wheelbarrow, and she clenched her teeth.

"Ugh!" she groaned, blowing her hair away from her face. The horse snorted and bobbed her head in reply. "Shut up. How much do you eat anyway?" she complained.

"Having trouble?" She glanced up and saw Derek leaning against the frame of the doorway.

"I think you feed these horses too much." He laughed and moved toward her, reaching for the pitchfork. "No, I can do this without your help," she insisted.

"We need to get going or we'll never be finished by lunchtime."

"Then you do it if you're in such a hurry." She pressed the tool into his hands and stormed toward the tack room.

His laughter followed her and she felt her palm itch to smack the smug expression she was certain he was wearing from his handsome face. She reached for the bucket, which was full of brushes, curry combs, and hoof picks, and carried it out to the mare, deliberately ignoring the man in the stall. She looked at the bucket, trying to remember which brush came first.

"Curry comb." She heard his voice call to her as he pushed the wheelbarrow out the back door of the barn.

"I know that," she returned, glaring at his back as she reached into the bucket for the circular rubber tool.

She had no idea what she'd done to cause this change in him since last night. *Maybe it isn't him. Could it be me?*

She'd lain awake most of the night, wondering if she had her priorities wrong. She spent so much of her life making plans for her father, hiding her need to help him behind a mask of ambition, that she isolated herself from life. She'd never had friendships with classmates or evenings out for drinks with coworkers. She was perfectly content to hide behind her façade of icy reserve, where no one could reach her or find out about her father and use that against her. As a result, she had no meaningful relationships at all. Not that she'd ever felt something missing—until Derek Chandler had awakened every nerve fiber in her body.

She dropped the curry into the bucket and reached for the soft brush, stroking the horse from behind her ears down her neck, letting the movement sooth her agitation. Derek walked by on his way to get his gelding from his stall.

"This one first." He plucked the brush from her fingers and replaced it with the hard bristled brush before walking away.

Angela clenched her jaw, barely controlling her desire to throw the brush after him. "Hey!"

Derek spun on the low heel of his boot, turning to meet her gaze. His eyes glinted mischievously, but he sighed dramatically. "What?"

Angela walked up to him until she stood toe-to-toe with him and tipped her chin up. She wasn't sure if she was more angry at him or herself.

"Stop." She poked her finger against the hard muscles of his chest and recalled her cheek against them the night before. "I am doing the best I can."

"Your *best* is taking forever. I'm beginning to think you want me to do it for you."

She pushed against his chest, hating that he didn't even shift his weight. "You're a jerk." She walked back to her mare, ignoring the sound of his footsteps following her.

Her heart leapt into her throat as his hands landed on her waist, gently squeezing. Derek leaned over her shoulder. "How do you want me to act, Angel? Like I can't keep my hands off of you?" He slid his hands up her sides, skimming past the sides of her breasts and sending her heart racing. He reached for her shoulders and spun her in his hands, sliding one hand to her lower back and pulling her against him. She could feel his arousal against her belly. Heaven help her, but she needed his touch and that frightened her.

"Like the thought of kissing you again drives me crazy?" He buried his hand in her hair, forcing her to meet his eyes, and dipped his head toward hers, pausing when their lips were a breath apart. "Like I couldn't sleep for thinking about what I wanted to do with you while we were alone today?"

She couldn't catch her breath. With every word from him, a new flash of desire ignited in her body. Her mind screamed at her to run, to move away from his touch, but she felt paralyzed as the brush clattered to the concrete floor and her fingers sought the strong foundation his arms offered, clenching the solid muscles of his biceps.

Derek's eyes flickered over her face, searching. Suddenly, his lips spread in a slow smile. "Isn't this where you run away, Angel?"

"Oh, you jerk," she muttered.

She pushed him away and bent to retrieve the brush. She wanted to be mad, but one glance at his face washed away any trace of anger. He looked like a little boy waiting for Christmas morning. Childish exhilaration gleamed in his dark eyes.

"Don't be disappointed, honey. If we can get these horses saddled, I'll make it up to you." He bent and pressed a quick kiss to her pouting lips before heading to retrieve his mount.

ANGELA FOUND IT much easier to stay in rhythm with her horse today. Her legs were stiff but not as sore, due in part to a hot bath the evening before. She still hadn't been able to discover what Derek had planned for her as they headed across a pasture east of Mike's house. He'd quizzed her on the rodeo knowledge he'd imparted the day before, asking her about each of the events, and he seemed surprised when she remembered it all. She refused to admit that seeing the satisfaction in his eyes sent a shiver of delight down her spine.

They'd already ridden for thirty minutes and she was beginning to wonder how much property the ranch included. Her research had indicated that Findley Brothers was on a thousand-acre parcel of land, but she wasn't sure how that translated into miles.

"Shouldn't we be nearing the end of the property?"

"Just over those hills." He pointed off in the distance. "But we'll be stopping before we go that far."

They crested a small hill and he stopped his gelding at the top. Angela looked down into a valley where a small creek cut parallel to a large pasture broken up into smaller fenced areas. Each held a magnificent horse, some grazing, others simply milling along the fence lines. One looked toward where they stood and whinnied. Soon, several others joined in and the horses began to prance along the fences. To one side was a barn with what appeared to be an attached corral and several small pens jutting from the back of each stall. To the right of the barn was a concrete slab with the framework of a new house. Her eyes turned toward Derek. He sat a bit straighter in his saddle, taking a deep breath and relaxing before her eyes. She could see the pride reflected in his eyes. Derek smiled. "You feel like checking out the studs?" She cocked her head and gave him a disparaging look. He burst out in laughter. "Stud *horses*," he clarified. "Stallions."

She could feel the heat of her blush creeping up the back of her neck. "I thought you said we were going to see some of the bucking stock today."

He nudged his horse, cuing him to start down the hill. "We are. In the pens."

She heard a quiet hum of electricity as they road toward the barn. "Electric fencing?"

"It's safer for stallions." He dismounted at the corral and slid the saddle from his gelding's back. "They can be rowdy when we bring the mares in. We have the electric fencing sticking out a few inches from the inside of the wooden fences along the top and bottom. It keeps them from running into it and getting hurt when they get excited."

She frowned as she dismounted Honey. "But doesn't it shock them?"

"A little, but nothing bad." He helped her unsaddle her mare and turned their horses loose in the corral before leading her to the nearest pasture.

"Watch." He reached out and tapped the back of his knuckles against the wire. His hand reflexively contracted back toward his body as he made contact, shocking himself.

Her mouth hung open in surprise. "Why would you do that?"

He shook his hand and shrugged. "Couple reasons. One, to prove to you that it's not painful, although it gets the animal's attention. And two, I needed to check it anyway." He laughed when she grabbed his hand to inspect his barely reddened knuckles. "See, nothing there. And horse hide at this height is tougher than mine."

She shook her head in disbelief. "You're insane." She looked into the pasture as a beautiful golden stallion jogged toward where they stood and stopped without touching the fence. She looked at Derek. "Can I pet him?"

"Of course, Frisco here is a big teddy bear. Be careful to stay away from his nose though, he will try to nibble on you."

She pulled her hand back. "He bites?"

Derek slipped a hand to her lower back, edging his body behind her and causing her pulse to quicken as heat traveled through her limbs. "No, he nibbles. A lot of stallions do bite, but Frisco just likes to grab at things with his lips. Sometimes, he catches skin by accident." He rubbed his hand over the stallion's face and she watched the horse lean toward his caress, edging closer to the fence.

"He's going to shock himself," she warned.

"He knows the boundaries."

Unlike his master. Not that she wanted Derek to move away.

The stallion stretched his thick neck over the fence toward the pair. Angela petted him, marveling at his deep golden color and white-blond mane and tail.

"He's a palomino," Derek explained. "That one over there is a paint. On the other side is Jester and he's a roan.

Just different hair coloring." He reached for a strand of her hair and lifted it between his fingers, his eyes darkening. "Just like yours."

She wanted to ignore the desire in his eyes but felt her entire body throb in response. She looked around at the fenced areas, desperate for a distraction. "Why do you have so many? There must be at least twenty."

He didn't even look away. "Twenty-seven, actually. These are the studs for the saddle bronc riding." He pointed to a group of stallions on the other side of the pasture. "Those are for bareback."

Derek slid his hand over her arms and she shivered at his touch. He smiled and clasped her hand in his before leading her toward the creek. Pleasure coursed through her. She pointed toward a massive framed building on a concrete slab. "What's that?"

A broad smile filled with pride spread across his face. "I'll show you that in a minute."

Angela stopped, forcing him to stop with her. "You're not going to make me go swimming again, right?"

"No," he laughed. "This is just a short break before I take you over to see the mares."

"How many horses do you guys actually have?"

Derek shrugged. "I'd have to really think about it. Between the animals we're breeding, the foals and the working stock, we probably have about three hundred horses at any given time."

"But you don't ride them all, right?" She still wasn't sure why they would have so many horses when less than seventy were usually used in the rodeo performance. It seemed that the more she learned about what he did, the more questions she had.

"Most of them are bucking horses, bred because of their parents' proven ability to make great bucking stock. Look up 'Born to Buck' when you do research. I'm surprised you haven't heard of it already. We have a lot of bucking stock so that none of the animals ever get overworked."

She sat on the damp earth at the edge of a swiftly moving creek, dropping her crossed arms over bent knees. He surprised her, scooting behind her and sitting with his thighs pressed against hers. It was an intimate gesture that sent butterflies spiraling in her stomach. She fought the urge to curl her arms around her knees, withdrawing from his connection. He lifted the hat from her head and laid it on the ground beside him before he leaned back on his palms. He didn't pull her back against him or lean into her. In fact, the only part of him touching her was his legs, as if he was waiting for her to make the first move toward him.

Everything about this budding relationship was foreign to her. He was so unlike any of the men she'd dated briefly before. Whenever they'd tried to breach her tough exterior, she broke off any communication. But Derek wouldn't take no for an answer and continued to press past the barriers she built, intent on revealing the vulnerabilities beneath the surface she'd taken great pains to hide.

And, there had never been anyone who made her feel the aching desire to touch and be touched. She wasn't sure if it was his flirty smile or his country-boy charm, but somehow he was slipping past her usual defenses. It was exhilarating and frightening, as appealing as it was dangerous. Angela wanted to lean back against him, to feel the support of the solid wall of masculinity behind her, but allowing even that simple connection would open her up to risk—risk of exposure, of giving up the future she'd worked so long to achieve.

"What's going on in that pretty head of yours?" he asked, his fingers playing with the long waves cascading down her back.

Angela rested her cheek on her wrists, looked at him over her left shoulder, and shrugged.

"You're tense," he pointed out, his fingertip outlining her ear.

She felt warm tremors course from his fingers down her neck and across her shoulders. The way this man could make her body respond with a mere touch was incredibly frightening. She closed her eyes, unsure how to respond. How could he read her so well in such a short time?

Derek's fingers slid her hair to one side, exposing her left shoulder. He leaned forward, curling his body around her back. She wondered if he hadn't given up, would she have made the first move? Would she have leaned into his heat? His lips found the hollow behind her ear and icy fire shot through her veins, burning and tingling at the same time, leaving her entire body languid and warm. She leaned back against him, shutting out the fearful warning threatening to creep in.

Derek wrapped his arms around hers, enveloping her

within his embrace. "Angel, you are the most stubborn woman I've ever known." His lips continued to caress the flesh of her neck, assaulting her will to distance herself.

Angela sucked in a breath as his teeth nipped at the sensitive skin at the back of her neck before his lips kissed the flesh. She couldn't fight her desire any longer. Derek reminded her that she was a woman, feminine and desirable, worthy of love. In his arms, she was protected and cared for, cherished and adored. Foreign sentiments, even in her childhood. Derek forced her to relinquish control, and for the first time she found herself completely trusting a man.

She had to feel his lips against hers, to show him how much his affection was releasing her from her self-imposed, emotionless prison. She twisted in his arms, coming to her knees in front of him. Her palms cupped his unshaved jaw, loving the rasp of his whiskers against her palms as her lips found his, tentatively at first, quickly losing herself in the kiss. Angela silently begged him to understand her need, the ache that she was finding more difficult to fill when he wasn't around.

DEREK'S ARMS TIGHTENED around her, pulling her against his chest. It was the first time she had initiated any contact between them, and he reveled in the knowledge that she was just as affected by this fire between them. His ice queen was melting and leaving a woman with burning desires. He brushed his fingers along her jawline before burying his fingers in the hair at the back of her head. Her tongue touched his lower lip before sweeping against his, and he felt his restraint snap. He'd never responded to another woman the way he did with her. He groaned and lay back on the grassy bank, dragging her with him.

His hands found the hem of her shirt, searching for the smooth perfection of her skin. Every nerve ending sizzled as his fingers found their prize. His large hands splayed over her lower back, sliding up her spine. He couldn't get enough of the taste of her as his mouth sought her neck. She arched her head backward, allowing him access as she gripped his shoulders like a lifeline. He understood her need. He was alive only when they touched. His fingers continued up her spine, trailing over her ribs, his thumb brushing against the flimsy lace covering the softly rounding curve of her breast. With a flick of his fingers, he released the straining mounds, cupping them in his hands. She cried out as his thumb brushed against her peaked nipple. He massaged her flesh, driving himself wild with a need to taste her as she writhed under his touch. Her hands slipped under his shirt and every inch of his body burned with longing. He wondered if she would stop him from taking her here on the grassy bank.

Derek groaned, forcing himself to retreat, every part of his body rebelling against him.

"Angel," he whispered against her lips. "We have to stop." He could feel his arousal straining against his jeans uncomfortably and groaned as she shifted over him, pressing into closer contact the core of her desire. "Angel, you're killing me," he growled against her lips.

As if realizing the need she'd unleashed, she tried to pull back. But he refused to allow her to move away, tucking her head under his chin. He could tell she wasn't ready to face the desire she'd revealed. He was surprised she didn't fight him, but he was content to lay by the creek all day if it meant she would stay in his arms.

His heartbeat began to slow as he trailed his fingers over her back, encouraging her to relax. Her breathing soon became slow and even and he wondered if she'd fallen asleep.

"Can I tell you something?" She laid one hand over the center of his chest and rested her chin on top, looking at his face.

Derek folded one arm under his head and brushed her hair away from her face. "Anything."

He realized he meant it. He still worried about what her story might do to the stock contracting company, but he couldn't ignore this connection he felt with her, as if fate had bound them to one another. It was unlike anything he had ever experienced, and he couldn't explain it any more than he could fight it.

"I have never felt as welcome as your family has made me feel." He could see tears brimming in her eyes. "I don't want to ruin them." She sighed and tried to roll off of his chest, and he could see her walls being re-erected.

"Whoa, don't you go anywhere." He reached out for her as she sat up and adjusted her clothing. Derek pulled her back between his legs. "Don't run away this time."

She rolled her eyes toward him. "I can't do this."

"Do what?" He circled his arms around her and kissed her temple.

"This," she said, flinging her hands out. "This story, you, me, your family . . ." Tears slipped down her cheeks, unchecked, in contrast with her usual detachment.

"Angel, I'd like nothing better than for you to drop this story. But I also know that when you do, you'll leave." He tipped her chin up so that she was forced to meet his eyes. "I'm not ready for that. Whatever *this* is," he said as he placed a gentle kiss to her lips, "I think we owe it to each other to explore it."

She returned his kiss, smiling against his lips. "But . . ."

"But nothing." He eyed her playfully. "I also think I should continue to explore this." He trailed his finger from her shoulder down her arm to the inside of her elbow, loving the goose bumps that rose on her skin. "Maybe a little of this." He slid his finger along her collarbone and watched her eyes darken to the deep emerald he'd seen only moments ago, and he frowned. "Maybe we should go take a look at the house after all," he suggested, nodding toward the wooden framework.

She turned to him as they reached the concrete foundation. "It's enormous."

Derek shrugged. "Scott thought it was about time I move out of Mike's house. I agreed, but I want to build it myself. We've been booked pretty heavily, so it's taking longer than I hoped."

"You're building this yourself?" She looked surprised.

"In case you haven't noticed, I'm pretty good with my hands." His eyes slid over her body before centering on her lips. He wanted to kiss her again. In fact, he wanted to take her back to Mike's house and disappear upstairs for the rest of the day. He forced his wayward thoughts back to the present but noticed the longing in her eyes, and he wondered if she wasn't thinking the same thing he was. He lifted her hand and pressed a kiss to the back of it, her pulse beating against his lips. "This is going to be the master bedroom."

He directed her around the skeleton of what would eventually be his home, describing exactly how he planned to finish each room and how it would look. He watched her reaction to each description, unsure of why he wanted to see approval in her eyes. He hadn't felt this nervous since he'd climbed on a bull on a bet at thirteen, but watching her look around with awe and appreciation made his confidence soar.

"It's going to be beautiful, Derek." She stopped and turned toward him. "You never wanted to do this instead of rodeo?"

He shrugged. "Rodeo is what we do. Building this is just how I unwind and find myself."

"You were lost?"

He knew she was teasing when she asked, but it felt like a knife plunged into his heart. He didn't think she noticed the change in him until she stopped walking and stood in front of him. "Open book, remember?"

Derek gave her a lopsided grin. "Why is it that *I* am an open book but you aren't?" He leaned back against one of the beams and pulled her between his thighs, curling his arms around her back.

"Remember when I told you there was some tension between me and Scott?" She nodded and curled her arms around his waist, making it difficult for him to concentrate. "I've always tended to be the 'black sheep,' the one who never wanted to grow up and accept responsibility."

"Who, you?" He knew she was trying to keep the mood light, but he had to get this off his chest. He had to make her see why he couldn't let his family down again, what kind of man he really was, even at the risk of losing her. His chest ached as he forced himself to go on.

"Last year that irresponsibility almost got Sydney killed. I got involved in something that got out of control quickly. I let myself be conned into doing something completely self-serving and by the time I realized I wanted out, it was too late. Sydney was hurt, and the stallion we'd planned on building our entire breeding program on was killed." He clenched his jaw, trying not to relive the anguish he'd felt over the pain he'd caused. "I nearly destroyed everything my family had been working for, and Sydney paid the price for my selfish irresponsibility."

ANGELA COULDN'T IMAGINE him deliberately doing anything that would harm his family. She recognized the self-loathing in his eyes and could see he blamed himself for what had happened, whether or not it was his fault. Maybe he hadn't always been the man he was now. Maybe his mistakes had shaped him. She certainly understood how circumstances and decisions, especially painful ones, altered the future.

Surrounded by his arms, the home he was creating to find himself again, and his vulnerability, something inside her broke. She didn't want to carry her burden alone, any more than she wanted him to bear his in silence. She fingered the chain on her neck, wanting nothing more than to erase the pain in his eyes, even if it meant sharing her most painful memory.

"I understand what it is to live with regrets." She brushed her hand over his jaw. "My mother died when I was eight years old. I remember hearing my parents fighting in their room. They were always fighting." She stared at the center of his chest and gave a bitter laugh. "I ran into their room and yelled at Mom to leave him alone. Not because she was wrong, but I knew if they kept fighting Dad would just start drinking again. I'd seen it happen before," she whispered.

She shook her head at the memory. It had been years since she allowed herself to think about that night. She didn't want to lose herself in the emotions completely. Derek's hands were warm on her hips, holding her against him, supportive without being forceful. He shared her pain rather than turning away from her grief the way her father had done. Even Joe, in their long friendship, hadn't allowed her the opportunity to open the vault of her heartache and purge it. But Derek welcomed the downpour of her pain with a sensitivity she'd hadn't expected.

"Mama didn't listen. They kept fighting. I don't even remember what it was about. The next thing I knew she was heading for the front door and ran out into the rain. My father followed her out the door, yelling at her to get out." She laughed bitterly. "He tried to kick *her* out."

"Angel," he whispered. He pressed a kiss to her forehead and wiped the tear slipping down her cheek. That one word on his lips gave her the courage to press on, trusting him with her vulnerability.

"I followed them to the stoop and she ran into the street." Tears coursed down her cheek now and her hands fisted against his chest. "She never saw the car coming. I held her hand until the ambulance took her away, but she wasn't conscious."

She looked up at him. "I didn't even go to the hospital. I took care of my grief-stricken, drunk father instead of going with her. I never got to tell her goodbye." Her voice was barely a whisper.

Angela could read sympathy in his eyes, but there was more: bitterness and anger bubbling behind the tenderness he directed toward her. "Angel, I can't imagine facing that choice as a child, but you took care of him. Your mother wouldn't want you to shoulder this blame." His brushed her hair from her cheek, kissing her eyelids. "You have no idea how much it means to me that you would share this."

He sighed and she felt the tension fall over his shoulders. "My mistake was different. It was made by an immature, spoiled man, deliberately and selfishly. There will never be anything I can do to bring back what was lost or make up for the pain it caused."

His voice echoed with his self-contempt as he looked

around the framework of his house. "I don't deserve this, or the forgiveness my family has given me." He cupped her face, his lips meeting hers in a soft caress filled with heartache. "Or you. But I need you to understand what sort of man it's made me. I can never disappoint them that way again. Not even for you."

Chapter Twelve

ANGELA PUT HER fingers to her lips, which still tingled from Derek's kisses, as she drove her sedan toward town. It had been an emotionally draining morning but she felt oddly relieved after telling Derek about her mother's death. She wasn't sure why she'd opened that door and allowed him to see the depths of her pain. She'd never even told Joe what had happened that night. Maybe she wanted him to know she understood the sorrow of his regret, or perhaps it was because she felt safe with him, as if he could rescue her from the grip of her past.

You better get control of yourself. He's not a knight in shining armor. You don't know this guy well enough to let him in this way.

She twisted the volume button on the car stereo, hoping some music would sooth her mind. Her Instead, she could only think about the way she'd draped herself across Derek's chest with her hands wrapped around his neck, her lips on his, and his hands covering her breasts. She felt a blush creep over her shoulders and neck. How could she have been so shameless? A slow sizzle of desire circled in her stomach as she remembered whimpering with pleasure at his touch. How could nothing more than a thought of him cause a reaction like this when no other man had so much as stirred a single flutter?

Her phone chirped from the center console of the car and she glanced at the caller ID, pressing a button on the steering wheel to answer it, grateful for the distraction from her carnal thoughts. "Hey, Joe. I hope you have good news for me."

"You on the way to talk with the vet?"

"I am. Depending on what I get from him, I'll have a better idea which direction this story will take."

She heard the pause from the other end of the phone. "What do you mean, 'which direction'? I thought you already knew that." He sounded suspicious. "What's going on out there, Gigi?"

"Nothing," she denied quickly. "But right now there's nothing to indicate abuse at all. In fact, what I've seen disputes all of my research. Maybe we should try taking the other side," she suggested.

"Are you kidding?" His voice rang with impatience. Joe was known as the Tyrant of Channel 12 for a reason—it was his way or no way.

"I'm just trying to think outside of the box. There are plenty of stories covering animal cruelty. What about one that proves the animals aren't hurt?"

"You were the one who brought me this story. You insisted on heading out there to prove your theory and now you're telling me you don't have a story after all?"

"Well, I'm just thinking . . ."

"If there's no abuse, get your ass back here and quit wasting my time." The threat in his voice caused panic to ripple down her spine.

"There might be a few leads to follow up on after the interview today. And I still have the rodeo this weekend. I'll let you know then."

"Follow up on them today and call me." She could hear the finality in his voice. Friend or not, he wouldn't allow her to cost the station any unnecessary time or money. "And, Gigi, call your dad."

"Is he okay?"

His voice immediately returned to that of her friend. "He's fine, but he misses you. He needs to hear your voice."

She sighed but was glad to have the concerned note back in his voice. "You know, you're kind of a nag, Joe."

His chuckle filled the car. "And you're still my favorite reporter. But they are bugging me to get you back on the air. They're convinced people won't tune in if they don't get to see your pretty face soon. Monica just isn't as good as you are and viewers aren't talking. When they aren't talking, they aren't watching." He hesitated, as if unsure how to say what he wanted. "Gigi, I can't lose you," he confessed.

"Joe, I . . ." She let her words hang. She wasn't sure how to respond. She'd always been honest with him about her feelings, or lack of them, and he knew she needed to leave to help her father. Every time he reminded her of his affection for her, guilt ate at her, threatening to overwhelm her, reminding her of how easy it would be to stay in the pitiful circumstances she found sadly comfortable.

"Just call me tomorrow and let me know the status of the story." He hung up before she could even respond.

"DR. BRADFORD," ANGELA greeted the vet, thrusting out her hand. "Thank you so much for taking time to talk with me today."

"It's my pleasure."

She took a seat across from his massive metal desk. The office was decorated with various awards and degrees framed on the wall, in addition to several cards, pictures and collages of animals that he'd treated. The entire wall behind the doctor was covered with files sporting multicolored tabs. Angela inhaled the scent of antiseptic and looked around her, impressed by the cleanliness, before glancing back at the man sitting with his hands folded over a slightly round belly. He appeared to be about fifty, and his hair, what was left of it, was completely white and stood in messy tufts. His eyes were filled with humor, as if he were waiting for the punch line of a joke, and he gave her a friendly smile.

"I understand you're looking for my professional opinion about rodeo."

"I have a few questions, but mainly specific questions about the care of the animals."

"Shoot." He leaned back, his chair creaking loudly.

She pulled a small recorder from her purse and held it up. "Do you mind?" Dr. Bradford stuck out his lower lip and shook his head. She placed the recorder on his desk and pressed the button. "Dr. Bradford, can you please state your occupation."

"I've been a large-animal veterinarian for the last thirty years, operating my own practice for twenty-two of those."

"Have you ever been called out to a rodeo in a professional capacity?" She skimmed her notes.

"I've worked as the vet for several local rodeos, both professional and amateur, and I've attended several ranch rodeos."

Angela looked up and frowned. "What's the difference?"

"A ranch rodeo is simply an event that a ranch owner puts on. Anyone can do it—provide stock, make up their own events . . . whatever. An amateur event is usually very similar to a professional rodeo but isn't sanctioned. It's usually where most cowboys, and girls," he clarified, "get started. Then there are professional rodeos, those sanctioned by a governing branch, complete with rules. The purse at a pro rodeo is much bigger than at an amateur."

"So it's like a baseball player starting in the minor leagues before going to the majors?"

"Exactly."

She jotted down a reminder in her notebook of the comparison. "What about stock contractors? Are they all the same or are there amateur and professionals with them as well?"

"Absolutely. But just like the cowboys, stock contractors have a number of requirements they have to fulfill to be considered 'professional.'" He tilted his head at her. "Looking at someone specifically?"

Angela bit her lower lips. She didn't really want to bring up Findley Brothers but couldn't ignore his direct question. "Maybe," she hedged. "What about the animals themselves? Any requirements for them?"

Dr. Bradford shrugged. "That depends on what you mean by requirements. They need to fall within certain ages or weights for some events. They must be considered healthy."

"Who decides that?"

"Well, that's where it gets a bit sticky. The rules don't really say and most people assume it's the vet on site. But, if the stock contractor is less than . . . conscientious about their animal care then . . ." He shrugged, not finishing his sentence, leaving his meaning clear. There were times the animals performed when they weren't "healthy."

"Who polices the stock contractors?"

"It's supposed to be the judges. The same judges that the stock contractor hires. It's a bit of a catch-22." He raised his bushy brows, waiting for her to make the connection and ask another question.

"In the rodeos you attended, were animals injured?"

Dr. Bradford chuckled quietly. "You better define 'injured' because that could be a very broad spectrum. Animals are injured in pastures every day. I couldn't begin to tell you how many times I'm called out to patch up a horse that has run through a fence or has been punctured by a branch on a tree. I love what I do, Angela, but we aren't dealing with an overabundance of intelligence in many cases. Even the best-trained horses can hurt themselves, in a stall or at a rodeo. But, assuming you mean significant injuries requiring veterinarian care, I have been needed only once in over fifteen years and probably forty or fifty rodeos."

Angela frowned. Her story seemed to be falling apart in the middle of her interview. "That's it?"

"Not what you were expecting? That one time was for a mare that got overexcited in the chute and began flailing. When she wouldn't calm, the stock contractor opened the chute and let her loose. As she was turned loose, she kicked at the gate and appeared lame when she was in the pen afterward. She was treated with bute on site and brought here after the rodeo for X-rays, which showed a small crack in the coffin bone. We had a farrier called in for special shoes, and after returning home she was confined until it healed. I heard they retired her to pasture and to be a broodmare afterward—due to her temperament, not her injury."

"But I've seen several videos with animals, especially cattle, injured in the roping events."

"It can happen, but it's usually when a green cowboy or horse is involved. Stock contractors can use those calves for only a short time because they outgrow the weight and age limitations, so most don't keep a ton of them on ranches. If cowboys injure them, they are forced to purchase more. I've seen a few contractors go after the cowboys for fines because their horse choked a calf by pulling backward in a roping event." He shook his head and smoothed back a few stray tufts of hair on the top of his head. "Like I said, it happens, but I've never seen an injury from it."

Angela continued to interview the vet but was surprised by several of his answers. There *might* be a story here, but the evidence was for the other side. Joe wasn't going to be happy, and she could see her hopes of an anchor position slipping away. She flipped through a few pages of her notes.

"You mentioned 'bute' earlier, what's that?"

"Phenylbutazone. It's an NSAID for horses. Like ibuprofen. It's used for pain relief, reducing inflammation, things like that."

"Could that be considered a performance-enhancing drug?"

He puckered his lips and bobbed his head from side to side thoughtfully. "Maybe. I guess if the animal was injured and you didn't want anyone to know. I would be more likely you'd see that from the horses trailered in for roping events or in barrel racing than from the stock contractor though. Even then, the livelihood of that cowboy depends on his animal, and running an injured animal will only break it down faster. Cowboys know that. There are others—bronchodilators, stimulants—but they are used more often in horse racing than rodeo. I've never personally seen anything used by contractors or competitors. Then again," he pointed out, "I've never tested for any of them either."

She read through her quickly scribbled notes again. "I think that's all of my questions, doctor. You've been incredibly helpful. I appreciate the unbiased answers. It was exactly what I was looking for." Angela rose from her chair and turned off the recorder.

"Have you thought about talking with Mike Findley, from Findley Brothers? He's not too far from here."

"I'm actually heading back out to the ranch. Mike has been kind enough to let me stay there to see a few professional rodeos first hand."

Dr. Bradford walked her to her car. "You won't find a nicer man than Mike, or his partners, the Chandlers. They love what they do. But, like I said, not all people are like them. I wish they were."

She turned and looked him in the eye. "Off the record, Dr. Bradford, do you support rodeo?"

The vet took a deep breath, considering his words before answering slowly. "I'm not unsupportive of it. I've seen far worse abuse, neglect, and animal cruelty outside the rodeo arena than I ever saw inside."

"Earth to Derek."

Derek shook his head, dragging his thoughts back to the present as his brother held the wire clippers toward him. Scott shot him a knowing grin. "You going to finish this fence or fantasize?"

Derek grabbed the tool from his brother and snapped

off the end of the fencing, bending the rough edge back into the fence post for safety. "What the hell are you talking about? I was listening."

"Really?" Scott raised his brows in disbelief. "Then you have a suggestion for this weekend?"

"What about this weekend?"

"Good to know you're listening." Scott removed his gloves, slapping them against his thigh as he stood up. He caught his brother's frown. "I'm just kidding. Man, what has you all riled up?"

Derek shook his head and tucked his work gloves into his back pocket. "Nothing."

Scott tossed the tools into the truck bed. "You've been awfully quiet today." He crossed his arms over the side of the truck and looked at his brother across the truck bed. "You okay?" He opened the small ice chest in the back of the truck and tossed a bottle of water across to Derek.

He caught it and opened the bottle, chugging half in one swallow. "I guess I'm worried about Angela wandering around the rodeo unsupervised all weekend."

Scott shrugged and shook his head. "Don't sweat it. You know we take care of our animals. We take every precaution for the cowboys. There's nothing for her to find." He took a second bottle of water from the ice chest, offering another to Derek. "She's not the first activist we've ever dealt with. Why are you so worried?"

"No thanks. Because she's the first one I've dealt with on my watch," he admitted. "You and Mike always took care of them. I wasn't around, remember?"

"So?"

Derek cocked his head at his brother as if the answer should be obvious. "I don't exactly have a track record of good decisions, Scott."

"You need to stop this." Scott crumpled the plastic bottle and tossed it into the back of the truck before opening the passenger door and climbing inside. Derek followed and started up the truck. "You can't punish yourself forever for Liz. You aren't the same person you were."

Derek knew that coming from Scott, considering how strained their relationship had been over the past few years, his comment was the highest praise he could imagine. He felt his chest swell a bit knowing his brother recognized all he accomplished in the last year. He quickly shoved away any feelings of pride as he thought about the fact that they'd had only ten foals this year instead of hundreds over several years because of his selfishness and immaturity. He couldn't let this situation escalate into another mistake like last time.

"Thanks for taking time out from flirting to help me with the fence today." Scott could barely hide the smile as he cupped his chin in his fist on the window.

"You're an ass." Derek shot his brother a glare but wasn't about to deny he'd enjoyed the time he'd spent with Angela the past two days.

Scott laughed and raised his palms toward Derek. "Just saying, it must be hard to find time to work when you're busy riding with someone who gets a rise out of you just walking into the room."

Derek arched a warning brow at his brother. Scott's

double meaning wasn't missed. "I'm sure it's been so long since you and Sydney met that you barely remember."

Scott chuckled. "Yeah, right. And I remember fighting it just like you're doing. Don't bother. You might as well give in and enjoy it. It won't do you a bit of good to fight, anyway."

Chapter Thirteen

_____

ANGELA STARED IN awe at the buzz of activity around
her. The sun had barely crested the horizon and cowboys, trucks, and trailers filled with animals were scattered everywhere she looked. As Sydney loaded several
horses into the trailer, Scott directed other cowboys to
take two of the rigs into the east pasture to load the bulls
he'd separated. Mike took the lead loading the cattle for
the timed events and prepping the truck while he was on
the phone with the stockyard they would stop at on the
way to the rodeo to water the animals.

Her eyes found Derek across the busy corral. Amidst
the hectic activity and stress, he still found a moment to
share a laugh with one of the older cowboys. She admired
his easygoing humor, even in the face of immense pressure. She bit her lower lip as she watched him head into
the barn, returning with a saddle over each shoulder. He
was an impressive specimen of a modern cowboy. The

baby on her lap slapped her hands against her chest playfully, distracting her from appraisal.

"Looks like Kassie needs your attention more than Derek," Silvie pointed out.

A blush flooded Angela's cheeks at being caught watching him, and Silvie laughed, wiggling her fingers in front of Jennifer's little boy, Blake. "Don't you worry, Angie, I doubt anyone else is even paying any attention."

Angela was just about to deny watching Derek when her cell phone rang. Her heart jumped into her throat. She knew it was Joe again, wanting to know if she'd dug up any dirt. She needed to continue to avoid his calls until she could find something—anything—that might get him to send a news crew to the rodeo this weekend.

"I can hold Kassie if you want to take that," Silvie offered.

Angela shook her head, praying that Joe wouldn't call back until she was on the road. "It's fine. I'll call them back later." She pushed the button to reject the call.

Silvie eyed her but refrained from commenting as Mike approached, folding the papers in his hands and shoving them into his back pocket. "Angela, are you planning on driving, or did you want to ride in one of the trucks?"

"I was planning on driving." Angela shrugged. Just remembering the touch of Derek's lips on her own, his hands burning her bare skin, kept her tossing and turning into the early morning hours. It was going to be a long day if she was driving after a sleepless night.

"I just figured riding in one of the trucks would give you a more authentic experience. We have plenty of room. You could ride with Scott and Sydney, if you don't mind the baby," he said, chucking Kassie's chin and making a silly face at her. "Or you could ride with Derek."

Her heart picked up speed at Mike's suggestion. As much as three hours of close confinement with Derek might send shivers of anticipation over her flesh, she wasn't sure she was ready to be alone with him after yesterday. She didn't want to face their troubled pasts, and who knew where the conversation might lead. But riding with Derek would give her an excuse for not returning Joe's call.

"Great then that's one less car we need to worry about at the rodeo." It didn't sound like he was actually giving her a choice.

"Whatever is easier, Mike. I don't want to be any trouble. And I'm going to try to get a crew there at some point this weekend, if that's still okay with you."

Mike nodded and jotted himself a reminder on the papers from his pocket. "Just don't let me forget to get them press passes when they arrive. Are you packed?"

"Sydney loaned me a few outfits since I didn't have long-sleeved shirts. It's a good thing we are about the same size."

"I'm going to make sure everything else is well under way. We're pulling out in about two hours."

"How is this chaos going to be ready to leave in two hours?" Angela whispered to Silvie as Mike walked back toward the barn.

Silvie laughed. "That man is a magician. You'll see. Just make sure you're not the one holding up the show." She rose and carried both babies into the house for breakfast.

DEREK GLANCED AT the woman seated next to him in the truck. Whose bright idea had it been to put them in a truck together for three hours? The last fifteen minutes of awkward silence was enough to make the tension between them obvious. So far, Angela had spent each mile ignoring him, making it clear she had no interest in conversation. He wasn't sure what had happened since yesterday afternoon at his house, but it hung in the air, dragging out every second into a roar of silence in the cab. Maybe knowing what sort of man he was had extinguished any attraction she might have had. It was probably for the best, but he couldn't help feeling disillusioned.

He reached over and turned on the radio. A country song blared through the speakers of the truck. If she wanted to ignore him, he could do the same. She glanced his way, and then turned back to the window almost immediately, watching the miles of scenery slide by and fade into the distance. After another twenty minutes, he couldn't take it and clicked the radio off.

"Did I do something to piss you off?"

She glanced his way, looking bored. "What are you talking about?"

"You're acting like I have the plague." Derek's hands squeezed the steering wheel and he took a deep breath. "So, what'd I do?"

Angela shook her head and shrugged. "After yesterday I just . . ." The ring of her phone interrupted what she was about to say. She glanced at the screen, biting her bottom lip nervously. "Crap. I have to take this," she explained as she pushed the button.

Derek wondered if she really didn't want to take the call or if she was just avoiding talking to him. He saw a flicker of nervousness in her eyes and she sat upright, looking straight ahead.

"Hey, Joe." He could barely hear a muffled male voice on the other end of the line. "I know, but it's been a busy morning. We're already on our way to the rodeo grounds."

Was that a tremor he heard in her voice? Where was the confident woman who usually argued with him?

"It went well. I might have a lead, but I can't really talk right now."

She glanced at Derek and he arched his brow at her in question. *A lead?* That didn't sound like it would bode well for his family. "You aren't coming until Saturday? That might be a bit of a problem."

She sighed and he wondered who this Joe might be. Obviously it was someone she worked with, but he didn't like the worried tremor in her voice any more that he liked the direction the conversation was taking.

"I can't get into it right now. I guess Saturday will be fine. I'm doing the best I can," she muttered through clenched teeth into the phone before disconnecting the call.

"Trouble?" He wanted to press her for information, to find out what her "lead" might be, but he also wanted to find out what had brought the shadow of apprehension to her eyes again.

"My boss," she said, pocketing the phone as if that should explain everything.

"I know how that is. Damn demanding bosses." He glanced sideways to see if she'd detected the teasing note in his words. He caught her trying to hide a smile, even as she bit on the corner of her lower lip nervously. What he wouldn't give right now to nibble the soft flesh, even in the face of her indifference today.

"Look, I don't know what happened yesterday after you went to town, and you don't have to tell me, but are we okay?"

She looked him in the eye and he could see the apology there. It was the last thing he wanted to see in her eyes. It meant she was about to do something that would damage the tenuous connection they were building, something she felt the need to apologize for. She shrugged and looked back to the window.

Derek clenched his jaw and looked out the windshield. "So, we're back to this? You're the reporter bound to blow the whistle on the villainous rodeo industry, and I'm the depraved stock contractor abusing animals for fun?" He shook his head in disgust.

"I didn't say that."

"You didn't have to, Angel." He couldn't look at her. He was afraid she would see his disappointment and regret. He hadn't been able to change her mind.

"I don't have a lead, and I don't know what I'm reporting," she confessed. "That's the problem."

"Why can't you just report the truth?"

"Because they don't want the truth," she pointed out. "And there's not a damn thing I can do to change their minds." She turned back to the window, effectively ending the conversation.

This was going to be a long weekend.

WHILE THE MEN unloaded the animals into various pens, Sydney asked Angela to help her prepare lunch at her trailer. Angela hesitated to join her, worried Sydney might see through her confident façade, but she didn't want to take her frustration out on the other woman. Joe was furious with her lack of details, refusing to send a crew until late Saturday evening, after the performance. If she didn't come up with something in the next two days, Joe was going to pull the story and crush her chance to get her father into rehab.

After her conversation with Dr. Bradford, she recognized there was no animal abuse, at least not with this stock contractor. Sure, there were ways professional rodeos could eliminate some of the risk for the animals, but this was an issue filled with gray areas. Without any evidence of abuse, she was having a difficult time finding another angle that would make this story worth the station's time.

Angela slathered condiments on the bread Sydney had spread over the counter and table as they prepared sandwiches for the entire crew in assembly-line fashion. She sighed, wishing that one breath could convey all of the frustration, anger, and misery she felt. She refused to entertain the thought that she might be returning to her apartment sooner than she ever anticipated and without any hope to offer her father.

"You're kind of quiet today. Are you okay?"

"I guess." She reached for the lunchmeat, slapping slices onto the bread. "I've just got a lot on my mind."

"Anything I can help with?" Sydney glanced at her as she put cheese onto the sandwiches. "I'm a pretty good listener."

Normally Angela would have refused. She didn't like listening to others complain, and she wasn't one to confide her secrets with strangers, but she was at a loss. She had nowhere to turn for solutions. "I'm not sure what to do about this story. It's pretty obvious you guys aren't abusing your stock. I've tried to get the station manager to spin the story the other direction, making you the victims of a witch-hunt, but they aren't having any part of it. They want the ratings that controversy brings, and making you guys out as the hero won't cut it."

Angela slumped into the chair as Sydney finished the sandwiches. "If I can't find a story before tomorrow, I'll be back on the air doing ribbon cuttings and covering charity events by Monday." She rested her chin in her hand, watching Sydney pile the sandwiches onto a platter.

"You want more," she clarified. "I know that feeling. Can't you just go to a bigger station?"

Angela shook her head. "I can't give up this job until I have something better. I have . . . responsibilities I can't ignore."

Sydney arched a brow and tipped her chin up, staring at her curiously. Angela cursed herself for not being more careful with her choice of words, and she was grateful when Sydney didn't pursue it. "Can you take some time off?"

Angela shook her head. "They don't like when your face is off the air if you're the one pulling in ratings. I already had to pull some strings to get them to let me off now. They aren't happy about it and they're getting impatient."

"I have an idea," Sydney said, motioning for Angela to grab several bags of potato chips and a tray of sandwiches. "Let's get these boys fed and we can work on the details over the weekend. I think between the two of us, we can convince your boss to take this angle." She winked at her. "I'd bet Derek would be happy to help us."

Angela rolled her eyes as they headed out to feed the crew. Apparently the attraction between them hadn't escaped anyone's radar. If everyone else could already sense it, Joe would be sure to notice it when he came out to shoot video. How in the world was she going to hide it from him?

THE ANIMALS HAD been rested and watered at the stockyard, reloaded into the trailer, and unloaded a second time at the rodeo grounds. While the cowboys made sure the animals were settled, Angela helped Sydney take care of the baby and set up a buffet style meal of barbecued hamburgers, potato salad, fruit salad and grilled asparagus. Once the meal had been eaten and cleared away, Sydney had brought out several chocolate cakes, frosted to perfection. She refused to allow Angela's assistance in cleaning up, insisting that she sit and take notes.

With full bellies and gregarious companionship, Angela sat outside Sydney and Scott's trailer with several of the cowboys she'd met on the ranch, all circled around a propane fire pit. She was amused as they recounted stories she was sure they shared at every opportunity. Each cowboy tried to outdo the last, their exaggerations growing wilder with each tale, and she couldn't help laughing. Her eyes slid past Jake, the most boisterous of the men, as he spun another story about Sydney and Scott's first meeting. She glanced at the pair standing just outside the circle, their young daughter asleep against Scott's chest and Sydney curled under his other arm. It wasn't hard to see they were very much in love, but according to Jake's recounting, Scott had run her over with his horse and she'd insulted him. Angela laughed with the rest of the crew and sipped her bottle of water.

She searched the faces around the fire pit for a particular cowboy missing from the festivities. She spotted Derek leaning against the back of a horse trailer, watching from a distance. He stood with his arms crossed over his chest, listening but not participating. She could barely make out a faint smile on his lips and wondered why he didn't join in the fun. She rose, dropping her notebook onto the folding chair before walking toward him. He straightened and tucked his hands into his front pockets nonchalantly when he noticed her approach. She wondered at his segregation.

"Having fun?" His voice was deep and slightly raspy after hollering at the crew while unloading.

She smiled. "Those guys are something else. I thought I could tell a good story, but they are amazing."

He returned her grin. "Yeah, well, you probably shouldn't believe half of what they say."

Angela glanced over her shoulder in time to see Sydney wink at her while the rest of the group continued to laugh loudly at Jake's story. "I don't know." She looked back at Derek, his face half hidden by shadows, and her heart skipped at his rakish appearance. "They've had quite a few tales about you. You seem to be quite the ladies' man."

His face grew serious. "Like I said, you probably shouldn't believe even half."

Angela took a step closer to him, closing the physical distance between them but unsure how to close the gap her story was widening between them. If she and Sydney could come up with a better story, she prayed they could bridge it. Her fingers itched to touch the rasp of his day-old beard growth. She laid her hand on his chest, feeling the muscles twitch beneath her fingers. Her breath quickened as he wrapped his fingers around her wrist gently.

"What is it you want from me, Angel?" His voice was husky, vibrating her nerve endings with shivers of delight.

"Why do you call me that?"

"Why wouldn't I call you that?" His eyes were completely shadowed now, only the distant fire reflecting and giving them a dangerous gleam within. "I'm just not sure where you've been sent from."

It hurt knowing he didn't trust her, but she couldn't blame him. She'd opened up to him, only to close herself off with the phone call from Joe, making it clear that her job came first. What if Joe forced her to pursue this story for ratings? Would she sacrifice this family and destroy their business to propel her career and help her father? Could she trust herself to make the right decision, even at the cost of her own future, or her father's?

She leaned closer, feeling his breath on her face as she looked up at him. "I'm sorry for . . ." She wasn't sure how to finish. He saw her as a threat and her shallow words wouldn't change that. "I'm doing the best I can to not hurt anyone. I'm sorry I can't make you any other promises right now."

"Angel, promises aren't what I want." His thumb traced the line of her jaw, running along the outer shell of her ear. She could hear the rasp of desire in his voice as he stared at her lips. "But I can't give in to anything that will jeopardize this family, not again. Unfortunately, right now, that includes you."

She felt her heart sink. He had no idea they shared the same risk—the future of her family was at stake if she didn't get a story. In a sick twist of fate, getting her story might just make her future bittersweet now that she'd met a man who could scale the protective walls she'd built. Derek dropped his hands and walked to where the others stood around the fire, leaving her trusting that her father's chance at sobriety was worth the price of her broken heart.

Chapter Fourteen

ANGELA GROANED AS the alarm sounded the next morning and Sydney slipped from the bed. "You have fifteen minutes while I feed the horses to jump in the shower," she warned as she laughed. "The baby will be up in about thirty minutes so you'll be getting up either way."

Angela cracked one eye open just enough to see Sydney pull a sweatshirt from the small closet before heading outside.

"Why does everything seem to happen early with you people?" Angela asked as she pulled the sheet over her head and snuggled under the warm blankets, wishing she could go back to her dream. She knew Sydney wouldn't feel one ounce of sympathy about making her take a cold shower if she went back to sleep.

"Ugh!" Giving up, she pushed back the covers and closed the sliding door between the bathroom and the kitchen. The water was warm, loosening the muscles in her shoulders that were still a bit sore from her riding lessons with Derek. She yawned, wishing one last time for a lazy day to sleep in. Angela reached for the bottle of shampoo and was rinsing the suds when she heard the front door of the trailer open.

"I'm almost finished, Sydney, then I'll start breakfast."

She wrapped a towel around herself, stepping into the bedroom to get dressed. She slipped a camisole over her wet head and pushed her arms through a long-sleeved Western shirt before pulling on a pair of Sydney's Miss Me jeans. She'd been unsure about wearing them, opting for jeans that wouldn't cost so much, but Sydney had insisted that her first "real" rodeo was a special occasion and she needed to look good. She slid her hands over her hips to her thighs, loving the way they fit. No wonder they cost more than her clothing budget for the month.

She brushed her teeth quickly and ran a comb through her tangled hair, letting the waves fall to her waist as they dried, pulling the sides back with a barrette. She glanced at her reflection. She would worry about makeup later so Sydney could get her shower before the baby woke up. She slid the doorway open and hurried down the three stairs, running into Derek at the kitchen counter.

"Oh!" She stopped with her hands against his chest, his arms circling her waist, keeping them both from falling against the counter. "I didn't see you there."

He didn't remove his hands from her waist and she could feel the heat from his fingers through both shirts as he moved her so her back was against the counter. "I gathered that," he laughed.

His grin was infectious and she prayed the rest of their day would be this carefree. *Please, can I have just one more day?*

She pushed thoughts of Joe, the story, and her father to the far reaches of her mind, promising herself she could worry about them tomorrow. "Coffee?" He opened the cupboard to remove two cups but didn't release his hold on her. "Although, I'm not sure you need it if you're moving so quickly already."

"I thought you were Sydney. I was trying to hurry so she could get a shower before Kassie wakes up."

She couldn't help but notice how dark his eyes looked this morning, or how much she loved the cinnamon-musk scent of him. Without warning, Derek dipped his head and brushed his lips against hers, sending a jolt of pleasure to her core. His hands slid up her spine, molding her to his chest. He groaned and deepened the kiss, searing her senses as she met his desire with her own. Her fingers slid around his neck, winding in his hair and pulling him down to her. She couldn't get enough of him, wanting to be closer, hating the barrier of their clothing between them.

A quiet whimper broke through their hunger and Derek sighed against her lips. "Sounds like someone else needs attention more than I do." He smiled and pressed one last kiss to her surprised mouth before moving to the portable crib his sister had set up by the couch. "Good morning, little lady." He scooped up the baby and curled her against his chest, tucking her dark head under his chin.

The child instantly quieted and Angela couldn't help but smile at the sight of the big cowboy with a curly-haired baby nestled against his muscular chest, looking so small in his arms. Angela's heart thumped in her chest and she suddenly understood the desire to marry and have a family. It was such a foreign concept for her, she stepped backward, and the smile slipped from her lips. After seeing her parents' relationship she'd promised herself she would never put a child through that. Now, as Derek pressed a kiss to his niece's head, she realized she'd been duped, assuming all marriages ended up like her parents.

She couldn't catch her breath, and her hands shook as she reached for her mother's ring. It was a tangible reminder of what happened when you loved the wrong person, someone you didn't know well enough, someone who didn't love you back. If there was ever a man she was wrong for, it was Derek. She turned her back on him, trying to pour herself a cup of coffee, and only managed to spill on the counter.

"Damn," she cursed under her breath, reaching for a towel.

"You okay?" He passed her the towel as he rocked Kassie slowly from side to side. Derek was so at ease with the child in his arms she could imagine him with several of his own.

"I'm fine." She threw the towel on the sink and headed toward the door, desperate to put some space between them.

She ran down the steps of the trailer and headed

toward the pen where the horses ate quietly, crossing her arms over the railing and putting her forehead against her arms. They were as different as two people could be. They wanted entirely different things from life. He deserved marriage and a family. She couldn't offer him that sort of permanence. The heat between them might flare into an inferno, but that fire would destroy both of their futures. She didn't realize she was crying until she felt the tears soak through the arm of the shirt.

She had never cried over a man. But this was more than that and she knew it. It was the realization that she might never have the things she'd never admitted wanting before: marriage, children . . . family. It was easy to say you didn't want something when there was a possibility to have it *someday*. Now that she was faced with making a choice between her career and a family, she didn't want to choose. She knew she was being selfish, but she couldn't help herself.

"Angel, are you okay?"

She felt his hands on her shoulders and it shattered her heart. He'd seen that she was upset and had come after her. He had no idea he was tearing her heart out, making her miss even more what they could never have. A sob escaped her and he spun her to face him, looking into her eyes.

"Honey, what is wrong?" He brushed the tears from her cheeks and pulled her into his arms, smoothing his hands over her back, pressing a kiss to her temple. "I can't help if you don't talk to me."

"It's stupid," she muttered against his chest, her lips

burned from his heated flesh beneath the cotton t-shirt, even as she wrapped her arms around his waist.

He brushed his hand over her hair. "What's stupid?"

"Me, crying over this." She looked up at him. "And there is no *this*."

Derek cupped her face, his thumbs running along her jaw, and he grinned at her. "There *could* be a this."

"No, there can't. You've said so yourself. You don't trust me, and I don't blame you. I wouldn't trust me either. I can't fall for you. I barely even know you."

He leaned forward until their foreheads touched and smiled down at her. "You're falling for me?"

"Yes," she admitted, blushing. "I mean ... I don't know. But I can't fall for you because I don't *do* relationships, ever. I ..." She tried to pull away from him, pushing against his chest.

"Oh, no you don't." He pulled her back into his arms, holding her wrists loosely behind her and backing her against the metal corral panels. "You're not going to run away this time and you're not going to hide behind any walls." She laid her cheek against his chest, pressing her lips against his shirt. Derek tipped her chin up with one hand. "And you're not going to distract me with that sweet mouth."

He let go of her wrists and curled one hand at the base of her neck causing shivers of heat to trickle down her spine, hypnotizing her with languid tenderness. She could read the raw emotion in his eyes and it scared her. "I know what my reservations about this relationship are, but tell me yours."

"I don't have relationships. I don't know how." She glanced over his shoulder to see several of the cowboys beginning their workday. Soon everyone on the crew would see them together and begin speculating.

"So, you've had a few bad break-ups. We all have." He shrugged.

"No, I've never had a relationship that lasted more than a few dates. I don't let people close. I've never seen a relationship work out well so I just don't have them."

She tried to push past him but he grabbed her hips and held her in place. "Huh-uh. Right here." He pointed to his eyes. "You're afraid. I get it. You don't want to trust me any more than I want to trust you." She looked down at his chest. She hadn't thought of it that way. Derek brushed back her hair and her eyes found his. "I see those wheels turning."

She wanted to squash the questions beating at her mind in time with her racing heart; it was safer to retreat behind the wall, to patch the holes he'd chipped in it and hide again. But, seeing the hope gleaming in his eyes, the unspoken promise of what could be, she couldn't ignore the longing coursing through her veins.

"Just for today, Angel, let's forget about that crap. Forget about your story, our past mistakes, or whatever worries we have about the future." The pad of his thumb traced her lower lip. "For today, it's just you and me and *this*." One of the horses chose that moment to bump her shoulder with his nose and make his presence known. "And my job," he added, jerking his chin toward the horses with that grin that melted her will to refuse him.

He grew serious. "Let's just see what happens today, and then we can make some decisions."

"But, how can we . . ."

Derek slanted his lips over hers, silencing her skepticism, his tongue sweeping away any trace of uncertainty and replacing it with his quiet confidence. "Just one day," he whispered against her lips.

Angela wanted what he offered more than she'd ever wanted anything else. What harm could one day do?

SHE KNEW SHE should be taking notes or at least recording a few observations while she watched the preparations. Mike had taken her down and shown her how to slip a horn wrap over the cattle in the chute before they let each one loose into the arena. He explained that letting them loose helped the animals feel less stress and made them perform in a predictable fashion for the ropers, since these particular cattle were used for only the team roping event. Once all of the cattle were returned to their pen, horn wraps still intact, they let the steer roping calves into the chutes.

Angela was surprised at how forthright Mike was in answering every question she asked. If he was unsure he would admit it, a trait she found lacking in most people she interviewed. He passed her off to Scott who took her behind the rough stock chutes and patiently showed her the equipment and tack they used. She tried to focus on what he was showing her but she couldn't help but make comparisons between the brothers. Scott was so serious, without a hint of humor behind his eyes, and she wondered what Sydney had seen in him. He was handsome, but he lacked Derek's quick smile. Both men were tall compared to most of the cowboys working for them, but Scott lacked the sheer mass of his younger brother.

Angela found her gaze straying from the equipment to where Derek sat astride his black gelding at the end of the arena, talking with the announcer and one of the rodeo representatives. As if expecting her to be watching him, his eyes met hers and he shot her a cocky grin. She arched a brow in rebuke but laughed. He was far too sure of himself where she was concerned.

She looked back at Scott, trying to concentrate on what he was telling her about the fleece flank strap and how it helped the horse buck in a more natural fashion, but her thoughts continued to stray back to Derek's last kiss and the slow burn it created in her belly. The radio on Scott's hip beeped before she heard Mike's voice.

"Scott, the vet is down here. Do you want to inspect the animals with him and Jake?"

"We're at the chutes, so send them my way." Scott spoke into the radio before tucking it back into his pocket. "Want to inspect the stock with us?"

She glanced one last time at Derek across the arena, biting her lower lip. "Sure, but I won't know what I'm looking for."

He chuckled. "I didn't think you would, but it's a chance for you to see how we do it."

Angela followed him from the chutes and down the stairs to the pen of horses. She stood to one side, petting the neck of one gelding when he dropped his head over the railing. It still awed her that these sweet animals could turn into bucking monsters when they entered the chute with a rider. She watched Scott enter the pen with the two men and halter one horse at a time, inspecting everything from the top of the animal's ears, pointing out any bumps or scrapes, to lifting the horse's feet and checking the bottoms. Two animals were culled out by Scott as unfit for the performance. One had a small cut on the front of his leg, and the other, according to Scott, had favored his right foot when he exited the trailer. Both were moved to another pen. They moved into the next pen where the bareback broncs were finishing their breakfast and repeated the process.

She followed them to the first pen of cattle, wondering how they were going to inspect them. She wasn't overly surprised to see that they weren't able to inspect them as closely since they were more skittish than the horses. She heard the vet mention that he'd already watched them as they went through the chutes earlier that morning and indicated one calf by number he felt shouldn't be allowed in the performance. Scott had one of the crew move the calf into a separate pen where the vet inspected him more closely.

"I think this guy may have been kicked on the ride over, Scott." She edged closer to hear better over the bawling calf. "See, right here." The vet pointed out a scrape on the calf's hide where it had a scab already forming. "Just put some ointment on it while you're here and he'll be fine."

So much for the theory that they were putting injured animals into the draw. The rodeo hadn't even started yet and nearly every complaint she'd researched had been disproved. Her phone chirped from her pocket and she glanced at the screen. Her stomach fell when she saw the caller: Officer Miller. She stepped away, not wanting anyone to hear her end of the conversation, and made her way toward the fifth-wheel. "Hello?"

"Angela? We have your father again." Her stomach dropped to her toes and she closed her eyes slowly. It wasn't even lunchtime yet. How could he be drunk already? What was she going to do now with no savings left and no way to get him out? Why hadn't Joe been watching him?

"Officer Miller, I . . . I don't have the money to bail him out right now. I'm going to need to make some calls."

"I just came on shift, so I'll try to keep him in holding as long as I can."

"Thank you." She breathed the words as she hung up.

Guilt flooded her, squeezing the air from her lungs. She couldn't fault Joe for not watching him. He wasn't Joe's responsibility. She was sitting at the table in the fifth-wheel trying to steel her nerve to call Joe and ask him to bail her father out when Derek came inside.

"I thought you were with Scott?" She shrugged as he made his way to the refrigerator for a bottle of water. "Maybe we should both take a break, then." He reached for her hand and pulled her to stand, circling his arms around her waist and pulling her close.

She couldn't believe he had the power to send her

senses into an uncontrollable spiral of desire in spite of the dire predicament she was facing. He looked down and frowned, pausing with his lips mere inches from her.

"What's wrong?" She shook her head and tried to force a smile. How could he read her so easily this soon? She couldn't tell him about her father. This was exactly the kind of worries they'd vowed to avoid today. "Angel, I can't help if you don't tell me."

"It's just something I have to figure out on my own." Her phone rang and she reached for it on the table: Joe. He was the last person she wanted to deal with right now, but she knew she couldn't avoid this conversation. "I have to take this."

She answered the phone, glancing at Derek, who seemed content to remain and listen to her conversation. He sat in the chair across from her and leaned back, crossing his ankles in front of him.

"One of these days, you'll listen to me." She could hear the reprimand in Joe's voice. "I told you to call him."

"I need your help."

Derek slid the bottle of water onto the table and crossed his arms over his chest. She could see a flicker of emotion in his eyes and knew he was hurt that she was asking someone else for help, that she was letting someone else in. She cocked her head at him, silently begging him to understand. They didn't know each other well enough for her to unload this on him.

"I can't give you another advance, Angela. You're already borrowing off next month's salary." Joe sighed into the receiver. She could hear the exasperation in his voice and dreaded asking him to bail her father out. "What do you need me to do?"

Derek arched a brow at her. "Joe, can you hang on for a second?" She hit the button to mute her call. "What?"

"You're going to ask your boss for help, but you won't even tell me what's going on? Why won't you let me try to help?"

"This isn't your problem," she argued.

"Today it is."

She stared at him, unable to fathom his need to come to her aid. There was such determination in his face that she almost missed the despair in his eyes. She'd promised him today they would trust one another. She took a deep breath. Trusting him meant confessing her failure as a daughter. She closed her eyes. "Okay."

She pushed the button, reconnecting her call with Joe. "Sorry about that. I'm going to have to call you right back." She hung up, ignoring Joe's protests coming from the phone's earpiece.

Derek's victorious smile faltered when she grew quiet. "My father is an alcoholic. He's in jail, and I need to bail him out."

He reached across the table for her hand. "Where?"

She stared at him, her mouth falling open slightly. "Just like that?"

"Scott can cover for me and we'll take my truck to get him."

Angela slapped her hands on the table, shaking her head. "You're incredible, you know that?" She wondered why she was angry at Derek when he was so ready to help without judgment. "You don't even know where he is."

"Why are you yelling at me?"

She rose and began pacing. "Because, you're just . . . ugh!" She spun and faced him. "I don't have the money to bail him out again. This will be the third time this month."

He reached for her hand and pulled her toward him, forcing her to sit on his lap. "I'll give you the money." She glared at him. "Okay, call it a loan. You can clean stalls to earn it off when we get back to the ranch." He laughed quietly at his own joke but grew serious when he saw the tears of frustration misting her eyes. "Angel, let me help you."

"I can't," she whispered. "This is my problem. I'm going to have to go back." She dreaded saying the words aloud. It gave them a power—a reality—she didn't want them to have.

"Why don't we go get him and take him back to the ranch? You can keep an eye on him there, and maybe the time off would do him some good."

"He doesn't work," she admitted.

"You support both of you?" He tipped her chin up, and she couldn't hide the tears of frustration burning in her eyes. "And you've already bailed him out twice this month?" Derek sighed and pinched his lips into a thin line. "No wonder you didn't know what to do," he muttered. He lifted her onto her feet. "Give me a few minutes to talk with Mike and let him know what's going on." He stood and pressed a kiss to her lips, grabbed his water bottle, and headed out the door without waiting for her response.

Angela watched him go, still shocked at what he was offering. She wasn't sure this was the best idea. Having her father with her would solve the problem of keeping an eye on him, but he could just as easily cause trouble at the rodeo, where everyone could witness her humiliation.

Chapter Fifteen

DEREK REACHED FOR her hand as they walked into the police station. Several officers nodded at her as they passed. That was not a good sign. He wondered again if he wasn't making a mistake, getting far too involved in this woman's troubles. But one look at the apprehension in her emerald eyes and he knew he couldn't change his mind. He wanted her to trust him, to understand she could rely on him, even if she'd never been able to rely on anyone else before, *especially* because she'd never been able to rely on anyone.

As they approached the desk, Angela stopped suddenly. "Joe?"

The man at the counter turned around and his eyes slid over Derek, almost immediately dismissing him, before hurrying to pull Angela close.

"What are you doing here?" she asked.

He tipped his head at her like a parent scolding a

child. "Your dad called me. Since you didn't call me back . . ." He eyed Derek again and cleared his throat. "Who's this?"

"Who're you?"

Angela stepped between the two men. "This is Joe, my boss and one of my oldest friends. Joe, this is Derek Chandler, part owner of Findley Brothers Stock Contractors."

Derek didn't want to shake his hand. He didn't like the way he looked at Angela, a cross between anger and desire. He grasped Joe's hand with an overly firm grip, letting the man know he was staking his claim. Derek didn't care how long this guy had known her, Angela was his.

"Thanks for coming down, Joe, but we'll take it from here." Derek stepped up to the desk and pulled out his checkbook.

"I've got this." Joe brushed past him, glancing at Angela for her agreement. "I'll take him home."

She bit at her lower lip and Derek wondered about her uneasiness. "Actually," he said, slipping an arm around her waist, "we're taking him back to the rodeo with us. Angela thought the fresh air would do him some good."

Joe arched his brow, ignoring Derek and looking at Angela. "I see." By the tone of his voice he didn't, and he wasn't thrilled with her silence. "I guess you don't need me then." He tucked his checkbook back into his jacket pocket. "I'll see you at the rodeo tomorrow, Chandler." Joe nodded in his direction.

Angela's head snapped up. "You're coming?"

"Skip and I are the only two available so we'll be out

in the morning." He glared at Derek. "Unless you need me sooner?"

"Tomorrow's fine," Derek assured him.

Joe looked to Angela, as if waiting for her to contradict him. She shrugged and pressed her lips together, making Derek speculate at her uncharacteristic behavior. She almost seemed afraid to say anything and he wondered if there wasn't more to her relationship with Joe than she let on. She'd told him that she didn't *do* relationships, but this went beyond a working association or old friendship.

The tension should have disappeared with Joe's exit, but Angela's nerves were ready to snap by the time the officer escorted her father into the room. She finished signing the paperwork and Derek handed over the money.

"Derek, this is my father, Robert. Dad, this is Derek Chandler. I'm doing a story on his family business, so we are going to be staying with them for a little while."

Derek held out his hand in greeting, but her father eyed him suspiciously, shoving his hands into his pockets. "I just want to go home."

Ignoring her father's rudeness, Derek pulled out his keys. "Why don't we go get you some clothes before we head back to the rodeo grounds?" He saw the blush creep over Angela's cheeks as she clenched her jaw.

"I'll give you directions," she offered, helping her father into the backseat of Derek's truck. He promptly closed his eyes and began snoring.

Derek shut the door behind Angela as she buckled herself into the passenger seat, easing behind the wheel.

Angela glanced over at him. "Thank you for this."

"You're welcome, Angel." He glanced at the sleeping man behind him. "Hopefully he won't be too hungover." Derek reached for her hand, kissing the pulse racing at her wrist. She looked over her shoulder at her father and he wanted to somehow ease her mind. "He's a piece of cake compared to Scott when he's had a few too many."

"Most of the time, he doesn't stay sober long enough to find out."

Derek silently vowed to do anything to make this easier on her. As she gave him directions, they drove through several blocks of questionable neighborhoods, each becoming worse than the next. It wasn't a slum, but in a town of golf courses and upper-middle class, it couldn't be considered a good neighborhood. Broken-down cars balanced on cinder blocks, half-covered by torn tarps, decorated several driveways. A young boy pedaled by with an even younger girl riding on the handlebars of his bicycle and waved at Angela.

"You know them?"

"Yeah, they live downstairs from us. Right here," she said, pointing at the driveway of a small apartment complex. Derek pulled into an empty parking spot, barely fitting the big truck under the canopy. Her father woke with a start and, realizing where he was, opened his door, hitting the post roughly before stumbling toward the staircase leading toward their apartment. Angela looked at the ding in the truck and shook her head.

"Are you sure you want to do this?" she asked quietly.

He grasped her chin in his thumb and forefinger and

looked into her eyes. "Yes, I'm sure. He's just sobering up. It's fine."

"No, it's not. Look what he did to your truck." She watched her father head up the stairs toward their apartment.

Derek pressed a kiss to her lips, wanting to remove the remorse from her eyes. "That's why we call it a 'work truck.' Don't worry, we'll manage."

He wasn't letting her run away from him that easily, and he certainly wasn't about to let the situation with her father ruin the woman he'd seen blossoming during the past few days. She smiled at him sadly before following her father up the steps. Derek looked around him one last time and pressed the button to lock his truck. He hurried up the stairs and into her home. He knew you could learn a lot about a person from their home and wondered exactly what he would learn about someone as reticent as Angela.

"I'm going to see if he needs any help," she informed him as she headed down the narrow hallway to her father's room.

Derek wandered into a small living room sparsely furnished with a tattered light brown couch, dinged coffee table, and a small entertainment center. The apartment was impeccably clean, as if no one actually lived inside, and had only one small photo nestled in a silver frame near an old television set. He reached for the picture of a woman holding a small girl, beaming up at her mother with adoration.

There was no mistaking that Angela was the child.

Angela couldn't have been more than six when it was taken. She was the spitting image of her mother but with green eyes instead of her mother's blue or her father's deep-brown.

"Mom," Angela said, nodding toward the frame in his hands.

"You look just like her." Derek hadn't heard her return. He slipped the frame back on the empty shelf. There was nothing in this apartment that spoke of warmth, and the coldness made him uncomfortable.

She shrugged and he could see the dejection settling around her shoulders like a worn blanket, threatening to strangle her. He glanced toward the hall, eager to get her out of the apartment and away from the apathy he could see creeping in. "Is your father ready?"

She leaned her shoulder against the wall and crossed her arms. "Just about."

"This place doesn't seem very . . . you."

Her brows arched in surprise. "What do you mean? I've lived here forever."

Derek frowned and tucked his fingers into the belt loop of her jeans, pulling her into his arms. "You're all fire and this place is all ice."

She looked around the room, sadness filling her eyes. "To be honest, I didn't plan on coming back until I was ready to move him out for good. But . . ."

"That explains all the boxes you brought." Derek gave her a knowing grin. He looked around him at the narrow halls, small rooms, and low ceiling. "I don't know how you do it. I'd feel claustrophobic."

She gave him a sardonic smile. "That's because you have been spoiled by fresh air, large rooms, and this thing we poor, working-class call money, cowboy. Not all of us have been as fortunate."

He didn't take offense; he *had* been spoiled. He'd been lucky to grow up on the ranch. It might require hard work, but his family had always supported him, even in his irresponsibility. There was always a place he could return and be accepted. Angela had never had the luxury of a supportive family, trust, or much of a home.

"Do we really have to do this?" her father asked, dragging his duffle bag behind him.

"Yes. You might actually have fun, Dad."

"Doubt it," he muttered under his breath.

Derek took the bag from his hands and carried it downstairs while Angela locked the door. Her hand paused over the lock, making him wonder if she was debating staying or praying to never return.

ANGELA TRIED TO ignore her father's small talk throughout the entire ride to the arena, wishing he'd just go back to sleep. If only she could have been that lucky.

"I don't remember a lot about the night Angie was born, but I remember thinking she looked just like her mother."

Derek glanced over at the man in backseat. "I saw the picture by the television. They look almost identical."

"Almost." Angela saw a frown furrow his brow for a moment before quickly passing, like a shadow. "Her mother was a beautiful woman, too pretty for the likes of me." Angela had heard her father talk about her mother through the years and couldn't remember him sounding this tender and reminiscent. He usually sounded like a man wracked with guilt, but today he seemed to remember only the good times. "My Angie-girl has her spirit too."

"Really? I never would have guessed that." Derek glanced at her and gave her a knowing smile. She was grateful Derek seemed to understand she didn't want his pity. She took a deep breath, holding it for a moment, willing herself to have patience. Her father talked far too much when he'd been drinking.

As they turned into the rodeo grounds, Derek pulled to the back and several trailers came into view. A few horse trailers were pulling out now that some of the roping events had finished, and it looked like the barrel racers were preparing for their rides. Angela sighed, irritated her father had cost her an entire day she should have been working on her story. Who knew what she missed while she retrieved him from jail yet again. Her anger sparked at his selfishness. How could he be so narcissistic to take her away from her job, the only means she had to feed him and keep a roof over his head?

As Derek pulled to a stop, she jumped out of the truck and slammed the door. She couldn't bear to look at her father, and she was too embarrassed to talk to Derek. "Dad, I'm going to try to get some work done. Take your things to that trailer and get some sleep. Don't go anywhere without telling either Derek or me."

Her father glanced from her to Derek. "I could have stayed home."

"Dad," she said with a sigh, feeling guilty for her sharp words. "I couldn't leave you there alone. Derek and I have work to do. He runs the rodeo and took time out today to drive me to pick you up. You should thank him instead of acting ungrateful."

"Come on, Mr. McCallister. I'll show you where you can get some rest. We're almost done for today anyway."

Angela saw her father's eyes light on the various trailers and equipment, making her hesitant to let him go. "Dad, please stay out of trouble while you're here, okay?"

Her father frowned. "I'll be fine. If you were so worried . . ."

"Sir, let me introduce you to Mike Findley. He actually started this company with my father."

She mouthed a quick *thank you* to Derek as he turned to take her father toward the trailer. Angela was grateful for Derek's interference. His kindness and patience with her father were more than she could have ever hoped for. She could see the annoyance on her father's face. He'd made it clear to her in their apartment he didn't want a change of scenery. Why would he? Here he was under her watchful eye again, and in such close proximity the likelihood of slipping a drink past her was pretty slim.

She headed to the announcer's booth where she could watch the barrel racers from their entry to their exit. She was determined to focus on the rodeo and her story, even with her father near. She frowned, watching her father enter the trailer with Derek, but shoved her worries about

208 T. J. KLINE

him aside. She needed to have some sort of story ready for
Joe when he arrived.

She looked toward the gate when the announcer
called the name of the next competitor, Alicia Kanani.
She watched the animal hopping onto its back feet from
behind the closed gate with its rider tugging on the reins,
barely keeping the animal under control. The horse's shod
feet kicked up dust as she turned the horse so it couldn't
see the gate. As a cowboy opened it inward, she spun her
paint, charging into the arena. Steering the horse sharply
to the right, Angela gasped as the horse curled his rump
under him and slid toward the barrel, leaning precari-
ously. She saw the barrel tip as the rider bumped it with
her knee somehow managing to keep it upright as she
kicked the horse on to her second turn.

The horse veered out, away from the second barrel
before cutting sharply to the left and appeared to circle
the barrel without moving forward. The cowgirl kicked
her legs and heels against the horse's sides as the animal
bolted toward the last barrel at the end of the arena. Again,
the horse spun around the final barrel before charging
toward the end of the arena and the closed gate. As she
leaned forward, her horse pinned its ears back, stretching
out and eating up the arena. She crossed a laser beam of
light, set up along the side of the fence, and triggered the
timer to stop. Angela glanced at the clock reading: 16.56
seconds. Good enough for third place.

Angela glanced back at the cowgirl, who had her horse
under control as he jogged out of the gate and headed back
toward her trailer while the next contestant repeated the

pattern. She watched as the first rider slowed her horse to a walk, the animal's sides heaving as he caught his breath from the sprint. Instead of stopping and dismounting immediately, she watched as the cowgirl headed back to the warm-up arena and walked her animal for several minutes, cooling him down. She continued to watch the other performers, keeping her eyes out for any sort of animal neglect, but saw nothing for her story.

She glanced toward Derek's trailer and saw him exit. Taking a moment to appreciate his masculine perfection, she watched him tighten his mount's cinch before hopping into the saddle. He rode through the gate and into the arena, looking like her knight in a cowboy hat at that moment.

DEREK RUBBED HIS jaw with his thick leather glove. He needed to concentrate on their final event, but he wasn't sure what to do about Angela's father. He couldn't let him wander around, finding any alcohol the crew might have. He would need to find something to keep the man occupied, where he wouldn't need to be watched 24/7.

Derek unlatched the rope he had on the front of his saddle as the first bulls were sent into the chutes and rode to his brother's side. "You know Sydney hates it when you insist on being in here."

"You made it back pretty quickly." Scott gave him a confident smirk. "And Sydney knows it's part of the job."

"And I know my sister-in-law. What did you promise

her in return?" Derek arched a brow, guiding his horse closer to the chutes, watching the animals intently.

Scott laughed. "I promised her we could start trying to have another baby."

Derek looked back at his brother, surprised. "You sure it's worth the price? She drives a hard bargain."

"Would you mind having another one like Kassie around? Besides, I missed being in here." Scott shrugged. "You know how it is. It's a rush and when you don't have it, life seems a bit slow."

"I'd be happy with slow right now." He shifted his gaze to Angela in the announcer's booth.

Scott arched a brow at his brother but remained silent as the announcer started the heavy metal music meant to get the crowd excited for the coming bull riding event.

They rode together to stand at the corner of the arena as the rodeo clowns entered, rolling padded barrels in front of them. "Are you sure this is trouble we even want to deal with?"

Derek glared at his brother but knew it was a legitimate concern. "It will be fine."

Scott shook his head, looking down at his saddle. "I sure hope so. Has Angela given up yet on her story?"

"Not exactly." Derek didn't want to explain Angela's reasons for not dropping the story to his brother. He was just starting to understand what drove her, especially after meeting her father. She claimed to need the story to land a better job, but he recognized the truth. The reality of the situation was that Angela was trying to escape the origin of their loss and wanted to help her father do the same.

ANGELA HEARD THE commotion below the announcer's booth and looked over the edge in time to see a bull in the chute tossing his head as one of the riders tried to settle on its back. She heard cowboys shouting as the announcer was commentating the ride already taking place in the arena. The bull in the arena thrashed, twisting wildly and rocking from his front legs to his back. She thought she recognized the bull in the arena as Buffalo, one of the animals Derek had shown her. She'd petted the sweet, docile animal at the ranch. Seeing him in the arena with a cowboy hanging on to the flat rope wrapped around his massive chest, she was awed by the extent of power he exuded. It was a raw, dangerous explosion of strength and might. The cowboy hung on, his body shifting forward and back, sliding slightly to the right as the animal spun to the left just moments before he fell from the animal. The cowboy reached for the part of the rope hanging but couldn't grasp it.

Derek and Scott immediately moved their horses in closer as the rodeo clown ran straight for the bull's head to distract the animal. Derek moved his mount close to the bull's left side as Scott edged behind the bull rider. A second clown moved in and released the cowboy's hand before running to jump into the padded barrel. Scott reached down, helping the cowboy onto his horse's back as the bull turned its filed horns toward Derek, twisting his head before turning his attention toward the clown on the ground. The clown urged the bull to follow him toward the barrel. With the rider moved to safety, Derek signaled the cowboy manning the back gate and herded the bull toward it and his pen.

Angela breathed a sigh of relief until she realized that she would be forced to watch Derek in the same danger with every ride for the next two days. She looked around for Sydney, wondering how she dealt with the strain of watching her husband in this position every weekend. She glanced at the trailers and saw her seated in a folding chair with Kassie sleeping against her chest while she talked with one of the barrel racers she'd seen compete earlier. Angela wondered if she'd stayed at the trailer because of Kassie or because she couldn't bear to watch her husband in the arena with these massive beasts.

She looked away from Sydney in time to spot her father leaving the trailer he was sharing with Derek and Scott. Looking back at the arena, she sighed, realizing she would miss the rest of the event. Her father was her responsibility and she had to keep an eye on him, even here. She hurried down the wooden staircase behind the chutes, wondering where he might have disappeared. She found him searching a nearby ice chest.

"Looking for a cold one?" She shook her head as she approached him.

"I'm thirsty."

"You can't drink here."

Her father scoffed at her. "Take a look around." He waved toward a stand nearby selling beer and hot dogs. His voice was hoarse with sleep and sobriety.

"No, *you* can't drink here." She took a step closer to him. "We are guests. This is my job. If I don't get this story, we're done."

"We'll manage. We have before. I want to go home," he complained.

Why couldn't he seem to understand? If she didn't get this story, they didn't have a home to go back to. She'd already spent rent on his bail. She would give anything to be able to walk away and never look back. But he was her father, even if he was a poor excuse for one, and she'd never doubted his feelings for her. He loved her in his own way.

"I have nothing left and spent rent the last time I bailed you out. If I don't get a story, we have no home." He started to interrupt her but she didn't give him a chance to speak. "I can't afford to bail you out anymore. We have *no* money left. None. I've been begging Joe for advances on my salary and he won't give me any more. The only reason you're even out now is because Derek bailed you out. You owe him your gratitude, not this . . ." she said, waving her hand at the ice chest.

Her father leaned back against Derek's truck and narrowed his eyes before giving her a tentative grin. "You like this guy."

Angela crossed her arms over her chest. She didn't want to get into a discussion about Derek with her father. The less he knew about Derek and his family, the better. But it was good to see a smile on his face, one that wasn't induced by alcohol. "I'm trying to keep you safe and out of jail again."

Her father took a deep breath. "I need a beer," he muttered.

"No," she insisted, arching a single brow, "you don't."

He sighed in resignation. "Can I at least get something to eat?"

Angela searched his face. "Come on, I'll see if there's anything in my trailer." She led him to the fifth-wheel, introducing him to Sydney before she went inside and urged him to sit at the table.

"I know what you're doing." He glanced up at her as she fixed him a sandwich.

"I'm not doing anything." She slapped a slice of bread on top and rolled her eyes.

Her father stared down at his hands in front of him. "You think you can fix me. Your mother couldn't, what makes you think you can?" He looked despondent as he buried his face in his shaking palms.

Angela stared at him, dumbfounded. She slipped into the chair across from him and reached for his hand. "I promise. I'm going to get you some help. Dad, I'm not giving up on you." She slid the plate in front of him. "You need some food. Eat." She bent and placed a kiss on his forehead.

She left him in the trailer and saw the stands emptying. Several cowboys headed toward a table Mike had set up behind the chutes with the rodeo secretary to distribute the day's purse winnings for each event. She glanced back at the trailer, praying her father would stay inside. She noticed her hands shaking and fisted them at her chest, longing for Derek's arms to chase away the hopelessness she'd heard in her father's voice and the despair she could feel creeping up on her. She'd hoped that one day her father would see all she was doing to try to help him, to save him from himself, and he would want to change, for her. But his question echoed in her mind: If her mother's love hadn't been enough to convince him to stop drinking, what could she do?

Chapter Sixteen

DEREK HAD NEVER felt so relieved to finish a rodeo. He glanced up into the announcer's booth and wondered where Angela had slipped off to. He rode the horse to his trailer, pulling the bridle off and clasping the halter behind the gelding's ears, trying to dismiss the uneasy feeling centering in the pit of his stomach.

"Mike," he called, "have you seen Angela?"

"Not recently. She was over at the trailer with Sydney earlier." He shuffled papers to the side and handed a check to a cowboy in front of him. "But I'm kinda busy, so I haven't been watching for her. If you see the rodeo secretary, send him my way."

"Will do." Derek spotted Sydney near the trailer putting Kassie into her playpen in the shade and jogged to her, scooping the baby from her kiddy-corral and tossing her into the air. Her giggle tickled him, and he couldn't help but smile up at his niece.

"Have you seen Angela?" he asked Sydney, cuddling Kassie against his chest as she reached for his hat.

"Not since she left the trailer. She took her dad inside to get him something to eat." Sydney's brows knit together in a frown that worried him. "She came out alone, but he left a few minutes later. Did you check the announcer's booth?"

Derek shook his head. "She's not there." He looked toward his trailers. "Have you seen her father since?"

She shook her head and Kassie copied her, making them both smile. "He didn't say anything when he came out, but he looked upset. He headed back toward where our trucks are parked."

Dread began to well up as Derek put Kassie back into her playpen. "I'm going to see if I can find her."

"Is everything okay?" He could hear the worry in Sydney's tone.

"I'm sure it is. I just don't want her to feel like she needs to deal with him alone."

She reached for his forearm as he turned to leave. "She told me she's trying to work out a new story. I get the feeling she's trying to run away from something. Is it him?"

"I don't think so." Derek couldn't help but think about Joe. "It's more complicated than that . . ." His voice trailed off, and he clenched his jaw. "Sydney, she's been supporting them both, alone." He shook his head in disbelief. "She keeps bailing him out and it's taking its toll on her. She can't keep doing this."

Sydney gave him a gentle smile. "You care about her."

He tilted his head at her and rolled his eyes. "I would do this for anyone. I'm just trying to help her out."

"Oh, sure." Sydney nodded at him, obviously skeptical. "Face it, Mr. I-Want-to-Save-the-World Chandler," Sydney began, tapping her finger over his heart, "Angela has you thinking with this instead of this." She touched her finger to his head.

Derek glared at her. "If you see her, tell Angela I'm looking for her."

ANGELA SLIPPED BEHIND the trailer, listening to her father's side of the conversation. When did he get a cell phone? She could hear the annoyance in her father's voice but wasn't sure if it stemmed from being dragged to the rodeo or from remaining sober all day.

"I don't know." His voice grated into the phone. "She said she's still working but I don't know what the story is about. She hasn't talked about it with me." Her father glanced back over his shoulder as Angela jumped behind the nearest trailer. "I think she has a *thing* for one of the cowboys. Seems like a nice guy. Yeah, the one who was at the jail. Tonight?"

He had to be on the phone with Joe, but why would Joe call him? *Is that where the cell came from? Maybe the phone was Joe's way to "keep an eye" on him while she'd been working on the story.* She felt that familiar flip of her stomach that always seemed to guide her reporter's instinct. Questions began to flit quickly through her mind like hummingbirds, never landing long enough for her to grasp answers to any of them.

"Angela?"

She heard Derek call her name and spun around, seeing him headed her direction. She didn't want him to know what she'd overheard until she had the opportunity to ask her dad about the call.

"There you are." Her voice cracked and she cleared her throat as she hurried toward him. "You made me nervous in the arena with those bulls."

He gave her a curious look but shrugged. "They're not so bad as long as you stay out of their way. Where's your dad? He's not in the trailer and I couldn't find him."

"He's on the phone right now." She thought it would be better if he didn't know her father was talking to Joe after the stand-off between the men at the jail earlier.

He slid his hands into her loose hair and pulled her to him, his lips capturing hers in a kiss that surprised and delighted her. She felt her body instantly react, melting against him, all tension disappearing. Her hands found his back as she held on to him. What had begun as an innocent kiss quickly turned into an inferno of need as his tongue brushed hers, igniting her senses. She sighed with pleasure, and he circled her waist with his arm, holding her so that every delicious muscle was pressed against her. She could feel his arousal and briefly wondered if they might not sneak off to his trailer.

"Eh-hem." Her father cleared his throat.

Angela's eyes widened and she tried to pull away from Derek, a blush burning her cheeks. Her father had never seen her kiss anyone, not even Joe during the short time they'd dated. Derek's arm remained wound around her waist, stubbornly holding her to him. She pushed her hands against the solid wall of his chest in an effort to loosen his embrace.

"Derek, please," she whispered through clenched teeth.

He inhaled deeply, releasing his breath slowly as he looked at her father, still refusing to release his hold on her waist. "Sir, I apologize." He looked into Angela's eyes and smiled. "The next time I kiss your daughter, I promise to show more regard for her reputation." He waited for her father to comment.

Her father's face split in a grin for the second time in one day and his eyes held a merriment she'd never seen in them before. She looked at her father, really looked at him, for the first time in months. His jaw was covered by graying whiskers, making him look even older than his fifty years, and deep wrinkles surrounded his eyes. His clothing was beginning to hang on him, a result of too much drinking and too little food since she'd left. He appeared weak and tired, as if time hadn't been his friend, and she could see the toll his grief had taken over the past fifteen years.

"Angel, why don't you make sure the shower is free so your dad can use the trailer before we head up to the barbecue."

"Barbecue?" Her father scrubbed at his jaw nervously.

"We always try to stay for the barbecue and dance so the rodeo committee knows we are supporting them. Why don't you let Sydney know we need to be up there in about two hours?"

She still wanted to ask her father about the phone call, but it was going to have to wait until later. Derek kissed her temple before she headed to find Sydney and lay a towel out for her father. It was going to be a full time job keeping him from drinking tonight. This day hadn't turned out the way she'd expected, but she was certainly learning she could trust Derek.

DEREK WATCHED ANGELA walk away, making sure she was out of earshot before he turned his attention back to her father. "I need you to steer clear of trouble tonight, sir." He wanted to show Robert the respect he was due as Angela's father but had to make sure his point was made: No drinking allowed.

"You better not hurt my daughter," Robert replied. Derek appreciated the older man's protectiveness even if the notion was coming far too late. Derek narrowed his eyes at Robert's warning tone. "I want her to be happy, but I'm not sure everyone would feel the same way. You should be careful though."

"Something specific you think I need to watch for?"

Robert shook his head and looked at the ground. "I don't know. I just have a feeling. But if I were you, I'd be prepared for trouble when that news crew gets here. I don't know much more than that right now." He wiped a hand down his face and over his whiskered jaw. "Just keep an eye on her. She stays pretty closed off—that's probably my fault—but I think she likes you. I've never seen her like this with anyone before."

"Is this about Joe?" Warning bells sounded in his brain, and he was sure Robert knew far more than he was letting on.

He clapped Derek's shoulder in a sympathetic gesture. "Do me a favor? Keep this conversation between the two of us. She'd be furious if she knew I told you any of this." He chuckled. "Definitely has her mother's fiery spirit."

Derek looked back toward Angela's trailer. The conversation with her father hadn't done anything but intensify the foreboding in his gut. Something was going on but he wasn't sure who needed his protection more: his family or Angela.

THE SMELL OF hickory smoke from the barbecue drifted to where the crew waited impatiently for the two women to finish getting ready. Derek could tell there was going to be a coup if they didn't leave soon. Several of the hands had already tried to convince Scott and Derek to allow them to sneak off. Kassie fussed in her father's arms, leaning sideways, trying to get her uncle's attention.

"Give her here." Derek reached out his arms just in time to catch Kassie as she lunged for him. He laughed and tossed her up into the air. "How's my cowgirl?"

"Today? Moody," Scott warned.

"Oh, so you're just like your daddy?" Derek caught his brother's glare and laughed.

His laughter died as he saw Angela emerge from the trailer wearing a white sundress with green flowers that matched her emerald eyes. The skirt was soft and flowing, reaching just to the tops of her borrowed brown dress boots, which matched the brown belt Sydney had loaned her. She'd pulled some of her flaming hair back, making her look young and innocent and oh-so-sexy, with the low-cut neckline showing off her ample endowment. Kassie shoved her fingers into his gaping mouth.

Scott laughed out loud as he took his daughter back. "Maybe if you didn't have your mouth hanging open, she wouldn't have done that."

Derek pecked a quick kiss to Kassie's hand. Angela was so beautiful she'd actually made his jaw drop, and Kassie had taken advantage. As she came near, Derek could see that Angela was blushing at his reaction. He winked at her.

"You look amazing."

She eyed him appreciatively. "You don't look too bad yourself, cowboy," she teased.

"Isn't Sydney ready yet?" Scott grumbled impatiently.

"I'm right here."

Derek didn't even bother to tear his eyes from the vision in front of him. "Hey, Syd."

"Here you go," Mike said as he approached and handed each person a ticket and a wristband. "These are for dinner and drinks. Angie, these are for your dad, wherever he might have gone." Mike looked around.

She bit her lip and looked at Derek. He immediately understood her concern. She didn't want her father to start drinking and get out of control. "I'll give them to him." Derek tucked the wristband and Robert's ticket into his back pocket, out of sight.

Angela mouthed a quick *thank you* to him as Mike shuffled the hands into the bed of his truck. Her father came out of the trailer to meet the group, freshly show-

ered and shaved, dressed in a pair of jeans and a borrowed Western shirt. She was surprised. She hadn't seen
him look this good in a long time.

"Dad, you look nice."

"Thank you." Her father pinched his lips together
and looked at Mike. Derek didn't miss the glance and
wondered if Mike hadn't already issued a warning to
Robert.

"Let's get going before these guys starve." Derek led
Angela to the truck and opened the back door for her. He
gave her a quick kiss on the cheek before leaping into the
bed of the truck, taking the spot beside Robert. "Here's
your meal ticket." He handed the man the slip of paper
and leaned toward him. "Save us both the trouble. No
drinking tonight at the dance, okay?"

"I'll do my best," Robert said. Mike leaned over and
said something to Robert Derek couldn't hear. "I'll try. I
mean it," he promised.

Most of the hands hopped out of the truck and headed
toward the food before Scott had even parked the truck.
Derek shook his head at Mike, saying, "They act like we
don't feed them."

Mike laughed. "They're just ready for some fun."
He jumped out of the truck and went to Sydney's door,
scooping Kassie from her car seat. "You can come with
Grandpa, little girl, and your Uncle Derek and Angie can
go get the food while we find a place to sit."

Derek wondered when Mike had started calling
Angela by her father's nickname. He nodded at Mike,
knowing that Mike was giving him an opportunity to

discuss Robert's concerns with Angela. Derek had asked Mike for his advice, but he'd assured him the family trusted Derek's instincts. He didn't understand their blind trust in him, but Mike insisted he had grown up over the last year. He wished he had the same confidence in himself that they seemed to have in him, but after what had happened to Sydney, Derek didn't trust himself when it came to Angela. She had him spinning in every direction, desire ruling his brain instead of logic, and he refused to take that risk again. He glanced over at Kassie cuddling against her mother's shoulder. As much as he wanted Angela, he had to protect his family first.

Derek slid his hand to Angela's lower back, testing his resolve, and led her toward the growing line while Scott pointed Mike and Robert toward a table near the back where the crew would have some privacy—at least until the band started playing.

Angela reached back and took his hand, sending a jolt of pleasure up his arm. The sizzle of fire and ice joined, creating a burning need he didn't want to acknowledge. The joyful anticipation he could read in her eyes shook him.

Get control of yourself. Family first.

"I've never seen anything like this," she said, dragging him into the lengthening line of hungry patrons. "There's a band?"

Derek tried to suppress his smile at her childlike wonder. "That's usually the case when there's a dance," he said with a chuckle, glancing back at the table and Mike's vigilant eye. "Angel, I need to ask you a question."

Apprehension immediately flooded her eyes at his serious tone, and he hated himself for causing the reaction when she'd been so carefree only moments ago. He put his hands on either side of her waist, his fingers splaying most of the way around, and pulled her toward him.

"What? What happened?" Her eyes sought his, worry darkening them.

"I need you to tell me the truth. What's going on with Joe?"

She frowned and looked away from him. "Joe? That's what you want to know about? I've known him since I was a kid. We went to college together." She bit her lower lip before continuing. "We both studied communications, and he became my boss. Why?"

"That's it?"

She shrugged. "I'm not sure what you want to hear."

Derek stared down at her, sure that she wasn't telling him the entire story. Joe was far too possessive to be nothing more than an "old friend." She was hiding something, but before he could push her the man in line behind them nudged Derek, letting him know the line was moving.

Derek tabled the conversation with Angela and introduced himself to the woman taking tickets, explaining that they needed twenty-three plates and pointed toward the table where the others waited, looking hungry and pathetic.

"I'll get some help and bring them all over there," she assured him as she counted out the dinner tickets for the entire crew, slipping them into her cash box.

"We'll help," Angela offered.

"Honey," the woman scolded sweetly, patting her shoulder, "you'll spill all over the front of that pretty dress."

"Pshh." Angela blew her lips and waved the woman off. "I'll just borrow one of those aprons." She reached for an apron at the top of a small stack set aside for the workers. "Is that okay?"

"Of course it is, dear!" the woman exclaimed. "But you don't have to do this. We can bring it to you. You've been busy all day."

Angela tossed an apron to Derek. "Don't just stand there, cowboy. We have twenty plates to get over to your starving crew before they gnaw their arms off." She shook her head at him. "You don't want me to report the way you abuse your crew, do you?" she teased. Derek was finding it hard not to laugh at the humor in her voice. This was not the same woman who showed up trying to flirt her way to an interview less than a week ago. That woman hadn't thought about anyone but herself, and she certainly wouldn't have gotten dirty serving "manure jockeys."

Watching her now, her eyes lit with playfulness and excitement, he was having difficulty reconciling the hard-hitting reporter with his Angel. The fact she could switch roles so quickly made him second-guess his judgment more than anything else had. He couldn't allow himself to be so hung up on a woman that he couldn't recognize if he was being played for a fool.

As Angela approached the table with two plates, Sydney jumped up and took them from her, passing them to the cowboys seated at the far end. Angela hurried back to the barbecue and grabbed more, not stopping until everyone had a plate in front of them. Little beads of sweat glistened at her temples as the sun began its descent and a breeze caressed her face, lifting strands of her hair gently. He followed her back to the barbecue one last time and took the apron from her hands, laying it on one of the nearby tables.

"What's gotten into you?" He brushed a tendril of hair back from where it stuck on her face. "Slow down."

"I'm having fun, Mr. Chandler, for the first time in a very long time." Her face was flushed from the warm evening and the exertion, but her eyes gleamed with elation.

One of the crew passed them on his way to get a drink, saying, "Thanks, Angie."

When did everyone start calling her that?

She gave him a bright smile. "You're welcome."

"Better watch out, boss, or one of us is going to steal her away," the crewman warned. Angela laughed, but Derek glared at him. The cowboy held up his hands. "I'm just kidding," he said as he hurried back to the table.

Her laugher died when she saw his expression. He wasn't usually the jealous type, but this woman seemed to bring out traits he hadn't realized he possessed. His family might come first, but he wasn't about to give her up without a fight—not to one of his crew or to Joe.

Derek slid his arm around her waist and pulled her to him, feeling her breasts against his chest. Desire pulsed through him as steady as his heartbeat, and he moved her into the shadows, where they were hidden from sight. He covered her mouth with his, sliding his fingers into her hair. His kiss was meant to brand her, making sure she realized what they had was special, but it backfired on him. Yearning raged through him like a wildfire. Derek groaned deep in his throat, his tongue plunging into her sweetness, tasting her. The scent of her drove him mad. Her fingers clutched at his shoulders, pulling him down to her, and knowing she shared his longing was enough to still the doubts circling his mind. Derek's lips found her neck and she arched against him with a soft whimper of delight. He needed to get control of his rebellious body, and she was making it incredibly difficult. His lips stilled and he sighed against her neck.

"I'm debating dragging you down to one of those trailers without letting you eat dinner." He lifted his head to look at her.

Angela's eyes were dark with desire, glittering like jewels, and she gave him a coy smile. "I'm not really hungry anyway."

Derek groaned and closed his eyes. "You're killing me. You know that, right?"

She laughed softly and kissed his jaw. "Actually, I'm teasing. I'm starving."

He shook his head and brushed her hair back from her temple. "Don't take too long to eat. I'm kinda looking forward to having you in my arms tonight."

Her eyebrows shot up in surprise. "Really? You're awfully confident, aren't you, cowboy?"

"Dancing," he clarified. "After the barbecue, the band will . . ."

Derek noticed the man approaching the table where Robert and Mike were chatting. He narrowed his eyes, trying to place where he knew him from, when he saw the camera bag over his shoulder. Joe.

"Shit." He saw Robert point toward where he and Angela stood together. "What are they doing here tonight?"

Confusion marred her brow as Angela slipped out of his arms. "Who?"

Derek put his hands at her shoulders and spun her to face the table. "The news crew."

She looked back at him. "They're early. Joe told me they were coming in the morning. I . . ."

Derek didn't wait for an explanation. Spinning on his heel, he moved to leave. Angela grasped his forearm. "Derek, I have no idea why they're here now."

He left her standing in the shadow of the trees, staring after him, and stormed back to where the news crew was talking with Mike.

"Thought you were coming tomorrow?" Derek didn't bother to hide his animosity as Joe met him partway.

Joe shrugged. "I told Angela. I assumed she let you know."

Derek glanced back at her, still standing by the tree, looking slightly dazed. "Did you? Must have slipped her mind."

"Oh, I'm certain you've kept her busy with plenty that might cause her mind to be slippery." Joe glared at Derek, making him wonder again at their relationship. "Don't worry, cowboy. She's a pro. She's probably already finished the story and has it all ready for me. Now she's just enjoying the spoils of her victory."

"Excuse me?"

"You really think you're the first guy she's used to get a story? Come on, you've got to realize you're not exactly her type, and we all know reporters tend to use whatever means necessary." Joe laughed quietly and glanced at Angela, who was now heading toward them. "I remember this one politician she seduced. She got him on a story of falsifying documents. You're not the first guy to fall for her, but you would be the first one dumb enough to have her move in and give her full access. I knew cowboys were known for their brawn, but you must have no brains at all."

ANGELA STARED AFTER Derek, wondering what had just happened. One minute, they were having a good time, sharing a kiss—and that kiss! She still felt her entire body tingling, as if she had touched an open current and still had electricity running through her veins. The next minute, he was storming away to face off with Joe. She looked toward the table, where Skip sat with her father while Joe made a beeline for Derek.

"What the hell?" she muttered, forcing her feet to catch up to the two men. Joe glanced her way as she reached them.

"Don't worry, we'll stay out of your way, maybe just film a few things here and there tonight for our B-roll. You know, background footage," he explained condescendingly.

"Like hell." Derek growled, his fists clenching at his sides. "You can come back in the morning."

"Joe, what are you doing here? I thought you weren't coming until tomorrow." Why didn't he call her before coming? She certainly wasn't camera ready. She looked at Skip's camera bag on the table. There weren't any lights. He couldn't be getting any video tonight without lighting. None of this was making sense.

Joe waved her off. "I told you we were coming on the phone, remember? This way we can get every bit of tomorrow's rodeo, from sunup to sundown."

"There's nowhere for you to sleep," Derek interrupted.

She looked from him to Joe. The two men stood facing one another, and she was sure one of them was about to throw a punch any second. She wasn't sure why they disliked each other so much since they'd met only once, but the tension between them was palpable.

Joe eyed Derek and smiled confidently. "We'll manage. We've done it plenty of times before. We don't need your charity." He looked at Angela expectantly. "Unless there's no story?"

"It's not the story I originally thought we'd have." She stalled, looking from Joe to Derek. With his arms crossed and his eyes darkened with fury, Derek's entire demeanor let her know their evening had come to an abrupt end.

"Good, then let's pack up and head home. We'll figure out something else and get you back on the air." Joe reached for her arm and pulled her toward him. "Chalk this up to a few wasted vacation days." He smirked at Derek.

Angela slipped her arm from Joe's grasp, and Derek took a step toward him. There was far too much testosterone in too small an area.

"No, I'm not going anywhere yet."

Joe's brows shot to his hairline in disbelief. "If there's no story, why are we wasting any more time here?"

"Wait a minute." Sydney rose from the table while heads spun toward her. "Angela told me about her new idea. I think it's even better than animal cruelty. Rodeo: America's Most Dangerous Sport. It would have people glued to their seats and show how dangerous rodeo really is." She laughed and reached for Angela's hand. "It'll make Shark Week look like child's play."

Mike's face brightened. "I love it! You can interview the cowboys and see why they do it, what motivates them." He smiled at Joe.

Angela could have kissed Sydney. It was a brilliant idea. People loved tuning in to see blood, guts, and gore. Rodeo events certainly fit that description, providing more danger to the cowboy than any of the animals. She looked to Derek, hoping he would give her an indication of his thoughts, but he only narrowed his dark eyes and crossed his arms over his massive chest, looking impervious. His jaw clenched and she could just make out the pulse in his temple.

Mike ignored Derek and concentrated on Skip and Joe. "You are both welcome to come stay at the ranch. Jen and Clay have an extra room." He sounded like a kid planning a sleepover. "As for tonight, you can stay in our trailer. Derek and Scott can sleep on the couch in yours, right?" He looked at Sydney.

She returned his grin. "We'll figure something out."

Joe glared at Derek before turning his dark gaze on Angela. "Come here," he ordered, pulling her aside, out of earshot. "Is this the story you want to do? You really think *this* is going to get you noticed by another station?"

"It's a great idea, Joe. It's worth taking the chance."

"No, it's not. You're already on thin ice at the station. They are tired of you rocking the boat, Gigi. If you stick with this nonsense and the story doesn't get ratings, the station is going to let you go. You realize that, right?"

Angela took a deep breath, trying to think rationally. She looked over at her father, who was seated beside Mike. For the first time in years he looked content, and so far the change in scenery and companionship had kept him out of trouble, stirring a hope in her she'd never felt before. It wasn't the first time Joe had issued the warning, but it was the first time she'd ever been this close to putting their past behind them. But if this story didn't pan out and she had to return to their apartment, or worse, if she got fired . . . Angela didn't even want to consider that alternative.

Sydney and Mike looked at her expectantly. They'd gone out on a limb for her, something no one but her mother had ever done for her. Even Scott had showed her more kindness and support than Joe. She couldn't understand why he was balking at this story. It was far better for her career than the mall openings and puff pieces she'd been doing for the past two years. She frowned, looking at Derek, realizing he was the reason Joe was pushing her to drop the story.

Joe followed her gaze. "What's going on with the two of you?"

"Nothing," she assured him, tearing her eyes away from Derek. Glaring at her and Joe, Derek looked callous and uncompromising; the tender man she'd been kissing only moments before was gone.

"I don't believe you."

"Joe, you gave me a two weeks to bring back a killer story. The station owners agreed to that."

"You know I can't stay at their ranch or do several of these." He waved his arm at the crowd of people waiting for the band to start playing. "I have a station to run, and other reporters who are bringing me regular stories that go on the air every day." He glanced back at Derek and reached for her hand, drawing her into an awkward embrace. "It's not the story I'm worried about. I'm worried about you getting your heart broken by some redneck cowboy with a girl waiting for him at every rodeo. He probably has a few here tonight."

She felt his lips moving against her hair, and she shivered as her entire being objected to his intimate caress. Joe stepped back and cupped her face in his hands. "Even if you don't want to be with me, I don't want to see you end up being just another romp in that guy's bed."

Chapter Seventeen

"WHAT THE HELL, Robert? I thought you said she didn't have another story." Joe wiped his hand over his face and rubbed his eyes. "I do not want to be stuck sitting at this rodeo all weekend watching her with that horseback Romeo."

"I said I didn't know," Robert reminded him.

Joe threw his hands into the air in frustration. "She's going to get hurt."

Robert twisted his mouth and pinched his lips. "I thought you wanted to see her happy."

Robert glared at him. "Of course I do, but with me."

Robert laid a comforting hand on Joe's shoulder. He might not have been sober throughout most of Angie's childhood, but he'd seen enough to know that Joe thought he was in love with her. He was secretly glad things hadn't worked out between the pair. Joe was far too possessive and domineering. The more he saw the two of them together, the more he realized Joe quenched the fire in his daughter. Derek Chandler challenged her, making him a far better match for her. "Let her go, son. There's a girl out there for you. It just isn't my Angie."

"What are you talking about?"

"It's pretty obvious she and Chandler have a connection."

"She can't possibly be serious about him. She barely knows him." Joe frowned. "Maybe she's just using him for the story."

Robert snorted. "Not if the kiss I saw earlier was any indication." He patted Joe's shoulder again. "Let her go."

Joe brushed his hand away. "You might not care enough to stop this, but I'm not going to sit by and let Gigi get hurt."

"She's a big girl. I'm warning you. You're making a mistake, Joe. Leave them alone."

"She's a girl in a woman's body." Joe narrowed his eyes as he watched Angie talking with Sydney. "She has no idea what she needs or wants." Robert didn't like the storm he could see brewing in Joe's eyes.

ANGELA STOOD IN the trailer staring at the roll-out bed. There was no way that Scott and Derek would both fit on it. With each man well over six feet tall, their legs would dangle from the end. She and Sydney could share it but they wouldn't have room in the bed for Kassie, whose playpen was put away since there wasn't enough room now. This was a mess, and she blamed Joe for showing up unannounced.

Derek entered the trailer and, seeing her standing by the bed, made his way to the other side, tossing his change of clothing on the floor farthest from her. He'd ignored her for the rest of the evening, heading back down to the trailers. This was the first she'd seen of him since he stormed off. Instead of a magical evening dancing under the stars and culminating wherever his kisses might lead, they'd somehow made a wrong turn where she now stood face to face with his contempt, and she wasn't even sure why.

"Would you mind telling me what I did? One minute you're kissing me, the next you won't speak to me." She crossed her arms, waiting for his explanation.

Derek sat on the edge of the bed and pulled his boots off, standing them by the wall alongside the bed. He removed his socks and stuck them inside before rising, turning to look at her. She could see his disappointment clearly. "We had a deal: one day."

"Okay?"

He unbuckled his belt and pulled it from the loops on his pants. "I asked you to tell me the truth and you lied to my face." He tucked the huge silver buckle into a boot and stood with his hands at his hips, waiting for her response.

"I didn't lie." What in the world was he talking about? Derek shook his head and shrugged. Turning his back to her, he pulled his shirt over his head, laying it across the top of the boots.

"Derek, I don't know . . ." He turned back toward her and her brain stopped working.

He was chiseled perfection. She couldn't have imagined a more perfect specimen of manhood. She couldn't keep her eyes from his bare chest. His bronzed skin gleamed in the light from over the small stove, casting shadows over every valley and crevice. The muscles of his chest tensed under her gaze and she tried to ignore the way his broad shoulders tapered to a V at his waist with just the slightest trail of dark hair ending at the waistband of his pants. The sight of him struck her dumb, and she couldn't recall what he'd just said.

He covered the space separating them in two steps. His hands cupped her jaw as he pressed his lips to hers. His tongue found hers and danced, sending spirals of pleasure coursing over her skin. Lightning shot through her veins and she reached for his shoulders to hold herself upright. The touch of her fingertips on his skin was more than she could bear. She sighed against him, whispering his name.

"Tell me you don't feel that, that this is just another story."

She could hear the anger and frustration in his voice, but his touch was tender as his mouth trailed to her throat, moving the strap of her dress aside. His lips found her collarbone, burning kisses over the bared skin.

"No," she whispered, her fingers curling against his upper arms.

Coherent thoughts were no longer a function of her brain as she reveled in the desire swirling through her body, surrounding her with heightened sensitivity to his touch. He pressed a kiss against the swell of her breast, just above the bodice of her dress, and the rasp of his jaw made her cry out in pleasure. She wanted to feel his skin against hers, and she pressed herself against him, lost in the fierce longing he'd ignited. No man had ever taken her to this place of need and want and hunger. His hands trailed up her spine, arching her toward his lips, pressing their lower bodies together. She gasped at the contact.

The footsteps on the stairs registered only seconds before Sydney opened the door. She paused in the doorway, seeing the two of them. "Um," she hedged, glancing back at Scott over her shoulder. "Scott, I can you go with me to get something from the truck."

Heat flooded Angela's cheeks, a blush rushing upward from her toes.

"Don't worry, Syd." Derek looked down at Angela and his eyes hardened. "I was just leaving." Grabbing his shirt and boots, he brushed passed Sydney and Scott.

Sydney hurried to move out of his way as he hurried down the stairs, and Angela straightened her dress quickly. She knew there was nothing she could do about her kiss-swollen lips or the red marks on her shoulder from his whiskered jaw. She could barely catch her breath.

"What's gotten into him tonight?" Sydney asked Angela, worry creasing her brow.

"I'll be back in a second." Scott followed Derek toward the truck as Sydney shut the door.

DEREK WAS SO angry he hadn't realized he'd walked to his truck barefoot until he stepped on a sharp rock and the pain broke through the haze of his indignation. "Damn it!" He hobbled the rest of the way to his truck and turned on the inner light to inspect his foot.

"What in the hell are you doing?" Scott braced his hands on the door of the truck and shook his head.

"Checking my foot."

"I don't mean your foot, you idiot. I mean with Angie, and you know it."

"Is everyone calling her Angie now?" Derek asked sarcastically, looking up at his brother. He wanted to assure Scott he had the entire situation under control, to deny his desire for her, but he knew he couldn't. Scott knew it, too, which was probably why he was standing here instead of heading to bed with his wife.

Derek ran a hand through his short hair and sighed. "I have no clue," he admitted.

"You'd better figure it out, because right now you're spun out of control and you're making mistakes. This isn't like you."

Derek hung his head. "I'm doing the best I can, Scott. At least it doesn't look like the story is going to happen."

"I'm not talking about the story." Scott threw his hand up before slapping his thigh. "Man, you really aren't thinking right now. I'm talking about that woman in there. I thought I was in denial with Sydney but you're making me look like a genius."

"I'm not going to be used again, especially for some story," Derek spit out. He didn't want to believe it, but, remembering the woman who'd tried to con her way into an interview, Derek couldn't deny Joe's accusation was likely.

Scott closed his eyes and put a hand to his forehead. "Are you even listening to yourself? You said she couldn't even flirt when you first met her, remember? Do you really think she could flip a switch and be good enough, overnight mind you, that she could get a story out of you?" Derek could hear the frustration in his brother's voice. "Look, I'm not one to push anyone into a relationship, but she's fighting with her boss to come up with *any* sort of story to stay close to you!"

"She needs a story to get her father away, to get a promotion. She just wants to move on to bigger and better things and avoid going back to their old neighborhood." Derek sighed, got out of the truck, and stood in front of his brother. He outweighed him by at least twenty pounds of solid muscle and was almost half a head taller, but Scott didn't back down a bit. "I'm not the only man she's tried to seduce for a story, okay?"

Scott shoved Derek's shoulders, knocking him off-balance. "She's not even doing the story on us anymore, you idiot. You are so stubborn. Sydney's right, you don't deserve her."

The fight instantly drained from Derek. He trusted Sydney even more than his family and she knew him better than any of them. "Syd said that?"

"Yes," Scott said, not bothering to hide his irritation. "I suppose her opinion matters more than mine."

Derek rolled his eyes and shrugged. "Well, yeah."

Scott laughed. "Whatever. Look, I had my doubts about her when she first came, you know that, but so far Angie hasn't done anything to warrant this. I appreciate how you've stepped up and taken over, and you're doing a great job, but don't let this"—he waved a hand at the trailers—"rob you of someone you care about. Go talk to her."

He shook his head, jutting out his jaw. "She lied to me. She looked me in the eye and lied. How can I trust anything she says?"

"Are you sure she was the person who lied?" Scott looked pointedly toward Joe and Skip talking quietly outside the trailer. "Be careful whose word you take."

"I HAVE NO idea what happened." Angela sat at the edge of the roll-out bed while Sydney rocked Kassie on her hip. "One minute he was fine, the next he was furious and accused me of lying to him." She looked up and shrugged. "I don't know what I did."

"Did you? Lie to him, I mean," Sydney asked quietly.

Angela wracked her brain. There was nothing she'd blatantly lied about, although there were plenty of things she'd avoided discussing with him. She recalled his question just before Joe and Skip arrived, his reaction to their arrival, and the dark fury in his eyes whenever she spoke with Joe. Pieces started to fall into place. For some reason, this was about Joe. She told Sydney her suspicions.

"Oh my goodness," Sydney exclaimed, "he is more like Scott than I thought. Stupid, fool men," she ranted and began to pace. "I should punch him. He probably thinks you're using him to make Joe jealous. You have to understand, Derek is big on loyalty, all of the Chandlers are, and if they suspect anything even remotely traitorous, they turn tail. I know from experience."

"Sydney, there is nothing between Joe and me. And, as much as I love your idea for a story, unless rodeo is as dangerous as you say . . ."

"It is," she said soberly.

"If it's not, it really won't matter how Derek or I feel because I'll be back doing feel-good pieces on Monday."

"Don't give up yet. I'll talk with Derek in the morning and see where his head is. All of us can see he cares about you, and with Derek, that's enough for him to take the risk."

ANGELA LAY STARING up at the ceiling, the sound of Sydney's even breathing and an occasional quiet snore from Scott were the only sounds breaking the silence in the trailer. She heard a quiet giggle from Kassie as if she were laughing in her sleep. The near silence grated on her frayed nerves. She couldn't stop thinking about her conversation with Sydney. Didn't Derek realize how much she was beginning to trust him, or how much it meant to her that he returned that trust? At least, she'd thought he did. She shifted on the roll-out bed, trying to find a spot that wouldn't press uncomfortably into her back.

She had seen Derek talking with Joe before she was able to get close to them and wondered what was said to send Derek into such a foul mood. She had seen the look that passed between them at the police station, as if she were a bone to fight over, but could Derek really think she would respond the way she did to him if she was in love with Joe? What kind of woman did he think she was?

She wiggled and tried to adjust the pillow under her head, punching it, realizing his assessment might not have been too far from the truth a few weeks ago. In the past, when she wanted a story, she hadn't hesitated flirting to get an inside scoop or lying to get ahead of the competition. And she'd never spent any time worrying about who might get hurt in the process, whether it was her subject or a fellow reporter. Somewhere in the past week, she'd done what she'd sworn she never would—become emotionally attached to the subject of her story.

She swiped at the tear burning a path down her cheek. "And this is why you don't, you idiot," she whispered in the darkness. She sighed and swung her legs over the side of the bed, reaching for the quilt Sydney had laid at the foot. Wrapping it around her shoulders, she silently crept from the trailer and slumped in one of the lawn chairs outside, staring up at the stars.

She still marveled at how the stars could be so brilliant away from the city lights in the night sky. Only a single light at the other end of the arena marred the perfection of the slivered moon. She twisted the blanket around her and curled her legs under her, wondering if her mother was watching her now and whether she would be proud of the way her daughter had turned out. She hated to admit she didn't feel optimistic at the thought.

Her gaze strayed to the trailer where her father was sound asleep. How was she going to help him stay sober? Did he even want to? She had no clue what to do about him after this weekend. Taking him back to the apartment was bound to lead right back to the destructive path he'd been on. Mike had offered room for both of them at the ranch, but would he even want to go? As much as it would make things easier for her, it wasn't fair to Mike or the Chandlers.

She'd never met anyone like Mike or the Chandlers. They knew what she did for a living, knew she could destroy them professionally, yet they had opened their home and their hearts to welcome her. She'd never experienced that sort of selflessness. Her life had been repeated lessons in learning to take from people before they took from you. She used people before she was used by them. Angela had never known a time when she didn't have to scrimp and claw her way just to reach mediocrity, and she refused to be shackled there by guilt and recriminations of her past. But in her need to get ahead, leaving guilt behind, she was becoming someone she hated, forced to stifle more guilt when she backstabbed a coworker or tricked someone into giving away something in order to make her interview more controversial.

She saw the shadow of the horses wandering inside their pen in the darkness. *I guess they don't sleep either.*

Angela made her way toward the makeshift corral. She had lost her fear of horses, thanks in part to Derek's patience and Honey, the gentle mare he'd taught her to ride. She leaned on the top rail of the corral fencing and laid her chin on her wrists as Honey walked up to her, nudging her for an apple. She'd developed a habit of bringing the mare a treat when she visited her, hoping to remain on her good side.

"I don't have anything for you tonight, girl." She rubbed her hand over the mare's velvety nose. The horse hung her head over Angela's shoulder and she patted the mare's neck. "You pretend that you're so tough and unapproachable but you're really just a sweetheart, aren't you?" She pressed her cheek against the mare's warmth.

"Reminds me of someone else I know."

Angela jumped and spun around, surprising the mare, causing her to jump backward and snort as she bumped one of the geldings. "Stop *doing* that," Angela whispered.

Derek chuckled softly. "Doing what?"

"You keep sneaking up on me," she scolded. "If I didn't know better, I'd think you were stalking me." Without a hat, in the faint pre-dawn light, he looked dark and mysterious, almost dangerous, and her heartbeat quickened.

He hooked his thumbs in the corner of his jean pockets. "Can't sleep?"

She turned back to the mare, who had returned to the fence and was edging closer to Angela, and shook her head. "No, you?"

She sensed Derek moving closer, the heat from his body warming her through the quilt she pulled tighter around her shoulders. Fisting her hands, she tucked them inside the blanket to keep from reaching out to him. She ached to touch him, but after what had happened with their last kiss she was hesitant to take the risk.

His arms circled hers, over the blanket, and he laid his cheek against her hair before inhaling. She tried to convince her heart to slow down before she had a heart attack. Shivers of desire raced through her.

"Cold?"

She wanted to tell him she was burning up, that he'd ignited a flame in her she'd never known was lying dormant.

This wasn't going to work.

She knew what she had to do, and it felt like someone was ripping her heart from her chest.

Angela bit her lower lip before she answered him. She could feel the tension emanating from him, in spite of his tenderness. "I told you I'm no good at this. We gave it one day and it was a disaster."

"Angel . . ."

"No," she said, turning in his arms to face him. "I didn't lie to you, but neither of us is willing to let go of our distrust long enough to believe the other." She tried to blink back the burning tears forming in her eyes. "It's always going to be something, Derek."

"Whose idea was it to change the story?"

She sighed and wondered if it really mattered at this point. "I realized there was no evidence for the animal cruelty angle pretty quickly, so I tried to convince the station to take the other angle, but they wouldn't do it. Sydney came up with this new story idea." She could see him searching her eyes for the truth, wanting to believe her but still uncertain.

"This is why there can't be anything between us."

She pulled away from him, starting toward the trailer, when he grasped the edge of the blanket and jerked her back into his arms. She stepped on the edge of the blanket and tripped, falling against him, knocking them both to the ground.

Derek's chest shook with laughter. "So much for being romantic," he teased. "At least I broke your fall."

She loved the sound of his deep timbered laughter and couldn't help but join him. She laid her cheek against the wall of his chest and giggled. These were the moments when she felt completely at ease with him, when nothing else in the world could quite reach them. She sighed. "You're quite the charmer, dragging a lady into the dirt." Angela wound her arms around his waist, savoring this brief moment, knowing it couldn't possibly last.

"It was exactly what I meant to do," he joked. Derek ran his thumb over her jaw and rolled so she lay beneath him, balancing his weight on his forearm under her neck. His eyes, black in the near darkness, grew serious. "I want to trust you."

"Then trust me," she pleaded. She reached her hand up to his rough jaw. "I don't know why you think I lied."

"Open book?"

She hesitated. Agreeing to be an open book with him would mean complete honesty. He could ask one of a million questions she didn't want to answer about her past. But if they were going to take the next step, if she wanted to keep him in her life, she had to be vulnerable. "Open book," she said, nodding.

"What's going on between you and Joe?"

"Joe?" Of all the questions that must have been weighing on his mind, she was surprised he chose that one first.

"Nothing. He's my boss and runs the station. I told you we've been friends for years."

"What aren't you telling me?" His eyes probed hers, drawing the entire truth from the depths of her soul.

"We dated for a short time." She wasn't sure how to explain what had happened with Joe, but she wasn't willing to lose what she could have with Derek for what would never be with Joe. "He thinks he loves me and I care about him but not the way I love . . ." Angela caught herself, realizing what she'd almost revealed. She couldn't possibly have fallen in love with Derek in this short amount of time, could she? "I don't love him the way he deserves to be loved."

"And he knows it?" he asked.

"I've told him several times that I will never love him, and we are just coworkers and friends," she swore. She lifted her other hand to his jaw, cupping his face between her cold fingers. "Open book."

Derek stared down into her eyes, and she wondered if he was seeing whatever it was he was searching for. His body remained over hers, hovering between desire and self-preservation. She could feel the proof of his need against her lower stomach and she fought her own longing to arch against him.

"Angel, you're lucky we're sharing a trailer with my brother tonight." His eyes gleamed in the faint light. "I don't think I'd be able to keep my hands off you otherwise."

Hope began to blossom in her chest. Did that mean he believed her? Angela was certain Lady Luck wasn't playing in her favor because, right now, she didn't want him to keep his hands off her. She wanted those hands everywhere.

DEREK WOKE THE next morning with auburn hair splayed across his chest. Angela's fingers were spread across his stomach under his t-shirt and his loins ached with unreleased desire. She lay curled against his side, her head resting on his chest with one hand fisted under her chin. Her lashes brushed against her cheekbones as he felt the urge to kiss her eyes open from slumber. He brushed her hair back from her face, loving the way it fell through his fingers like silk, landing over her shoulder.

He'd used every ounce of willpower he possessed to lay beside her in the wee hours of the morning and not touch her. It had nearly killed him to lie in bed with her, holding her, without tasting her sweet lips or allowing his fingers to glide over the satin skin of her back. Even now he felt his body cursing him for even contemplating slipping out of the bed before she woke. What he wouldn't give to stay in bed with her all day.

As if responding to his presence, Angela sighed in her sleep and twined one leg with his, trapping him in place. He gave in and curled his arms around her, savoring the moment before reality chose to rear its head on their bliss. Within moments, Kassie began fussing in the next room and Derek knew either Scott or Sydney would be up. He wanted to save Angela the embarrassment of anyone seeing them sharing a bed, even platonically.

He pressed a kiss to the top of her head, her peach-vanilla scent shooting desire straight to his lower body. He cursed his response and dragged himself from under her hands, her fiery halo pooling around her head. He stood, shifting his jeans, trying to make them somewhat comfortable in his aroused state, and saw his brother standing with Kassie at the top of the stairs. Scott arched a brow and smirked but refrained from commenting as he reached for a bottle of water, warming it in a cup in the microwave.

"Aren't you supposed to boil it on the stove? That's how Sydney does it."

"Aren't you supposed to marry the girl before you sleep with her?" Scott countered.

Derek glared at his brother. "You're one to talk." He glanced back at his Angel, still sleeping. "We both still have our clothes on."

Scott chuckled and wiggled his brows. "There's a lot of fun to be had, even with clothes on."

"Nothing happened, Scott."

"Then I'm disappointed in you," his brother said, laughing quietly and cuddling with his daughter. "I remember those days with your mama."

Derek shook his head and made his way out the door, pulling a flannel shirt over his t-shirt to ward off the chill that still hung in the air. He tossed alfalfa to the horses and hay to the cattle and checked on their water. He waved to Mike as he saw him coming out of the other trailer.

Mike yawned as he approached. "I need coffee."

"Scott's feeding Kassie right now, but I'm sure that's next on his to-do list."

"Did I see you sleeping in the back of the truck last night? I thought you were staying on Sydney's couch?"

Derek nodded. "I was out here for a while then I went inside."

Mike cocked his head and narrowed his eyes. "Everything okay?"

"It's fine, Mike. Just ironing out a few details." Derek didn't want to rehash his discussion with Angela when he wasn't even certain what they had decided. He still wasn't certain he wasn't being used but he knew he couldn't give her up. The rest they would try to figure out as they went along.

Mike looked at him for a moment longer then slapped his shoulder. "Then let's get this show ready. It's going to be a scorcher today."

"Mike, what are we gonna do about Robert? I'm sure Angela is going to be busy with the news crew here."

"What are you thinking?"

"We could always have him help behind the chutes, putting on wraps, moving stock, things like that. At least it would be easier to keep an eye on him."

Mike stuck out his lower lip, contemplating Derek's suggestion. "It's not a bad idea. I've been talking to him a bit. He's a good guy, Derek. I think there are some fences he and Angela need to mend, though. Speaking of Angela, any idea what her plans are after this weekend?"

Derek shrugged. "I know she said she's getting some video this weekend behind the chutes and interviewing cowboys before and after. I think she's planning on trying to interview the ones who hit the next rodeo, too."

"Then she's coming back with us?" The older man's eyes gleamed mischievously.

Derek clenched his jaw, trying to hide his grin and nodded. "It looks that way. Are you happy with yourself?"

"Son, I only want to see you three kids happy. Whether you realize it or not, you're happier with her."

"In case you haven't noticed it, we're not kids anymore. I'd think you'd stop matchmaking by now. And I'm fine with things just the way they are."

"No, you're surviving, but that's not living." Mike glanced at Scott exiting the trailer, leaning forward to kiss Sydney. "And I'll stop matchmaking when I make a mistake. So far I'm two for two with you kids, and I'm betting you make it three for three." He winked and made his way toward Scott.

Chapter Eighteen

ANGELA PULLED SKIP to her side, pointing toward the cowboys settling on the back of the saddle broncs in the chute. She'd already interviewed most of them and was shocked to find out how many had been injured or hospitalized, but drove away, refusing treatment, in order to compete in the next rodeo a few days later. Mike reminded her that if they didn't ride, they didn't get paid. Angela knew from experience that hunger was a strong motivator.

"Head back there and stick that camera over the back of the chute or head up to the announcer's booth and shoot down. I want it to look like we are seeing things from the cowboy's angle," she ordered. "Get as much of the sound as you can, too. Think 'reality show.'"

Joe leaned back against the panels, looking bored. "Think we could hurry this along? You're just repeating the same sorry tale over and over with a different cowboy.

Got hurt, rode through it, ignored the paramedics, and went to the next rodeo." He sighed. "All you're proving is that these guys are idiots."

Angela smiled at him sweetly, wishing he'd just head back to the station. He wasn't helping and had complained all morning. "I know how busy you are, Joe. If you need to head back, I'm sure Skip and I can finish up today."

"And leave you here with the Marlboro Man to get your heart broken?" He blew air between his lips. "I don't think so. Besides, I'll take your dad home with me tonight. It will make it easier on everyone."

Angela bit her lip, wondering how to break it to Joe that she was taking her dad back to the ranch. Mike had already insisted they both come, and she wondered if he understood her predicament. Having her dad close would help her keep him safe, and it would be much easier to keep an eye on him if he was secluded from nearby bars. Mike was giving her an opportunity to do her job and keep her father safe—something Joe hadn't been able to do while she was away. But Joe wouldn't see it that way. He'd take it as a personal affront and a lack of confidence in him.

"Dad's going to come to the ranch with me. He'll be away from all the pressure at home."

Joe cocked his head and rolled his eyes. "What pressure? Watching you go to work every day?"

Angela arched a brow at his sarcasm. "He's coming with me to the ranch, Joe. I'll be there until after the next rodeo. Then Skip and I will come back to the station and edit the footage." He opened his mouth to argue. "You agreed to two weeks if I had a story, remember?"

Joe closed his mouth, his lips pinching into a thin line. She knew he was angry, but she wasn't backing down this time. Now that she'd taken a bite of this story, she knew she was on the right track. It had every component to make it a feature story—good-looking cowboys, Western culture, danger, drama—it was sure to be a hit. Skip was convinced they would turn it into a series.

"Fine," he snapped, pushing himself off of the panels, causing them to rattle loudly, ruining her shot. "Since you seem to have everything in order and don't need me, I'll just head up to the announcer's booth and see what I can get up there."

"Joe," she called after him. She hated when he was angry at her, but he was being so difficult. It was just easier to let him go cool off. She sighed as he hurried away.

"He'll cool off, Angela. I'll get a better shot from the chutes." Skip glanced over his shoulder and leaned back, trying to get a good look at the rough stock chutes. "I think if I can get behind the chute crew, it will give me a clear shot, and I'll still get all the commotion down there. You're gonna want that on camera."

"Thanks, Skip. You really are the best cameraman around." Skip frowned at her, looking at her as if she'd grown a third head. "What's wrong?"

Skip shook his head. "Nothing's wrong. You know, that's the first time you've ever given me a compliment."

"No, it's not." She waved him off with the back of her

hand. "You know I always request you for my location shoots."

"Yeah, I know you do," he agreed, "but you've never been this excited about a story. And you've never told me I do a great job." He shrugged and lifted the camera to his shoulder. "It's just nice to hear every once in a while. And it's really nice to see you enjoying yourself for a change."

Angela realized he was right. She wasn't rude to her crew, but she'd never thought of them as people with feelings and needs. She'd seen them as pawns in her daily grind, to be ordered around, never giving any thought to the work they put in or how good they made her look. Her selfishness hit her square in the chest. While none of them ever complained, at least not when she was around, they certainly hadn't been lining up to work with her. She'd been demanding and difficult and cold as ice. While it might have made her a good reporter, it made her a terrible person.

She reached for Skip's elbow. "I'm sorry, Skip. You've done so much for me and I should have never treated you the way I have. I . . ." She wasn't sure what else she could say to make up for her pretentious attitude. There was no excuse for her actions. She shook her head and couldn't look at him. "I'm sorry."

He laughed, nervously. "I'm not sure what's come over you with this story, but I kinda like this Angela. She's a lot more relaxed." Skip hurried up the stairs toward the chutes, immediately finding a spot to stand behind the cowboys where he could get video he wanted without being in their way.

She looked at the broad-shouldered cowboy guiding a bucking horse out of the arena. Derek was a big reason for the change in her. He was forcing her to release her need to be in charge, her desire to control every circumstance, and her tendency to squeeze every ounce of self-preservation out of situations. He was teaching her that vulnerability wasn't a weakness, and others were noticing the gentleness he was drawing out of her. She liked the person she was becoming under his affection, even if she was afraid of her. She was letting go of the pain and bitterness that colored her every decision and relying on a newfound faith in the future.

Angela admired Derek from a distance as he focused on helping a rider onto the back of his mount, away from danger, and then setting him safely on his feet again. He didn't realize it, but he was doing the same for her.

JOE FOUND ROBERT in the announcer's booth and glared at him. "What the hell? You were supposed to tell her you wanted to go home, now you're going back with her?"

"What difference does it make where I go?" He flipped his hand at the younger man irritably.

Mike had offered him this opportunity to help out by keeping track of the scores, and, while he hadn't held a steady job since Angela was a little girl, he was surprised at the odd sense of renewal he felt. It made him feel like he had a purpose, at least for today. It had been a long time since he'd felt any desire to impress someone else,

260 T. J. KLINE

and he was grateful for the reminder of how it felt to be a provider instead of a burden.

"If she stays here, we both know she's going to hook up with him and get her heart broken."

"It's about time she falls for someone." Joe's outrage almost made him laugh. "Relax, nothing is going to happen. You know better than anyone that Angie won't get close enough to fall for anyone," he reminded him. "Let her live a little. Besides, if he breaks her heart, you can be there to pick up the pieces." It didn't take a genius to see that Derek had fallen hard for Angie, and he doubted the cowboy would hurt her, but Robert would say anything right now if it would get Joe to shut up.

"You realize if this story does as well as she thinks it will, she'll be moving to one of the bigger stations in Sacramento or San Francisco. Maybe even L.A. And where would that leave you?" He jerked the pen out of Robert's hand, forcing him to look at him. "If you think she's planning on taking you, you're wrong. She can't wait to get away."

The announcer turned off his microphone. "Do you two mind? I'm trying to work here. If you want to talk, get out," he ordered, turning his mic back on and adding some commentary to the ride happening in the arena.

Robert wasn't sure if Joe was repeating something Angie had said or just trying to get a reaction from him. "We'll talk about this later," he whispered.

"I have a job for you while you're there, Robert. Just be sure to find me before I leave. And, just so you know, if you don't do this, I'll make sure you're sorry. You'll wish you were in jail again when I get through with you."

DEREK WAS KICKING himself. He'd tried to work out at least one hundred different scenarios to get Angela alone, and nothing seemed feasible. He watched her from the end of the arena while the specialty act performed for the crowd. The bull riding was next, their last event before they ran the evening slack, and he wondered if she was getting the footage she needed. He'd seen her talking with several of the competitors before and after their events, hovering in the medical tent while several minor injuries were treated.

She was a vision and he couldn't seem to tear his eyes from her. Even seated beside her father and Joe in the announcer's booth, her hair gleamed like it was lit from a fire within. She'd borrowed another Western shirt from Sydney, and she looked good enough to eat in her dark green shirt and jeans, with rhinestones on her perfectly round rear. He'd heard more than one of the contestants talking about her behind the chutes, and had he not been a professional he might have put a few of them in the medical tent himself. She was a woman who demanded a man's attention without even trying.

"Hey, you gonna stare at her all day or get ready?" Scott sidled his paint gelding beside Derek's horse.

"I'm ready." He crossed his forearms and leaned them on the saddle horn.

"Maybe I should finagle a way to get Sydney and Kassie to a hotel tonight, huh?"

Derek glared at his brother. "It's not like that."

"The hell it's not." Scott rolled his eyes and looked back at the animal act in the arena. "Why don't you take her out tonight? Find someplace in town for dinner. I'm sure I can convince one of the other guys to run the slack with me. It's just timed events."

"And if one of these guys gets hurt and she's not here to get it on film?" He shook his head. "She'd never forgive me." His eyes found her again and he clenched his jaw when he saw her lean close to Joe.

"I don't trust him," Scott said, his eyes following Derek's.

"What am I supposed to do? He's her boss."

"He's also up to something. You need to keep an eye on him," Scott warned.

"I know, but I'm not sure what I can do right now. Unless he threatens the company, he's just like any other reporter with a press pass." Derek sighed and winked at Angela as she met his gaze across the arena and smiled. He felt his body immediately respond and shifted uncomfortably in the saddle. Damn, that woman could play him like a fiddle if she wanted to. He didn't miss the glare Joe shot him. "But I don't think it's us he wants to threaten."

DEREK FOUND ANGELA after the end of the bull riding in the medical booth, interviewing a cowboy who lay on a gurney while the doctor checked out his ribs. "How many times have you broken your ribs?"

"Who knows?" The cowboy winced as the doctor

pressed against the bruised flesh. "I crack them at least once a year, sometimes more."

"Yet, you continue to ride?" Derek caught the cowboy's nod in greeting. Angela followed his gaze over her shoulder. "Why?"

"What do you mean, why?" he laughed. "Even on a bad day, this beats any eight-to-five job I could get working construction or behind a desk. I get to do what I love."

"You love being injured?" Derek laid a hand on her shoulder, unsure if he was doing it because of the aching need to touch her or because he wanted to make sure everyone realized she was his.

"I love this sport. We're just like any other athlete. Football players, baseball players, skiers, mountain climbers . . . they can all get hurt. We're no different."

"Except you're riding a two-thousand-pound animal determined to get you off its back by any means necessary."

He gave her a lop-sided grin. "Yeah, well, there is that."

Angela smiled back at him and Derek felt the urge to drag her away from any other men nearby. She laid her hand on the cowboy's forearm. "I think we have enough for now. Are you really going to try and ride next weekend?"

The cowboy glanced at the doctor, who frowned down at him. "I'm about ninety percent sure you have at least two cracked ribs."

"Yeah, I'll be riding next weekend."

She laughed with him, even as he grimaced in pain,

and the medic shook his head. Angela turned to Derek. "Are you finished?"

"No." He frowned when he saw Joe and Skip waiting for her at the trailer. "We still have to finish the timed events."

"I thought those were finished a long time ago." She twisted her lips in an expression he wanted to believe was disappointment.

"The slack is the overflow of competitors who weren't able to compete in the time allowed during the performances," he explained. "We had a lot of calf and team ropers this weekend so we'll take a short break and then get them started. Hopefully, it won't last too long tonight."

"Need my help with anything?"

Derek snuck one arm around her waist and pulled her close, spinning her so that he leaned back against one of the trailers and she stood between his thighs, away from the view of prying eyes. "You have no idea," he murmured, dipping his head toward hers. His voice was low and hoarse with desire.

He had to spend some time with her alone tonight. He gently touched his lips against hers, trying to keep his kiss light against her lips until her fingers clenched against his chest. He deepened the kiss, slipping his tongue past her lips to taste the sweet nectar of her mouth. He felt himself grow hard as her hands snuck over his shoulders and around his neck and she pressed herself against him with abandon. Her mouth stoked the fire in him until it was threatening to consume every shred of self-control he retained. He growled low in his throat and spanned her waist with his hands, moving her backward until she was arm's distance away.

"Good God, Angel. I have never wanted a woman the way I want you." He saw her eyes glimmer and dismissed the notion that it might be tears. She wound her fingers around his wrists, moving his hands to circle around her.

She leaned forward and pressed a kiss to his jaw. "Mr. Chandler, the feeling is mutual," she whispered.

She leaned backward to get a better look at a commotion near the arena and, heaven help him, the movement pressed her breasts closer to his chin. He took a ragged breath, his hands sliding up her back and pulling her upright.

"If you do that again, I'm going to drag you inside and take you here and now and forget everything I know about being a gentleman," he warned, every nerve ending in his body vibrating with desire.

"And I just might . . ." He saw her face pale. "Derek, they need you." Her voice held a note of panic.

Derek moved her aside and ran to the arena with Angela right behind him. He saw the cowboy riding out of the arena, his arm clutched to his stomach, blood pouring from a fresh wound.

"Skip," Angela called. Derek barely glanced at the man as he ran toward them, the camera immediately on his shoulder.

As the cowboy dismounted and was settled on the gurney, the doctor began to inspect his bleeding hand. Blood dripped down his palm, splattering in the soft earth and forming droplets at their feet.

"Found it!" someone called from the arena and Derek saw another cowboy run toward the table. "Here ya go, doc."

Derek turned and began to walk away as the doctor slipped the top of the cowboy's thumb into a bag of ice as one of the paramedics on site helped the cowboy into the back of the ambulance. Angela paled and moved away from the cowboy, shying away from the gore. She shook her head at Skip and he backed away as they closed the doors, still filming as the ambulance pulled out of the rodeo grounds. She turned to the doctor.

"How often does that happen?"

"It's not common but it happens in the roping events. Usually it's when the roper dallies the rope around the saddle horn. The tip of his thumb can get caught, and when the rope pulls taut"—he smacked his lips together and flipped his hand up—"there goes the end of the thumb."

"Are they going to be able to fix it?" He could hear the horror in her voice. She glanced at the cowboy who'd found the digit before looking back at the doctor for his answer.

"They'll try, but there's a good chance they won't be able to do anything."

She looked at Derek and then at the cowboys around her with incredulity. He could see how it might be difficult for her to grasp the fact that no one seemed overly worried about the thumb. It was just part of the culture: a "cowboy up" attitude. Besides, it was just a thumb.

He leaned in and pressed a kiss to her cheek. "I have

to get back in the arena and finish. Are you going back to the trailer?"

She glanced at Skip, who jerked his chin toward the cattle chutes at the other end of the arena. "I can get some good shots down there, Angela, and if anything happens I'll be right there."

"Okay," she acquiesced. "Then I'll head over to the trailer and start the copy with Joe."

Joe was the last person he wanted to leave her alone with, but he didn't see that he had a choice. This was her job and Joe was her boss. He spotted Sydney heading into the trailer. "Why don't you work inside the trailer? It'll give you some quiet, and I'm sure Syd could use some help with Kassie while she starts dinner for everyone."

At her nod he felt a measure of relief. At least with Sydney present he would feel safer knowing that she would eavesdrop. Sydney was a master when it came to finding out information people didn't even know they were giving.

DEREK ROLLED HIS shoulders backward, trying to loosen up his stiff muscles. The slack had lasted far longer than he'd thought it would, and they still had one performance left tomorrow. He locked the back gate as the last contestant pulled out. What he really wanted to do was to head back to the ranch and spend a few days working on his house. Working on it always seemed to give him time and distance to put anything troubling him into its proper perspective.

Perspective was exactly what he needed right now, when every instinct was telling him Angela was "the one," but every circumstance seemed destined to drive them apart. How could a city girl and a cowboy ever make a relationship work? He knew he could never move, and the only place she wanted to go was up: bigger city, bigger stories, bigger fan base, bigger paycheck. As much as he wanted her, he wanted something that would last, and he just couldn't see past their differences. However, logic wasn't enough to stop the electrifying jolt of yearning he felt as soon as she came into view.

Angela set out plates of food on a long table for a buffet-style meal for the crew. He chuckled as Kassie reached across Sydney to grab a fistful of Angela's long hair. He saw the smile that graced Angela's face as she reached for the child, catching Kassie as she lunged before cuddling her close. She was quickly letting go of her ice queen demeanor. There was joy in her eyes now; contentment had replaced the haunted desperation he'd seen there last week. It surprised him how easily her smile surfaced now. Knowing what he did about her past, it probably surprised her too.

Kassie spotted him behind Angela and reached for him, causing Angela to turn and see what had attracted the child's attention. She flashed him a bright smile and his heart pounded against his ribs.

That is not a good sign, cowboy.

He scooped the baby from Angela's arms and kissed her cheek, making her giggle. "Hey, cowgirl. And one for you," he said, leaning down and pressing a quick, perfunctory kiss on Angela's cheek.

He didn't want it to appear too intimate with others around, but he couldn't help but touch her. Kassie watched them intently, and Derek laughed when she opened her mouth, wanting another kiss. The pair obliged the baby while the crew began dishing up their plates.

"Where're Joe and Skip?" He shifted Kassie to one side of his chest and held her in the crook of his elbow, bouncing her occasionally as he searched the faces nearby.

"Joe's by your trailer, probably pouting. He's not happy about the turn of the story but he's agreed to one more week, although he would like me to head back sooner if possible." She pointed to several of the crew seated with her father, Skip on his right. "Skip's over there with Dad. I guess they are going to share the couch in your trailer tonight, which doesn't really leave you many options again, I'm afraid."

"My truck or your couch again," he filled in. The thought of sharing the roll-out bed with her last night stirred a fire within him, again overruling the discomfort still tormenting his back. "Hmm, who's staying on the couch with me, you or Scott?"

She tipped her head and gave him a reprimanding look. "I overheard Sydney say she was heading back tonight after dinner." She allowed Kassie to grasp one of her fingers in her pudgy fist. "This one might be coming down with the same thing her cousin has." As if on cue, Kassie coughed hoarsely.

She met Derek's gaze, her eyes dark with longing. "I'm not sure what the sleeping arrangements are going to be tonight."

"Don't worry, Angel. Your reputation will be safe. Scott and I will take the couch and you can have the bed."

"I can't do that! You guys won't fit on that couch." She paused, looking as if she wanted to say something, and he wondered if she was thinking about how he'd managed to fit on the couch with her in his arms last night.

"We'll figure something out." Derek cringed at the thought of sharing any bed with his brother. He'd done it enough in the past to know it would be a tugging match for blankets. He didn't anticipate getting much sleep tonight, especially when the person he wanted to be lying next to was only a few feet away.

"Why don't the two of you take the bed and I'll sleep on the couch?" she suggested, looking pleased with her solution.

It wasn't the solution he had in mind. "We'll figure it out." He turned toward the food. "Dinner looks good." He reached for a plate and set it on the table, trying to spoon homemade pork and beans onto it without spilling on the baby in his arms.

"Here, either give me Kassie or your plate." She reached for the child, who whined and clung to her uncle. "Okay, then I'll take the plate," she laughed. "She's pretty smitten with you."

Derek smiled down at the little girl tucking her head between his neck and chin. "Yeah," he agreed. "This little girl has a special place in my heart." Angela turned and looked at him intently, as if trying to read his thoughts. He could see concern creeping into her eyes and wondered at her hesitation.

"That's sweet."

Derek didn't miss her clipped tone. "Angel," he said, reaching for her waist and pulling her close, "are you jealous?"

"Why would I be jealous?"

"Let's take our food over there," he said, jerking his chin toward his truck. "I think we need to talk for a second."

Angela dished up a plate for herself while he waited. She walked toward the truck, carrying both plates. He lowered the tailgate and she set the plates down, glancing at Kassie, now asleep in Derek's arms.

"You want me to take her so you can eat?" she asked softly, unable to keep the gentle smile from curving the corners of her lips.

"No, go ahead." He wasn't sure where to begin. He stalled, twisting the cap from a bottle of water and drinking half before setting it down. Angela played with her food but remained silent. He could tell she wanted to ask about his earlier statement but wasn't sure how to bring it up.

"I told you Scott and I didn't get along, but last year I helped Scott's ex keep him and Sydney apart. The only thing it accomplished was getting Sydney hurt, almost killed." Derek could taste the shame on his tongue, bitter and vile, and he looked away from Angela. "I promised her I'd make it up to her. That I'd never let my family down again, and she's family. Kassie's . . ."

"The part of Sydney that you *can* have," Angela finished. He could hear a note of sadness in her voice as she put her fork down. "I get it."

"No, I ... damn it." Derek tossed his hat into the back of the truck, and for the first time Derek wished for someone else to hold Kassie. "Angel ..."

"Don't call me that," Angela murmured, shaking her head and tossing those fiery waves around her shoulders.

He reached his free hand out, grasping her chin in his fingers. "Sydney isn't the person meant for me."

"Because she's with your brother?" Her eyes burned with anguish and he hated himself for causing it.

He was making a mess of this. How could he show her that it wasn't Sydney he wanted? He took a step forward and slid his fingers into her hair at the back of her head, pulling her toward him. His lips met hers with a fiery passion, burning uncontrolled as he let the dam of emotions loose. With her hands between Kassie and his chest she gasped for breath but didn't pull away from him. He hoped it was a good sign.

"It's you, Angel," he whispered against her lips. "I don't know whether it's safe or not, but I want you."

Kassie stirred in his arms. "Wait here." She nodded but looked like she might run away. "Promise me." She rolled her lips inward and nodded again.

He hurried toward Sydney and Scott, every part of him feeling exposed and raw. If he wasn't careful she was going to panic and run the other direction. He couldn't let her think she was a substitute for his brother's wife, a woman who had never stirred him the way Angela did. He wanted to protect her, not cause her more regret.

"Here," he said, sliding Kassie into Sydney's arms. "Angela said you're leaving tonight?"

Sydney looked at Scott. "I have to get Kassie home. She was running a slight fever, so Scott's going to drive me after we finish eating. I think she might have a touch of what little Blake caught."

"I should be back in time for the performance tomorrow," Scott assured him.

"Is everything okay?" she asked.

"I'm about to find out." Derek looked at his brother. "Be careful driving."

Scott nodded and chuckled. "Don't do anything I wouldn't do."

ANGELA SAT ON the tailgate of the truck. She shouldn't have bothered to wait for him to return. Nothing he said would change things. The light in his eyes whenever he held Kassie, the connection she'd seen between him and Sydney, spoke volumes. He and Scott were close, but the signs were there. Derek was in love with Sydney and she would never be more than a substitute. She couldn't be a stand-in for any man, even temporarily. Her heart ached at the thought of emotionally walking away while still physically working in close proximity for the next week.

She looked up in time to see him jogging back to the car without Kassie, and she knew he must have taken her back to her mother. A heavy sigh escaped and she felt tears beginning to burn in the back of her eyes. She closed them, willing the tears away, reached for her anger, and wrapped it around her, tucking her heart behind the chipped wall that had surrounded it before she'd allowed Derek to break through. How could he accuse her of lying about her relationship with Joe when he hadn't told her about Sydney? She was quickly turning into her mother, falling in love with a man who would put her behind his first love. She couldn't let history repeat itself.

Derek stepped between her legs, his hands drifting along her thighs. His touch burned through her jeans just above her knees, sending hot desire shooting up her legs to areas she assumed were long dead until meeting him. She fought the yearning pulsing through her body, wishing she had the strength to push him away. She clenched her fists at her sides and dug her nails into her palms, focusing on the pain in her hands and her knuckles pressing into the hard metal of the tailgate instead of feeling the agony in her heart.

"Let me try this again." His hands slid to her hips and he pulled her toward him, staring down into her eyes. "I've been jealous of my brother my entire life and it's always caused contention between us, even as kids. If he had something, I wanted it: his horse, his friends and, yes, his girlfriends." He shook his head and looked down at her lap. "I have no idea why I thought he had it so easy. I just always knew that he was the one everyone saw as a 'man' and I was the 'boy.' I hated it."

She watched Derek clench his jaw, struggling to make her understand. "But I was so immature. I was good at playing on the sympathy everyone showed me since I was the kid who never knew my parents. I got whatever I wanted. I was a spoiled brat. By the time Sydney came into the picture, Scott and I were barely on speaking terms. I wanted her because she was his. I nearly destroyed their relationship and almost got her killed."

Derek met her gaze, and she could see his eyes misting. She could read the guilt and pain in his eyes ... and the shame. She understood the helplessness of living with that sort of shame and guilt. She knew how it felt to have guilt driving every action, every decision, every breath. She wasn't sure how to remove the pain from his eyes, to help him push away the guilt gnawing at the edges of his heart now that she'd pressed him for an explanation, but she knew she had to do something to comfort him. Angela knew she was risking her own heart as she cupped his jaw between her fingers. "Derek," she whispered, joining her lips to his.

He tore his mouth from hers but remained only a breath away, his forehead pressing against hers. "I never loved her. I thought I did but it's nothing like ..." He stopped and her heart paused mid-beat, waiting for him to finish his thought. "There is nothing but friendship between Sydney and me. I am not in love with her. Kassie is special to me because she is a living reminder of the forgiveness I've received, how I can never go back to being that person. I will always put my family first."

Angela felt her heart pounding against her ribs, wondering what he'd almost said. She couldn't assume he felt the same way about her that she was realizing she did for him. But now that he'd told her about his past with Sydney, she'd seen his soul completely exposed—baring the ugliness he saw inside himself—and she had no doubts about his honesty. This man took being an open book to a new level, and she wondered if she could return his trust with her own vulnerability. Angela bit her lower lip and he groaned in his throat.

"Angel?" She lifted her eyes to meet his gaze and saw the desire smoldering in the depths. "Unless you want me to take you right here, in the back of my truck, you better stop looking at me like that."

"Like what?"

"Like I'm your dinner and you're starving." The corner of his lips curved in a cocky grin and his eyes crinkled at the corners. He was trying to lighten the mood but she couldn't help rising to the bait.

She pulled away from him, leaning backward. "I am not!"

He slid her closer until her butt was barely on the back of the truck, his hands curved around her hips. With her body fitted against him, she could feel the evidence of his desire through their clothing. Flames of longing licked at every nerve fiber. She wanted to rip his shirt off and feel his skin under her fingertips. She did the best she could and slid her hands to his biceps, bared by his t-shirt, her hands tingling where she touched him.

He gave her a grin that could have melted butter. "Yes, you are," he assured her as he leaned toward her, nuzzling his lips against the hollow behind her ear.

She couldn't help the shiver that coursed through her body and down her spine, and he chuckled against her neck. "You taste like you smell, like vanilla." His arm came around her back and she arched against him, pressing her breasts against his chest. A soft whimper of delight slipped out as his lips found the magical spot where her collarbone met her neck. Her fingers wound around the back of his neck.

He growled against her throat, his chest rumbling against her. Spirals of pleasure trailed across her breasts and settled in her stomach knowing that she affected him as much as he did her. She felt a ripple of power and ran her fingers over the front of his shoulders to his chest and over the rippled muscles of his abdomen, allowing her fingertips to rest on his waist as his lips crashed against hers again.

"Angel?"

"Yes." She smiled against his lips.

"You're making this really difficult."

"What?" She knew exactly what he meant, but she was enjoying his kisses too much to ask him to stop.

"You know *what*." He couldn't fight the grin tugging at the corners of his mouth, and he finally pulled away. "Grab the plates and hang on."

"What?" She squealed as he spun his back toward her, quickly sliding his hands under her thighs and lifting her off the truck, piggyback. "What are you doing?" She laughed, feeling like a kid as she tried to not to spill the food left on the plates.

"You must weigh a ton," he teased.

"Brave words from a man with pork and beans only inches from his head," she warned.

He hitched her up higher on his back, pretending to have difficulty carrying her, as they closed in on the crew seated around the fire pit. "Any chairs free for this nosy reporter I found back there?"

Skip and Robert laughed as he pretended to stumble from her weight on his back. Joe glared at the pair before rising and storming toward his van.

"Take mine. I've got to get going." Sydney glanced at Angela. "Unless you want to help me for a second?"

"Sure."

Angela slid from his back to follow Sydney to the trailer but Derek held her hand for an extra moment, as if it pained him to let go of her.

Sydney rolled her eyes at him. "She will be right back."

"She better be, or I'm coming looking for her."

"You two look cozy." Sydney smiled at Angela as she packed Kassie's bag.

"I think we're coming to . . . an understanding."

"Derek's a pretty amazing guy, who doesn't realize how rare he really is." Her eyes held a tenderness and Angela felt a stab of jealousy.

"What happened between you two? You mentioned it once and he told me a little, but . . ."

"You want my side?" She paused with her hands in the bag. "You know, one of these days, you're actually going to have to trust someone. You're going to have to take them at their word and stop wondering if they are lying or hiding something from you."

"I'm not," Angela began to deny. "I just . . ."

"I am married to Scott Chandler, King of Distrust. Someday I'll tell you about it. But"—she pointed her finger at Angela—"I see the same look in your eyes. You want to believe, but you're afraid to."

Angela turned away from Sydney and grabbed a few dresses from the closet. "I trust him," she hedged.

"But?" She took the dresses from her hand, dropped them into the suitcase lying open on the bed beside Kassie's, and put a hand on her hip. "Loving someone is not going to kill you. It's going to make you stronger."

"It killed my mother," she pointed out.

Sydney pulled her into a sympathetic hug, wrapping her arms around Angela. Angela hugged her back, appreciating the support of another woman as tears burned the back of her eyes. She squeezed them shut, forcing the tears away. She didn't want to admit she was afraid, but the fear bubbled up before she could squash it. She didn't want to fall in love with a man who would break her heart.

Sydney held her shoulders and drew her back to look her in the eyes. "Derek is not your father."

"I know, but . . ."

"I have never seen him look at another woman the way he looks at you."

"Not even you?" If she was surprised by her question, Sydney didn't show it.

"I'm not sure what he told you. We are friends, and he has always been there when I needed him, even if he isn't perfect. I love him but it's completely platonic. I swear."

Angela had seen plenty of people lie. She'd interviewed politicians, lawyers, judges, criminals and other reporters. She'd seen through propaganda and falsehoods from people who lied for a living or kept dark secrets hidden from prying eyes. Looking into Sydney's eyes, there was nothing but complete honesty.

Angela wound her arms around Sydney again. "Thank you."

Sydney smiled. "For what? I just want to see you both happy. And I think you make him happy." She zipped the suitcase closed and carried it to the door of the trailer. "Scott's heading right back here after dropping Kassie and me at home. Don't waste the privacy while you have it." She winked at Angela.

Chapter Nineteen

ANGELA WAVED AS she watched Scott pull out of the rodeo grounds. Mike locked the gate behind them as the sun set just past the trees, turning the sky various hues of orange and pink. It was a beautiful evening, and she felt bad that Scott wouldn't be enjoying it with his wife beside the fire the way they'd planned. Derek's arms circled her waist and pulled her back against his chest, pressing his lips against the shell of her ear, causing shivers of delight to radiate down her spine as butterflies took flight in her stomach.

"I wish we were heading home," he murmured against her neck. His words sent waves of desire over her skin, causing goose bumps.

"One more day, cowboy," she whispered, speculating on what he had in mind when they arrived back at the ranch.

Jake walked past them and motioned for Derek to

follow him. Derek growled at the interruption. "I'll be right back."

She watched the two men as she wandered toward Mike's trailer. It was too early to head to bed, but she didn't want to join the rest of the crew around the fire pit, laughing and telling stories. She saw Jake motion toward Joe and her father, who were talking with Mike near the fire.

Angela watched her father as he laughed at something Mike said before taking a drink from a bottle of water. Her father had surprised her since they'd arrived. He'd been on his best behavior, not causing any sort of commotion, and she had yet to hear him complain in the slightest. It wasn't like him but she wasn't about to question any positive change she saw in him. Maybe she wasn't the only person Mike and his crew was softening.

"DEREK, I'M TELLING you, you need to have a talk with him."

"What am I supposed to say—'Stop talking about Angela'?" Derek shook his head and shoved his hands into his pockets. What he really wanted to do was punch something, or someone. He shot a glance at Joe. "What kind of man does that?" He couldn't understand Joe's motives, even if what he said was true. Doubt crept up on him, making him wonder if Joe might not be telling the truth. Maybe she was just playing him for a fool.

"Wait a minute," Jake said, shoving Derek's shoulder and forcing him to meet his gaze. "Do you believe him?"

"No." Derek answered quickly and frowned. Did he?

His heart thudded against his ribs painfully. Why would Joe say something that would ruin the reputation of his best reporter, even if he wanted her for himself, unless it was true? Doubts swirled like smoke in his mind, but he was unable to grasp any sort of proof to dispute Joe's claims. "I mean, I guess it could be. We don't really know her."

Jake threw his hands up and turned his back. "Are you kidding me?" He spun and faced Derek. "You're an idiot."

Derek noticed a few of the crew looking at them and stepped closer to the man he'd known all his life. "You think you could lower your voice, Jake?" he growled. "I will shut Joe up. The rest of it is my business, understand? Butt out."

Jake's jaw clenched and his eyes hardened, disappointment evident in his scowl. "Yes, sir," he snapped, turning to walk away. "Scott would've taken care of this *before* it became an issue."

Derek glared at Jake's back. It was a low blow, but it had the desired effect, and he felt like a bronc had just kicked him in the gut. He let out a long sigh.

"Joe," he called.

He saw the man glance his way before sauntering toward him with an arrogant swagger, pausing to make sure Angela was watching them intently from her trailer. Derek knew she was going to grill him about this so he didn't want it to look like an argument.

"What the hell is your problem?"

Joe laughed as if he knew what Derek was about to

284 T. J. KLINE

say. "I wondered when one of these flunkies would run and tell you."

Derek was surprised by his forthright answer. "Are you trying to piss me off?"

"I'm trying to warn you, but you don't want to listen. I was hoping that maybe one of these guys could talk some sense into you."

"By calling Angela a whore?"

Robert waved his comment off. "I never said that. I just told a few of these guys to watch you and make sure you weren't falling too hard for her game."

"Her 'game' being using me to get her story?"

Joe shrugged as if the answer were self-explanatory. "I told you, you aren't the first. I've watched her do this for years. Ask Skip what people at the station call her. She's known for being callous and cutthroat."

"You make me sick." Derek fisted his hands at his sides and forced himself to consciously take a deep breath to calm down. "If I hear that you've said one more word about me or Angela, you'll wish you were—"

"Easy, cowboy," Joe interrupted, laughing out loud. "I'll leave first thing in the morning. But when things go south, don't say I didn't warn you."

ANGELA WATCHED THE two men talking. Joe looked amused, but Derek was furious. He stood rigid with his hands clenched in fists at his sides and looked ready to kill someone. Even from this distance she could see the rage building in him. When he looked her way she saw him relax, and she felt a wave of pleasure that she could affect him the same way he did her. She wasn't sure what they could be discussing, but she wanted Derek to be assured of her trust.

She turned her back on the two men and went into the trailer, grabbing her laptop from the bedroom and booting it up on her lap as she sat cross-legged on the couch. She wasn't sure how to explain it, but when Derek was near she didn't feel the need to be in control of every situation. She was learning to relax and be herself, without worrying that she'd fall short of being worthy. She caught herself smiling as she thought about Derek's arms around her waist, warmth spreading into her stomach and radiating outward.

She opened her Internet connection and checked her email. Another message from Joe, sent during the rodeo today from his phone. She didn't bother to skim the message, saving it for later. She frowned and wondered why it seemed like he was trying to sabotage this story. She knew he didn't want to see her to leave the station, but he had to realize that she wasn't going to get any promotions reporting the new hardware store opening downtown. She sighed and wondered if he was becoming more of a boss and less her friend. She closed her email and opened a search window for reports of cowboy injuries. She was shocked at how many pages were listed, far more than she'd seen in her research for animal abuse.

She clicked on the first link, a bull rider who was hospitalized for a head and face injury. The next was an interview with a sports medicine specialist about the various injuries cowboys received most often in rodeo. She clicked on a video after reading the interview and watched a montage of footage from various rodeo injuries. It was brutal, and she found it hard to comprehend what drove them to get up and head to the next rodeo. She clicked on a link that led to a page raising funds for a cowboy's family to pay for his medical bills.

The door opened and she glanced up as Derek yanked his hat from his head and ran his fingers through his short hair, sighing.

"Are you okay?" she asked quietly. He no longer looked angry, but lines were forming around his eyes, making him appear weary.

He didn't answer. Instead he tossed his hat on the table and closed her laptop, moving it to the couch beside her. He grabbed her hand and pulled her to her feet. Without giving her a chance to protest, he buried his hands in her hair at the back of her head and his lips found hers. Her fingers clenched at his forearms, trying to hold herself upright as the earth seemed to lurch under her. Derek's arm wound around her waist and pulled her against him roughly. Her breasts molded against his chest as his tongue plunged into her mouth, sweeping away any objection her mind might conjure.

His lips trailed over her jaw to her neck as she dropped her head backward. A soft whimper escaped her lips as he sucked at the sensitive flesh. Her hands slid over his arms and shoulders and she buried her fingers in his hair, pulling him closer to her. His hand slid from her back, over her ribcage, and moved to cup her breast, his thumb brushing over the skin peeking from the lace at the top of the camisole top under her Western shirt. Explosions burst in her core, shocking her with the intensity, making her knees go weak. Her surprised gasp was caught by his mouth as he kissed her deeply, fully, leaving her clinging to him. Angela heard the pop of the snaps on the shirt she borrowed from Sydney as he tugged it from her waist and down her arms, leaving her standing in nothing more than a thin camisole and jeans.

He pulled away only enough to look down at her, his gaze scorching her with his longing. Her chest heaved as she tried to catch her breath from the sweet onslaught of his kisses. Derek's finger traced the chain of her necklace to the ring, hanging just above her cleavage, her skin tingling wherever he touched. She blinked up at him, afraid to say anything for fear that he would stop.

Please, don't stop.

His hand left her hair, slid over her side to her hip, and pulled her against him, his fingers curling into the flesh of her rear. She could feel his arousal against her and bit her lower lip nervously. His breath was as ragged as hers. Derek was the first man who had breached the wall she'd built around her. She'd never desired any man before Derek. Her one experience had resulted in Joe plying her with alcohol in college to convince her to even allow him to touch her. His touch hadn't held a candle to the way Derek could light her body aflame. Only Derek could put out this inferno.

"Angel?" Derek's voice was thick and husky, his eyes nearly black with desire. "Do you want me to stop?"

She couldn't speak. Her outspoken, self-assured façade had disappeared at his touch. She shook her head and looked up at him through her lashes.

He growled deep in his chest and lifted her into his arms. She wrapped her legs around his waist as he turned and carried her up the stairs to the bed, laying her on the mattress gently. He lowered himself over her, his weight pressing her into the mattress, covering her from chest to toe with his heat. Derek's fingers brushed her cheeks and he followed the line of her lower lip with his thumb before replacing it with his mouth. He sucked at her upper lip slightly before slipping his tongue inside to mate with hers.

His fingertips trailed over her collarbone, sliding the strap from her camisole down her shoulder, and icy fire burst in her chest. She arched against him and he smiled against her lips. Bracing himself on his elbow, his fingers found the bottom edge of her camisole, sliding it up and over her flat abdomen. She shivered as his palm heated the flesh of her stomach, his fingers splaying toward the bottom of her bra. Angela couldn't help herself as her fingers found their way beneath his t-shirt to caress the heated flesh, the hard muscles flexing under her touch. She ran her hands up his sides, feeling the ridges of muscle over his stomach.

Derek pulled away from her only long enough to reach over his head and grasp the back of his shirt, pulling it off and tossing it aside. His eyes gleamed as he slid her camisole over her head, the breath rushing from his lungs. "You're beautiful," he whispered reverently.

She looked at him, a perfect specimen of manhood. He was a solid mass of muscle from his shoulders to the ridges over his stomach. She ran her fingers over him and watched as goose bumps broke out on his skin. He closed his eyes. "Derek?"

He ran his thumb over the thin padding of her bra and she felt her body respond, lightning shooting through her limbs. She bit her lip to keep from crying out.

"Angel," he whispered, laying his cheek against her stomach, the rasp of his day-old beard growth delicious against her skin. He pressed his lips to the sensitive flesh. "I need you. Real or not."

Angela looked down at him, confused by his words. Meeting his gaze, she saw the raw emotion in his deep brown eyes. She knew hers held the same yearning. She could've sworn she saw a flicker of insecurity before he reached behind her and removed her bra, tossing it aside with his shirt, releasing her breasts to his perusal.

His eyes caressed her body, from the top of her head to her hips. "You're perfect." His thumb traced the outer edge of her breast and she moaned, closing her eyes as his hand covered her and he stretched out beside her. She felt warmth flood her lower body as his mouth replaced his fingers. She arched against him again, her legs tangling with his, her nails digging into his back with pleasure.

"Please," she begged.

He smiled against her flesh, humor tingeing his voice. "Please what, Angel?" He curved one arm under her, holding her body close, his mouth trailing kisses down to her stomach. The rasp of his beard drove her over the edge as his hand slid to her denim-encased thigh. His finger caressed the center of her pleasure as he sought the button, slipping it open. "You're wearing far too many clothes."

His teeth nipped at the rounded edge of her abdomen and he grasped the jeans at her hips and slid them down her legs, his fingers gliding over her skin, tickling behind her knees and back up her inner thighs. Derek traced a finger over the edge of her lace panties, hesitating as he reached the juncture of her thighs. A tremor of anticipation shook her, even as she fought the urge to cover herself.

Derek stood, turning away from her, and he unbuckled his pants and slid them down his legs, followed by his underwear. He kicked off his boots as she watched the muscles of his backside flex and move. He was massive, and for a moment fear gripped her. She'd been with only one man, and she had bordered on tipsy at the time, but even then she'd given him only her body. That had been sex, and she'd been able to remain distant and closed off. With Derek, she couldn't separate herself. She wanted to, but she didn't want her heart involved. If she couldn't hide her vulnerability, if he saw how much she cared, he could use it against her eventually.

This was too dangerous. Panic swirled in her mind like smoke, pressing her need and desire aside in favor of self-preservation. Derek turned and looked at her, his gaze hot with lust, and her arms came to cover her breasts, tears leaping to her eyes as she tried to hide herself from him.

He dropped to a knee on the mattress and slid alongside her, turning her toward him, cupping her face in his palm. "Angel, honey, what's wrong?"

"Nothing, I . . ." She wasn't sure how to answer his question.

How could she explain that she couldn't give him anything but her body, that she wanted him to take her body but not her heart? She brought her hands against his chest between them, trying to creating some distance for her to think. Her breath hitched as she felt the shaft of him against her thigh. His fingers trailed down her arm and settled on her hip at the top of her panties.

He closed his eyes as if struggling for control. "Do you want me to stop?"

Did she? A part of her did. The ugly fear inside her wanted to run and hide behind the wall of unsatisfying, emotionally void relationships. She wanted to protect herself from turning into her mother, living for a man who wouldn't love her more than he loved himself and dying in the street because he refused to try. Her heart cried out to let go, to allow Derek to see all of her, even the ugly fear—as he had done with her—and to let his touch cure the ache inside, to let him prove all love wasn't painful or angry or self-satisfying.

"No," she whispered. Derek continued to stare at her and she wondered if he'd heard her. "I want this."

"I heard you." He closed his eyes again. When he opened them he put his finger under her chin and lifted her face to look in her eyes.

She could see the agony in his eyes, could feel the evidence of his desire between them, yet he was willing to deny himself for her. She felt the crack he'd managed to chip in the wall around her heart break completely. She had never felt so cherished. She rolled onto her back and pulled his mouth down to hers.

"I have never wanted anything more," she whispered against his lips. She meant every word.

He brushed away a tear that slid from her eye over her temple. "Then why are you crying?" His mouth found the hollow of her throat and chills raced over her flesh, her nipples tightening into tight buds against his chest.

She shook her head, unable to answer him as desire forced her fear to retreat. He sighed against her skin, his breath fanning over her breasts as he cupped one, his jaw scraping her skin.

She mewed and arched against him again. "Derek," she moaned.

He slipped his fingers over the lace at the top of her panties, lifting her hips slightly and removing them before brushing his fingers over her mound. He nipped at her inner thigh and she yelped in pain until his tongue laved the spot. Fires burst over her skin and she reached for him. Derek brushed her hands from him and she clutched the blanket on the bed.

"You're so sweet," he whispered against her skin as he slid a finger into the slick heat at her core. He groaned as he found the nub of her pleasure and she bucked beneath him.

Angela's body trembled and vibrated with . . . something. She felt as if she were straining, reaching, and unable to find what she sought. Derek's fingers wreaked havoc on her senses, and she could only cling to his shoulders. When his lips found her breast while his fingers worked their magic, she felt herself burst into a thousand shards of light and cried out his name.

Derek slid up her body, every inch of her that only moments before felt satiated now electrified and came alive again. She gasped at his erection pressed at the entry of her heat. He leaned to the side of the bed and she protested, arching against him unintentionally.

"I'm not going anywhere," he chuckled and grabbed his wallet from his pants, plucking the foil packet from within, tossing the wallet back to the floor. "Trust me, Angel. Wild horses couldn't drag me from you right now."

Derek pressed himself against her for too brief a moment before moving away, sliding the condom over himself, and returning to her side. She felt him move between her thighs and she reached for his shoulders, her entire body needing to feel his flesh against her own. He ravished her mouth, his tongue dueling with hers as he slid into her, inch by pleasurable inch, with agonizing slowness. Her nails dug into the sinewed muscles of his back, silently pleading for more.

She threw her head back, arching, his hands holding her spine as he stoked the fire within her. His mouth found the curve of her throat, licking, sucking, and drawing out a wantonness she had never known existed. She knew she would be embarrassed by her reaction to him later, but right now she could only rock with the sensation of Derek joined with her flesh and soul.

"Look at me, Angel." She obliged, opening her eyes and focusing on his face—that sexy mouth that had driven her mad only moments ago, and his eyes, nearly black with his own barely checked desire. "Don't hide from me." He drove her closer to the edge again, pulling back and slowing as she neared the precipice.

"Derek. Oh, Derek," she whimpered, needing to be closer to him.

She wrapped her legs around his hips, and her eyes widened as he plunged into her once more before she grasped his waist, crying out in pleasurable agony as she reached the heights again. Derek thrust into her, joining her waves of release, arching his back before falling, spent, by her side.

His fingers trailed over the thin sheen of sweat between her breasts and she shivered. "Cold?"

She laughed quietly. "Hardly." She laid her fingers on the scruff of his jaw. "Derek, I don't . . ."

He covered her mouth with his, stealing the words from her lips, sucking her lower lip into his mouth, releasing it with a loud pop before getting up and walking into the bathroom. He returned and lay on his back, pulling her onto his chest. She giggled and laid her head on him, sighing as she ran her fingers over his chest and his flat nipples tightened into hard buds.

"I think you're the one who's cold."

She smiled against the heavy wall of muscle. She wasn't sure what had driven him to kiss her in the first place but he'd seemed angry when he first entered the trailer. She kissed his ribcage, tasting his saltiness on her lips. She knew she should be ashamed of herself and she might regret it in the very near future, but right now, curled in the warmth of his embrace, her skin still vibrating from their lovemaking with Derek's fingers tracing patterns on her shoulder, she couldn't feel anything but adored. She wrapped her arm around his waist and wondered if all relationships were like this . . . or was Derek something special? Right now, satiated, she didn't care. That worry could wait for morning.

Chapter Twenty

_____

"Angel."

She sighed as she felt lips gently pressing against her
forehead and eyelids.

"Time to wake up. Coffee is ready in the kitchen."

She blinked and groaned. Morning already? She felt
like she hadn't slept at all. Derek's lips brushed hers
lightly and the memories of last night flooded back. A
rush of heat filled her cheeks. Had she really attacked
him during the night, climbing onto him and straddling
his hips, begging him for her release? Derek smiled down
at her.

"So you *do* remember?" His fingers slid under the
sheets and cupped the curve of her breast, rubbing
his thumb over the taut peak of her nipple. White hot
lightning seared her, and her body responded without
her consent, arching into his hand. "You are no angel,"
he teased, running his tongue over her lower lip before
thrusting it into her mouth.

She tried to scoot away from him. "I'm sorry, I can't believe that I . . ." She chewed at her lower lip, embarrassment still coloring her cheeks.

"Don't you dare apologize."

He brushed the sheets back from her naked body and his heated gaze stroked her frame as desire flooded her again. This man drove her wild. She couldn't get enough of him.

"I would make love to you right now if I had the time," he growled, pressing his whiskered jaw against her shoulder, kissing the curve of her breast before taking her fully into his mouth.

"Damn animals," she agreed, her eyelids heavy as he sucked at the flesh, flicking the nipple with his tongue and sending shivers of delight over her flesh.

"Mmm, but they need to eat." He moved over her, his knee between her thighs. His free hand grazed her hip before his finger followed the line of her pelvic bone and hesitated at her inner thigh. His denim-encased thigh brushed against her sex and she moaned.

"I wasn't talking about them," she said, twining her fingers at the back of his head. "I meant us." Her voice was husky with longing.

Derek chuckled. "Someone else can feed." He slid his finger into her wetness. Her hips bucked against him as his thumb found the spot that drove her crazy.

She crested the waves of desire, reaching for the moment when the rest of the world ceased to exist. She protested when he moved away from her, kicking off his boots and dropping his jeans to the floor. She heard the rip of foil tearing and he returned, pressing into her in one swift movement.

A sigh escaped him and he dropped his head backward as she felt him shudder. "You're like heaven . . . my angel."

He leaned forward before rolling onto his side, pulling her with him. They both realized too late that there was no mattress beneath him and fell the short distance to the floor in a tangle of naked arms and legs.

"Ow! Shit!"

Derek had broken their fall, landing with his perfectly rounded buttocks on his boots. She burst out laughing as he tossed them aside.

"Are you all right?" She tried to stop laughing, praying that nothing important was injured.

Derek glared at her and arched a brow. "You think this is funny?"

"It's hilarious." She giggled, burying her face in his chest.

He lifted her to straddle his hips and slid her down the length of him. She groaned with pleasure. *Nothing broken here.*

Cupping her breasts, Derek took her to new peaks of gratification before joining her in the heights. Afterward, she collapsed onto his chest, praying for the ability to move as his fingers traced the trail of her spine.

DEREK LOOKED DOWN at the woman on his chest and his heart clenched. He hadn't missed the conflict she fought through last night. Seeing the fear that had flooded her eyes, he almost gave in and confessed his feelings for her, but he'd been around enough to know you couldn't smother fear. She pulled away, retreating into her protective shell, and the only way to draw her heart back to his was tenderness. A night of passion wasn't worth giving up what was developing between them, even if his body was in direct opposition with his heart. Derek wondered if she regretted their lovemaking. Her body clutched him, still buried within her, and he groaned in his chest. If she did, it wasn't enough to avoid repeating their mistake several times. And he couldn't silence the pessimistic voice warning him he was making yet another mistake.

He hadn't meant for them to end up in bed last night. In fact, he'd entered the trailer furious about the fact that he couldn't completely refute Joe's accusation. As much as he wanted to believe that she wasn't using him and his family to launch her career, she'd already admitted she would do whatever it took to get ratings. The reporter he'd met at the rodeo grounds that first day wouldn't have thought twice about sleeping with a man to get ahead, but he was having a difficult time seeing that woman in the one he held in his arms.

His fingers brushed her hair back from her temples and he looked at her closed eyes, a slight smile curving her lips. As much as he warned himself to keep his distance, if only to protect his family from the ramifications of negative press, his heart had tumbled ahead, refusing to listen.

Derek knew this wasn't lust, although that hadn't been lacking. The more he was around her, the more he felt like he was seeing the real Angela—someone *she* didn't even know—and he couldn't seem to get enough of her.

"I really do have to get up, Angel," he said pressing a kiss to the top of her head.

"Do you have to?" she complained.

"Yes," he laughed, "unless you want Jake or Mike to come walking into the trailer and find us lying naked on the floor."

Her eyes grew wide and a blush crept over her cheeks. It made her look innocent and adorable. She scrambled to grab a blanket from the top of the bed and wrap it around herself as she stood up.

"Don't you dare cover up." He stood and pushed the blanket from her shoulders, his hands finding her waist and pulling her against him. He pressed a kiss to her cheekbone before moving to her eyelid and forehead.

"They could come in any second," she protested.

"The door is locked." He grinned at her as she looked up at him, annoyance written all over her face. "How else was I supposed to get you up?" He laughed and winked at her as he let go of her and pulled on his pants. "I do have a job to do today, you know. As much as I'd love to stay for this rodeo, there's one out there I already committed to."

She pursed her lips in mock anger. "Get out and let me take a shower."

He crossed the small room in only a few steps. "Woman, stop teasing me. I don't have time to keep servicing your insatiable needs."

"Out!" She pointed her finger at him, picking up a boot and tossing it toward him.

Derek caught the boot and slipped it on, laughing as

he made his way into the kitchen and poured a cup of coffee for each of them. "Cream or sugar?" he called.

"Both, please."

He heard the shower turn on and was hard-pressed to distract himself from thinking about the warm water sluicing over that perfect satin flesh. He was failing miserably, his body responding to the mere thought of the way the water would be covering her breasts, sluicing through the valley between them. He was considering sneaking into the shower with her when the handle of the trailer rattled and a knock followed. He sighed and unlocked the door, forcing his fantasies to wait until tonight when he could act on them.

Scott entered, looking exhausted. "So, what's new?" He took one of the cups of coffee Derek had poured and sipped it.

"I don't kiss and tell." Derek reached for another cup as the water stopped in the bathroom. He closed the curtain blocking the bedroom and bathroom from view of the kitchen, making sure Angela had some privacy.

"Then there was kissing?" Scott's eyes were filled with humor. "I'm sure Sydney and Jen will be happy to hear that."

Derek shot him a look of warning, unsure how Angela would tolerate teasing this morning. He wasn't sure she was ready for their relationship to be made public just yet.

"Why don't we just keep all of this between the two of us for now," he suggested as he sipped the brew.

Scott shrugged it off. "Derek, the entire crew is hoping the two of you end up together. It's good to see the fun Derek back again."

Derek frowned. "I thought it was time for me to 'grow up and take responsibility,' remember?"

"Yes, but that doesn't mean you stop living and having fun." He sipped his coffee. "You've been trying so hard to be *me* that you've forgotten how to be you."

Derek shook his head. "Do you always get this deep when you've been up driving all night?"

"I slept a few hours before I left." Scott looked up as the curtain between the rooms moved. "Morning Angela," he said, tipping his cup to her.

"Good morning, Scott. I didn't expect to see you back so soon." She took the cup of coffee Derek held out to her, her cheeks coloring.

Derek wondered if she'd heard their conversation and needed to find out where her head was, with the story and their relationship.

"Mike wants to head back to the ranch tonight after the rodeo." He caught her frown. "We'll have to rest the bulls a bit before we take off, but we would still be home by dark."

Derek finished his coffee and placed the cup in the sink. "I hate unloading the animals at night."

"It's not so bad since we put in the extra lights now." Scott yawned. "I'm gonna go catch a little sleep while you get started."

"I'll come get you in a couple hours," Derek promised. "Thanks for making it back so fast."

"We have a rodeo today, so try to keep your hands off each other and stay focused."

She'd been quiet during their discussion but choked at his parting statement. Derek patted her back.

"He's only joking," he assured her. He put his own cup into the sink and pulled her close for a kiss.

She held her hand against his chest. "Derek, we need to talk."

He frowned, noting the disapproving tone of her voice. This sounded like "reporter Angela," not the Angel he'd come to know, and he didn't like the sound of it. "We will when we get back to the ranch, I promise. But for now, can we just enjoy this?"

She glanced up at him through dark lashes fanning against her brows. How had he not noticed how long her eyelashes were?

"*This* is what we need to talk about."

He wasn't going to let her analyze what happened between them like it was research for one of her reports. He kissed her eyes closed before moving to her sweet lips, his tongue sweeping inside her mouth to taste her. She leaned into him, allowing him to draw her against him, and he felt himself go hard. Damn if this woman didn't excite him more than anything he'd ever experienced.

"We'll talk on the way home tonight." He forced himself to hurry out the door before he carried her back into the bedroom and ravished her the way his body was begging him to do.

DEREK SAT ON the gelding as the sun beat down on him. It was hot and humid and his shirt stuck to him as he glanced toward the announcer's booth where Angela waited. He heard her talking with Joe earlier about the story, trying to convince him to make it a series. She was heading to the rodeo in Folsom with them on Friday, since she had four cowboys to follow up with: one bull-dogger with a fractured wrist, as well as the bull rider with broken ribs and two bareback riders with shoulder injuries. Nothing too dangerous, but the injuries had been caught on tape when they happened, and Angela was able to interview them in the medical tent. As much as it wouldn't help her story, he just wanted to finish this rodeo without any further trouble.

His gelding hung his head as Derek untied his rope and dropped it over the saddle horn. The crew began loading the first bulls into the chutes. Through the slats he saw a commotion in the pen. The crash of a massive animal against the metal panels echoed over the loud-speaker. Derek nudged his horse to move toward the back gate to inspect the chaos.

"Jake, what's going on back there?"

"It's Devil May Care boss. He's acting like it's his first time out. He's already kicked one of the boys in the thigh."

"You want to pull him?" Scott asked as he rode up. "Is he hurt?"

"Naw, he'll just have the medic look at it. He'll prob-ably have a doozy of a bruised thigh, though."

Derek sighed, irritably. "The bull, Jake," he clarified.

"Oh, no." He waved them off. "He's fine, not a scratch on him. I think he's just cranky today because it's hot and he doesn't want to work."

Derek hated days like this. None of the animals performed well in this kind of weather, which in turn gave the cowboys more to complain about. He'd already heard from several of the bronc riders because the horses hadn't bucked as hard as they expected, bringing the scores down for those competing for national titles. These were the days when less-than-honest cowboys would break the rules, trying to sneak small electric prods or over-tightening straps on the animals to get them excited. Animals, on the other hand, became unpredictable, which lead to injuries, both animal and human. With Angela's news crew videotaping every move, it was the worst scenario for him. Derek motioned for Scott to head back to his spot in the corner of the arena across from him.

"Mike," Derek called. He already spotted Joe and Skip near the bullpens this morning, inspecting the stock closely. It made him nervous.

"I've already got eyes back here," Mike yelled as if he'd read Derek's thoughts. "Nothing illegal."

Derek couldn't shake the churning in the pit of his stomach as apprehension crept over his shoulders. The nagging premonition of trouble gnawed at him as he sat on his gelding at the far end of the arena while the bulls were shuffled into the bucking chutes. He watched several cowboys straddling the top rungs of the chutes, slipping ropes to the side of the bull while their traveling partners hooked the rope underneath the bull and helped them get their knots right. There was nothing amiss, and he frowned watching the first cowboy settle over his left arm, his right holding the gate in a light grip. At his nod, the bull burst from the chute, immediately turning right and coming down on his front feet. Derek knew the bull and saw that he wasn't bucking the way he usually did. His normal routine was to buck hard and straight. But after a few turns, the bull stalled and remained still. The crowd groaned and the cowboy bumped him with his heel. The bull jerked a bit but refused to move.

The announcer cracked a joke about the bull being stubborn and proclaimed that the rider would be allowed a re-ride. Derek cringed, knowing that would run the rodeo longer, especially if several of the bulls acted this way due to the heat. There was a slam of metal gates, and one of the cowboys jumped from inside the chute to the top rails. He glanced at his brother across the arena. Devil was already a difficult bull to ride, one of the best in the nation, but if he was unpredictable, it could be dangerous. Scott shook his head and gave him a thumbs-up sign.

The next two bulls came out and performed well, but both riders were green, coming off well before eight seconds. The bull in the arena, a stubborn red beast, wouldn't exit when Scott and Derek rode behind it, so Scott tossed a loop around his horns, guiding him back to the open gate leading to the holding pen behind the chutes. Dropping his rope, he let one of the crew pull it from the bull's horns in the safety of the pen and grabbed another through the fence.

Devil had finally settled down in the chute and Derek went back to his corner, hoping it was a good sign that the rest of the rides would go smoothly. As Devil's rider climbed onto his back, scooting forward over his arm,

Derek glanced up at the announcer's booth where Angela was deep in discussion with Skip, pointing at the chutes. He had to get her out of his head and concentrate.

The rider shifted and jerked his head, signaling his readiness. The chute gate slammed open and cowboys on the ground scrambled out of the bull's path. Derek breathed a sigh of relief when he saw the rider had worn a protective vest and helmet. Devil bucked hard, unlike the bulls ahead of him. His legs jerked into the air as he twisted before coming down on his front feet with a jolt. Derek had never seen him buck this hard and fast. The animal jerked his head, gearing himself for another twisting jump as the rider rocked back and forth, almost laying against Devil's back as he kicked high behind him. The buzzer sounded and the crowd cheered for the ride. The cowboy threw his leg over the bull's head, coming off clean but dropping to his knees from the impact.

Derek and Scott hurried closer as the bullfighters rushed in, distracting the bull as the cowboy jumped up and climbed the chain link fence on the side of the arena. As the clown ran, the bull followed, dropping his head and charging. The clown dodged the animal's attack, sticking his tongue out at the bull to the delight of the crowd. As the bull moved closer to Derek, he formed a loop with his rope and tossed it over the bull's horns, guiding him toward the gate ahead of Derek's gelding. Devil jogged toward the gate and Scott hung a short distance behind him.

Without warning, Devil stopped, snorting loudly. Derek shook the rope, allowing it to slap against the bull's back slightly. Devil turned on Derek suddenly, kicking his back heels, charging Derek's horse. Derek kicked the gelding in the side as it spun to get away from the massive beast, and Derek dropped the rope. As the bull charged, the horse kicked out, connecting with the bull's shoulder but causing the gelding to stumble and fall to its knees.

Derek knew his horse was going down with the bull still loose in the arena. He shoved himself out of the saddle as he felt his gelding's shoulder hit the soft dirt. His mind ran through several scenarios in seconds. It wasn't the first time he'd come off his horse in the arena, but it had never happened in a situation this dangerous. If he could reach the panels he'd be fine, and Scott could get the bull out with the help of the clown.

He crawled away as quickly as he could and heard the clown yelling at the bull, trying to get his attention. He glanced over his left shoulder as he leapt up onto one of the empty bucking chutes to see his gelding up on his feet and running past unharmed. He breathed a sigh of relief, since it was his best pick-up horse.

"Derek!"

Scott's voice reached him just as he saw the massive creature barreling toward him from the right. Devil slammed against his thigh, knocking him from the gate. Pain blasted through his leg as he hit the ground and the bull came at him again. Fighting the black tunnel sweeping over his vision, he scrambled on his hands and knees to get away from the infuriated animal, one leg dragging behind him useless. The bull ducked his head and crashed into Derek with enough impact to toss him several feet into the air. He hit the ground with a thud that was far less painful than the impact he'd just endured from the solid skull of the beast. He wanted to move his limbs, but they refused to cooperate, and inky blackness swirled at the edges of his vision. Flashes of color were in front of him, and he realized it was their rodeo clown, teasing the bull away from his trampled body. Fighting to remain conscious, he saw the bull chase the clown toward the barrel just before Scott blocked the rest of the arena from his sight. He heard several other cowboys hurry into the arena, forming a line the bull wouldn't challenge. Seconds later, the bull exited the arena.

Scott leapt from his horse's back, dropping the reins as he hurried to Derek's side. "Don't move."

"I don't want to," he groaned.

"Get the ambulance," Scott ordered Mike. "Quick."

Before he could finish, the back gate was already opening and the ambulance was driving through. Derek glanced up at his brother and saw the worry.

"It's fine, Scott, I can feel my hands and legs. I just don't want to move because it hurts." He started to laugh and coughed. "Crap, that hurts," he clutched his right side.

Medics rushed to his side with the backboard, moving past the crowd of cowboys surrounding him. Derek wasn't about to let them take him out on the board. He was sure he'd broken a few ribs and knew there was a chance his leg was broken, but he was walking out of this arena, even if he needed help to do it.

"Help me up." He waved Scott to his side.

"I think you should stay on the board and let us carry you out. If it's a broken rib you could puncture a lung," the medic warned, giving Scott a pointed look, "or worse."

"I am *not* going out of here on that thing." He waved the medics off and forced himself into a seated position.

Pain exploded through his side and he couldn't catch his breath. He clenched his jaw as he looped his arm around Scott's shoulder. Jake hurried to his other side and helped lift him to a standing position. Derek gritted his teeth, a groan slipping from his throat, as they carried him toward the gate quickly. The announcer hyped the crowd, calling for a cheer, but the pain enveloped him, muffling the sound as if it were coming from the end of a long tunnel. Spots danced in front of his eyes as they exited the gate, and he caught a glimpse of Angela already in the medical tent, waiting for him. She looked horrified, and tears coursed down her cheeks.

"Grab him!" Scott yelled at a nearby cowboy. "He's slipping."

I will not fall.

The thought came just seconds before his vision closed in and everything went from gray to black.

HER HEART FELT as broken as his body looked. The cowboys crowded around Derek in the medical tent, blood and dirt covering his handsome, pale face. She could barely look at him, focusing instead on the medics as they moved swiftly to stabilize his condition. It reminded her too much of the night when her mother lay in the streets and she sat helplessly beside her until the ambulance arrived to transport her to her final moments. When she heard the second ambulance arriving at the rodeo to transport Derek to the local hospital, she wasn't sure she couldn't do this. Could she endure watching him risk his life each weekend? It was selfish, self-preservation at its worst, and she despised herself for it. The thought of watching Derek die paralyzed her.

"Angie, aren't you going with him?" her father asked quietly, reaching for her hand.

Panic flooded her, and she couldn't catch her breath. "No," she whispered. She caught a glimpse of Skip with his camera focused on the trauma unfolding in front of him, and she felt sick to her stomach.

Angela ran for the trailer. She locked herself inside as tears began to fall, coursing down her cheeks. Sobs wracked her body as she reached for the necklace at her throat, recalling her mother's last moments: the ambulance driver offering to let her ride with her mother, the blood soaking through her clothing, her father on his knees on the sidewalk with his eyes silently pleading. Her entire life she'd blamed her father for the fact that she hadn't been with her mother in her last moments, but it hadn't been his fault. She'd been too afraid to go with her mother. She'd run and hid, like she was doing now, because she couldn't face the pain and loss. Instead, she lived with the guilt and regret.

She stood, forcing her fear to retreat. She couldn't do it again. Angela couldn't live with the shame of not being with Derek. She loved him too much to abandon him when he needed her most. She might not be able to promise him forever, but she could be with him now. She hurried outside, tears blurring her vision, in time to see the ambulance pull away from the arena, lights flashing silently. Moments later, the siren sounded in the distance as it rushed toward the hospital.

In the midst of the activity, she hadn't noticed the final rides finishing while other cowboys from the crew filled in as pickup men. Scott saw her approach and brushed past her on his way to the arena. She looked away, swiping at the tears of disgrace slipping down her cheeks.

"Is he going to be all right?"

He stopped and spun to face her, loosing his anger. "Now you care? He needed you and you weren't there."

"You don't understand." She wasn't sure she understood either.

"You're right, I don't. But I think you forfeited the right to ask." He clenched his teeth, trying to control his temper, and scanned her with his eyes. "I guess we were all wrong about you."

She didn't have to ask what he meant by the comment; she knew. Silvie and Sydney had warned her. They were a close family, bound by strong bonds of loyalty and trust. She'd proven unworthy of that trust. She wanted to apologize, to explain her actions, to tell Scott that she loved his brother, but he wouldn't even look at her.

Scott shook his head and mounted his gelding, which was tied at the back gate of the arena. "You've got your story now, so I guess nothing else matters." He didn't give her an opportunity to respond, leaving her staring after him.

"Guess this didn't go the way you planned, did it, Gigi?"

She turned to see Joe leaning on the railing below the announcer's booth. He was the last person she wanted to see. "Not now, Joe."

He shook his head, sympathetically. "I get it. You're upset." He walked down the last few stairs and pulled her stiff frame into his arms. "I'll head back with Skip. We've already edited a few commercial spots and teasers to run this week." He tipped her chin to look at him. "Go back with them and make sure he's okay. Finish this and we'll run your story next week. I'll call you tomorrow."

"Thank you," she whispered. She hadn't expected this compassion from him, but she appreciated it. Maybe she hadn't been fair to him. Maybe he was her friend after all. Right now, he might be the only one she had left.

Chapter Twenty-One

ANGELA RODE BACK to the ranch with Scott in silence. She knew he was furious at her, they all were. Mike had barely glanced her way before they left, but she'd seen the disappointment in his eyes. How could she tell them that she was more heartbroken by her choices than they could ever understand? Only her father had looked at her with pity, as if he understood the disgrace and guilt she felt.

"Scott?" She had to make him understand the pain Derek's accident had dredged from the depths of her past.

He ignored her, clicking on the radio and turning it up, making it clear he had no interest in conversation with her.

A country break-up song filled the cab and his hands squeezed the steering wheel, the knuckles turning white, giving away his emotional state. Angela bit her lower lip, wondering if she dared to push him to listen, when a commercial echoed through the truck.

"This week, Channel 12's Angela McCallister investigates rodeo and the stock contractors who sustain this brutal sport. What may seem like harmless fun for spectators is anything but for the animals dying to entertain," the announcer bellowed. "Watch our four-part series, beginning Monday. You may never go to another rodeo again."

Scott reached out and turned off the radio, the hatred in his eyes scorching her, and she moved farther toward the passenger door. "Nothing really matters as long as you get your story, right Angela?" Bitterness dripped from his voice even as it remained calm—too calm.

Angela's heart dropped into her stomach. Joe had lied to her. He'd ignored the story she'd worked on and used her connection with Mike to take video of what he'd wanted, twisting it to make Findley Brothers look like villains. How could she even defend herself to Scott? She'd already lost their trust because of her treachery against Derek, they would never believe she didn't have a part in this.

She had to find a way to kill this and prove to Derek that he mattered more to her than any story.

DEREK HEARD THE hushed voices amid the beeping and whooshing of various machines and cringed. He recognized the sounds of a hospital but wasn't sure why he was there. For a couple of measly broken ribs?

He tried to turn his head but realized he was already braced up and lying on his right side. Pain gripped his chest as he tried to take a breath, and he could only groan.

"Derek?" Sydney moved around the bed and in front

of him. "Oh, thank God!" She hurried to the door and called for a nurse.

A nurse rushed into the room and checked his vitals before informing him that she would notify his doctor.

"What happened?" he croaked. His voice sounded weak and he wondered how long he'd been out.

"You have several broken ribs from that bull, but then someone even more thick-headed refused to be carried out of the arena and punctured his lung." She frowned at him. "Did you really have to act so macho?"

He gave her a weak smile and winked. "Cowboy up."

She glared at his attempt at humor. "Yeah, well, that just incapacitated you for the next six weeks. Jen and I were worried sick about you, you jerk." Sydney rolled her eyes at him.

Great, we have five rodeos scheduled for the next six weeks. How am I going to cover those now? Way to let the family down, Derek.

"Angela?"

A shadow crossed her eyes and she frowned. Derek knew that look and it wasn't good news.

"Where is . . ."

"Mr. Chandler, it's good to see you awake. How are you feeling?" Derek looked at the woman, who appeared younger than he was, as she laid a clipboard on his bed. His questions about Angela would have to wait, but not for long. He would get some answers from Sydney.

"Can't breathe," he struggled to get even the few words out.

She nodded. "That's to be expected. You need to try to take slow, deep breaths. You did puncture your right lung, but we were able to aspirate so you will most likely go home today. You're going to need plenty of rest and no strenuous activity for at least six weeks." She pulled a sheet of instructions from her clipboard. "These will give you a few other suggestions, but take ibuprofen for pain, 800 milligrams, and icing your ribs will help any swelling. Lying on the ribs will help as well. Most importantly, take deep breaths at least every hour." She smiled at him and folded her arms over the clipboard. "You're pretty banged up, but you were lucky."

"Thank you, doctor," Sydney said.

The doctor looked her way before looking back at Derek. "Any more questions for me? No? Then I'll send the nurse in to take out your IV and start getting you ready for discharge."

Derek nodded as the doctor exited and turned back to Sydney. "Angela?" He wasn't letting her run away.

ANGELA STARED AT the boxes on her bed. She couldn't stay at the ranch. She needed to find a way to rectify this situation, but she couldn't expect Mike's generosity when they suspected her of lying to them. She packed her meager belongings and needed to inform her father to be ready to leave.

She probably should have left last night, but she couldn't bear the thought of leaving without seeing Derek one last time. She had to know he was all right, and no one but Silvie seemed inclined to speak to her. How could she explain her decision to leave, at least until she killed the story? She worried that Derek wouldn't believe her, either. Why should he? The very thing she'd set out to do had happened and she'd as much as incriminated herself from the beginning with her talk of ratings and anchor positions for controversial stories. How could she have ever been so blind as to even consider selling her soul for a future she never really wanted, sacrificing relationships and the lives of others to further her own?

There was a knock at the door. "Come in, Dad."

"It's me." Silvie poked her head around the door.

Angela fought the tears that sprang to her eyes. Had it been anyone else, she could have reached for the bitter anger that seemed to surround her heart since Derek's accident as she shouldered a new guilt and shame. Silvie had only looked her way with sympathetic eyes.

"What's all this?" Silvie looked around at the boxes at the foot of Angela's bed.

"I think it's better if I leave. I need to somehow get this story off the air and I can't do that here."

"Hmm, I see." She sat on the side of the bed and folded her hands in her lap. "Have you told anyone else?"

Angela smiled sadly. "No one else is talking to me."

"So, about this story?" There was no note of condemnation or judgment in her question, but Angela felt shame smother her and turned her back on Silvie.

"I don't even care about the story. And the story they're airing isn't mine." She met Silvie's gaze, praying the woman would believe her.

"Then why in the world would you leave?"

"I can't stay here, Silvie. Everyone thinks I've lied about it and used Derek to get information."

"Have you?" Silvie's gaze was intent, but held no blame.

Tears sprang to Angela's eyes. "I care about him, Silvie. I never meant to, but I do."

Silvie smiled and wrapped her arms around Angela. "Aw, Angie, I know that. So does Mike." She ran her hands over Angela's head, soothing her like a mother would her child. "Don't worry. We'll fix all of this and you don't need to go anywhere. Besides, I need your help."

"Me?" Angela pulled away from the housekeeper's comforting embrace.

"Well, everyone else is going to need to do more work since Derek will be laid up for six weeks. Clay and Scott will have to run the rest of the rodeos with Mike. Jen will be doing double duty around here, and Sydney will be at the rodeos, so I'll be taking care of both babies and Derek. That's an awful lot for an old woman like me."

Silvie's eyes gleamed and Angela recognized a guilt trip when she heard one. It might have worked flawlessly if it hadn't been for the fact that staying would mean falling even further in love with a man who thought she'd used him. Her heart lurched against her chest at the thought of seeing him today.

Angela shook her head. "I can't. I just . . . I can't."

Silvie pursed her lips. "I see." She brushed her hands over her thighs and stood up.

"I have to stop this story from airing." A tear slipped down Angela's cheek and she swiped at it quickly.

"And you can't do that from here?" She tilted her head to the side. "Don't you think he deserves to hear your side directly from you?"

"Yes," she whispered.

"Then why are you really leaving?"

"Because I can't lose him." Silvie looked at her, thoroughly confused. "I can't face him when he looks at me and believes the worst. He'll believe I lied, Silvie . . ."

Silvie laughed quietly and patted her shoulder. "Honey, you're not going to lose that boy. I raised a smart man, and he's so head over heels for you that nothing would make him believe that."

"Silvie, you don't understand. When I first came, I *was* using him, all of you," Angela admitted, hating the woman she'd been only a short time ago.

Silvie laughed out loud. "We knew that, too. You're not nearly as sly as you think you are." She tapped Angela's cheek. "Life is full of unplanned and unexpected moments. Some good, like falling in love when you least expect it, and some"—she paused as she touched Angela's necklace—"well, some aren't so good. But you get through the bad times because the good times are worth fighting for."

She stood and headed toward the door. "I've seen the way you look at that boy. And I've seen the way he looks at you. If you give it a chance, it will be worth any bad you face because you'll face it together."

THE TRUCK PULLED down the driveway and Derek cursed every divot and pothole in the gravel, holding a hand to his ribcage. He glanced over at Sydney. "Why are you being so close-lipped about Angela?"

"She's at the ranch, for now."

"What does that mean?" He wasn't sure if she sounded bitter or disappointed. While it disappointed him that she hadn't come to the hospital, it hadn't surprised him. He knew she still hadn't dealt with her mother's death, hadn't even gone to the hospital then.

"According to Scott, she's planning on leaving." Sydney's declaration shocked him from his thoughts.

He clenched is jaw tightly, frustrated that she couldn't give him more than a few words at a time. "Did she say why?"

"The story is ready to air." Her voice was tense and he could tell she wanted to say more but was refraining.

He was tired of this game and stared out the window. This wasn't like Sydney, so he knew something was wrong, and it obviously involved Angela. He turned his mind back to the morning they'd spent together, just before he'd gotten hurt.

We need to talk.

He'd promised her they would talk that night, but they'd never had the opportunity. She'd sounded so somber at the time, and he'd been late to get ready for the rodeo so he hadn't wanted to talk. He wasn't ready to hear her regrets over what they shared the night before. Was that why she wanted to leave now? Or was Joe right, and now that she had her story, she had no further use for him?

ANGELA STARED OUT the window as Sydney's truck pulled into the driveway, watching from a distance as

Scott and Clay helped Derek out of the car. Mike grabbed the small bag the hospital provided from the backseat as she saw him disappear onto the porch beneath her. Had anyone spoken, she could have heard every word. Instead, the strained silence was deafening.

She looked back at the boxes by the bed. She should have taken them down to the car already, but after her conversation with Silvie, she felt guilty for leaving. She heard the awkward clunk of clumsy steps on the staircase as her phone rang. She glanced at the screen and saw Joe's number. As much as she needed to talk with Derek, it might be better to let him get settled into his room. She bit her lip, refusing to entertain the thought that she might actually be stalling, hoping that she'd convince herself to stay at least one more night.

"Yes?" she answered. She hadn't figure out how to kill the story yet and was waiting on a call back from Skip. She had to know what part he'd played in falsifying the footage. Joe didn't know she'd heard the advertisement.

"I haven't heard from you. How's your cowboy doing?"

She felt the bite of suspicion in her belly. "I guess that depends."

"Is he still in the hospital?" She could tell he was trying to lead her into a discussion about Derek, and she wasn't about to let him manipulate the conversation. She didn't want to talk to him about Derek, or the fact that he'd nearly died.

She feigned boredom. "I guess."

"You guess?" She could tell by his voice he wasn't buying her act. "Your new 'boyfriend' is knocked from his horse and almost gored, and you don't know if he's still in the hospital?"

"He is not my boyfriend. Why would you care anyway? It sounds like you have your *story* after all." She spit the words out like they were venom.

"Skip got some great footage. He showed me some of the raw clips last night. It's great!"

So, Skip was involved. She felt bile rise in her throat and her stomach clenched at the thought of watching the footage of Derek's attack. She swallowed, disgusted by the enthusiasm she heard in Joe's voice and the pleasure he was taking in the brutality of it.

"So, you can head back now. The story will air Monday."

She hated the arrogant tone of his voice and wondered if he was more pleased with his falsified story or because Derek had been hurt. "So I hear. I heard your teaser on the radio."

Joe grew quiet, and she could almost feel his tension mounting through the receiver. He cleared his throat. "That was done before you changed your story. We can change it. But you need to get back here, Gigi."

"I have another week's vacation time coming. You have your story."

"They don't like you being gone this long, Gigi. They're talking about . . . never mind."

"What? What are 'they' going to do?" She didn't even care about holding back her temper any longer. "And who is 'they,' Joe? Are you sure you don't mean *you*? I'll be back when I get back, and the more you push, the more I'll think about taking *my* story, the *real* story elsewhere." She ended the call without waiting to see what he might say, hoping he wouldn't call her bluff and fire her.

DEREK COULDN'T HELP but hear the conversation through his closed door. It wasn't like Angela was trying to be quiet, but he knew he should have at least tried not to listen. He glanced at his brother, who had remained in the room after Jennifer and Clay headed downstairs, pretending to ignore the conversation they could all hear.

"What do you think that's about?"

"We both know what it's about." Derek tried to take a deep breath but grimaced and reached for his side, scooting into a more comfortable seated position against the headboard of his bed. "Are you mad at her too?" Derek knew that his brother didn't trust easily and wasn't sure where he stood on Angela now.

Scott frowned and shrugged. "I'm not sure."

"If I'm not mad, why are you?"

"How are you not mad?" Scott shook his head. "You really don't think she used you, or us?"

He couldn't help the agony worming into his heart, squeezing at his chest worse than any pain in his side. The entire conversation they'd overheard could be a ruse, but he wouldn't know until he saw her. He wanted to reserve any judgment until then. "It's what I've worried about since she first wanted to interview Mike. But my gut tells me she's being honest."

"Yeah, well . . ." Scott shook his head, not finishing his thought out loud. Derek didn't need him to. He knew exactly what Scott was thinking—this wasn't the first time his gut was wrong.

ANGELA STEPPED INTO the hall as Scott closed Derek's door quietly behind him. He looked up, meeting her eyes, and she could easily read the hostility in them. His jaw clenched as he brushed past her without a word and headed down the stairs. She stared at the door, desperately wanting to talk with Derek, to see him less broken than she had at the rodeo, to rid herself of the image of his beaten and bloody body that had haunted her.

Her hand fell on the knob, but she pulled it back as if the metal were molten. She couldn't face him yet. She had to make some decisions before she saw him. Regret choked her, stealing her apology for avoiding the hospital. Her chest constricted, squeezing the breath from her lungs, and panic began to creep in. She pressed her hand against her chest, trying to still the pounding of her heart against her ribs. She needed air.

Her boots clapped against the wooden stairs as she hurried out the front door. She wanted to run, but there was nowhere to hide that wouldn't make her think of Derek. She looked for somewhere she wouldn't be forced to face the judgmental eyes of his family, where she could allow her burning tears to fall freely. She caught a glimpse of her father in the main aisle of the barn, pushing a wheelbarrow. The shock of seeing her father doing

326 T. J. KLINE

manual labor was enough to shake the panic threatening to overtake her.

"Dad?" She started toward the barn, ignoring the slam of the screen door as someone exited the house behind her. "Dad?" she called again.

He turned as she reached him and a wide smile split his face. She couldn't remember her father ever being this happy or smiling as much as he had since bringing him to the rodeo, unless it was induced by too much alcohol. "Angie-girl, I was wondered where you'd disappeared to once we got back."

She furrowed her brow, trying to figure out why he was cleaning stalls. "I was packing. We're leaving remember? What are you doing?"

He wrung his hands around the pitchfork nervously and frowned. "We need to talk." He sat on the bales of straw near the stalls and patted the spot beside him. "Mike offered me a job and I think I'm gonna take it."

She opened her mouth, but he wouldn't let her speak. "I know what you're gonna say, and you're not wrong. I haven't been the best father. In fact, I've been a terrible father."

"Dad . . ." She wanted to disagree with him but couldn't bring herself to argue with his honest assessment.

"Mike and I talked a lot at the rodeo last weekend. It's time I let you live your life and I need to take care of myself. I haven't had a drink since you bailed me out." He glanced at her to gauge her reaction, but she could see the glimmer of pride in his watery brown eyes.

Angela bit her lip. She'd been so caught up with Derek

and her story that she hadn't even realized her father had been sober. It was the first time he'd gone so long without drinking since she was a child, before her mother died. Tears of shame filled her eyes. She hadn't even noticed, had barely given him a thought other than making sure he wasn't causing trouble. She'd been relieved to have someone else take the responsibility from her shoulders.

"I didn't even realize," she muttered, swiping at the tears on her cheeks.

"Angie, it's okay. You aren't supposed to be watching my every move. I've let you take care of me for far too long. I forced you to grow up and be the parent. That wasn't fair to you." She saw the tears mist his eyes. "I'm so sorry, Angie-girl. But I'm going to stop drinking and be the man I should have been a long time ago."

She should have been proud of the change in him, should have been excited for his future, but she felt the anger lodging in her throat, trying to burst forth in a storm of uncontrolled fury at the unfairness of it all.

"You can stop because Mike talked to you?" She rose from the bale of hay. "No amount of begging from me or tears from Mom ever made a difference to you but when a *stranger* says something you can quit?" She pushed him backward with her finger in his chest. "Mom died because you couldn't stop drinking and stop fighting with her."

Rage flooded her chest, tears slipping down her cheeks to the dusty concrete floor. She could see the pain her words were causing, but she needed to purge the misery that haunted her childhood. Because of his weakness, she'd been trapped in a life of guilt and shame and loss.

"I grew up without a mother or father. I've had to fend for myself since I was eight. A child shouldn't know how to cure a hangover at ten."

"Angel, I know . . ."

She clenched her teeth together, turning her back on him. "Don't call me that. Mama called me that." Her eyes burned with tears that wouldn't stop falling, even as she willed them to cease. "You don't get to call me that."

She felt his hands on her shoulders as he turned her and pulled her into his embrace awkwardly. The fight left her and she realized she was trembling.

"I know I don't deserve you. I never have." He smoothed a hand over the back of her head as she gave in to her tears, letting the sobs wrack her body. "I didn't deserve your mother, either," he muttered. "It was my fault, all of it. I felt guilty because I couldn't give her the life she deserved. All she wanted was for me to love her, and I was so blinded by my guilt it drove me to the bar and her into another man's arms. When I found out, I chased her out of the house. It was all my fault."

His words broke through the haze of her pain. "What?" Angela pulled away from him. "Are you saying Mom had an affair? How dare you!" She shoved him away from her.

"You don't remember?" He looked confused. "Craig confessed to me at the bar that night, how he'd been there for her when I wasn't and how they were in love." He shook his head with recriminations. "I don't blame her, I never did. I was never there for her. But I was drunk and so angry when I found out. I went home and made accusations. You came out of your room just as she ran out the front door and . . ." His words trailed off.

"Uncle Craig?" She saw the flash of loathing in his eyes before it was replaced by anguish. "That's why he . . ." As much as she didn't want to believe it, the pieces were falling together to form a picture she'd never imagined. She took a step back and ran a hand through her hair, pulling on it in an attempt to clear her head.

"He's your father, Angie," her father whispered.

She looked back at him with disbelief, shock robbing her of the ability to speak. Was it possible her mother had an affair? How could he have lied to her all these years? She thought about each time she'd been called by the police to bail him out of jail, the many nights she'd drug him from the bar and put him to bed. "You're not my father?" she whispered.

"I'm sorry, I couldn't bring myself to tell you. Not after . . ."

"My mother died because of you and I didn't even get to say goodbye to her because I stayed to take care of *you*," she accused, reaching for the ring on the chain at her throat. "You think an apology will make it better? I lost everything that night."

He stared at the ground. "I can never make it right, Angie. I can't give you back your mother but I can give you the truth and your freedom. You deserve to live your life without worrying about me, to find someone who will love you, who you *can* love. I'm so sorry."

Tears clouded her vision. Years of wasted time, lies, and desperation. She should have left years ago, lived a life filled with happy memories and hope and love instead of the recriminations and responsibilities that haunted each sunrise. Her breath came in ragged gasps as she curled her fingers around the ring, feeling her nails digging into her palm, the biting pain fueling her anger. "It's not enough; it will never be enough."

"Angel."

Derek's voice broke through her fury like a bucket of cold water and she spun to face him. Her brow furrowed with worry, and she saw him grimace in pain as he walked toward her.

"You're not supposed to be . . . You need to be in bed."

"Don't say anything you can't take back." He reached his hand out, his fingers cupping her cheek, his thumb brushing her jaw. She could read the compassion in his eyes. "Regret is a painful partner."

She knew all about regret. "You don't understand what he's done." She glared at the man she'd thought was her father.

"I heard." He glanced over her shoulder at her father—Robert—behind her. He pried her fingers from the ring and twined his fingers through hers. "We all have regrets—you, me, Robert. Come back inside with me."

"You followed me out here?"

Derek must have stood silently, knowing she would need him, in spite of the pain his injuries must be causing him.

He stepped closer, moving between her and her father, cupping her face between his hands and pressing his forehead against hers so that she could look only into his

forehead against hers so that she could look only into his face. "I promised you we'd talk once we were back here. Let's go have that talk."

She felt his breath against her lips, warming her, drawing her back to the present instead of reliving her painful past. She nodded, afraid if she didn't go with him hate would take over, poisoning her soul.

reminded her of that, so that she could hold on to the
face. "I promised you we'd take one . . . we'll look back
. . . we'll have that talk."

She felt his breath against her lips, warming her,
drawing her back to him, giving her the gift of living, but
punishing her, too, because she knew she couldn't hold
him, that nothing would soothe his grief . . .

Chapter Twenty-Two

DEREK'S RIBS FELT as if they were being crushed in a
vice. He shouldn't have followed her downstairs, but
when he heard her footsteps, he worried she was leaving.
He'd known that Mike had offered her father a job and
that he'd accepted, but it was supposed to be a blessing in
disguise, to keep her close.

Derek ran his fingers through the long red waves that
fell over her shoulder as she lay against his left side with
her hand on his stomach, away from his injured ribs. He
held her while she cried, until her tears were spent and
she'd fallen into a deep sleep. He glanced down at her as
her lashes fanned over her cheeks, still red from crying.
He heard her breath hitch from the sobs that had shaken
her small body.

He'd held her wordlessly as she purged the grief she'd
never allowed herself to feel over her mother's death and
the betrayal she felt at her father's hands. *Not her father,*

he reminded himself, and wondered if Robert had confessed the truth to Mike.

Now he understood why she'd balked when he called her Angel, knowing it was a reminder of her mother. He didn't want to cause her more pain, but he didn't feel he could think of her any other way. She was his Angel. Maybe he should let her leave, move on to a bigger station, and help her put some space between her and Robert, giving her a chance to enjoy her freedom. His heart lurched painfully at the mere thought. He'd never felt the need to protect a woman the way he did this one. Somehow she'd grasped his heart and he couldn't let her go. This need he felt for her scared him.

Her fingers curled against his abs, and he stifled a groan as desire rushed through his blood. He hated himself for his lack of control and inhaled sharply as she woke slowly, her breasts pressing against his side. Her breathing changed, growing shallow, and he knew she was awake.

"Ready to talk?" His fingertips feathered over her forehead. He saw the tears mist her eyes again as she bit her lip.

"I shouldn't be here," she whispered, looking up at him.

"Here on the ranch or with me?" She didn't answer and he could see the agony in her eyes. "With me," Derek answered his own question, swallowing the lump forming in his throat and pressing his lips together. Joe's accusation haunted him, but he didn't want to face the truth of it.

She sat up on the edge of the bed, pulling away from him, and cool air filled the space between them. He wondered if it was from the air conditioning or the chill in her demeanor. She ran her fingers through her hair and looked backward at him over her shoulder.

"I need to go home." Her tone was flat and he couldn't read her thoughts. She'd disappeared behind the cold façade he thought had crumbled already. "Especially now. I can't stay here with him."

Derek didn't have to ask who she meant. "Angel, we both know you can't turn your back on him that easily. If you didn't do it already, you won't do it now."

She stood quickly. "You have no idea what I've been through. For nothing."

She took a step away from the bed but stopped as his fingers circled her wrist. "He's your father."

She laughed bitterly and the sharpness in her voice pained him. "Apparently, he's not. Didn't you hear?"

"He's the man that's raised you." Derek struggled to rise from the bed. "Even if he's done a poor job of it. Everything you've gone through has made you the woman you are today. If you've stayed and cared for him through all he's put you through, does knowing any of this really change how you feel about him?"

"No," she whispered. He ran his thumb over the pulse racing at the inside of her wrist and heard her breath catch, her eyes darkening with slumberous desire. "Derek," she whispered.

"Please come back here." He pulled her toward him on the bed. "I can't stand that long."

She allowed him to draw her back to his side as she sat on the bed beside him. He slipped an arm around her stiff form. "Relax," he encouraged. "I'm not going to bite." He gave her a wicked grin. "Unless you want me to."

She sighed and started to rise again. "I'm only kidding," he promised, holding her to his side, ignoring the pain the movement caused. He tucked her head against his chest under his chin, his fingers trailing over her spine. "I know this came as a shock. But you don't have to hurry off because of Robert. I'll send him to work over at my place. You won't have to face him until you're ready."

She glanced up at him. "You'd do that for me?"

"Of course I would." He pressed a quick, chaste kiss to her forehead. He inhaled the sweet scent of her and wanted to do so much more.

She sighed against his throat and he felt white hot desire plunge to his groin.

"I have to go back. Something is going wrong with the story. I'm just not sure who is to blame."

"Do I get two guesses?" Derek asked. She glanced up at him. "Since he couldn't get you to give up the story, Joe is going to do whatever it takes to get you away from me."

She leaned backward and looked up at him. "I told you, there is nothing between us. That was a long time ago and even then . . ." She shook her head before laying it against his chest.

"Angel, you have no idea your power over men," he

said quietly. "Just because you don't feel anything for him doesn't mean he feels the same. That man wants you. It's in his eyes every time he looks at you, and I don't think he's planning on giving up easily."

He heard the jealousy in his voice but couldn't seem to help himself. He needed to gain some control because if there was any chance that she was still using them, or playing him for a fool, he didn't want her to know she was taking his heart along for the ride as well.

"I'm sorry I didn't go to the hospital, Derek. I panicked, and when I came out the ambulance was gone." Her words spilled from her and he knew she was telling the truth.

His heart clenched, a stab of pain radiating through his chest, and he held his breath, waiting for her to finish. "You have no idea how scared I was."

As afraid as I am that I'm about to lose you, Angel?

His fingertips grazed her temple and cheek. "Of what?" She shook her head, burying her face into his chest.

"Angel, you interviewed a lot of those cowboys. They all said the same thing. It's not *if* you'll get hurt, it's *when*."

She pressed her lips together tightly. "I know."

"That includes us. This was sort of a freak accident, but it's just a few broken ribs. I'll be back out there next week."

She lifted her head to look at him. "You will not." Derek arched a brow but refrained from arguing with her.

Angela pulled away from him, sitting up on the bed. "You were lucky, Derek. It could have been so much worse.

You were lying there so pale, bleeding everywhere." She ran her fingers near the cut on his cheekbone where he'd needed four stitches. "I don't think I can watch you kill yourself."

"Angel," he whispered, curling his fingers at her neck and pulling her down so their lips met, "I'm not going to kill myself."

He tried to contain his passion, to kiss her gently, reminding her of their night together, of the shared vulnerability and how they had complemented one another, but once their lips met he couldn't suppress the longing he felt for her. His tongue swept into her mouth, dancing with hers, igniting a fire within him.

ANGELA HADN'T EXPECTED his kiss, although she hadn't thought about much else since their night together. She'd wanted to explain why she couldn't stay on the ranch, but once his lips touched hers, all logic and reason was lost. She could barely remember her name as his good arm pulled her against his chest, trapping her arm between them with her free hand on his stomach. She desperately wanted to touch him but was afraid of hurting him. He groaned and shifted, rising above her, leaning on his elbow, and she worried about his ribs. His right hand found her hip and he gripped her, his thumb trailing under the hem of her shirt.

"You're hurt," she reminded him.

Derek slid his hips between her thighs and pressed kisses along her jaw. She felt his arousal pressing against her thigh. He gave her a rakish grin and ran his tongue over her lower lip. "I'm just fine, obviously.

"Angel, the other night," he began as he pressed kisses down the side of her neck. His hands slipped under her shirt, his palm spanning her stomach, burning her skin with the intensity of his heat. "I'm sorry if I pressured you."

She cupped his face in her hands. "You didn't." She shook her head. "We didn't do anything I wasn't ready for." His fingers slid over the lower edge of her bra and she gasped as lightning flickered over her skin, igniting the tinder of her emotions.

"And what about now?" He looked down at her while his thumb continued to trace tantalizing lines of fire over her flesh, chasing away any fear or worry about the future.

"I need you, Derek," she whispered.

She wasn't sure she could stay and watch him put himself in harm's way, wasn't sure if her heart could stand to see him hurt, or worse. But she was certain that she couldn't walk away from him, not tonight. Not when she could see the desire in his eyes or hear the passion making his voice husky. Not when his hands were scorching her flesh with his desire. Silvie's words came back to her. Derek was one of the good ones worth fighting for.

She arched, her back curving to press her breasts against his seeking fingers, and he slid the shirt up her sides. She pulled it over her head and threw it aside as he unsnapped the closure of the bra with one hand.

"Talented," she teased.

"I try." When she was exposed, she watched his eyes light up with reverence. "You are the most beautiful woman I've ever known." His lips found the skin of her stomach before he laid his cheek against her heated flesh.

She wanted to argue with him, to point out the ugliness she felt inside, the pain and bitterness and betrayal, but even when she showed him a glimpse, he brushed it aside. He made her feel beautiful and cherished and loved. She pushed the thought away. He couldn't possibly love her, not after the way she'd abandoned him. Even if he didn't love her, she loved him. She blinked back her tears as his lips kissed the curve of her breast, his tongue blazing a trail over the tight nipple.

Her fingers curled against his neck as she pulled his head toward her, needing to feel his lips, to lose herself in his strength. Derek had far more than she'd ever hoped to find in a man: goodness and strength and loyalty. All things her father had never been for her or her mother, and he offered it all to her with complete disregard to himself. He had no idea how broken she felt, how helpless to let go of her need for control, or how courageous he made her feel, willing to love him in spite of her fears.

She clutched at his shoulders, her fingers digging into his flesh, desperate to touch him. Reciprocating her need to touch and be touched, he pulled away from her long enough to grab the back of his t-shirt, pull it over his head, and throw it aside. She almost sighed as her fingers slid over his skin, the ridges of every muscle taut under her hands. Angela whispered his name as his hands fondled her, his lips and teeth nibbling at the sensitive flesh of her neck and collarbone.

The metal of his belt buckle pressed into her hip painfully but she didn't care; it was a reminder of the pain she had caused him. She wanted to stay with him. The word *forever* floated though her mind like mist on a spring morning. She brushed it aside, unsure if they could have a "forever." He would continue supporting his family, and, thanks to Mike, she was no longer responsible for the man she'd been raised to think was her father, since he was attempting to stand on his own two feet.

Her future had suddenly become uncertain. She was free to go where she wanted, do what she wanted, with no one to worry about but herself. She felt the desperation that had clung to her heels for so many years lose its grip.

"What are you thinking about?" Derek asked, looking down at her. "You're here, but you're not here."

A smile spread over her lips. For the first time in her life, she was exactly where she wanted to be: in the arms of a man who cared about her, free to pursue her career without the weight of her father's mistakes hanging over her head and threatening her. She trailed her finger down his chest, her hand lighting on his uninjured ribs.

"I'm thinking about how quickly you seem to heal." She leaned forward, her lips meeting his in a kiss that warmed her to her toes.

"You're lying," he murmured against the base of her throat. "But if it puts that smile on your face . . ." He slid his hand to the button of her jeans. "I can think of a few other things that might make you smile," he said, tugging at the material.

She laughed as he tried to unbutton them with one hand. "Not so talented now. Need some help, cowboy?"

She popped the button loose and unzipped them. Derek brushed her hands away, sliding his one hand over her hip bone and between the material and the lace underwear she wore, his fingers curling into the muscle of her rear. He groaned deep in his throat, and his shoulders shook as he pressed her hips against his, sliding her jeans over her thighs. She heard his quick inhale and realized the movement must have hurt his ribs.

"Wait." She slid from under him carefully and instructed him to sit on the edge of the bed. "Let me help."

She wiggled out of her pants, watching his eyes darken with desire as she removed her clothing for him, making her feel powerful and feminine at the same time. It was an alien feeling, and she doubted that anyone but Derek could have made her feel this way. She kneeled between his thighs and reached for his buckle, pressing a kiss to his chest and feeling the muscles contract beneath her lips. She pulled the buckle and unbuttoned his pants, removing his boots and encouraging him to stand so she could remove his jeans and underwear. She was careful of the massive bruise on his thigh where he'd been hit by the bull's skull. He stood in front of her in his naked glory and she couldn't help but stare at him, his desire for her evident. *Dear God, this man is magnificent.*

He gave her a lopsided smile. "You have more clothes on than I do." His eyes flicked to her lacy panties. They covered next to nothing. "Enough games, Angel." He wrapped his left arm around her waist and pulled her against the hard wall of his chest. "I'm in pain and it has nothing to do with my ribs."

He backed her toward the bed until her legs hit the edge and lowered her onto the mattress, kneeling before her. His fingers found her breasts, teasing them into tight peaks, and she bit her lower lip to keep from crying out as desire and delicious pain swirled within her. His hand slid up her calf, tickling the sensitive flesh behind her knee before he kissed her inner thigh. His hands skimmed over her thighs to her hips, his fingers hooking on the edge of the thin lace before pulling it down her legs.

His breath was hot against her, fanning over the most intimate recess of her. She gasped as his mouth found her, his fingers creating a storm within her that raged out of control.

"Derek, wait," she panted, pleading with him, her fingers digging into the blankets on the bed.

"This is what you do to me, Angel. This is how I feel." He continued his tender assault on her, his tongue flicking, his fingers devastating her senses. She knew she had lost control of her response to this man as she plunged into the oblivion of ecstasy, her release washing over her as she trembled. Derek stood, reaching into the table beside the bed before lying on the bed beside her.

He allowed his finger to trail between her breasts, and she shivered, goose bumps breaking out over her heated flesh as she tried to slow her breathing. "You're the most beautiful woman I've ever seen, Angel."

She felt the blush creep over her body, flooding her cheeks, but she couldn't deny her pleasure at knowing he found her beautiful. She bit her lower lip, wondering if he realized how deeply she felt for him, or that he had somehow slipped past the massive wall that had been built around her heart the day her mother died. She loved him. There was no use denying it, hiding it, or pretending it wasn't true. This was more than desire.

She wouldn't ask him for more than he'd already offered her, nor could she speak the words to him. But she could open her heart to him in an attempt to *show* him. Wherever that led, she vowed she would follow, even if that meant pain or loss.

She pressed her lips against his chest, curling her arm around his waist. "I need you," she whispered against him. It was as close as she could admit to him right now.

Derek looked down at her and kissed her forehead, her eyelids, and the tip of her nose before taking her lips hostage. He moved away only long enough to tear the foil package and roll onto his back, placing the condom over himself. She took the opportunity to carefully swing her leg over his hip, straddling him.

His eyes closed and he moaned as she touched him, feeling the hard strength in every part of his body.

"Woman, you are evil," he ground out. He guided her, arching his hips, slowly impaling her on his shaft.

Her head fell back with the pleasure of it. He rocked against her as she rode him, her nails digging into his left side as she tried to be careful of the injuries on his right. Derek's hand snuck into her hair as he pulled her down to ravish her mouth with his tongue. She leaned over him, her hair forming a curtain, hiding them from the world, creating a place of privacy where only their ravenous need for one another existed.

As they found their release together, she collapsed on his chest. He inhaled sharply and she scrambled to move off of him. "I'm so sorry."

"Angel, don't you move," he ordered, holding her against him. "My ribs will never hurt so badly that I want you to move." He kissed her, the touch gentle and languid.

She tucked her head under his jaw, inhaling his unique scent, and then heard her phone ringing in her room.

"Do you want to get it?" he asked.

"I don't ever want to move."

"Good." His hand trailed over her spine lightly. She felt herself relaxing in his arms, dozing in and out of consciousness, feeling completely safe. "Angel?"

"Hmmm?" She tried to open her eyes, but exhaustion won over her will to relish every moment in his arms.

"Are you leaving?" She thought she shrugged her shoulders, but she wasn't sure. "I'd like you to stay," he clarified. "I think I love you."

"Mmm," she murmured and curled one arm around his neck. "I love you, too," she whispered just before sleep completely claimed her.

"I DON'T KNOW what she's planning to do, Joe." Robert had always tolerated Joe, but the demanding questions and details about his daughter's plans were getting aggravating. He was beginning to hate how this cell phone gave Joe instant access to reach him. "She's a grown woman. I don't have the right to demand anything from her."

"When I suggested you tell her the truth, you were supposed to tell her to come back here," the voice in the phone growled. "Are you trying to ruin everything?"

"She deserved to know the truth, and I know you don't agree, but she deserves to be happy. I think Derek Chandler is the best thing that's ever happened to her."

"You've been drunk most of her life. You don't know her or what she needs." Joe's voice had taken on a note of frantic desperation. "Are you sure she's even there? She's not answering her phone."

Robert didn't need the reminder about what a poor excuse of a father he'd been, and it only served to make him dislike Joe a bit more. "She's in the house. When I see her, I'll tell her to call you."

He considered deliberately forgetting about the message, but the longer Angela remained away from the news desk, the more burdensome and demanding Joe was becoming. This was beginning to border on obsessiveness.

"Don't bother. Did you put that vial into the refrigerator in the barn Angela told me about?"

Robert thought about the vial Joe had given him at the rodeo and decided in that instant to give it to Mike instead. He might have known Joe longer, but Mike had earned his loyalty. The way Joe had been acting was starting to worry him.

"Sure," he lied. "But I don't know why . . ." The call disconnected in his ear.

Robert tossed the pitchfork into the wheelbarrow. He pushed the tools into the corner of the barn, near the bales of straw piled almost to the ceiling. He didn't want to think about Joe, but something in his voice sounded off—more irate than this situation should warrant. He needed to find Mike and let him know about what Joe was planning and how he'd asked him to plant drugs on the premises to frame them.

Chapter Twenty-Three

THE NEXT MORNING dawned bright, but Derek didn't mind the sunlight filtering through the blinds. He'd been dreaming about waking with his Angel in his arms since their first night together at the rodeo. Jen and Sydney's voice carried from the kitchen, sprinkled with giggles from one of the babies. He wondered if he and Angela would still come over to have breakfast with everyone once his house was finished. Derek stopped mid-thought. He knew he thought of Angela as his, but there wasn't any sort of permanence to their relationship.

There could be.

He curled around her back, his legs curving around her rear. Derek hardened as he kissed the back of her neck. He'd told her he loved her last night and she'd said the same. Why shouldn't they make it permanent?

The smell of her tempted him, tantalizing his senses and making him want to fill himself with her. He inhaled deeply, memorizing the mixture of vanilla, peaches, and sunshine that was uniquely his Angel. He brushed his thumb across her breast, smiling against her skin as the nipple tightened to a peak. She sighed, arching her back as she stretched, waking slowly.

"Time for breakfast, and it smells like Silvie has the coffee brewing for you," he pointed out, knowing how she hated mornings. He kissed the arc between her shoulder and her neck and chuckled as goose bumps broke out over her skin. "Cold?"

"Not exactly." She rolled over, their legs twining, and he knew she could feel his arousal against her. She kissed his chin before flicking her tongue to lick the rasp of his jaw.

"Evil Angel," he growled, rolling so she lay beneath him. "I have to work today."

Her brow furrowed. "But your ribs . . ."

"I'm fine," he assured her, ignoring the twinge of pain that came with every breath. "There is plenty to do that won't require physical work. I'll call the contractor out to work on the house more since I'll have time to meet him out there now." He pressed his lips to hers quickly as his stomach growled loudly, and he climbed off the bed. "Feed me."

He pulled on the jeans he'd tossed to the floor the evening before and turned to look at her still twisted in the sheet. It was far more see-through than she realized, and she presented a tantalizing picture. He considered climbing back into the bed with her when he heard a door slam downstairs and his brother's voice. Derek sighed. *Time to get to work.*

"Should I ask Sydney or Jen to bring you up something?"

She glared at him and he laughed. "I'm getting up," she groused, pulling the sheet so that she could wrap it around her body as she searched for her clothes. "I hate morning people," she grumbled.

"You're so cute when you're grouchy in the mornings." He laid her bra and shirt on the edge of the bed. "Would you like me to get you some clothes from your room? Or I could cover the hall for you while you sneak in there?"

She shot wide eyes toward him. "You don't think they know, do you?"

He laughed. "Of course they do." The corner of his mouth lifted. "You aren't exactly quiet."

She couldn't have stopped the adorable blush that flooded her cheeks if she'd tried. He pulled a clean t-shirt over his head and pulled her into his arms, his hands at her hips, and kissed her thoroughly. "You have the look of a woman who's been completely satisfied."

Angela frowned, her lips forming a thin line of disapproval. "Watch the hall and make sure no one comes." She clutched her clothing to her chest.

The knock at the door froze her mid-step, and she stared at him like a deer caught in the headlights of an oncoming truck. "Derek, can you tell Angie that there's a news van coming down the driveway?"

Her blush returned. "I'll do that," he called back.

The furrow on her brow deepened. "They already think I'm using you."

"Are you?" he asked, getting right to the heart of the matter.

She lifted her chin defiantly, but he could see the hurt in her eyes. "Do you really need to ask me that?"

Derek waited until the footsteps receded from the hall. "I thought Skip went back to the station."

"I have no idea who it could be. Or why they are back."

"I overheard your conversation yesterday. I'm assuming it was with Joe."

She scooted closer, wrapping her free arm around his waist and looked up at him through her thick lashes. "Derek, open book? I promise, I don't know."

She looked vulnerable and frightened. Derek slid his finger through the ring on the gold necklace. He wanted to trust her completely, but Scott's words and his past mistakes gnawed at the edges of his mind, holding him back. She knew the pain of betrayal better than most people ever could. Maybe if he could twine her heart with his, even if it was nothing more than desire right now, she would think twice before turning her back on him. He had no doubts that her need for him was real.

Derek curled his hand around the back of her head and kissed her. He poured his heart into the kiss, praying she could hear his declaration without speaking it. When he broke the kiss they were both short of breath. He pressed his forehead against hers.

"I get the feeling you like me a bit, Angel."

Her eyes were dark with desire but they sparkled with humor. "Maybe a little. Now, go make sure there's no one in the hall so I can get dressed." She shoved him toward the door.

Derek opened the door and checked the hall, finding it empty. Stepping across the hall, he opened her door and stood at the top of the stairs. "Angela, there's a news van coming down the drive," he said, loud enough for everyone downstairs to hear.

She glared at him as she hurried across the hall into her own room. "Go," she mouthed, waving a hand at him.

He laughed and leaned forward as she scooted past him, stepping on the back of the sheet dragging on the floor. She realized too late as she dropped her clothing at her feet and stood just inside her doorway, completely nude.

"Good morning, Angel," he drawled.

She spun, giving him an eyeful of gorgeous satin-skinned woman before slamming the door. "Jerk!"

He chuckled. Her voice carried through the door as he headed down the staircase, knowing she would be furious when she came down but that the view had been absolutely worth it.

"MORNING." DEREK WINKED as she made her way into the kitchen in clean jeans and a t-shirt. He held a cup of coffee out to her, and she took a tentative sip.

"Good morning," she muttered as the others took their seats around the table and began dishing up their food.

Sydney tore tiny pieces from a plain pancake for Kassie and dropped them on the tray of her high chair while Jen fed Blake a bottle. Both glanced her way but without their usual friendliness. Neither Scott or Clay said anything.

Silvie tried to alleviate the palpable tension in the room and rubbed Angela's shoulder. "Sit and eat," she ordered.

"I'm going to see who's here," she said, heading for the front porch.

They probably thought she was trying to escape, and she was, but she wanted to know who Joe sent out and why. He already had the footage they'd taken at the rodeo, and he would be editing the first part of his bogus series. She held the mug between her hands and eyed the van as it came down the long driveway and parked in front of the house. Joe climbed from the driver's seat.

"Hey there, Gigi." He bounded up the porch stairs and leaned toward her as if he was going to kiss her cheek, stopping short. "What? You're not happy to see me?"

He was the last person she'd thought would dare set foot on the ranch. She sipped her coffee. "What are you doing here, Joe? I told you yesterday I won't do that story."

His lips thinned to a sharp line and he arched a brow, his eyes glittering with outrage. "I am still your boss." His voice took on a threatening note. He might have appeared calm, but she could feel the animosity radiating from him. He crossed his arms over his chest, daring a retort from her.

She accepted his challenge, taking a step closer to him. "For now," she replied quietly. "I wonder what the studio would say if they knew you were threatening your reporters and falsifying stories."

"What the hell is your problem?" he asked through clenched teeth, grasping her elbow and dragging her down the porch stairs toward the van.

Coffee sloshed over the side of her cup and onto her hand. "Ow!" she said, shaking her hand and jerking her arm from his grasp. "Let go of me."

She saw her father standing in the open doorway of the barn watching them. Worry creased his brow before he disappeared inside again. She was tired of feeling alone, of no one protecting her. She spun on Joe. "I am not a child. I will come when I'm ready."

"What the hell has gotten into you since you decided to take this story? You've changed." He looked her up and down disdainfully. "Wait, I *do* know." He glanced toward the house. "How many of these cowboys are you sleeping with?"

"You're disgusting." She wouldn't give him the satisfaction of letting him know his insult had actually stung.

Joe shrugged. "Look, there's nothing wrong with slumming, I guess, but I came to save your ass. The station wants to fire you."

She felt the blood drain from her face. Joe didn't look like he was bluffing. Even knowing she didn't have to be responsible for her father—for *Robert*, she corrected—she still needed a way to take care of herself. She bit her lower lip.

"You are going to come back with me today. If you don't, we'll run the story without you."

She glared at him but didn't miss the determination in his eyes. There was no pretense. "Don't threaten me."

He grasped her chin between his thumb and first finger. "Oh, it's not a threat, sweetheart. I'm making you a promise. If you don't come back with me, you'll be fired and I'll run my story. The one filled with sex and lies and how a reporter buried a story of animal abuse in rodeo because the stock contractor seduced her. I have plenty of reporters who will sit at that desk and report anything I tell them to."

He cued up a video on his phone and she watched the clip showing a cowboy's wrist as he gave steroid shots to the bull that had attacked Derek. Other footage showed barbs slipped into the fleece lining used on bucking horses and bulls. It never showed faces but it didn't need to. With copy stating the name of the contractor, it would destroy Findley Brothers. "Where did you get this?" Horror flooded through her limbs, weighing her down. "Skip?"

He crossed his arms and leaned on his shoulder against the van, smirking with his perceived victory. "Please, Skip isn't smart enough to manage this."

"You drugged those animals? That was why they acted that way." The pieces began to fall into place with an ominous thud. "You drugged them and nearly got Derek killed."

She glanced toward the house and saw Derek and Scott step onto the porch, watching her.

"You better decide what you're planning to do before they come over here. If you don't come back with me, I'll destroy them and you. You won't have a career left when I get finished."

"I thought you were my friend," she whispered.

"I thought you'd eventually come to your senses and realize that we belonged together. I never pegged you for a tramp. I guess we were both wrong." He narrowed his eyes, looking through the passenger window at the brothers standing on the porch. His anger snapped and he grasped her wrist, yanking her toward him. "You barely let me touch you after years of friendship, but you whore yourself for him in a matter of days?" She saw Derek start toward the stairs and Scott put a hand on his shoulder, stopping him. She could see the pain even that movement caused him. He was in no shape to fight Joe right now, even if Joe wouldn't be a match for him under normal circumstances.

"Angel?" Derek called.

"Isn't that sweet?" Joe whispered, laughing viciously. "Angel?"

"Let me go." She jerked her wrist from Joe's grasp and took a step backward so she could see Derek. "I'm fine, we're just talking." She tried to make her voice sound light, but it sounded strained. If Derek came over here, she was afraid he'd end up with more than a few ribs broken. She turned on Joe. "You can't do anything. You have no proof."

A sadistic smile spread over his too-thin lips. "Who needs proof? All I need to do is report it. People will believe anything they see, true or not. But you're wrong, I have proof, right here on their own ranch. It's your choice. You can destroy your own career and take them down with you. Or you can come back, renew your contract, and we'll do your story about injuries in rodeo. He can come out a hero and you stay with me. Either way, you'll say goodbye to your boyfriend."

She wanted to slap the overconfident expression from his face. How could she have ever thought he was a friend? Or that he would help her? She wondered how many times she'd trusted him to talk with the executives at the station on her behalf. How many times had he sabotaged her stories to keep her stuck in the newsroom, under his thumb? Joe didn't care that all of this was completely untrue. He only wanted her, to bend to his will again. And he'd found his bull's eye in Derek and her feelings for him.

She glanced back at Derek. This morning, waking in his arms, she realized that she couldn't leave him, in spite of her fears. Being without him would be like going without air. But Joe had her trapped with nowhere to turn. Derek's family, this legacy to them, meant everything to him, and he meant everything to her. If all he loved was ruined because of their relationship, he would never forgive himself. She couldn't let Joe destroy what this family had built—even if it meant ripping her heart out and leaving him behind in order to protect him.

"Fine," she whispered. "I'll go get my things."

"Oh, and *Angel*," Joe began, grabbing her jaw between his thumb and finger roughly, "this stays between us or deal's off. I almost killed him once. I'll make sure to do it the second time." He kissed her, crushing her lips against her teeth.

Joe followed her as she walked around the van, into the sight of the men on the porch. Mike and her father had joined them, both looking concerned for her welfare.

"Hey, Robert." Joe greeted her father cheerfully, ignoring the other men entirely.

Her father looked away. Angela didn't have time to worry about him. She wanted to get Joe away from the ranch, away from Derek, as quickly as possible. She deliberately avoided walking past Derek and went to the back door, through the kitchen. She put her coffee cup in the sink.

"Did you want breakfast?" Silvie asked, looking at Joe. "I could warm it for you both."

"No thanks, Silvie," Angela assured her. She hurried up the stairs to her room with Joe following closely. She wasn't sure if it was better to have him with her to keep an eye on him or to send him back to the van while she packed. "Do you really have to follow me?"

"I'm not letting you out of my sight for a second, *Angel*. Who knows what you might try to pull."

"I'm not the liar here," she said in hushed tones.

They entered her room and he closed the door behind him, cutting her off from any safety. She'd never been truly afraid of Joe before, but today he'd proven he was completely unpredictable.

The door opened with a crash. "What the hell is going on?" Derek's eyes flashed with fury, turning them completely black. He looked at Joe. "Get out."

"I'll leave when she's ready to go."

Derek took a step closer, and Joe's smug grin faltered. "You will go when I say. Now get out of my house," he ordered.

"Go wait at the van," she muttered to Joe. Joe shot a glare at Derek, clearly not happy about being forced to leave. "Fine, but remember, Gigi, our conversation was confidential. One misspoken word could derail your entire story."

As if she didn't understand his warning the first time. How could she convince Derek she wanted to leave with Joe when the mere thought was splintering her heart? "Get out," Derek warned through clenched teeth, "before I throw you out the window."

Joe shoved past him and Angela saw the flicker of pain in his eyes as Joe jarred his ribs. Derek shut the door behind him. He didn't speak as he watched her lift her boxes onto the bed. "What are you doing?"

"I'm leaving." She tried to appear nonchalant through the tears that were threatening to choke her. "They need me back at the station."

"I thought you were following up with some of the cowboys this weekend."

She busied herself with the boxes to avoid looking at him. If she did, she would break down. "I might make it to the rodeo, but I've got to get the copy ready and edit the first night's footage. They need me to . . . ."

Derek reached for her hand and pulled her into his arms. "*I* need you."

She had expected his anger or his hurt, but she hadn't expected this confession. "I . . . I have to go. It's my job."

Derek cupped his fingers at the back of her head, tipping her chin so she was forced to meet his gaze. His thumb traced the line of her jaw as she stared up at him. His eyes softened as he looked down at her. "Angel, I'm not sure how, but somehow you and this beautiful smart mouth have worked your way under my skin. I can't let you go."

"Derek," she began.

She looked at the door, worried that Joe could be standing outside listening. Before she could say anything else, his lips found hers, making her forget everything. His tongue slipped between her teeth and dueled with her own. It wasn't like the other kisses they'd shared. She could feel his desperation, and her response was filled with the grief and sorrow flooding her soul.

She tasted her salty tears on their lips, mixing with desire. She pulled away from him, turning her back toward him so he couldn't see her cry. "I'm leaving. I came for a story and I have it."

"You're saying that last night and this morning, you lied?" Derek's voice sounded dubious. "And that's all you're leaving with, your story?" She swiped at the tears on her cheeks as he grabbed her waist, spinning her so she faced him. His thumb brushed away the moisture under her eye. "You know you're leaving with more than that. I love you, Angel. I didn't know it was possible to feel this way about anyone in this short of a time, but I do."

"I *have* to go." She wanted to tell him she loved him, to let him see how her heart soared at his declaration. But

360 T. J. KLINE

she couldn't allow Joe to destroy his family with his lies. She couldn't figure out any other way than to go back and report her story instead of Joe's fake one. She hoped that someday she could tell him the truth and Derek would forgive her and understand that she had done it to protect his family. "I don't want to, but—"

"Then don't." He made it sound so simple. It wasn't simple. She'd run every scenario though her head on the way upstairs. "Is it your father?"

His question surprised her. "It's not him. I know I have no right to ask you this, but can you and Mike watch over him? He wants to please Mike, and I've never seen him want to please anyone before." She was still angry at her father, his betrayal stung, but she worried what would happen to him now, without her to watch over his habits and to bail him out of trouble.

"Angel, you can ask me anything." Derek brushed his knuckles over her cheek. His eyes turned as hard as stone. "It's Joe."

She heard the anger rising in his voice and saw his shoulders tense. She couldn't look him in the eye and lie. She dropped her forehead against the strong wall of his chest, content to draw from his strength for a moment. She could hear his heart beating against her ear, and she wanted to melt into his embrace and let the sound of his heartbeat block out the voices in her head, which berated her for her selfishness for wanting to stay. She wound her arms around his waist.

"Do you want to stay?"

"Yes, but I can't, Derek. I have to clear up the mistake

with the story." She couldn't take Joe's threat lightly. He'd almost killed Derek the last time. "If I don't go back, I'll lose my job."

His arms stiffened around her. "Then you'll come back after?"

She looked up and cupped his face in her palms, loving the feel of his raspy jaw against her skin. She pressed her lips against his and lost herself in his kiss.

DEREK KISSED ANGELA back. His arms tightened around her, causing his ribs to twinge with pain, but he ignored it. If she walked out the door, she wasn't coming back. She didn't have to say the words, he knew in his gut something was wrong. Derek couldn't shake the suspicion there was so much more to this situation. The tears brimming in her eyes, the fear he'd seen on her face, all indicated that she was worried about far more than simply returning to the newsroom to report a story. If that were the case, all he had to do was call her and they could see each other. This rang with a finality he couldn't explain.

She wouldn't look at him, hadn't responded the way he'd expected when he told her he loved her. He knew she cared about him; she'd admitted it last night as she fell asleep. But he wondered if he were a fool for believing a slumberous declaration if she couldn't say it in the light of day. Every nerve in his body was on edge, vibrating the way they did when a lightning storm approached. Trouble was brewing, he could feel it, but he couldn't figure out how to stop it. She pulled away from him with a tortured groan.

"I have to go," she insisted as she reached for a box and headed out the door, leaving him no option but to follow her down the stairs.

"Okay," he agreed, deciding to take a different approach. "Then I'll call you tonight."

"No!" She spun to face him on the stairs. "You can't."

She sounded horrified, and he'd never heard this tone in her voice before. "Why not?"

She sighed and hurried out to the van. The blood drained out of her face when she saw Joe waiting for her. Derek could almost feel the despair radiating from her as she loaded the boxes into the back of her car and rushed past him to grab another. He couldn't let her leave with Joe. He saw his brother and Robert standing on the porch. Scott waved him over as Angela headed back to her room.

"Provoke him. He's blackmailing her."

Derek looked at Joe leaning against the white van beside the car, gloating. He would kill him.

"We have proof, just be careful." Scott nodded at Robert who pulled out his cell phone, holding it at his side, out of sight.

Derek didn't need the details. The fact that this snake would threaten Angela was enough to rile him to violence.

"What the hell did you say to her?" Derek said, approaching Joe.

"Just reminded her of the truth, pal." He pushed off

the van and stepped up to Derek. He was either extremely brave or knew about Derek's ribs, giving him overconfidence in his abilities to fight Derek right now. "I tried to warn you that she'd use you. You wouldn't listen. But, hey, thanks for the great story."

Derek held his hands up, taking a step backward so that he was no longer chest to chest with the smaller man. "You seem awfully sure that's what she's doing. But maybe she isn't, and you can't stand it that she chose me over you."

"Cowboy, I'm warning you. You better take another step back or someone is going to get hurt." Joe stepped forward and punched Derek's chest.

Derek grimaced as pain exploded through his ribs. Stars danced in his vision as he fell to his knees. He heard the box hit the porch.

"Stop, please!" Angela ran down the stairs toward them.

Derek felt the second impact from Joe's foot against his jaw.

"I warned you." Joe laughed breathlessly as he took a step back.

Angela shoved Joe away from Derek as she kneeled by his side, coming between them. "Scott!" she yelled. His brother rushed to his side, helping him stand while Robert walked toward them, his cell phone pointed at the group in plain view.

She spun toward Joe. "What is wrong with you? I'm packing the car. Can't you just leave? I'll be at the station tonight." Angela turned to look into Derek's eyes as he struggled to breathe. She didn't take her eyes from Derek's face. "Are you okay? We need to get you back to the hospital."

"You know, this video should come in handy if you decide to press charges, Derek," Scott commented with a laugh.

"What video?" Joe looked from one face to another and spotted the phone in Robert's hand. "Robert?"

"I've seen you manhandling her enough. I'm not letting you blackmail her, too," Robert warned.

"Well, isn't that heroic coming from a lying drunk?" Joe reached for the phone but was surprised when Robert deftly shifted it from his reach. Joe glared at the older man. "Give me the phone."

Scott took the phone and held it up, continually videotaping Joe. "Why don't you come through me to get it?"

Joe turned to Angela, glaring at her. "Is this your choice then?" Derek stood to his full height in spite of the pain in his ribs and put his arms around her protectively. "I'm going to destroy you both." He pointed at them.

Angela slipped from Derek's arms. "I have to go," she whispered, looking sorrowful, as if she couldn't believe what she was saying. Derek was sure his face registered the shock he was feeling.

"I'm not letting you go anywhere with him." Derek looked from Joe to Angela. "What is he talking about?"

"You're an idiot for inviting her here. I have enough footage that I can bury you. I can make it look like you're doing your animals, abusing them . . . whatever I want it to look like. I even have the drugs planted here."

Derek took a step back and looked at Angela. Scott laughed. "By all means, keep talking. You do realize this is all still being videotaped, right?"

Angela laid a hand on Derek's chest, and he could see the tears forming. "I refused to do the story."

"She's lying," Joe argued. "She made sure Skip had all the footage he needed. Who do you think planted the drugs?"

"You mean this?" Mike pulled the vial from his pocket. "Robert already told us how you wanted him to plant it."

"I don't know where they got the footage or how. It's not even of you." Angela glanced from Derek to Scott and back to Joe.

"But he wants to make it look like us," Scott predicted. Angela nodded, the tears spilling onto her cheeks. "And if you went with him?"

"He promised to bury the falsified story and let me report mine. He was going to ruin Findley Brothers."

Derek ran a hand through his hair and down his face, his fingers resting on his swiftly bruising jaw. "And you believed him?"

"I couldn't take a chance, Derek."

He placed his hands on her shoulders. "When are you going to trust me? Why didn't you just tell me?"

"I couldn't. He said that if I told you . . ." She couldn't meet his gaze. "I was doing it for you. Please understand, Derek. I had no choice."

366 T. J. KLINE

"You." Derek pointed at Joe, looking far more confident and smug than he should. "You're going to leave and there will be no story at all. Nothing. If I so much as hear the word rodeo mentioned on your station, I'll take the video I have, clearly showing your face, to the police."

A dark cloud of fury settled on Joe's brow. "You can't do that!"

"Watch me. I can and I will." Derek looked at his brother. "I don't think we ever signed a release for any video of our rodeos to be used, did we?"

"Nope," Scott answered with a smile, shaking his head. "I think the paper is still lying on my desk at the house. Now that you mention it, I don't recall ever seeing a press pass on this guy either." He clicked the button on the phone, turning off the video.

"You know, none of this would ever hold up," Joe warned.

"Maybe, maybe not," Derek said, shrugging. "But I'm sure the other stations around here would love to have footage of you beating up an injured cowboy and to hear how you've assaulted your own reporter. And there's always the accusation of sexual harassment."

"What accusation?" Joe narrowed his eyes at Angela. "You're finished," Joe threatened, pointing his finger at her. "Not only are you fired, but you'll never work at another station again."

"I have a feeling that once our lawyers contact your station, you'll be the one looking for a job, not Angela."

Joe edged toward the front of the van. "This isn't over. Not even close."

"Don't ever threaten her again," Derek warned as he stepped toward Joe. The smaller man jumped backward, in spite of his earlier sucker punch, and hurried to the driver's side of the van. Derek could see the worry creasing Angela's forehead as the van backed up and headed down the driveway toward the road. He brushed his thumb over her forehead, smoothing out the lines.

"When are you going to learn to trust me?"

"I do," she insisted. "But he said . . ."

"I don't care what he said. Open book means you don't hide *anything* from me, Angel." Derek noticed that Silvie, Jen, and Sydney had found their way onto the porch, probably at some point during his fight with Joe. "Or them."

"Derek, he's not going to let this go that easily."

Derek looped his arm around her waist and pulled her close. "We'll take care of Joe. First, you need to kiss me and thank me for rescuing you." He bent down, taking her lips hostage, tasting her. Robert cleared his throat.

"Yeah," Scott agreed. "Thanks for making that awkward for the rest of us."

"All right," Mike teased. "Show's over. Let's all go back inside and get some food. You guys *do* still work, right?"

As everyone headed back into the house, Angela remained on the porch. Derek wrapped his arms around her waist as they stared out over the corral.

"Actually, I don't," Angela said. She looked discouraged as she glanced at her father, who was retreating into the house. "For the first time in my life, he has a job and I don't."

Derek shrugged. "Then stay here longer." The thought of her staying indefinitely sent spirals of desire to his loins.

She gave him a sarcastic grin over her shoulder. "Are you asking me to shack up, Mr. Chandler?" He didn't miss the gleam in her eye and knew she was joking. Suddenly, it didn't seem like a bad idea.

He grabbed her hips and turned her in his arms, giving her a lopsided grin that he hoped was charming. "Might be fun."

"And do what? Live off Mike's hospitality?" She shook her head. "I need a job."

"Well, there is this thing we call the Internet. I think I know this sexy reporter who constantly used it to do research. And I know this guy who could get you into any rodeo you want." He paused for effect. "You could report on every event, with behind-the-scene access and interviews, and broadcast it."

ANGELA'S EYES LIT up at his suggestion. A web show? She could certainly edit her own film; she'd done it before. To do what he was suggesting would take some time to build an online following but no more than putting together a new reel and landing another job. She bit her lower lip. It was definitely within the realm of possibilities.

"Don't do that," Derek groaned.

"What?" She looked up at his dark eyes, wondering how in the world she'd ever come to this place, in love with a cowboy.

"Bite your lip like that. It makes me want to nibble on it, too." He smiled down at her and she could see the mischievous gleam in his eye. "You know I love you."

She smiled up at him. "I think you mentioned that earlier." She saw the flicker of amusement in his eyes.

"You love me, too," he assured her.

"I don't recall ever saying that," she teased, knowing with every fiber of her being that it was completely true.

He nodded. "That's where you're wrong. You did say it. Last night."

Angela furrowed her brow. "I think I would have remembered."

"Not if you were falling asleep at the time." A blush crept up her neck to her cheeks as she vaguely recalled their conversation after they made love and she began to drift to sleep. "See, *now* you remember."

He sucked at her bottom lip, nipping the soft flesh with his teeth. "Marry me, Angel."

She gasped—whether from his request or his kiss she wasn't sure. "You barely know me."

He unclasped the necklace and slipped the ring from the chain. Grasping her hand, he slipped the ring onto her finger. "I'm pretty sure I know you better than anyone else ever has. Do you want to say yes?"

She looked at her mother's ring on her hand. She'd lost so much as a child and carried so much regret that she'd never allowed herself to live. Derek had shown her that she could be vulnerable and still remain strong. She could love someone and be loved in return in spite of her flaws. He'd shown her how to lay her burdens down in order to grasp happiness with both hands. Her mother and father might have been in love at one time, but they pushed each other away. Derek wasn't her father, and she wasn't her mother. She reached for his waist and pulled him closer, sliding her hands up the corded muscles of his back, and looked up at him.

She nodded, blinking back tears that clouded her vision. She wasn't sure if they were tears of joy or anxiety.

He ran his thumbs over her jaw. "I know you're scared. But I know this is right."

"Say yes already." Mike's voice was loud through the screen as Derek and Angela spun to see the entire family watching them. She laughed.

"We'll have as long of an engagement as you need." He twined his fingers through hers, her mother's ring pressing against her finger. "I love you, Angel."

She searched his eyes and saw that he meant every word he said. He would wait for her as long as it took for her to be ready. "I love you, Derek. I have never met a man like you."

He gave her an impish smile, and she could see a remnant of the boy who must have tugged at Silvie's heartstrings. "Will a week be enough time to convince you to marry me?"

She laughed as Jen and Sydney burst through the door and hugged them both. Scott and Clay clapped Derek on the shoulder, causing him to wince and then laugh. She looked over Derek's shoulder in time to see Mike's arm around Silvie, looking proudly over their family. Her father stood in the background, smiling, his eyes watery as if he were about to cry. She moved away from Derek and met her father at the door.

"I don't understand why you lied, but you're the only father I've ever known." She wound her arms around his waist and pressed herself against his chest. "I know it's going to take time, but I want us to be a family."

"Angie-girl, you have no idea how happy that would make me." He ran a hand over her hair and looked at Derek. "He's a good man," he whispered to her. "He'll take good care of you."

"Thank you," she whispered, and she felt another chipped brick fall from the wall she'd built around her heart.

"No, thank *you* for all that you've done to try to help me since you were little. I'm so sorry, Angie."

"We're moving forward from here. No more looking backward."

Angela realized she meant it. She didn't want to live in the past with its regrets and recriminations any longer. There was too much for her to look forward to. Derek's arms circled her waist, and she heard his sharp intake of breath.

"We need to get you to the doctor," she insisted.

"I'm fine. Listen to you, already nagging like a wife." He nuzzled her neck.

She frowned at him. "To the car, now."

"Yes, ma'am."

"Get used to it. This is just the beginning." Scott laughed as Sydney punched his arm.

"You sure you don't mind marrying a manure jockey?" he teased.

A blush flooded her cheeks at the memory of their first meeting. He'd taught her so much about herself in a short period of time. "I think I can manage to be happy as Mrs. Manure Jockey." She kissed his jaw where it was beginning to swell from Joe's attack. "Now, get into that car before I give you another goose egg on the other side."

Epilogue

ANGELA TURNED OFF the computer and leaned back from the desk, raising her arms above her and stretching the stiff muscles of her back.

"Done?" Derek leaned against the doorway of her office.

"For now. I have more editing for next week's segment, but the voiceover copy is done." Since leaving the station, she'd started an online rodeo show and had been picked up by a small local news station. She loved being her own boss without the stress of someone telling her what to report and when. She reported what she wanted and it allowed her to go to every rodeo with Derek.

His eyes flashed with mystery. "Then come here, I have something to show you."

"Is it from the lawyer?" She knew they were expecting the finalized court documents against Joe. Derek's lawyer had contacted the station and Joe had been fired, but he'd decided to try to take his story public. It back-fired when Findley Brothers sued him for libel and won, forcing him to pay far more than he'd ever be able to afford.

"No, I forgot to tell you we got those yesterday, along with the restraining orders. I think Joe's learned his lesson about tangling with a cowboy." He winked at her. "But I think you'll like this even more."

She followed him through the house. It had taken nearly six months to finish it to Derek's exact specifica-tions, but it had turned out beautiful: a majestic three-story cabin with plenty of room for the large family they were talking about starting right after their wedding next week, on her mother's birthday.

Derek curled his fingers around her hand and pulled her through the front door toward the stream. She could see it from a distance: a magnificent wooden gazebo overlooking her favorite spot by the water. As they neared the structure she could see personal touches, from intri-cate carvings of her favorite flowers on the pillars to their initials and wedding date carved into the designs on the railings. She ran her fingers of the carved surface, awed by the effort and beauty of his creation.

"This is beautiful. I can't believe you made this."

Derek shrugged off her praise. "I had help."

She wound her arms around his waist. "I love it. I'm glad it's still warm enough that I can use it."

"I thought we could use it this weekend." He leaned back against the railing and pulled her to stand between his legs, his hands curving on her spine, molding her

body against his. "We could get married in here. Put some lights up there and a few flowers."

She looked around her at the arches and carved vines twisting around the beams. "I think it's perfect the way it is." She pressed her lips against his, allowing her desire to ignite his, her hands finding the back of his head. She curled her fingers into his hair and drew him closer. "Cowboy, do you have any idea how happy you've made me?"

"I'm hoping you're going to take me back inside and show me." He gave her a wicked smile.

"I think I can take care of that."

Derek grew serious and he leaned his forehead against hers. "You're sure you're ready for this?" He brushed the back of his knuckles against her cheek. "I want you to be completely comfortable with this decision."

She kissed him, stepping closer, pressing herself against him, and she heard him groan deep in his throat. "I can't wait to marry you."

Derek stood, lifting her as he did. She curled her legs around his waist as he carried her back to the house, took her into their bedroom, and laid her on the top of their new king-size bed. He'd made everything about this house an oasis for her, reminding her how much he cherished her, and she wanted to show him she adored him for it.

"Derek," she whispered as his lips worked magic over the tender flesh of her neck. She pulled her shirt over her head. "I have a wedding present for you."

His palm slid over her hip to the button of her jeans. "I know. You told me you wanted to buy the . . ."

She shook her head. "I didn't buy this." He drew back to look down at her, and she smiled up at him and reached for his hand. "I know you want to start trying to have a baby right after the wedding." She moved his hand to her stomach.

"Angel, if you want to wait, we can."

"It's a little late for that," she laughed. "We're going to have a baby next spring."

"What?" His eyes grew wide as he looked toward her stomach, where his hand splayed over her flat abdomen.

"You're going to be a father." She pulled him down toward her again. "And you'll be a great father," she whispered against his lips.

Derek laid his cheek against her flat stomach. "A baby?" he whispered. "Angel." He sounded awestruck. "Are you okay? I mean, can we . . ."

She laughed, cupping his jaw in her palms. "You better not even think of stopping now."

He smiled rakishly, the rasp of his day-old stubble rubbing against her flesh as he moved up her body, driving her wild. She squirmed beneath him as need vibrated over every nerve ending. Derek kissed her, sending her senses spinning as she slid her hands over the ridges of his muscled chest.

"Cowboy, you were the best story I never reported," she teased.

"Huh." He nuzzled at the curve of her neck. "I knew you were trouble the first time I laid eyes on you."

"Open book?" she asked.

He returned her smile at what had become their inside joke. "Of course."

She grabbed his hand and laid it over the left side of her chest, just above her breast, feeling warmth spread over her. "You've knocked down every wall I built. I trust you more than I ever thought I could trust anyone. And somehow you managed to rebuild a relationship with my father I'd given up on."

"Angel, if it hadn't been for you, I'd still be trying to live up to a phantom image of who I thought I needed to be. Because of you, I know the man I am is enough." He cupped her jaw in his calloused hand. "You make me enough."

Tears sprang to her eyes at his tender admission. She hadn't been looking for him, but fate had been generous and brought him to her anyway. She couldn't imagine where her life would have ended up without him. He'd helped her find her way in her career and face the recriminations of her past, and he'd taught her to hope for a future.

"You gave me back my hope, Derek."

"You are my hope, Angel. Everything I ever hoped for and more." His hand slid over her stomach again. "I think we have a name if it's a girl." He smiled against her lips.

Hope. She would be the culmination of their dreams together.

"Hope," she whispered as his lips claimed hers in a scorching kiss that spoke of a future filled with love and promise.

Want more rodeo?
Check out T. J. Kline's first book in the rodeo series,

RODEO QUEEN,

to see Sydney and Scott fall in love.

An Excerpt from

RODEO QUEEN

THE DRAWLING VOICE of the rodeo announcer boomed over the loudspeakers. "Ladies and gentleman, we'd like to welcome you to the Fifty-first Annual West Hills Roundup Rodeo! But first, let's have one last look at the ladies vying for the title of your rodeo queen!"

The array of glitter, sequins, and beads was dazzling in the April sunlight, nearly blinding her. She patted her dapple-gray stallion to calm him as he shifted eagerly at the end of the line, kicking up dust in the newly tilled rodeo arena. Sydney looked down the line of young women on horseback, spotted her friend Alicia first in line, and gave her a reassuring smile.

"First, let's welcome Alicia Kanani!" Sydney watched as her best friend coaxed her gelding from the line, taking off into a slow lope along the fence. Alicia cocked a two-fingered salute to the crowd, her black tuxedo shirt glittering with silver and gold sequins, before filing back

382 T. J. KLINE

into the line of contestants. The next seven contestants duplicated Alicia's queen run. "And, last but not least, Sydney Thomas!"

Pressing her heels into Valentino's sides, Sydney made a kissing sound to the stallion as he took off from the line like a bullet from a gun. Leaning over his neck, Sydney snapped a sharp military salute while facing the audience. The sequins of her vest were a blinding flash of red light as Valentino stretched his body into a full run, his ears pinned against his head. Sydney reveled in the moment of flight as she and the horse became one, his hooves seeming to float over the tilled earth. As they rounded the last corner, Valentino slowed to a lope and Sydney sat up in the saddle. Reaching the end of the line, Sydney sat deep into her saddle, cueing the horse to bury his hocks in the soft dirt and slide to a dramatic stop. As the blood pounding in her ears subsided to a mild roar, she could still hear the audience cheering.

"There you have it, ladies and gentlemen, your contestants for West Hills Roundup Queen," the announcer repeated. "May I have the envelope, please?"

Glancing at the fence line, Sydney caught her brother's gaze as he winked and gave her a thumbs-up. She smiled, appreciating that he had come to cheer her on when he had his own event to prepare for. The "crowd" was sparse in the morning hours before the rodeo actually began. It was mostly family and friends of the queen contestants and a few rodeo competitors who performed before the rodeo due to too many entrants in their events.

"Without any further fanfare," the announcer paused

for effect as the meager crowd immediately quieted to a hush. "Your princess this year is ... Alicia Kanani!" Cheers erupted from the grassy hillside where Alicia's family was seated with Sydney's. She cheered from the line, excited for her friend. "And now, the moment we've all been waiting for ..."

Sydney's heart raced. She felt it in her throat and in her toes at the same time as she waited for the name of the new queen to be called. Only her brother, Chris, knew how many hours of training and preparation had gone into this competition, all in hopes of having her name come to be associated with the best horse trainers in rodeo. As queen, she would be attending rodeos all over California, meeting and networking with stock contractors and other rodeo participants. She hoped that it would all lead to more exposure for her mounts, which meant more horses to train.

"The new West Hills Roundup Queen is ... drum roll, please ... Sydney Thomas!" The applause rose to a roar on the hillside again as Sydney's family rose, laughing, cheering, and hugging one another. Sydney edged Valentino forward as the previous year's rodeo queen placed the silver-and-rhinestone crown on her red cowboy hat. She was soon encircled by the other contestants, who offered congratulations as they exited the arena and headed for the horse trailers.

They'd barely dismounted at Sydney's trailer when Alicia tackled her with an enthusiastic hug. "I can't believe we did it! You won!"

Sydney opened her mouth to respond but was cut off

by the massive arms that lifted her from behind and spun her around. "Congratulations, Queenie."

"Chris, put me down," she squealed. As her boots touched the ground she slapped him on the shoulder. Her brother might be a year younger than she was, but he'd inherited their father's tall, lanky frame.

"Ow!" He rubbed his arm. "You'll never find a king acting like that," he teased.

"Please. That is the last thing I'm looking for." Sydney rolled her eyes and turned to tie Valentino to the trailer.

"What about you, Alicia? Want to be my princess?" Chris asked as he snuck his arm around her shoulders.

Chris was a hopeless flirt. At nineteen, he was striking with his jet-black hair, aqua eyes, and broad shoulders—everything a girl would imagine from a cowboy, including the drawling charm. The fact that he and his roping partner were consistently ranked in the top of the national standings for team roping made him a pretty hot ticket around the rodeo circuit. But he'd never shown any indication that he would ever settle down with one girl.

"Why don't you go find yourself one of those 'buckle bunnies' that hangs out behind the chutes?" Alicia asked, shaking his arm off.

One of the drawbacks of rodeo were the women fans, young and old alike, who wanted to snag a cowboy. Too often, Sydney found the cowboys around the circuit expected all of the other women to do the same.

"No thanks." Chris laughed. "When I find the right girl, she's going to outride and out-rope me."

"Good luck with that." Sydney laughed.

Alicia pulled her cowboy hat off, exposing her long, dark hair, and set the hat on the back of the truck. Sydney didn't miss the look of appreciation Chris shot her best friend. "You never can tell, sis." He tapped the red line her hat had left on her forehead before stepping back. "I'll never understand why you girls wear hats that tight."

Sydney slipped her sequined vest over her arms and unbuttoned the tuxedo shirt, grateful for the tank top underneath, and hung her shirt in the tack compartment of her horse trailer so she could wear it again once the pre-rodeo events finished. "You guys should try doing a queen run sometime. If that hat hits the ground with a crown on it, my head better be in it. Rule number one."

She flipped the front of her brother's cowboy hat, knocking it to the ground. "Unlike you ropers, no one picks up our hats when they come off in the arena," she teased as she pulled a light cotton Western shirt from the trailer, wishing again that short sleeves were allowed. "Okay, I'm going to head back to find the stock contractor and see what they'll allow us to do during the rodeo."

It was typical for the stock contractor to allow the rodeo queen and her court to carry the sponsor flags for the events, but Sydney was hoping to network a bit and charm her way into being allowed to clear the cattle from the arena in the roping events. It was good exposure to show off Valentino and her accomplishments as a trainer. She exchanged her red cowboy hat for a baseball cap, pulling her russet curls through the opening in the back.

"Can you keep an eye on Valentino for me?" Sydney

spotted their families heading toward the trailer. "Here comes the crew," she said, jerking her chin in their direction. "Let them know I'll be right back."

"Talk with Mike Findley," Chris instructed. "He's in charge. He should be pretty receptive to you."

"Thanks. I'll be right back."

Chris glanced toward Alicia, who was being hugged by both of her parents. "No hurry." Sydney smiled, wondering if the dance tonight wouldn't be the perfect opportunity to give Chris and Alicia a little nudge to take their friendship to the next level.

Sydney rolled up the sleeves of her shirt to her elbows and pulled the shirt from her chest in an attempt to cool herself. It was only April, but her shirt was already sticking to her skin at nine in the morning. She couldn't help but smile and take in the smell of alfalfa, dust, and leather as she made her way through the jumbled maze of trucks and trailers, most with horses tied in the shade, dozing before their events. She knew how lucky she was; most people couldn't honestly say that they loved their life, but she loved every minute she'd spent growing up in rodeo.

Sydney heard the unmistakable pounding of horse hooves on the packed ground behind her and moved closer to the vehicle on her right. Usually there was more than enough room for riders and their rigs in the walkway, but with the unexpected turnout at the rodeo today, there was barely room to maneuver. The horse was jogging pretty quickly and she didn't have anywhere else to go, especially since another truck and trailer had chosen that moment to pull out of the gate ahead of her. The driver of the truck spotted her and waved her on. She tried to hurry through the opening he'd left her at the gate, but the rider behind her chose to slip between them, his mount's shoulder knocking her into the gatepost on her right.

Sydney reached up to massage her shoulder before registering the surprise on the face of the driver of the truck.

"Are you okay, Sydney?" It was Bobby Blake, a friend of her father's who must have been delivering some panels in the back of the arena.

"Yeah, I'm fine," she assured him before raising her voice. "I guess chivalry really is dead," she yelled at the cowboy's back.

She saw him jerk his mount to a stop before glancing back over his shoulder at her. "Look, honey, I don't have time for you girls who don't belong back here. This area is for contestants, not their groupies."

"Want me to set him straight?" Bobby asked.

Sydney smiled her appreciation. "No, but thanks Bobby. I've got this."

"Go get him, honey," he teased. "He doesn't know who he's dealing with. By the way, congratulations."

"Thanks, Bobby." Sydney made her way toward the obnoxious cowboy seated on the sorrel. "Look, I don't know who you think you are, but around here we tend to have a sort of unspoken code. When that walkway is packed with cars and horses like that, you slow down and you certainly do not push your way between a truck and someone walking. I don't really appreciate hoofmarks across my back."

She looked up at him as she came closer, refusing to let him intimidate her from his seat on the horse. "And as for being a groupie, I could probably outride you any day of the week," she challenged.

The cowboy arched his right brow and a slow smile spread across his face. "Maybe we'll have to see about that later." With a tap of his heels, the horse jogged forward a few steps toward one of the stock pens.

Sydney narrowed her eyes as he left. What a jerk, she thought. Shaking her head, she rubbed her shoulder again and searched the back of the arena for the stock contractor's trailers, noticing a lanky cowboy setting up folding chairs beside a Findley Brothers stock trailer.

"Excuse me," Sydney began, making her way across the short grass. "Can you tell me where I might find Mike Findley?"

A weathered face returned her smile, and Sydney realized he was much older than she had first assumed. "What's that?"

Sydney realized that he probably couldn't hear her over the clattering of stock panels as the cattle moved into the pens. "Mike Findley? Do you know where I can find him?"

"Oh, no, I'm not Mike. I'm Jake," the man hollered.

"Hi Jake, I'm Sydney Thomas." She raised her voice as well. "I was just crowned rodeo queen and I'm looking for Mike to see if we might carry the sponsor flags or run cattle for him today."

Jake turned and faced her, crossing his arms. The cattle had quieted so he toned down his voice as well.

"Well, Mike's up with the announcer right now working out of a few details. But he's not who you'd want to talk to about that." He leaned back against the trailer, crossing his ankles as if getting relaxed for a long conversation.

Sydney raised her brows in expectation. When Jake didn't say anything, she pressed. "So, who should I talk to instead?"

"That'd be Scott Chandler."

Sydney sighed, finding it difficult to restrain herself from punching something. First she'd been shoved into a fence post and now a cryptic cowboy was obviously enjoying a joke at her expense.

"And where would I find Mr. Chandler?"

The Cheshire-cat grin on Jake's face made her heart sink. No, life couldn't possibly be that cruel. Her gaze followed the direction of his finger as he pointed to the cowboy atop the sorrel at the stock pen, obviously eavesdropping on their conversation. Swallowing the dry lump that had suddenly materialized in her throat, Sydney squared her shoulders and raised her golden eyes to meet the black eyes of her foe.

"Well, I think you just finished telling him off." Jake grinned, anticipating the showdown to come.

Sydney had a few choice words that might have suited this moment if her mother hadn't ingrained in her how unladylike it was to curse. A blush crept up her cheeks as Scott Chandler dismounted his horse and bowed deeply before her.

"Your Majesty," he mocked. "I am at your disposal."

She realized that the noise from the stock pen hadn't

kept him from overhearing her conversation with Jake. "I'm sorry. I didn't know who you were."

Sarcasm colored his chuckle. "Somehow I don't think it would have mattered if you had. Now, I am busy, so what did you need, Miss Thomas?"

Sydney took a deep breath and ignored the warmth flooding her cheeks. "I came to see about carrying the sponsor flags and returning the cattle during the rodeo."

"Experience?"

"Well, I've worked for Marks' Rodeo Company for the last four years doing both, as well as training for the last eight years, five of those professionally." Sydney's chin rose indignantly as she felt his gaze weighing heavily on her. She felt suddenly self-conscious in her red jeans and red-and-white plaid Western shirt. Did she look like an immature girl?

Scott gave her a rakish, lopsided grin. "Oh, that's right. You can outride me." His brow arched as he articulated her words back to her. "Any day of the week."

It took everything in her to try to ignore how good-looking this infuriating man was. He towered over her, well over six feet tall, and the black cowboy hat that topped a mop of dark brown hair, barely curling at his collar, gave him a devilish appearance. With sensuous lips and a square jaw, his deeply tanned skin reflected raw male sexuality. She wasn't sure if he was actually as muscular as his broad shoulders seemed to indicate due to his unruly Western shirt, but his jeans left no imagining necessary to notice the muscular thighs. However, his jet-black eyes almost unnerved her. Those eyes were so dark that Sydney felt she would drown if she continued to meet his gaze.

So much for ignoring his good looks, she chided herself. "Give me a chance out there today to prove it."

"I don't see why she can't run them, Scott." Jake must have decided that it was time to break up the showdown with his two cents. "She is certainly experienced enough, more than most of the girls you let run flags."

Scott glared at Jake before turning back to Sydney. She caught Jake's conspiratorial wink and decided that she liked this old cowboy. Scott would be hard-pressed to find a reason to deny her request now that Jake had sold him out.

"Fine, you can do both. But if anything goes wrong, if a steer so much as takes too long in the arena, you're finished. Got it, Miss Thomas?" The warning note in his voice was unmistakable.

Sydney flashed a dazzling smile. "Call me Sydney, and it's no problem." She clutched her shoulder. "Unless I'm unable to hold the flags since someone ran me into the fence post."

His look told her he didn't appreciate her sense of humor. "I mean it. Rodeo starts at ten sharp. Be down here at nine thirty, ready to go."

As the sassy cowgirl walked away, Scott shook his head. "What in the world possessed you to open your mouth, Jake?"

"Aw, Scott, she'll do fine. Besides, you did run her down with Wiley at the gate. You kinda owed her one."

Scott watched Sydney head for the gate, taking in her

small waist and the spread of her hips in her red pants and down her lean, denim-encased legs. That woman was all curves, moving with the grace of a jungle cat. With her full, pouting lips and those golden eyes, it certainly wouldn't be painful to look at her all day. "I guess."

Scott mounted Wiley and headed to change into his clean shirt and show chaps, but he couldn't seem to shake the image of Sydney Thomas from his mind. He knew that she'd been attracted to him—he'd seen it in her blush—but he'd had enough run-ins with ostentatious rodeo queens over the years, including his ex-fiancée, to know that they simply wanted to tame a cowboy. It was doubtful that this one was any different, although she did have a much shorter temper. He chuckled as he recalled how the gold in her eyes seemed to flame when she was irritated. He wondered if her eyes flamed up whenever she was passionate. Scott shook his head to clear it of visions of the sexy spitfire. No time for that, he had a rodeo to get started.

About the Author

T.J. Kline was bitten by the horse bug early and began training horses at fourteen as well as competing in rodeos and winning several rodeo queen competitions but has always known writing was her first love. She also writes under the name Tina Klinesmith. In her spare time, she can be found spending as much time as possible, laughing hysterically, with her husband, teens and their menagerie of pets in Northern California.

Visit www.AuthorTracker.com for exclusive information on your favorite HarperCollins authors.

Give in to your impulses . . .
Read on for a sneak peek at three brand-new
e-book original tales of romance
from Avon Books.
Available now wherever e-books are sold.

FULL EXPOSURE
BOOK ONE: INDEPENDENCE FALLS
By Sara Jane Stone

PERSONAL TARGET
AN ELITE OPS NOVEL
By Kay Thomas

SINFUL REWARDS 1
A BILLIONAIRES AND BIKERS NOVELLA
By Cynthia Sax

An Excerpt from

FULL EXPOSURE
Book One: Independence Falls
by Sara Jane Stone

The first book in a hot new series from
contemporary romance writer Sara Jane
Stone. When Georgia begins work as a
nanny for her brother's best friend, she
knows she can't have him, but his pull is too
strong, and she feels sparks igniting.

Georgia Trulane walked into the kitchen wearing a purple bikini, hoping and praying for a reaction from the man she'd known practically forever. Seated at the kitchen table, Eric Moore, her brother's best friend, now her boss since she'd taken over the care of his adopted nephew until he found another live-in nanny, studied his laptop as if it held the keys to the world's greatest mysteries. Unless the answers were listed between items b and c on a spreadsheet about Oregon timber harvesting, the screen was not of earth-shattering importance. It certainly did not merit his full attention when she was wearing an itsy-bitsy string bikini.

"Nate is asleep," she said.

Look up. Please, look up.

Eric nodded, his gaze fixed to the screen. Why couldn't he look at her with that unwavering intensity? He'd snuck glances. There had been moments when she'd turned from preparing his nephew's lunch and caught him looking at her, really looking, as if he wanted to memorize the curve of her neck or the way her jeans fit. But he quickly turned away.

"Did you pick up everything he needs for his first day of school tomorrow? I don't want to send him unprepared."

His deep voice warmed her from the inside out. It was so familiar and welcoming, yet at the same time utterly sexy.

"I got all the items on the list," she said. "He is packed and ready to go."

"He needs another one of those stuffed frogs. He can't go without his favorite stuffed animal."

If she hadn't been standing in his kitchen practically naked, waiting for him to notice her, she would have found his concern for the three-year-old's first day of preschool sweet, maybe even heartwarming. But her body wasn't looking for sentiments reminiscent of sunshine and puppies, or the whisper of sweet nothings against her skin. She craved physical contact—his hands on her, exploring, each touch making her feel more alive.

And damn it, he still hadn't glanced up from his laptop.

"Nate will be home by nap time," she said. "He'll be there for only a few hours. You know that, right?"

"He'll want to take his frog," he said, his fingers moving across the keyboard. "He'll probably lose it. And he sleeps with that thing every night. He needs that frog."

She might be practically naked, but his emphasis on the word *need* thrust her headfirst into heartwarming territory. Eric worked day and night to provide Nate with the stability that had been missing from Eric's childhood thanks to his divorced parents' fickle dating habits. She admired his willingness to put a child who'd suffered a tragic loss first.

But tonight, for one night, she didn't want to think about all of his honorable qualities. She wanted to see if maybe, just maybe those stolen glances when he thought she wasn't looking meant that the man she'd laid awake thinking about while serving her country half a world away wanted her too.

"You're now the proud owner of two stuffed frogs," she said. "So if that's everything for tonight, I'm going for a swim."

Finally, *finally*, he looked up. She watched as his blue eyes widened and his jaw clenched. He was an imposing man, large and strong from years of climbing and felling trees. Not that he did the grunt work anymore. These days he wore tailored suits and spent more time in an office than with a chainsaw in hand. But even seated at his kitchen table poring over a computer, he looked like a wall of strong, solid muscle wound tight and ready for action. Having all of that energy focused on her? It sent a thrill down her body. Georgia clung to the feeling, savoring it.

An Excerpt from

PERSONAL TARGET
An Elite Ops Novel

by Kay Thomas

One minute Jennifer Grayson is housesitting and the next she's abducted to a foreign brothel. Jennifer is planning her escape when her first "customer" arrives. Nick, the man who broke her heart years ago, has come to her rescue. Now, as they race for their lives, passion for each other reignites and old secrets resurface. Can Nick keep the woman he loves safe against an enemy with a personal vendetta?

The woman at the vanity turned, and his breath caught in his throat. Nick had known it would be Jenny, and despite what he'd thought about downstairs when he'd seen her on the tablet screen, he hadn't prepared himself for seeing her like this. Seated at the table with candles all around, she was wearing a sheer robe over a grey thong and a bustier kind of thing—or that's what he thought the full-length bra was called.

He spotted the unicorn tat peeping out from the edge of whatever the lingerie piece was, and his brain quit processing details as all the blood in his head rushed south. He'd been primed to come in and tell Jenny exactly how they were getting out of the house and away from these people, and now . . . this. His mouth went dry at the sight of her. She looked like every fantasy he'd ever had about her rolled into one.

He continued to stare as recognition flared in her eyes.

"Oh my god," she murmured. "It's . . ."

She clapped her mouth closed, and her eyes widened. That struck him as odd. The relief on her face was obvious, but instead of looking at him, she took an audible breath and studied the walls of the room. When she finally did glance at him again, her eyes had changed.

"So you're who they've sent me for my first time?" Her voice sounded bored, not the tone he remembered. "What do you want me to do?"

What a question. He raised an eyebrow, but she shook her head. In warning?

Nothing here was as he'd anticipated. He continued staring at her, hoping the lust would quit fogging his brain long enough for him to figure out what was going on.

"I've been told to show you a good time." Her voice was cold, downright chilly. Without another word she stood and crossed the floor, slipping into his arms with her breasts pressing into his chest. "It's you." She murmured the words in the barest of whispers.

Nick's mind froze, but his body didn't. His hands automatically went to her waist as she kissed his neck, working her way up to his ear. This was not at all what he'd planned.

"I can't believe you're here." She breathed the words into his ear.

Me either, he thought, but kept the words to himself as he pulled her closer. His senses flooded with all that smooth skin pressing against him. His body tightened, and his right hand moved to cup her ass. Her cheek's bare skin was silky soft, just like he remembered. God, he'd missed her. She melted into him as his body switched into overdrive.

"What do you want?" She spoke louder. The arctic tone was back. He was confused and knew he was just too stupid with wanting her to figure out what the hell was going on. There was no way the woman could mistake the effect she was having.

She moved her lips closer to his ear and nipped his earlobe as she whispered, "Cameras are everywhere. I'm not sure about microphones."

And like that, cold reality slapped him in the face. He should have been expecting it, but he'd been so focused on getting her out and making sure she was all right. She might be glad to see him because he was there to save her, but throwing her body at him was an act.

Jesus. He had to get them both out of here without tipping his hand to the cameras and those watching what he was doing. He was crazy not to have considered it once he saw those tablets downstairs, but it had never occurred to him that he would have to play this encounter through as if he were really a client.

He slipped her arms from around his neck and moved to the table to pour himself some wine, willing his hands not to shake. "I want you," he said.

An Excerpt from

SINFUL REWARDS 1
A Billionaires and Bikers Novella
by Cynthia Sax

Belinda "Bee" Carter is a good girl; at least, that's what she tells herself. And a good girl deserves a nice guy—just like the gorgeous and moody billionaire Nicolas Rainer. Or so she thinks, until she takes a look through her telescope and sees a naked, tattooed man on the balcony across the courtyard. He has been watching her, and that makes him all the more enticing. But when a mysterious and anonymous text message dares her to do something bad, she must decide if she is really the good girl she has always claimed to be, or if she's willing to risk everything for her secret fantasy of being watched.

An Avon Red Novella

I'd told Cyndi I'd never use it, that it was an instrument purchased by perverts to spy on their neighbors. She'd laughed and called me a prude, not knowing that I was one of those perverts, that I secretly yearned to watch and be watched, to care and be cared for.

If I'm cautious, and I'm always cautious, she'll never realize I used her telescope this morning. I swing the tube toward the bench and adjust the knob, bringing the mysterious object into focus.

It's a phone. Nicolas's phone. I bounce on the balls of my feet. This is a sign, another declaration from fate that we belong together. I'll return Nicolas's much-needed device to him. As a thank you, he'll invite me to dinner. We'll talk. He'll realize how perfect I am for him, fall in love with me, marry me.

Cyndi will find a fiancé also—everyone loves her—and we'll have a double wedding, as sisters of the heart often do. It'll be the first wedding my family has had in generations.

Everyone will watch us as we walk down the aisle. I'll wear a strapless white Vera Wang mermaid gown with organza and lace details, crystal and pearl embroidery accents, the bodice fitted, and the skirt hemmed for my shorter height. My hair will be swept up. My shoes—

Voices murmur outside the condo's door, the sound piercing my delightful daydream. I swing the telescope upward, not wanting to be caught using it. The snippets of conversation drift away.

I don't relax. If the telescope isn't positioned in the same way as it was last night, Cyndi will realize I've been using it. She'll tease me about being a fellow pervert, sharing the story, embellished for dramatic effect, with her stern, serious dad—or, worse, with Angel, that snobby friend of hers.

I'll die. It'll be worse than being the butt of jokes in high school because that ridicule was about my clothes and this will center on the part of my soul I've always kept hidden. It'll also be the truth, and I won't be able to deny it. I am a pervert.

I have to return the telescope to its original position. This is the only acceptable solution. I tap the metal tube.

Last night, my man-crazy roommate was giggling over the new guy in three-eleven north. The previous occupant was a gray-haired, bowtie-wearing tax auditor, his luxurious accommodations supplied by Nicolas. The most exciting thing he ever did was drink his tea on the balcony.

According to Cyndi, the new occupant is a delicious piece of man candy—tattooed, buff, and head-to-toe lickable. He was completing armcurls outside, and she enthusiastically counted his reps, oohing and aahing over his bulging biceps, calling to me to take a look.

I resisted that temptation, focusing on making macaroni and cheese for the two of us, the recipe snagged from the diner my mom works in. After we scarfed down dinner, Cyndi licking her plate clean, she left for the club and hasn't returned.

Three-eleven north is the mirror condo to ours. I

straighten the telescope. That position looks about right, but then, the imitation UGGs I bought in my second year of college looked about right also. The first time I wore the boots in the rain, the sheepskin fell apart, leaving me barefoot in Economics 201.

Unwilling to risk Cyndi's friendship on "about right," I gaze through the eyepiece. The view consists of rippling golden planes, almost like . . .

Tanned skin pulled over defined abs.

I blink. It can't be. I take another look. A perfect pearl of perspiration clings to a puckered scar. The drop elongates more and more, stretching, snapping. It trickles downward, navigating the swells and valleys of a man's honed torso.

No. I straighten. This is wrong. I shouldn't watch our sexy neighbor as he stands on his balcony. If anyone catches me . . .